Second Story Used Books
18104 E. 10 Mile
773-6440

AN AFFAIR OF HONOR

Susannah Garland felt lost in a world of love beyond all rules.

There were two men in her life. One was Sir Jeffrey Stratton, whose seductive appeal she had vowed to resist, even though she felt herself inwardly yielding to it. The other was Miles Devereux, who filled her with mingled joy and fear when he told her that he did not love his faithless wife but loved Susannah instead.

Now these two men were about to meet in a duel, and the winner would surely seek to claim her as a prize.

But deciding which one she hoped would win was like choosing which sin she was willing to commit. . . .

FASHION'S LADY

SIGNET Regency Romances You'll Enjoy

(0451)

☐ **THE INNOCENT DECEIVER by Vanessa Gray.**
(094638—$1.75)*

☐ **THE LONELY EARL by Vanessa Gray.** (079221—$1.75)

☐ **THE SHERBORNE SAPPHIRES by Sandra Heath.**
(115139—$2.25)*

☐ **THE DUTIFUL DAUGHTER by Vanessa Gray.**
(090179—$1.75)*

☐ **THE WICKED GUARDIAN by Vanessa Gray.** (083903—$1.75)

☐ **THE WAYWARD GOVERNESS by Vanessa Gray.**
(086961—$1.75)*

☐ **THE GOLDEN SONG BIRD by Sheila Walsh.** (081552—$1.75)†

☐ **BROKEN VOWS by Elizabeth Hewitt.** (115147—$2.25)*

☐ **THE SERGEANT MAJOR'S DAUGHTER by Sheila Walsh.**
(082206—$1.75)

☐ **THE INCOMPARABLE MISS BRADY by Sheila Walsh.**
(092457—$1.75)*

☐ **MADALENA by Sheila Walsh.** (093321—$1.75)

☐ **THE REBEL BRIDE by Catherine Coulter.** (117190—$2.25)

☐ **THE AUTUMN COUNTESS by Catherine Coulter.**
(114450—$2.25)

☐ **LORD DEVERILL'S HEIR by Catherine Coulter.**
(113985—$1.75)*

☐ **LORD RIVINGTON'S LADY by Eileen Jackson.**
(094085—$1.75)*

☐ **BORROWED PLUMES by Roseleen Milne.** (098114—$1.75)†

*Price slightly higher in Canada
†Not available in Canada

Buy them at your local bookstore or use this convenient coupon for ordering.
THE NEW AMERICAN LIBRARY, INC.,
P.O. Box 999, Bergenfield, New Jersey 07621
Please send me the books I have checked above. I am enclosing $_____
(please add $1.00 to this order to cover postage and handling). Send check
or money order—no cash or C.O.D.'s. Prices and numbers are subject to change
without notice.

Name_____

Address_____

City _____ State _____ Zip Code _____

Allow 4-6 weeks for delivery.
This offer is subject to withdrawal without notice.

FASHION'S LADY

by
Sandra Heath

A SIGNET BOOK

NEW AMERICAN LIBRARY

TIMES MIRROR

NAL BOOKS ARE AVAILABLE AT QUANTITY DISCOUNTS
WHEN USED TO PROMOTE PRODUCTS OR SERVICES. FOR
INFORMATION PLEASE WRITE TO PREMIUM MARKETING
DIVISION, THE NEW AMERICAN LIBRARY, INC., 1633
BROADWAY, NEW YORK, NEW YORK 10019.

Copyright © 1982 by Sandra Heath

All rights reserved

SIGNET TRADEMARK REG. U.S. PAT. OFF. AND FOREIGN COUNTRIES
REGISTERED TRADEMARK—MARCA REGISTRADA
HECHO EN CHICAGO, U.S.A.

SIGNET, SIGNET CLASSICS, MENTOR, PLUME, MERIDIAN AND NAL
BOOKS are published by The New American Library, Inc.,
1633 Broadway, New York, New York 10019

First Printing, October, 1982

1 2 3 4 5 6 7 8 9

PRINTED IN THE UNITED STATES OF AMERICA

1

The statues and paintings for which Sanderby was famous were the only witnesses as Susannah Garland slipped secretly along the gallery of her uncle's house. She wore the pink taffeta gown she had finished barely an hour earlier, and over her arm was a heavy winter cloak which dragged behind her on the polished wooden floor. Pausing by one of the tall windows overlooking the magnificent park, she stared out, but it was quite dark now; the short January day had faded swiftly beneath the shroud of mist and winter clouds which had lain over this part of England all day. Glancing swiftly back along the gallery in case she had been seen after all and her purpose guessed, she hurried on. No one must know she was meeting her cousin Miles like this, least of all her uncle, Lord Devereux.

Dancing firelight from the open library door lay like a barrier across her path, and she halted in dismay, knowing instinctively that her uncle was there. Through the doorway she could see the elegant room where the firelight leaped over leather-bound books and turned the richly tasseled curtains to a deep crimson. Lord Devereux stood alone by the huge fireplace, gazing into the heart of the flames. His hands were clasped so tightly behind him that his knuckles were taut and white. The powdered wig he always wore lay on a nearby table and his bald head gleamed in the moving light. His heavy-browed face was cold and his thin lips were pressed together in that hard line which was a constant reminder of the evil temper which made him one of the most disliked men in the realm. The squat figure in its costly blue frock coat and beige breeches looked somehow demoniac in the glowing light, and his frightened niece melted back into the shadows of the gallery. He was her mother's brother, but she knew that he loathed her. She was a reminder of a past scandal, of a disastrous misalliance with an impoverished schoolmaster. Slowly she edged past the doorway and then almost ran on to keep her assignation with Miles. Her heart was thundering, a mixture of fear and excitement which was unsettling. She loved Miles Devereux very much, but she was terrified of his autocratic father. She descended the staircase to the echoing hall with its immense chandeliers and pink marble tables, and then at last she was outside in the icy night.

The pink taffeta gown with its little puffed sleeves and high waistline was too flimsy for such bitter weather, and she quickly put on the drab winter cloak, raising the hood over her tawny hair. In the darkness, where only some oil lamps pierced the gloom, her eyes looked almost violet, and her heart-shaped face was very pale. She waited a moment, still afraid that she had been seen, but everything was still and quiet, and so she gathered her skirts and hurried on down the wide, shallow steps toward the drive.

The mist which had lingered over the park all day was heavier now. It had risen early from the nearby Thames and spread slowly over the grounds until it enveloped the house. The ornamental lake and the protective fringe of evergreens which had been planted to screen the house from the busy London road were invisible now; she could not even see the lights of the lodge shining through the opacity of the night. It was impossible to imagine that London was barely five miles away or that Britain in 1804 was once again at war with France and had been these past eight months or more. The night was so calm and peaceful that there surely could not be something as ugly as war to mar it.

The wheel marks of Miles's curricle were still to be seen on the gravel drive as she crossed to the wet lawns and the looming shadows of the dripping rhododendrons. She gasped as one of her uncle's peacocks cried out suddenly, a jarring sound which was like a shriek of fear in the silence. Behind her Sanderby was already blurred and indistinct, but ahead she could see the embankment edging the tidal reaches of the Thames.

The river slid silently past the southern boundary of the estate, the tide high so that there were no ugly mudbanks to spoil the smooth water. Even at this hour there was still some traffic passing to and fro. A barque slipped downstream on the current, sitting low in the water, her sails limp and still as the flow of water took her effortlessly toward her destination. A Royal Navy longboat labored upstream, the sailors straining at the oars and an immaculately uniformed lieutenant sitting upright in the prow. It moved away into the mist and vanished from sight. For those men the war with Bonaparte's France was a reality, not a topic to be idly mentioned from time to time at the breakfast table or over a dish of tea.

The wash from the two craft lapped against the shore as she continued toward the boathouse, and she heard the wavelets gurgling and splashing around the little jetty where in the summer her uncle's fashionable Whig society guests would alight from their elegant barges.

A light glowed in the boathouse and she stretched up on her tiptoes next to a window to look in. Her uncle's golden barge rocked gently at its moorings and some upturned skiffs rested against the far wall. The floor was littered with nets and boathooks, and everything was lit by a dimmed lantern on the floor next to the barge.

Miles lounged thoughtfully in the barge, leaning back on the scarlet cushions and gazing at nothing in particular. His face was withdrawn, sullen almost. His golden hair was startling in the half-light and there was an air of fashionable indolence and refinement about him. He was finely made, almost beautiful, and only his dark eyebrows and pale blue eyes showed that he was Lord Devereux's son. Where Susannah's uncle was short and thickset, Miles was tall and graceful. Unseen, she watched him for a moment more. She had loved him from the first moment she had arrived at Sanderby, an orphan of only fifteen. She had been penniless, alone, and frightened, but Miles had made her feel welcome, he alone had been kind. She was twenty now, and still in love with him. How could she not fall in love with her handsome golden cousin?

He got up immediately as she came into the boathouse. "Did anyone see you?"

"No."

He relaxed visibly, flicking an imaginary speck of dust from his exquisite green velvet sleeve as he climbed out of the barge and came toward her. He kissed her, but it was such a brief caress—too brief. She couldn't help noticing how swiftly he released her or how he seemed to be avoiding meeting her eyes. Something was wrong. No, no, she must be imagining it. She chided herself for allowing her thoughts to run away with her.

Oblivious of the touch of the night air, she removed her cloak to show him the pink taffeta dress. She twirled once, and the rich material rustled pleasingly. "How do you like it? I worked and worked today to have it finished to show you tonight."

"It's very pleasant."

She stared at him, a little crushed by his lack of enthusiasm. "*Pleasant*? Miles Devereux, all my hard work and ingenuity went into this dress and all you can find to say about it is that it's *pleasant*! Shame on you, I swear I've a mind to be in a pet with you!"

He touched the taffeta sleeve, smoothing the heavy silk between his fingers. "The gown is very beautiful, Susannah. It would seem that you have inherited more than a little of your mother's brilliance with needle and thread, for this gown would grace any fashionable London drawing room. Who knows, it may even be good enough for a Chippenham farmer's wife!"

She flinched at the cutting reminder of her life before she had come to Sanderby when her dead mother, although a proud Devereux, had been forced to earn her living as a dressmaker. "Even farmers' wives can be particular," she said slowly. "And my mother—your aunt, may I remind you—was a very discerning dressmaker."

"I hardly need reminding that my aunt was a low dressmaker!"

"Miles!" She was very hurt by his whole manner now.

"It's hardly the thing to boast of such a connection," he went on. "The *beau monde* would regard it as most reprehensible."

"What's wrong, Miles? Why are you being like this?"

"Must there be something wrong for me to be ashamed of your background?"

"Please stop."

"Don't look at me like that!" he cried, turning away sharply and leaning his hands on the barge's golden rail.

"I . . . I think that I had better go, for I don't wish to quarrel with you—not with you, Miles."

He caught her hand then, pulling her into his arms and

4

burying his face against the tawny curls pinned high on her head. "Forgive me," he whispered, kissing her face then. "Please forgive me, for I did not mean to hurt you."

She held him tightly, her eyes closed. She could feel his body trembling and smell the perfume of costmary clinging to his clothes. The fragrance tingled in her nostrils.

He rested his cheek against her warm hair. "Why oh why did your mother have to make a misalliance with a damned schoolmaster? Why could she not have been as meek and obliging a bride as every other Devereux woman and make a grand match with some nobleman?"

"She loved my father."

"Aye, and there's the rub, eh?" He smiled at her, cupping her face in his hands. "I wish to God I were not going up to Town soon."

"Fibber. Nothing would keep you away from Sir Percy's gaming tables. Nothing at all."

"Am I that hopeless a case of gambling fever?"

"You most certainly are. Many families would have been ruined by activities such as yours—you are fortunate that the Devereuxs of Sanderby are so very wealthy that your debts can be absorbed."

"Yes, I fear you are right." He released her abruptly, a nuance of his earlier mood returning suddenly. "Gambling has indeed been my downfall, Susannah, you do not know how much."

"All gentlemen gamble, it is expected of them."

"But it is not expected that they shall always lose."

"Your excursions to Town *are* a little costly," she said with a smile. But she did not feel as lighthearted as her outward appearance would suggest. He was so strange tonight, so pale and tense, and how frequently his tongue passed nervously over his lower lip. It was a habit she recognized well; something had happened to upset him, and whatever it was made him want to take his anger out on her this time.

"Miles, something *is* wrong, isn't it?" she asked at last.

"Wrong? Why should there be?"

"Because you are behaving very oddly."

"I am devastated," he said with a short laugh. "Here I stand, the very epitome of all that is noble and elegant, and you tell me that I am odd. Now it shall be my turn to be in a pet."

His tone was light and bantering, but it was lacking in his

usual charm and ease. He leaned again on the rail of the barge, his head bowed as he kicked idly at a small stone, the tassels of his shining hessians swinging angrily to and fro.

Unease spread through her as she watched him. "Please tell me, Miles, I cannot bear it when I *know* you are not being honest with me."

His blue eyes were large and unhappy then. "Susannah," he said softly, "never forget that I love you."

"Forget?"

"When . . . when I return from Town this time my betrothal to Lady Agnes Winston will be announced."

The cold of the night suddenly washed bitterly over her. She stared at him, her body quite numb with shock. The air seemed to move, to whirl around her so that she could feel nothing but the heartbreak his words brought. "Betrothal?" she whispered.

"I am to marry her this summer."

"I did not know . . . you said nothing . . ."

"I don't want to marry her, you must know that."

"Know?" she echoed. "How would *I* know anything of what you do when you are away from Sanderby?"

"I have not deceived you when I've been away, I swear that I have not. The whole matter has been arranged without my knowledge, I knew nothing at all until tonight. She means nothing to me, Susannah, you must believe me."

Miserably she closed her eyes, and the tears pricked painfully. She could see Lady Agnes, so tall and beautiful with her magnificent red hair and penchant for wearing pink. "She is heiress to one of the greatest fortunes in England," she said slowly, "and she could not possibly be more politically acceptable to your father, as she too is a Whig of the first order. Politically and financially you could not make a better match, could you? She is the ideal future mistress of Sanderby, an Earl's daughter with vast lands adjoining yours, connections of the most exclusive kind, a veritable open sesame to the continued approval and patronage of the Prince of Wales! What could possibly be better for you, Miles?"

"She may be all of those things, but I don't love her and never will. I find her quite disagreeable, strong-willed, and overbearing. I believe she has agreed to this match because she thinks I will make a suitably meek husband for the future when it comes to her infidelities. I love you, Susannah."

6

"But you will not marry me. I'm nothing. Your father loathes the very sight of me because I bring back the awkward past. I'm not even considered fit to dine with your influential Whig friends because I may raise the memory of the blot on the Devereux escutcheon! When there are guests, I am confined to my room, most of your acquaintances are unaware that I even exist, and those who do could not describe my appearance in the slightest, as they have never seen me! I am anonymous, Miles, and I always will be. These past months with you like this have been a lie, and in my heart I knew that nothing would ever come of it. I just pretended that this day would never come." Her eyes were bright with tears.

He caught her hand and pulled her close. "I am forced to agree to this match. My hands are tied and there is nothing I dare do to halt it."

"What do you mean your hands are tied?" she breathed.

"I mean that unless I marry Agnes, then I shall of a certainty go to Fleet prison."

"Debtor's jail? If this is your notion of a jest, Miles . . ."

"It is no jest."

"But you are rich, your father is known to rival Croesus himself!"

"He is also known to want me to make a good match—and in this he has the whip hand. My gambling debts are so mountainous that I need a Croesus to save my neck. Unfortunately, Croesus cannot aid me as easily as once he could. He has made some bad investments, played recklessly with stocks and shares, and things are not as good financially as once they were. He has refused to save me from the duns this time, Susannah, unless I agree to marry money—Agnes Winston, to be precise. If I do not do as he says, then he will disown me and allow me to be flung in the Fleet, and if I ever get out again, I will not have Sanderby." He looked urgently into her tear-filled eyes. "Susannah, there are two things on this earth that I love. You are one, and the other is Sanderby. If I marry Agnes, then I believe I may keep both of those precious things that I love."

She stared at him.

He kissed her for a long while, his lips moving slowly over hers. "Nothing need ever change," he murmured. "We can go on as we now do, loving each other . . ."

"Nothing need change?" She moved sharply away, her eyes

wide. "But, Miles, *everything's* changed! You belong to her now!"

"What does that matter? It is a marriage of convenience, Susannah, not a bond of love!"

"It matters too much for me, Miles. You may have no scruples about this, but I have far too many. My honor would not permit me to continue to see you this way."

"Susannah . . ."

She shook her head slowly, bending to pick up the cloak and put it on. For a last time she looked at him, and then she turned to run from the boathouse and out into the cold night. Hot tears burned her cheeks as she ran along the path and onto the grass, and she didn't see the motionless figure on the little jetty.

Lord Devereux watched his niece's flight with great interest, his veiled eyes moving then to the dejected figure of his son by the boathouse door. So that was the way of it, eh? Lord Devereux took a jeweled snuffbox from his pocket and flicked it open. He inhaled the snuff deeply, snapping the box closed again and returning it to his pocket. Nothing must stand in the way of the Winston match; there must be no risk at all if the status quo of life at Sanderby was to be maintained. Miss Susannah Garland would have to be removed before Miles discovered that he had after all a little backbone to hold out for what he wanted. Yes, little Miss Garland would have to be sent away, and the farther away the better for all concerned. Entirely beyond the reach of mortal man, if necessary.

2

It was late the following afternoon and darkness was falling again before Susannah felt able to emerge from her room to face Miles and her uncle. She had cried so bitterly through the night that her eyes were swollen and red and she had felt too miserable to brave either the breakfast table or luncheon. In the morning she had sent word that she had a headache and would remain in her room. Miles had guessed the truth and had come to her door several times, but she had not answered him. If she spoke to him just yet, she knew that she would be sorely tempted to give in, to yield to what he wanted and agree to continue their affair even after his marriage. It would be so easy, such a salve to her broken heart—but it would also be very wrong and dishonorable. To sever everything now was surely the only course, for to delay would make it harder and more painful. But as she stood by the window watching her uncle's agent spurring his horse away from the house in the gathering darkness, she knew that ending her liaison with the man she loved would be the most difficult task she had ever had to face in her life.

The agent skirted the lake, and her dull eyes followed him to the lodge, where the gates were opened and he rode quickly out and turned in the direction of London, vanishing from sight in the gloom by the fringe of evergreens. Slowly she allowed her gaze to wander over the park, taking in the great curve of the Thames where ships plied to and fro on the high tide, and the beautiful grounds laid out by Inigo Jones. She had been fooling herself, she thought, refusing to face the inevitable. She would never be mistress of Sanderby, for no matter how much Miles loved her, he would not dare to defy his father by taking such a dowerless bride. It was all over now; she must resign herself to it and put on as brave a face as she possibly could.

She went to the small dressing table which was the only elegant piece of furniture in a room which was otherwise poor and threadbare. Not for Susannah Garland a grand chamber; she had a room on the top floor, almost among the servants in the attics. Her situation warranted a hard bed, a worn carpet, an upholstered chair which had been patched until it looked very sorry—and this beautiful dressing table which had once graced the late Lady Devereux's room. Susannah smiled wryly, for had there been a suitably battered dressing table somewhere in the house, no doubt she would have been given it. Maybe coming to Sanderby had been a mistake after all. Her father had died of consumption when she was only thirteen, but she knew that he had a sister who lived in Covent Garden in London—maybe life with Aunt Garland would have been less painful than life with Uncle Devereux. But Susannah's mother had on her deathbed extracted a promise from her daughter that she would go to Sanderby, not Covent Garden, that she would attempt to make a life for herself in the grandeur of the Devereux family and maybe one day make a marriage which was as advantageous as her mother's was not. And so Susannah had dutifully come to Sanderby, and from the outset her uncle had left her in no doubt that he was doing his duty, no more than that. But also from the outset there had been Miles. She stared at her reflection in the mirror. Only her love for Miles had kept her at Sanderby, made her endure her uncle's unkindness and spite. She had been expected to know her place and keep rigidly to it. What would Lord Devereux say if he knew how very much she had wanted to step out of her low station and reach up for the very stars themselves?

Opening a small drawer, she took out a japanned box of Chinese colors. She had saved for months out of her small allowance in order to purchase it, just as she had saved for the pink taffeta dress, and until now she had never brought herself to use any of the little colored papers inside. But tonight . . . tonight she would have to do what she could with her ravaged face if she was to sit down to dine with Miles and his father. Wetting the tip of her finger, she dampened a green paper and then rubbed it gently against her cheek. It left a rosy bloom which was a vast improvement on her previous pallor. Encouraged, she applied it to the other cheek. The white papers took away a little of the salt-reddened look around her eyes, and when she had combed and pinned her hair again, she thought that she would do.

The pink taffeta felt chilly as it slithered against her skin, and she quickly took up her white woolen shawl and the pink reticule she had made to match the dress. She smiled bravely again as she fluffed out the dainty skirts, for had it not been for her determination and the skill she inherited from her mother, she would have had to content herself with the plain wool her uncle considered suitable attire for his church-mouse niece. Not for her the delights of chiffons and other such elegancies, or the services of a maid to help her. But as she looked at herself in the mirror now, she thought that no outsider would have known. The gown was fashionable, her coiffure would not have disgraced Devonshire House, and her poise was quite befitting Lord Devereux's niece. The perfume of lavender surrounded her and her hair shone a deep honey color in the candlelight, but as the sound of the dinner gong echoed through the house, her guard dropped a little and the fear and unhappiness showed through again. Arranging her shawl until it was the way she wanted it, she turned to leave the cold, bare room and go down to the warm sumptuousness of the dining room.

A coal boy was tending the fire on one of the landings as she approached, but he took no notice of her as she passed. No one took much notice of Susannah; she was a nonentity in the house. The housekeeper, Mrs. Hunter, came out of one of the linen stores, her keys clinking. She bowed her head, her white mobcap trembling, and she smiled—for if Susannah was not of any importance, that did not mean that she was disliked.

"Good evening, Miss Susannah."

"Good evening, Mrs. Hunter."

The housekeeper watched her for a moment. What would His Lordship have to say if he knew of the goings-on in the boathouse? Yes indeed, what *would* he say? But who was going to tell him and spoil it for the young lovers? Not Abigail Hunter, to begin with. The housekeeper hummed to herself as she locked the linen cupboard and went to the back stairs which led down to the kitchens.

Susannah's hand moved smoothly over the polished handrail as she descended the sweeping staircase with its great Ionic columns and echoing marble. But when she reached the door of the dining room, a door which for once was not presided over by a red-liveried footman, the unguarded conversation from within made her halt and pay close attention.

Her uncle's voice was quivering with barely suppressed anger as he faced his son. "And I tell you, boy, that you'll do as you are told! It is all arranged—signed, sealed, and damned well delivered! The Earl of Winston has agreed the terms, and so have I!"

"I was not consulted!"

"The marriage is too important to consider your finer feelings!" snapped his father. "If you are to stay out of jail and if I am to keep Sanderby as it is now, then you must take a wealthy wife."

"Take one yourself, you are free!"

"Agnes Winston wants *you*, my dear boy, not me. She has a fancy for a pretty golden husband, so I believe."

"There are other brides."

"Not one with all the attributes of this one. I do not think I need to enumerate them yet again, do I?"

"No. But I still do not wish to marry her."

"No, you'd prefer to dally with that simpering miss I am to call my niece!"

Miles was stunned. "How did you know about that?"

"It doesn't matter how—just that I do and I am taking steps to put an end to it forthwith. If you think I am about to jeopardize this match because you have an itch for Susannah Garland, then you are sadly mistaken."

"I love her."

"Love? *Love*? What has that to do with this? Compulsion is the rule of this little game, my laddo, and you had better face that fact right here and now. Do not think I would shrink from carrying out my threats—I would willingly let the duns have you, willingly disown you if you go against my wishes. And believe me, refusing to marry Agnes Winston would be seriously going against my wishes." He said this last in a low, soft voice which made Susannah shudder as she stood listening.

"Right," went on Lord Devereux with some satisfaction. "I take it that that is the end of your tiresome objections?"

"I have little choice, have I?"

"None at all."

"I will marry Agnes."

"There was never any serious doubt of that. However, I fully intend making certain that any further notion of heroics on your part is squashed from the outset."

"What do you mean?"

"I mean that I intend sending Susannah Garland away. To my estates in Ireland, to be precise. That is far enough away to keep you in line."

"That is unnecessarily cruel to her!" cried Miles desperately. "At least allow her to go to her aunt in London—"

"And have her within five miles of you still? Allow me a little more intelligence than that! No, she goes to Ireland, and that is the end of it. I've sent my agent to London, he's to see that the *Jacqueline* is made ready to sail on tomorrow's morning tide."

Susannah stepped involuntarily back from the door, her eyes wide. She was to be sent away? Sent all the way to Ireland to keep her from Miles?

Something caught Miles's eye outside at that moment and he went to the window. "There's a carriage by the lodge, I can see the lamps."

"Damnation, I want no guests here tonight! Do you recognize the drag?"

"I believe . . . God above, I do believe it is Jeffrey Stratton's!" cried Miles in amazement. "What would that close little Pittite Tory want with this Whig stronghold? Yes, I see it more clearly now, it *is* Stratton's drag."

"We will have to receive him, dammit."

Susannah heard her uncle's steps approaching the door and she turned to run back up the stairs, reaching the landing above as his angry voice echoed through the house calling the butler.

In her room Susannah gathered her few belongings together in a large cloth bag. She had no clear plan in mind, just that she must escape from Sanderby if she was to avoid a life of imprisonment on her uncle's Irish estates, for that she would be a prisoner was not to be doubted. Lord Devereux would take no chance at all of her contacting Miles before the wedding had safely taken place—and probably not even then. Maybe his plans would be even more final. Tears blurred her eyes as she packed away her sewing implements, her Chinese box of colors, and the other little things which formed her only possessions. Picking up the bag when she had at last put on her old cloak, she paused to take a long, steadying breath. There was only one place she could go, and that was to her father's sister, for she had no one else in the world. With a last glance around the room which had been hers for the last five years, she went out.

No one saw her at all, and she reached the great staircase before she realized that she could go no farther, as Sir Jeffrey Stratton was waiting in the hall. True to his Whig leanings, Lord Devereux was keeping the notoriously Tory Sir Jeffrey waiting.

Jeffrey Stratton was a little taller and a little older than Miles, and where Miles was very fair, he was dark. His hair was wavy and fashionably disheveled and even from that distance she could see how gray his eyes were. They were shrewd eyes, they missed nothing, and they were just the eyes she would expect in a man of his reputation. Rumors always circulated about him, whispers which if all true made him a very dangerous man to cross. At least two men had died at his hand in duels, and more than one husband had been wounded after being foolhardy enough to call him out. There were unsavory rumors too about his bride's death, a death which left him conveniently rich after being previously only a little wealthy. Susannah's life at Sanderby may have been sheltered, but even she knew what was said of this refined, very handsome man. But looking at him now, it was hard to believe any of it. His appearance was one of absolute perfection, his coat fitting his slender figure as if molded to it, and there was not a single crease to spoil the discreet dark blue cloth which smacked so of Bond Street. His cravat was complicated without being in any way ridiculous, and his long legs were encased in spotless cream breeches which left little of his anatomy to the imagination. His movements were unhurried and graceful, and there was a faint smile on his lips as he removed his shining top hat and slowly teased off his kid gloves. He glanced at the morning-room door, where he guessed his host to be. He knew full well why he was being kept kicking his elegant heels in the drafty hall like this, and it amused him.

At last Lord Devereux emerged, having decided that he had timed Sir Jeffrey's punishment to a nicety. He came to stand on the far side of the pink marble table from his unwanted visitor, and from her vantage point in the shadows on the stairs Susannah knew instantly that there was very little love lost between the two men. Her uncle inclined his head briefly. "Stratton."

"Devereux." Sir Jeffrey sketched a bow which bordered on the insolent.

"I cannot imagine what possible reason you could have for coming here."

"Necessity named the tune, sir."

"I'll warrant."

"I must reach Windsor, and the bad roads have damaged my carriage."

"Windsor?" Lord Devereux's hard eyes glittered suspiciously. "You go to the King?"

Sir Jeffrey smiled enigmatically. "That is my intention."

"You go for Pitt? Yes, I see that you do! Something is afoot, and your damned Sweet Billy plans to return to power!"

"Do not hasten to the wrong conclusion, my lord, for although I do indeed go indirectly on Pitt's errand, it is not in connection with a change of government—at least, not directly."

"You may have learned how to hedge from your master, but you ain't got his style! Pitt *does* intend returning!"

Sir Jeffrey was infinitely patient. "I go to Windsor because there are rumors that the King is ill again."

Lord Devereux gave a short, triumphant laugh. "Insane again, you mean! I'll *warrant* Pitt has sent you scuttling on his behalf, for the King's illness means a regency, and a regency can only mean the Whigs in power instead of your wishy-washy Tory Addington!"

"My dear sir, I am far more concerned that the Prince of Wales may have charge of England's fate than I am with who it is who occupies Downing Street! The thought of that fat buffoon having a final say in my country's fate fills me with absolute horror."

Lord Devereux smiled unpleasantly. "I still fail to see why I should extend hospitality to you, Stratton. Why on God's own earth should I wish to accommodate your Pittite mission?"

"It is not a Pittite mission, sir, I go to Windsor because the King has commanded me to. Oh, he has also demanded to see Oliver Cromwell and Alexander, but unfortunately I am the only one of the trio available. I would hate to have to tell His Majesty, whose memory as you well know is most excellent even when he's ill, that I was unable to obey his command because a Whig lordling refused to help."

Susannah held her breath. Even in her state of fear and misery she could still admire Sir Jeffrey's coolness and still take a great delight in seeing him get the better of her unpleasant uncle.

A dull stain of fury spread across Lord Devereux's face. He turned and snapped his fingers at a nearby footman. "See that the barouche is made ready!" he said shortly.

Sir Jeffrey sketched another bow. "You are too kind, sir."

"Let us not beat about the bush a moment longer, Stratton. My reluctance to deal with you has nothing to do with our opposing ideas on politics, has it?"

"That is all in the past."

"Is it?"

"Oh, I still consider you palpably guilty of ruining my father, but—alas—I cannot prove it."

There was a cold smile on Lord Devereux's lips. "That is your misfortune."

"It is indeed."

"Your father was a fool."

"It is his son you face now, sir, and I strongly advise you to guard your tongue."

For a moment Susannah thought her uncle's temper would get the better of his common sense. His knuckles were white as he looked venomously across the table. "Do not think I will give you an excuse to call me out, Stratton."

"I rather think I need no reason beyond that which has been there ever since you decided to involve yourself in the affairs of the Stratton family." Sir Jeffrey picked up his hat and gloves. "I will not take up any more of your precious time, my lord." He inclined his head and walked to the door.

Susannah's uncle remained by the table for a moment, his deep hatred and great anger written large on his still face. She did not know what it was that lay in the past between him and Jeffrey Stratton, but it was obviously very bitter. But whatever it was, she did not care; all she wanted was for her uncle to leave the hall so that she could make good her escape from Sanderby.

At long last he turned on his heel and strode back to the morning room, slamming the door behind him so that the sound echoed through the empty hall. Susannah crept from her shadowy hiding place and hurried on down the stairs, running across the hall to the door.

With the precious cloth bag clutched tightly to her breast, she slipped outside and hid by the great Corinthian pillars of the portico. Her heart thundered as she pressed back in the shadows. Sir Jeffrey's carriage stood waiting at the foot of the steps, its glossy mirrorlike panels shining in the lamplight. The four perfectly matched black Hanoverians stamped and snorted as they waited, blankets thrown over their backs by their anxious coachman, who fussed around them. Sir Jeffrey himself stood by the lead horses, and she heard his voice quite clearly.

"Do you think you can get back to Berkeley Square, John?"

"I believe so, sir, though 'twill take a fair while."

Susannah gazed at the magnificent carriage. Everything about it, its trappings and team, was black and excellent. It was one of the most handsome and expensive drags she had ever seen—even here at Sanderby, where in the past some very grand equipages had been seen. The poor King himself would have been proud to possess such a vehicle.

She began to slowly descend the steps, her eyes on Sir Jeffrey and his coachman, but they were still too concerned with the team to even glance around at the cloaked figure on the steps. She reached the lawns and the shelter of the rhododendrons without being seen, and then she paused to take stock. A single glance at the lodge told her that she could not merely walk out of Sanderby, for the gates were firmly closed. There was no other way of leaving except by the river, and that was a route she did not dare to take alone and at night. Dismayed, she stood in the darkness, the cloth bag held close as she looked at the closed gates, which were quite plain to see by the light of the lantern the lodgekeeper held as he waited for Sir Jeffrey to leave. She knew the lodgekeeper, but she knew too that he would never consent to open the gates and allow His Lordship's niece to walk out unattended into the night. But she *must* get away; somehow she must escape from Sanderby and her uncle!

Sir Jeffrey's voice interrupted her thoughts as he spoke to the coachman again. "Ah, here is the long-awaited barouche. You had best begin the journey back to London, then."

"Very well, Sir Jeffrey."

She stared at the carriage, and without hesitating a moment longer, she hurried back toward it, keeping the vehicle itself between her and the two men. They saw nothing as she opened the door and climbed inside, lying down on the floor of the empty vehicle with her face pressed against the pale blue velvet upholstery, which smelled faintly of southernwood and tobacco smoke.

She heard her uncle's barouche draw up alongside and felt Sir Jeffrey's carriage sway as the coachman climbed back onto his box and prepared to leave. Her heart was beating wildly as she lay there listening to the barouche drive off, and she closed her eyes tightly as the coachman stirred the black Hanoverians into action. With each passing second she expected to hear someone shout, the carriage to halt, and the door to be opened to reveal her hiding place. But the carriage drove slowly on unchecked, and at last she sat up on the cold seat, looking out at the dark grounds slipping past.

The carriage skirted the lake, where she could vaguely see the white Temple of Apollo among the trees which tumbled down on the far side. She heard the sound of the little waterfall by the rustic bridge. At the lodge the coachman shouted to the lodgekeeper and the lanternlight slanted into the carriage for a moment. The gates clanged behind her and the carriage moved a little more swiftly on the London road, swaying from side to side on its springs as the team trotted through the darkness.

Susannah stared out without seeing. She was bereft of feeling suddenly. So much had happened in so short a time. Tears shone on her cheeks as she rested her tired head against the blue velvet. She felt lost and so very alone. And she was desperately afraid of what lay ahead for her now.

3

She hardly noticed the towns and villages the carriage passed through on the way to London, and it wasn't until the outskirts of the city itself were reached that she began to wonder about her aunt. She knew nothing of her father's sister beyond the fact that she lived in King Lane, Covent Garden, next to the sign of the White Horse. Would her aunt even want to see her, let alone offer her shelter?

The carriage passed through Tyburn turnpike and turned into Park Lane, where some very beautiful houses looked out over the shadowy expanse of Hyde Park. The lamplit streets were very busy, crowded with drays, wagons, horsemen, and elegant carriages, and there was such a lot of noise after the countryside Susannah was used to. There were so many horses, so many wheels, church bells sounding the hour of ten, and people shouting that she was sure her head would ache from it all. She gazed through the glittering windows of the Mayfair houses and saw rooms with rich silk or brocade walls, shining mirrors, and beautiful furniture. There was such wealth all around, so much beauty for the *beau monde* to surround itself with, that she could only gaze out in wonder. Sanderby had been magnificent and so very large. These houses were mostly small, but their grandeur matched the house by the Thames.

Berkeley Square was wide and its grassy center was planted with trees. The carriage came to a standstill outside Sir Jeffrey's austere, dignified house and the door opened as the head butler hurried out to see why the carriage had returned. As he spoke to the coachman, Susannah looked up at the

19

house. It was of brick with stone facings and its round-headed door was approached by three stone steps with balustrades. Arrow-headed iron railings sprang up into a graceful arch in front of the entrance and an iron lantern was suspended over the steps.

Satisfied with the coachman's explanation, the butler returned to the house, and the carriage moved on again, turning out of the square and into the narrow mews lane behind. Closely ranged tenements crowded in after the wide spaciousness of the square and the air was full of the smell of horses. There were lights burning in the loft over Sir Jeffrey's coach house and some footmen lounged in a doorway, their gold-braided coats unbuttoned and their hands in their pockets in a slovenly way which would never have been permitted in their master's presence. A string of washing was suspended across the lane and a woman shouted crossly as the carriage dragged against a white shirt. A dog began to bark and was silenced as the carriage at last came to a standstill. Some grooms hurried to unharness the sweating horses, leading them away to a well-earned rest in the comfortable stalls.

Susannah crouched on the floor of the carriage as some men pushed it carefully into its place beside the only other vehicle in the coach house, a smart black cabriolet which Sir Jeffrey no doubt tooled dashingly through the streets during the Season. She raised her head at last and saw the men carrying the harness away to clean it, while another man drove a dairy cow into a nearby shed where a milkmaid waited with two pails.

The minutes passed and everything became more quiet after the momentary excitement of the carriage's unexpected return. The horses had been groomed and were now contentedly chewing a mixture of corn and beans, and most of the men had adjourned to the loft, where a woman had brewed a large pot of tea. In the cowshed the milkmaid completed her task and carefully carried the two pails back to the main house. Silence reigned at last and Susannah dared to sit up on the velvet seat once more. But was it safe yet to leave the carriage?

Slowly and carefully she opened the door and slipped down onto the cobbled floor. The cow lowed softly, raising its head over the half-door to look curiously at her. Lifting her cloth bag down, she hurried out of the coach house.

After the relative warmth of the carriage, the bitter cold of the January night struck her forcibly, making her breath catch in her throat. The pall of coal smoke hanging in the frozen night above the city was heavy and impenetrable as she walked swiftly along the narrow mews lane, picking her way around ice-covered puddles. There seemed to be no one around now, for Sir Jeffrey Stratton was one of the few in Town before the commencement of the Season.

She heard the Watch calling as she reached Berkeley Square again. The bare plane trees loomed in the darkness and the parish lamps looked pale and watery. She could make out a mounted statue of the King dressed as a Roman emperor in the center of the square as she approached Bruton Street. She glanced frequently behind, still expecting to see someone giving chase, but it seemed that she had escaped from her uncle's clutches without anyone knowing at all. She wondered if her absence had been discovered yet back at Sanderby. What was Miles thinking? Was he sorry? Did he feel anxious for her safety? She bit her lip to fight back the easy tears. Yes, of course he would be worried, he had been speaking the truth when he told her he loved her.

She walked more slowly now, for she was in a narrow but fashionable street where there were still a number of people to be seen, mostly men who walked casually along the pavements, gazing in the sparkling windows of the shops where outside lamps played their light over the costly array of goods displayed inside. Gradually she became aware of the scarcity of other women, and those she did see were painted and brazen as they openly flaunted themselves. No *lady* would be seen out alone, she thought in dismay, and certainly not at this time of night.

But even as the thought struck her, a tall dandy dressed entirely in green silk stepped in her path, raising his quizzing glass as he perused her from head to toe. "Well, now," he drawled lazily, "and what have we here? Your name, Oh Divinity?"

"Please let me pass, sir."

He caught her arm. "Such a divine creature as you must surely be dedicated to gaiety and pleasure. Name your price."

"Leave me alone, sir! I am respectable!" she cried in growing fear, glancing around for help but seeing no one was taking any notice.

"Respectable?" He laughed. "Out in Bond Street at this time? Come, now, don't play games!"

She wrenched her arm away from him and began to run. His footsteps were close behind and she could hear him cursing furiously beneath his breath. Desperate to get away from him, she ran into the crowded yard of a small coaching inn, pushing her way among the people until he must lose sight of her. She could see him beneath the arched entrance, his rouged face angry; then he was forced to stand aside as a mail coach arrived and began to discharge its tired passengers. Touts and ostlers hurried about their business as she caught a last sight of the dandy. He took out a lace handkerchief and flicked it angrily over his green sleeve. There were others, he was thinking, he'd not waste time or energy on some little Venus with a mind to play hard-to-get.

She exhaled slowly with relief as he walked away from the inn. She glanced around at the mails and stages drawn up neatly and at some coachmen and guards who were arguing about lost time on the Oxford road. Bales of straw and leather buckets of water littered the courtyard, and the passengers were one and all grumbling about stiff limbs and aching backs as they made their way into the warm taproom from which emanated a delicious smell of roast beef.

Susannah's stomach was pinched with hunger at that appetizing smell, for she had not eaten all day and now felt both cold and faint. An orange girl sauntered past with her fruit tray, her cries ringing above the clatter all around, and a pieman's bell jangled loudly.

The smell of the hot pies was almost too much, and Susannah put out her hand to him. "A pie if you please."

As she took out her purse and counted out the coins, his shrewd watery eyes moved curiously over her. She was alone; he'd noticed her run in from the street with that dandy in hot pursuit—yet she didn't look the usual run of whore. He gave her the pie. "Business bad tonight, eh?" he asked.

Her face flamed immediately and she took the pie, turning away from him.

" 'Ere," he said more politely, "I didn't mean no 'arm. Anyone can make a mistake. Run away, then, have you?"

She stared at him, going suddenly cold.

He grinned. "Come on, now, if you ain't a streetwalker then you've got to've run away. There ain't no other way a wench like you'd be out alone. I've bin around long enough to recognize the signs, there's lots of 'em arriving here all the time. Come far, have you?"

22

"Far enough."

He nodded at the noncommittal reply. "Right enough, it's your business. But hark on now, you're very foolish to be out alone. Ain't you got nowhere to go? No friend?"

"I want to go to my aunt in Covent Garden."

"Well, *there's* a fashionable, respectable neighborhood for you!" he said with a guffaw.

She looked at him in dismay. Surely Covent Garden was not *so* disreputable?

He got over his mirth and spoke more kindly. "You've got money in your purse, I saw that. My advice then is that you take a hackney coach to get to your aunt's. Hackneys may not be grand or 'owt, but they're a damn sight safer than the streets. Old Joe over there's a hackney coachman, and a reliable one as far as they goes. It's only just over a mile from here to Covent Garden, so don't you let him charge you more 'n eight pence. Here, Joe, I got a fare for you!"

The old coachman looked up from where he sat with his mug of ale on the foot of the gallery steps. His face was wrinkled and weather-beaten and his old box-coat was dirty and worn. "Where to?" he called above the noise of the courtyard.

"Covent Garden," replied the pieman.

The coachman spat roundly on the floor and scraped out his blackened clay pipe as he considered for a moment, his rheumy eyes moving swiftly over Susannah as if gauging how much he could charge her.

The pieman grinned. "She knows it'll cost eight pence, you old rogue!"

Shoving his pipe into his coat and draining his mug, the coachman got up, scowling at the pieman. He sniffed, his breath silvery in the cold as he indicated a battered coach in a corner, its bony old horse standing with its head held very low. On the door panels she could still make out the family crest which showed that this sorry old vehicle had once been a prized possession of some fashionable aristocrat, but now it was scratched and the harness was patched.

As she climbed inside and sat on the musty, damp seat, she heard the coachman snap angrily at the grinning pieman, "Don't you want anyone to mek a honest living, Dan Parsons?"

"Aye, that's just what I *do* want," retorted the pieman, "and that's what I've just seen to, ain't it? Get on, now, she ain't the sort you should be fleecing, not a little maid like that! Shame on you, Joe!"

Still scowling, the coachman glanced at her. "Where to in Covent Garden?" he demanded ungraciously.

"Do you know the White Horse in King Lane?"

"I do." He slammed the door on her without asking anything more.

She just had time to raise her hand in thanks to the pieman as the coach rattled and bumped out of the yard, the glass in the windows rattling and the old springs complaining as the horse turned into Bond Street. She caught a glimpse of the dandy in green again, walking slowly with a plump, painted woman clinging to his arm.

The hackney coach rumbled eastward through the dark streets. Occasionally she saw carriages traveling in the same direction, conveying their passengers to the theaters and the opera house for which Covent Garden was famous. Occasionally too she saw animals being driven through the quiet streets on their way to market. Once the hackney coach had to halt while some red-uniformed soldiers marched past.

"Give Boney one for me!" shouted the coachman, waving his whip on high. "You kick the little frog off of the land and let Lord Nelson kick 'im off of the seas!"

Outside the White Horse tavern in King Lane the hackney drew up at the curb and the coachman climbed down slowly, rubbing his rheumatic knees and grumbling under his breath as he opened the door for her, his face sullen as he touched his hat and held his hand out. "Eight pence," he said shortly. He would have charged her more but for the pieman's interference.

She climbed down and paid him. He almost snatched the coins from her and then climbed back onto his perch, replacing an old horse blanket over his knees and coaxing the weary horse into life again. She watched the old carriage rattle away along the uneven street. She was alone again.

4

~

She looked around the dark street. The sound of laughter and the scratchy notes of a fiddle came from the smoke-filled rooms of the tavern. A drunken man reeled out, his breath reeking of brandy and tobacco as he staggered past her, weaving to and fro as he tried to make his way along the pavement. Across the street there was a coffeehouse, but the shadows moving against the upstairs curtains left her in no doubt as to the true purpose of the building. The whole street seemed to be an area of bagnios and bawdy houses, and there were several expensive carriages moving slowly along as their occupants appraised the various courtesans swaggering so brazenly everywhere, their breasts almost exposed even on such a cold night. A carriage came to a standstill and several prostitutes pushed toward the open door, thrusting their cards inside hopefully. One card was chosen, and with a triumphant glance at her conquered rivals, a woman in a striped dress and blue spencer climbed into the carriage, which then drove smartly off.

Susannah attracted some curious glances from the prostitutes as she stood so hesitantly outside the inn, but her demure appearance and obvious unease soon convinced them that she was no poacher upon their preserves.

Near where she stood, some small boys were throwing rotten fruit at a caricature of Bonaparte which someone had daubed cleverly on a wall. She stepped hastily aside as an orange splattered over the pavement near her feet.

After the minute of confusion when she had stood there just looking around, she turned to make her way to the house next to the tavern. It was a tall red-brick building with a light at one of its grimy windows. It did not look at all the sort of place she would have wished her aunt to live in, but now that she had got this far she did not have any choice but to go there. But even as she raised her hand to knock, a new sound carried through the night and she turned in horror. A coachman was shouting to his tired team, and it was a voice she recognized only too well. Peniston, her uncle's coachman! She stared down the street and saw Lord Devereux's dark red carriage turning the corner, the team straining as they sought to keep up their pace. Their flanks were foam-flecked, an indication of the breakneck pace at which they had been driven from Sanderby, and their breath was clearly visible in the cold air. What a fool she had been! She should have realized immediately that coming here would be the first thing her uncle would do! She could not move as the carriage came nearer; her legs would not obey her! And then at last she found the strength to hurry away from the door, going swiftly down the basement steps of the house next door and pressing back in the dark shadows as the carriage halted nearby.

She heard the door slam and a man's heavy steps approaching her aunt's door. Her uncle hammered his cane on the faded paintwork. "Open up, there!" he shouted, and Susannah noticed how very quiet King Lane suddenly was. Where a moment earlier the pavements had been crowded, now there was no one to be seen. The prostitutes had vanished and the small boys had run down an alley. It was so quiet that she distinctly heard someone in the house coming to the door.

A broad-bosomed woman with a fearsome face opened the door, standing with her arms folded as she surveyed her aristocratic caller. She seemed not in the least intimidated by him. "Well?"

"Miss Verity Garland?"

"No."

Susannah felt a surge of relief that this dragon was not her aunt.

"Tell her that Devereux of Sanderby is here."

"That might be difficult."

"Why?" he demanded testily, his uncertain temper threatening to snap.

"She croaked it two years back."

Susannah closed her eyes faintly. Oh, no . . . please, no.

"Dead, you say?"

"That's what I said. Croaked it."

"Has anyone else been here asking for her tonight?"

"And if there had, why should I be telling the likes of you?"

He spoke softly, his voice full of menace. "Because you would be better advised to tell me rather than make any foolish attempt to conceal the truth."

The woman's face lost a little of its composure then. "There . . . there's been no one come here at all, sir, I swear it."

"Have you seen a young woman, about twenty years of age, with honey-colored hair and blue eyes? A stranger."

"No, sir."

"If she does come here—"

"Then I'll see to it she's kept here while I send word to you," said the woman quickly.

"I'll be at my club—Brooks's in St. James. Ask for Devereux, *Lord* Devereux."

"Yes, sir . . . my lord." The woman bobbed a belated curtsy, wiping her shaking hands on her dirty apron.

Lord Devereux retraced his steps to the carriage, looking up and down the quiet street before climbing inside again. "My club," he said to the coachman.

Susannah listened as the carriage drew away, and when it had passed out of sight and hearing, she slowly emerged from the basement steps. She was not alone; the small boys came from their alley hiding place and the prostitutes returned to their parading. In a moment or so the noise of King Lane was as great as it had been before Lord Devereux's arrival.

Susannah looked miserably at the door of what had been her aunt's house. Aunt Garland was dead—now what was she to do? Looking across the street, she saw a board above a doorway: "MRS. HARPER'S LODGING HOUSE." There was nothing she could do tonight, but she must have somewhere to sleep. With a heavy heart she crossed the street to the lodging house.

The door was opened by a fat woman in a coarse brown dress. Her graying hair was pulled severely back from her pale face and a neat day-cap rested on her head. She did not smile.

Susannah swallowed. "I . . . I am looking for lodgings."

The humorless eyes flickered over her and then beyond to a prostitute who stood beneath a parish lamp. "Lottie? Do you know this one?"

Lottie came to the door, a hand on her swaying hips as she surveyed Susannah for a moment and then shrugged. "Don't know 'er."

"Not on the game, then?"

"Not that I know, but that don't mean—"

Susannah looked from one to the other a little angrily. "I am perfectly respectable!" she said. "I merely wish to take a room."

Lottie laughed. "Well, reckon she don't sound like no streetwalker, eh? Your lodging house's good name won't suffer from taking *her* in." Still laughing, the prostitute walked on, stepping quickly into the street as a barouche approached slowly.

The woman in brown looked at Susannah. "Rooms cost money, missy—have you money?"

"A little."

"Four shillings."

"For . . . for how long?"

"One week."

Susannah nodded, taking out her purse for the third time since leaving Sanderby. She counted out the money and looked in dismay at what was left. She had barely five shillings and nine pence to her name.

"The room's right at the top of the house, in the attic. Last on the left. Take it or leave it. I warn you now, if you have no money in a week's time, then out you go."

"I understand."

"Come in, then."

Susannah stepped into the musty, dark hallway, where only a dirty oil lamp gave any light at all. The woman gave her a lighted candle and then left her. Slowly Susannah ascended the creaking stairs, watched all the time by a black-and-white cat with amber eyes which did not blink even once. She heard sounds coming from the other rooms, low murmurings, an occasional burst of laughter, and from one the sound of someone playing a penny whistle. But at the top of the house it was very quiet. And so cold. Her breath made a silvery cloud as she at last came to the end door on the left.

The attic room was large but sparsely furnished. It contained a mattress lying in one corner, some old blankets folded on it, and a hard pillow which felt as if it had been stuffed with chips of wood. There was an old washstand and a chest of drawers with a cracked mirror. Worn beige curtains hung at the sloping window which looked out over Covent Garden Square and the market behind King Lane. There was no carpet or rug on the bare boards and she could hear mice squeaking and scratching behind the walls. Cobwebs hung from the low ceiling, and they fluttered constantly in a chill draft which found its way through the window and beneath the ill-fitting door.

Susannah held the candle high as she gazed around, and she felt as if she could have burst into tears—except that the tears would not come. She pushed the bolt across on the door and drew the curtains. Slowly she undressed and stepped shivering into her nightgown. Then she curled up in the blankets on the disgusting mattress.

The noise of the market droned on outside the window as porters shouted and carts and wagons rumbled to and fro with loads of fresh fruit and vegetables. Once she thought she heard a carriage halt somewhere close by and for a terrified moment she thought her uncle had returned, but as she listened and the moment dragged past, she relaxed again.

She felt completely drained, emotionally and physically, but she could not sleep. She lay looking up at the trembling cobwebs where they were lit by the lights from the market. How long could she survive alone like this? What was going to happen to her? If only she could turn time back and change the course of events, if only she could go to the boathouse again and find that Miles did not have any terrible news to impart. If only. But she could not. She had embarked upon a course of action the end result of which could only be guessed at. But as she lay there she began to wonder if her decision had been taken in too much haste. Would she not after all have been better off allowing herself to be dispatched to Ireland? As it was, fate could well have something far worse in store for her than mere incarceration on her uncle's estate.

"Oh, Miles," she whispered, the tears filling her eyes at last. "Miles, I love you so." Giving herself to weeping came as a welcome release. She hid her face in her hand and turned toward the wall, her whole body shaking as she wept her fear and misery.

The church bells were sounding three in the morning when at last she cried herself to sleep.

5

~

Late the next morning she left the lodging house to begin her search for employment. There seemed no other course open to her now. She carried all her belongings with her in the cloth bag, for she did not trust Mrs. Harper or the other occupants of the lodging house.

The woman who now lived in her aunt's house was outside beating a rug against the wall, but although she looked as Susannah passed, there was no indication that she connected her with the description Lord Devereux had given.

Turning a corner, Susannah found herself in the market she could see from her window. It was in a magnificent square which had once been the haunt of high society, but the aristocrats had deserted it now for the newer suburbs like Mayfair. The sprawling market had taken over now, and Sir Christopher Wren's beautiful church looked over a scene of incredible noise and bustle as porters shouted and jostled, baskets balanced precariously on their heads. Wagoners argued prices with market folk, and countrymen in smocks eyed everything with extreme suspicion. The market was a jumble of single-story shops and open-fronted booths which comprised the workplaces and homes of those who occupied them. Fashionable ladies rubbed shoulders with shabby flower girls, beautiful carriages eased past rickety old wagons; it was a contradiction, a strange mixture of wealth and squalor, and it was more noisy than anything Susannah had ever imagined. She picked her way through rotting fruit and vegetables, scattered haybands and cracked nutshells, holding tightly on to her cloth bag for fear of pickpockets or snatch thieves.

After walking for some time, she found herself in Tavistock Street, where she sat on a low wall to rest her tired feet. She had just been walking aimlessly, for she did not know what to do. What sort of work could she look for? Who would want to employ her without a reference?

There was a town chariot drawn up outside a tall house opposite, and as Susannah watched, a woman she recognized emerged from the green front door, pausing at the top of the steps to pull on her gloves. Emily, Lady Cowper, was a celebrated beauty, a Whig hostess of note who with her rather dull husband had been a frequent visitor to Sanderby—although, of course, she had never set eyes upon Lord Devereux's niece. She was a patroness of Almack's and extremely influential. She was also Sir Jeffrey Stratton's mistress, which fact had caused a great deal of surprise due to their disparate views on politics. However, as Susannah had overheard one of her uncle's male guests remark on the stairs one day, what had politics to do with what one did between the sheets?

Lady Cowper's complexion was that of a pale rose and her dark hair curled in clusters around her lovely face. Her rust-colored pelisse was trimmed with white fur, and rosettes bounced on her beaver hat as she descended to the waiting chariot, her dutiful maid following a step or two behind.

Susannah watched the chariot drive away, mingling with the crush of traffic thronging the street, and then she looked curiously at the house opposite again. It was an imposing building, three stories high with wrought-iron railings at the upper windows. In one of those windows was a display of elegant and fashionable hats, and an impressive chandelier was visible in the room behind them. A flight of steps led up to the door onto the street, and a maid was now busy polishing the lion's-head door knocker, having just completed the discreet brass nameplate.

Crossing the street between a brewer's dray and a hackney coach which was even more unroadworthy than the one she had traveled in the night before, Susannah stood on the pavement to read the nameplate: "MADAME HILARY. DRESSMAKER. MILLINER. BY APPOINTMENT TO T.R.H. THE PRINCESSES."

Madame Hilary. Susannah had heard of her, for she was one of *the* most fashionable dressmakers of the moment. Her latest designs were frequently illustrated in *The Ladies' Mag-*

azine of Modes, which Susannah had sometimes read when one of her uncle's lady guests had left a copy behind.

The French Revolution had eclipsed Paris' power over the world of fashion, and now London was the center of influence. Many French émigrées had fled across the Channel to continue their work from the safety of England. There were French dressmakers, milliners, and corsetmakers in London now, even Marie Antoinette's milliner Rose Bertin, but although Madame Hilary sounded fashionably French, she was most decidedly a Londoner. She was also far and away the most important and influential *modiste* in the kingdom, although as *The Ladies' Magazine of Modes* had slyly jibed, she still craved the final accolade, the royal warrant to the Queen herself. The Queen preferred her old German dressmaker and staid designs. Madame Hilary had risen as far as the Queen's daughters, but no further.

All this passed through Susannah's mind as she stood watching the maid polish the door knocker. The maid went inside and the door closed. Susannah read the nameplate again. Dressmaking was the one thing she knew anything about, for had she not learned all there was to know from her mother? Madame Hilary might be famous and intimidating, but she was still a dressmaker, and with the new Season about to begin, she would surely wish to take on new staff to cope with the rush of orders.

While the boldness was still upon her and before faintheartedness could rush in, she hurried up the flight of steps, but before she could take the knocker in her hand, the door swung open and a haughty young footman looked out.

His livery would not have disgraced Sanderby, his rich blue coat had long pigeon tails and was crusted with golden braid, and his waistcoat sported a handsome set of yellow buttons. He wore black plush breeches, white stockings, low shining shoes, and his calves were carefully padded to accentuate his already fine legs. He was obviously very superior and considered himself to be vastly important—as undoubtedly he was. He looked down his nose at her. "Yes?"

"I wish to see Madame Hilary," she said in a small voice.

"Have you an appointment?"

"Yes," she lied, looking him squarely in the eyes, her Devereux blood stirring angrily at his insolent demeanor.

"Your name?" He was a little uncertain of her, for although she looked insignificant in her drab cloak and her gray woolen dress peeping from beneath it, her voice was much more drawing-room than he had been expecting. "Your name?" he asked again when she did not reply.

"Miss Garland."

Immediately she knew she had made a mistake, for no lady would give her name to a footman like that *before* entering. A triumphant grin spread across his face and he began to close the door.

Furiously she propelled herself forward, determined to get inside somehow and see Madame Hilary. She caught him unaware and he stumbled back, allowing her to gain entry. In the small moment before he recovered, she saw a pale green hallway tiled in gray and white. Two large fires burned in marble fireplaces and a single red velvet sofa was standing against one wall. A magnificent staircase curved away from the far end of the vestibule.

That was all she saw, for the footman gathered himself together again and caught her arm very roughly, pulling her back toward the open door. "Out you go, Miss Cleverclogs," he hissed. "The front door ain't for the likes of you!"

"James!" An imperious voice cut across the hall from the staircase. "*What* is the meaning of this disturbance? I expect the Duchess of Glenbeigh at any moment!"

A sharp-faced, angular woman in black bombazine stood on the stairs. Her fair hair was powdered and piled high on her head beneath a black lace cap, and the stiffened bodice of her mourning gown was laced very tightly indeed. The bunch of keys suspended from her waist chinked together softly as she descended to the tiled hall. If this was Madame Hilary, then she chose to dress in far from the latest fashion.

"Well, James?"

"This . . . this person was attempting to gain entry, madame, and I was throwing her out."

"Were you indeed? It seemed to me that you were making very heavy weather of so simple a task."

"Yes, madame."

"Well, show her out now, you foolish fellow, show her out!"

Susannah snatched herself away from him. "Madame Hilary?" she cried desperately. "Please allow me to speak with you."

Again her well-spoken voice compelled interest. "Well?"

"I am seeking employment as a seamstress, madame."

The pale eyes flickered coldly. "This, my girl, is a *maison de modes*, not a bawdy house. Ladies come here for the delights of *chiffons*, they do not wish to encounter persons such as yourself or come upon such disagreeable scenes as the one I have just been witness too. Besides which, I do not concern myself with the employment of mere seamstresses, I leave that to my forewoman! Had you been acceptable, which you are not, you would have gone to the side door. Show her out, James."

The footman's hard fingers pinched her shoulder as he grabbed her again and bore her struggling toward the still-open door. Desperately she opened her cloth bag and took out the pink taffeta gown, tossing it across the floor to the dressmaker's feet, where it lay in a crumpled pile. "Please, madame," she cried, still struggling and making the footman's task as difficult as she possibly could. "Please inspect my work for yourself!"

She almost fell down the steps to the pavement, saving herself from sprawling in front of passersby by clinging to the iron railing. Breathless and close to tears of rage and humiliation, she remained there for a long moment, her head lowered to hide her face from the curious glances she was attracting. How could she have muffed it all so badly? How could she have been that foolish?

"Hey, you! You're to come back in."

She looked up at the footman. "Me?"

"There's no one else!" he snapped, clicking his fingers at her in a way strongly reminiscent of her loathsome uncle.

She straightened her cloak and then slowly retraced her steps to the hall. There was no sign of the dressmaker or of her taffeta gown.

"Madame will see you in the showroom," said the footman curtly, straightening his powdered wig and going up the staircase.

She followed him along a thickly carpeted corridor where many gold-framed mirrors hung on the silk walls. Doors opened off into small booths where ladies could view clothes in private, and at the end of the corridor were double doors which the footman flung open to reveal the showroom beyond.

After the elegance of the vestibule, Susannah had expected more of the showroom of the most important dressmaker in the realm. She was disappointed. The walls were a dull brown and there were bolts of cloth on shelves in the corners. The cloths tumbled down higgledy-piggledy to the floor, left where they were after being inspected. Cheval glasses stood along one wall, and above them some of the most beautiful and expensive dresses she had ever seen were hanging untidily from a picture-rail. In the middle of the room were two milliners' mannequin dolls, one *en déshabillé* and the other *en grande toilette*. They were dressed in perfect miniatures of real clothes, the stitchwork and trimmings impeccable in every detail.

There were three windows, and in the center one was the display of hats she had seen from the street below. She gazed at these now in admiration. One was a silver toque adorned with bird-of-paradise plumes in jade and black, one was an apple-green turban embellished with aigrets, and the last one was one of the new poke bonnets which were becoming more and more the rage with each new Season.

"Have you seen enough, missy?"

She turned with a start to see the dressmaker seated on an upright chair by the fire, the pink taffeta dress draped over her knees.

Madame Hilary gave a faint, chill smile and then nodded at the waiting footman. "Take the fashion dolls now, James, they are to be dispatched to Princess Amelia at Kew. I presume I can trust you to attend to it correctly?"

"Yes, madame." He picked up the dolls and bore them carefully out.

"And see to it that that fool of a messenger reaches Kew before nightfall this time! The Princess requires to see the new clothes as soon as possible."

"Yes, madame," came his voice from the corridor as he hurried away.

Madame Hilary looked at Susannah again. "I have little time to waste and so will come directly to the point. Did you make this garment?"

"Yes, madame."

"You would appear to be very talented, then."

"Thank you, madame."

"And you also appear to be most impudent, coming to the door of a fashionable *maison de modes* as if you were born to that privilege!"

"Forgive me, madame, I meant no impertinence."

"For a mere seamstress you speak very well. Who exactly are you?"

"My name is Susannah Garland."

"Have you testimonials from previous employers?"

"No, madame."

"Then how am I to gauge your character?"

"You cannot, madame."

The dressmaker stood, the taffeta dress sliding unnoticed to the dusty floor before the fire. She came closer, the keys chinking together. "I am curious about you, missy, and all I have elicited thus far is that your name is Susannah Garland. Are you from a good family?"

Susannah hesitated, a fact which the dressmaker did not miss. "Yes, madame," said Susannah at last. "At least, my mother was of good family, my father was a schoolmaster. My mother became a dressmaker and taught me all I know."

The dressmaker was thoughtful. There was far more to this than met the eye. However, for the moment she would let it pass. The girl was clever with her hands and had to be considered. "Your mother taught you? I have not heard of a *couturière* named Garland."

"She was only a country dressmaker, madame."

"Ah. The country." The tone was withering. "May one pray that you refer at the very least to Bath?"

"No, madame. Chippenham."

There was a slow exhalation of breath. "Oh, dear. Coney as distinct from ermine. However, my judgment must not be clouded by such a detail." She paced around Susannah. There was a mystery here; the girl had such an air of secrecy about her. What could she have to hide? Well, all that could be discovered in due course; for the moment it was more important to find out exactly how much the talented Miss Garland knew of the work.

Turning suddenly, the dressmaker lifted a court gown down from the picture-rail and displayed it over her arm. "Of what material is Lady Cowper's new gown made?"

"I . . . Genoa velvet?"

"Are you asking me or telling me?"

"Genoa velvet."

The dressmaker took down another. "And this?"

"Marguerite."

"Indeed it is. Tell me, how would you set about sciving the outer edges of a skin such as leopard?"

"I doubt that I would, madame, for it is generally too hard and thick on the outer edges."

"And if you wished to repair a hole in the same skin, how would you gauge the exact size of the patch?"

"It must be one-sixteenth of an inch smaller than the hole it is to fit."

Madame Hilary nodded. "You appear to be knowledgeable enough, Miss Garland. I think you could possibly prove to be quite an asset to me, both in the workroom and possibly here in the showroom too. Yes, indeed, in the showroom you could prove very useful in dealing with my ladies."

Susannah held her breath with excitement. She was to be employed? "You are offering me a position, madame?"

"Possibly. There are conditions to discuss. The hours are long, from nine in the morning until nine at night, and the work is very hard and exacting. I suffer no incompetence, no loose work or poor concentration. I will provide your luncheon and tea, but you must live elsewhere. I pay eight shillings each week and in return I expect perfection in every detail, from the keeping of time to the keeping of the last pin. Is all that quite clear?"

"Yes, madame."

"And the conditions are agreeable?"

"Yes, madame."

"Very well. In future you will never approach the front door of this house, and you will also never approach me unless bidden to do so. Is that also quite clear, Garland?"

The new state of their relationship was evident in the immediate change of tone. Now that Susannah had accepted the position, Madame Hilary felt free to treat her as she pleased. "One presumes you wish to commence this very morning?" went on the dressmaker.

"Yes, madame."

"Then you may do so. But remember, Garland, that from this moment on you are part of my temple of fashion. Here is to be found the most elegant display of taste and perfection in the whole of London, and I am the source of genius and invention from which these elegancies spring. My word and my will is the absolute rule." The dressmaker surveyed herself in one of the cheval glasses. "Everything I do for ladies of fashion and consequence gives the utmost satisfaction and pleasure, Garland, for I alone know what is right and wrong for them. My garments have clothed the bodies of the most beautiful and most influential women of the realm."

Yes, thought Susannah, well you may have—but not the Queen. Not the Queen.

The dressmaker turned sharply toward her, almost as if she had detected the disloyal thoughts. "My name is a byword in *couture*, Garland, you are merely a seamstress who will endeavor to bring to vibrant life the magnificence of my designs. You are a nothing, a nobody. *I* am omnipotent."

"Yes, madame."

At that moment the footman returned. "Madame, the Duchess of Glenbeigh has arrived."

"Very well, I will go to her. And, James, escort Garland to the workroom and inform the forewoman that she is a new seamstress and that I have taken the unusual step of engaging her myself."

The footman's eyes slid in amazement to Susannah. "Yes, madame."

For a moment the dressmaker's hooded gaze rested on Susannah again. Inquiries would have to be made in Chippenham, the truth about this young lady would have to be sought out, for there must be no hint of scandal attaching to the serenity of this establishment. With a slight inclination of her head, Madame Hilary swept out, her skirts rustling.

Susannah retrieved the pink taffeta from the floor and pushed it quickly into the cloth bag. James watched her, an unpleasant sneer on his thick lips. "So, you wormed your way in after all, eh? It'll make a change to have a *pretty* bit of muslin around."

She said nothing. She did not like him and saw no need to engage in pointless conversation with him.

"You're not going to be very popular, you know," he went on. "No, not popular at all. Coming to the front door like that, encroaching on Miss Chiddock's territory."

"Miss Chiddock?"

"The forewoman. No, Chiddy's not going to like this little lot one bit. Of course, *I* could make life much easier for you —if you're sensible, that is. And if you're nice to me."

She looked through him. Be nice to *him*? She would as soon cradle a viper to her bosom!

He shrugged. "Suit yourself. You'll learn quick enough how it is around here." Turning on his heel, he strode away along the corridor, forcing her to almost run to keep up with him.

Down in the hallway she could hear Madame Hilary greeting the Duchess. "Good morning, your Grace, and it is a very fine morning, is it not?"

"It is tolerable, madame, tolerable."

"And how may I be of service to you?"

"I am to present my niece's new husband at the Queen's next drawing-room, and I require robes of suitable modishness. They must retain modesty at the same time as extreme fashion, madame, for I have little desire to appear in these naked muslins which are so disgracefully prevalent."

"Your Grace shall have whatever she desires. Have you anything in mind?"

"I thought that perhaps a cream silk taffeta would be a little different."

"Oh, dear me, no," said the dressmaker with crushing firmness. "Cream will not do at all for a court gown."

Susannah leaned over the banister to look down. Her curiosity and surprise at the dressmaker's autocratic behavior made her forget James for the moment. How could *anyone* speak to a Duchess like that?

The Duchess looked flustered. "But . . . but I do not think white is *de rigueur*. Indeed I—"

"I make *only* white and gold court gowns, your Grace, for that is what is expected. And silk taffeta would be most disagreeable for you anyway. I have just the muslin in mind, it is so sheer that it cannot help but look like gossamer. Your Grace will look most fine."

The Duchess looked miserable, but she nodded her agreement.

Susannah gazed down in utter amazement now. Madame Hilary had obviously not spoken idly when she said she was omnipotent. Susannah had thought that a rather grand and affected word to use, but somehow at this moment it seemed the perfect choice. The unfortunate Duchess of Glenbeigh had come to Tavistock Street with a clear notion of being a little different at Court, but she was going to have to conform. She wanted cream but was to have white, she did not wish to look naked in muslin, but that was exactly what she *would* look! It had never occurred to Susannah that a dressmaker of Madame Hilary's standing could behave in such a despotic way and get away with it, but she had the evidence

39

of her own ears and eyes to tell her that this was indeed how it was. What a far cry this was from the rented rooms in Chippenham where her mother was meek and obliging and the *customers* behaved like tyrants!

"Garland!" hissed James. "Are you coming or aren't you? You'll be out on your ear if Madame sees you're still here!"

Quickly she left the top of the stairs then. But as she followed him to the back staircase, she was still thinking about the extraordinary scene she had witnessed in the elegant green vestibule.

6

The workroom was approached across a courtyard at the rear of the house. Someone was singing in the nearby kitchen and there was a smell of baked pork drifting appetizingly in the cold air. The courtyard was closed in and dark, for the buildings all around rose so high that they kept the daylight out. A small side door opened onto Tavistock Street, and a maid opened it to go out. For a moment the noise and bustle of the street was loud, and then the door closed and the sound of the city became muffled and indistinct again.

Susannah followed the footman up a flight of outside stone steps leading to a door in a brick building which appeared to have no windows at all. He paused to throw her a last malicious grin before opening the door, and she took a long breath to calm herself to face what lay beyond.

Inside the workroom it was darker than the courtyard; the only light was that which filtered through some grimy skylights, and it took Susannah a moment or two to become accustomed to the gloom. Rows of silent seamstresses worked at tables, and she noticed with surprise that they were all either a little elderly or were very plain. There was not one pretty girl among them.

She glanced around the lofty room. Bolts of rich, colorful cloth lay on racks at the far end and there were tall cabinets containing a great many drawers for all the trimmings, buttons, accessories, and implements needed in such an establishment. Half-finished garments hung on the walls, and one of the older women carefully moved a mourning gown to a safe distance so that she could tend the low fire which was all there was to warm the large room.

Some of the seamstresses were stitching, others cutting out, and still others were diligently laying paper patterns on some beautiful crimped silk gauze which had been laid out very carefully on a square of worn carpet in a corner. Rough drawings were pinned to a board on the wall by each table, and a large pile of pattern paper filled an entire wardrobe, the doors of which stood open as a wizened little woman, her fingers deformed from years of holding a needle, sorted through it.

The slither of material, the squeeze of scissors, and the scraping of busy fingers in bowls of pins were the predominant sounds when the woman tending the fire finished. Susannah noticed all this in those few seconds as she stood waiting by the door as James went to a woman who sat at a table on a dais at the head of the room.

Occasionally the woman glanced over her spectacles at the girls under her charge, but for the most part she contented herself with the study of some new design drawings which lay before her. She was somewhere in her thirties, but it was hard to tell if she was nearer thirty or forty, and her figure was inclined to be plump, the lacing at her waist being pulled in very tightly to give some semblance of shape. Like Madame Hilary, she still powdered her hair, a fact which was unexpected, for when fashion was turning more and more to the natural and classical, the greatest dressmaker in the leading fashion city of the world still wore the designs of the previous decade. The only concession to the latest modes was the forewoman's choice of a dainty sprigged muslin for the gown with its stiffened bodice and full, cumbersome skirt. There were sour lines at the corner of her mouth and her eyes moved swiftly around the room when she looked up. It was not a kindly face, and the atmosphere in the workroom was uneasy. No one looked remotely happy or contented, and the lack of any conversation at all was oppressive when so many were gathered together for so long.

The forewoman was not aware of the footman's approach, and she gave a start when he suddenly put his hand on her shoulder in a rather intimate way. Her face flushed with what was unmistakably pleasure and she hastily removed her unflattering spectacles and patted her powdered hair. Her eyelids fluttered like those of a young girl and she leaned toward him coquettishly.

He whispered a few words to her, nodding once in Susannah's direction, and the forewoman's smile faded. Those seamstresses whose tables were close enough for them to have heard what he said gasped aloud, glancing around to whisper to those behind. The forewoman rapped her knuckles sharply on her table, and immediately they all returned industriously to their tasks, but Susannah felt the close scrutiny she was now receiving from all sides.

Slowly the forewoman got to her feet. "But why was she not sent to *me* first? You *know* I choose everyone myself!"

"Well, Chiddy, it looks like this one slipped through your net, eh? Slipped in through the front door, no less."

If the previous silence in the room had been oppressive, it now became deafening. The forewoman stared at him and then turned slowly to look at Susannah. "The *front* door?" she breathed in horror.

"Like she was born to it."

The sprigged muslin swished heavily as he woman approached Susannah. Close to, her eyes were hazel and her skin a little more softened by the years than had appeared from a distance. She was much closer to forty than thirty. "I am Miss Chiddock," she said coldly, "and I am the forewoman here."

Susannah bobbed politely. "Ma'am."

"So, girl, you think you are worthy of the front entrance, do you?"

"I meant no impertinence, Miss Chiddock."

" 'Ma'am' will do very well."

"I meant no impertinence, ma'am."

"Indeed? How very fortunate for us all."

Some giggles rippled around the room, and Susannah said nothing, keeping her eyes firmly on the floor.

James was enjoying himself immensely. "Well, Chiddy, we've got a pretty one at last, after all these plain Janes you've been so careful to surround yourself with. Young and pretty this one is—just the way I like 'em."

Miss Chiddock's face was fiery. Satisfied that he had caused enough of a stir, he sauntered out of the workroom, whistling loudly.

The forewoman's fury was evident in her quivering voice. "So, girl, your impudence would seem to have gained you a position here—how vastly pleased with yourself you must be."

"I did not mean to—"

"Your name, girl?"

"Susannah Garland."

"Very well, Garland, we shall now see how capable you are—and how long you are likely to remain." The forewoman's eyes glittered malevolently and she turned to indicate a table where a thin, round-shouldered young woman was working on what looked like the arm of a spencer. "Jones, she will work with you."

The woman called Jones stood and bobbed. "Yes, ma'am."

"Garland," went on the forewoman, "you will do exactly as Jones bids you, and if I am not pleased with everything you do, then it will be your misfortune to unpick every stitch and begin again."

"Yes, ma'am."

Susannah removed her cloak and hung it with all the others next to the door. She knew before she took up a needle that Miss Chiddock was going to find fault with her work; it was a forgone conclusion. But as she went to sit at the table, her face revealed nothing of how miserable she felt inside. She wouldn't show them how unhappy and unsure of herself she was, she *wouldn't*! She had seldom felt more Devereux than she did in that proud moment as she took her place.

Jones was one of the least plain of the seamstresses, but even so, with her dull mousy hair and pointed nose, she was far from being attractive. She pushed the other arm of the rather large oyster-colored spencer toward Susannah. "Finish the seam. Here's the silk. That's the design, it's for Lady Ormanton, a German lady."

Susannah nodded, glancing at the drawing. It was not cleverly executed and showed a very stout woman in a fur-trimmed spencer, seamed and cut in the very latest fashion. To Susannah's mind a tightly fitting spencer in a material with a decidedly horizontal pattern was not at all becoming or suitable for a lady of Lady Ormanton's undoubted dimensions. The oyster cloth was very luxurious and the cuffs would soon be splendid with astrakhan, but its gathered upper sleeves and lines of straight braiding across the ample bosom would surely serve only to emphasize the wearer's unfortunate size! The sight of Lady Ormanton in this spencer would not do credit to Madame Hilary's tact or flair; in fact,

44

the more Susannah looked at the drawing, the more convinced she became that one of two things lay behind its conception. Either Madame Hilary was jaded and uninspired, or Lady Ormanton did not merit too great an effort.

She immersed herself in the work, but she was aware all the time of Miss Chiddock's constant surveillance and of the animosity surrounding her in the workroom. Jones said nothing; her face was stern and lacked humor, and Susannah's spirits grew heavier and heavier as the morning progressed. And then it happened. Just as the clock on the forewoman's table pointed to midday, Susannah reached across the table to pick up the dish of pins, and knocked it to the floor. It crashed loudly, scattering its glittering contents everywhere.

For a tiny moment there was a delighted air of anticipation in the room as Miss Chiddock swept triumphantly to her feet. "You clumsy wench, Garland! There is a chip out of the dish now, and the cost of replacing it will be deducted from your first week's wages!"

The dish had already been chipped, but Susannah bit back the angry retort. "Yes, ma'am" was all she said. She must keep this employment, she must live—and she would have to endure the forewoman's spite if she was to survive.

"If there is another display of such monumental clumsiness, I shall be forced to go to Madame Hilary concerning your continued employment."

"It will not happen again, ma'am."

"Pick every pin up," said the forewoman, glancing at the clock. "The rest of you may go to the kitchen now."

Benches and chairs scraped, pins rattled and scissors chinked, and the seamstresses went to form a neat crocodile by the door. At a signal from the forewoman, they filed obediently out.

Susannah was on her knees by the table, picking up the pins one by one under Miss Chiddock's eagle eye. When the last pin had been retrieved and the dish replaced, Susannah at last faced the forewoman.

"Garland, you would be better advised to take yourself elsewhere for employment, for you will never be welcome here."

"I'll do my work well, ma'am, and I'll try not to offend—"

"Your very presence offends. I give you good warning that I intend ridding myself of you, for I won't have someone like you anywhere near me, do you hear me?"

"But I've done nothing wrong!" protested Susannah, staring at her.

"You've come here. I need no more reason than that to despise you. Now, go to your luncheon!"

Slowly Susannah backed away and then turned to leave the workroom. Outside on the steps she halted, taking a long, shuddering breath of the cold, clean air. How long could she possibly endure this? How could she withstand such hatred and resentment?

She watched a small group of German milliners cross the courtyard to enter the kitchen, followed by an aloof party of Spanish milliners who emerged from the same doorway and who obviously considered themselves vastly superior. As the kitchen door was opened, she caught a glimpse of her fellow seamstresses seated at a long table, laughing and chattering together.

She looked at the main house, remembering Madame Hilary. Susannah Garland, she told herself determinedly, your work has been found acceptable by the most illustrious *couturière* in the kingdom—if you're good enough for that, you're good enough for anything!

She went down the steps and across to the kitchen. Inside it was warm and steamy, the windows running with moisture. Great dressers lined one wall, their shelves and hooks loaded with blue-and-white crockery. There were copper utensils on the wall by the immense black fireplace around which sat the cook and some of the scullery maids, enjoying a well-earned dish of tea.

The Spanish milliners sat stiffly at a small table in one corner, their backs toward the equally stiff Germans. The seamstresses occupied a long table down the center of the room, and their conversation died away as Susannah entered. The milliners forgot their petty differences for a moment to glance at one another as they all detected the instant change of atmosphere when the newcomer appeared. The scullery maids sniggered together, to be silenced by the red-faced cook as she ordered one of them to prepare another plate of the baked pork and potatoes.

One of the seamstresses, a large, bony woman with graying hair beneath her mobcap, got up slowly. She was obviously intent upon tormenting Susannah, and the way she swaggered across the floor to sketch an exaggerated bow confirmed it. "Oh, *do* join us, Miss Garland," she said affectedly, pretending to flick dust from her sleeve. "Pway sit down and tell us who you twod a measure with at Almack's last night!" The sarcasm brought hoots of mirth from the onlookers.

Susannah flinched inside, but she said nothing as she walked past her tormentor to take her place at the table. The woman followed. "Only the fwont door for you, eh?"

A plate of food was placed before Susannah by a giggling scullery maid, who immediately scuttled back to the fireplace to watch the proceedings with great glee. Susannah continued to ignore her self-appointed goad.

"Cat got your tongue, Miss Fancy?"

Susannah looked across the table at Jones, who sat opposite. "Would you pass me the salt, please?" she asked pleasantly.

She thought for a moment that there was a flicker of humor in Jones's eyes as she handed the salt cellar to her, but she said nothing.

To Susannah's relief, James entered the kitchen at that moment, and his arrival was a signal for a semblance of order to return to the room. The woman who had been tormenting her went back to her place, and Susannah began to eat her luncheon. She wouldn't let them draw her, she wouldn't!

The footman leaned on the table next to her, his sleeve deliberately brushing against her arm, although he appeared to be taking no notice of her whatsoever as he addressed the room at large. "I've some grand news for you all!" he said importantly.

"What?" asked Jones.

"What'll you do for me if I tell you, Jonesie?"

She gave a short laugh. "Think *I* want to lose my place here?"

He grinned. "Well, maybe I'd have to be pretty desperate anyway, wouldn't I?"

Jones flushed a little and went on with her meal; then she looked up again. "Well? What *is* this wonderful news, then?"

"There's going to be a grand wedding this July."

"A *royal* wedding? One of the Princesses?"

"No, but grand enough to suit Madame Hilary for all that. One of her best customers, in fact."

"Who?" demanded Jones in exasperation as he still kept the most tantalizing information from them.

"Lady Agnes Winston."

Susannah froze, staring at her plate without moving a

muscle. Lady Agnes came here for her gowns? Why hadn't she thought of that before? Of *course* she came here, didn't *everyone*?

"How do you know that?" cried Jones challengingly. "Lady Agnes hasn't been in Town for months!"

"No, but Lady Cowper came here this very morning. She and Lady Agnes were at some fancy Whig get-together at Devonshire House a day or so ago."

"Who's she marrying?"

"Lord Devereux's son."

A ripple of excitement ran through the room then, for no one could mistake the importance of such a marriage, uniting two such wealthy and influential families.

James took the salt cellar and poured some salt onto his finger, licking it as he looked around at the sea of excited faces. "It's not *certain* she'll come here for her wedding toggery, of course, but it's more than likely. And there's to be ten bridesmaids at the very least. *Won't* you all be busy then, eh?"

They all murmured delightedly together, wondering what the gown would be like, what color the bridesmaids would wear, and so on. James took the opportunity of attracting Susannah's attention. He put his hand on her shoulder in a way every bit as familiar as when he had greeted Miss Chiddock earlier. Coldly she removed his hand, but he only grinned. "Enjoying your first day, are you? Making you feel really welcome, are they?"

She didn't reply, and he laughed, strolling out of the kitchen whistling the same droning tune he had whistled earlier. Susannah was spared any further attention for the rest of the meal, for the news of the grand wedding took precedence over everything else. She finished her meal in peace.

Throughout the long afternoon and evening she worked on Lady Ormanton's spencer, but all she could think of was Miles's wedding. Somehow it had not seemed so very inevitable until now; it had all been like a bad dream from which she would eventually awake. But now there would be no awakening. Now it was all too painfully true; every terrible part of her sadly changed life and circumstances was true and could not be denied. The room at the lodging house was true, this terrible workroom and the hatred of her fellow workers was all true. Her fingers trembled as she worked, and she kept her head down for fear that her misery would be revealed.

After tea she finished her piece of work and took it to Miss Chiddock, who gave it a cursory glance and then shook her head. "That is hardly satisfactory work for an establishment of this reputation and standing, Garland. Unpick it."

Susannah carried the wretched spencer back to the table without a murmur.

It was very dark outside when at last the end of the long working day was reached. Susannah put away the spencer, which she guessed would be haunting her for many days yet if Miss Chiddock had anything to do with it. There was more than a hint of mist in the cold night as she went out through the little side door into Tavistock Street.

Jones stood on the pavement waiting. Susannah halted warily, but Jones smiled. "My name's Annie," she said.

7

Over the next few months Annie Jones's secret friendship made Susannah's lot much easier to bear. In many ways Annie's situation was similar to Susannah's, because she too came from a rather more well-off background than her present employment would suggest. Her father had once owned a haberdashery in St. Martin's Lane until the business had failed and Annie had been left to fend for herself by his premature death. She was very afraid now of losing her position at Madame Hilary's and so did not dare to be open about befriending Susannah, but she did all she possibly could under the circumstances. Susannah understood and was only too grateful to know that at least someone there was kind. But she did not tell Annie the whole truth about herself, telling her simply that her father had been a schoolmaster. She thought it wiser to keep her own counsel about her connections with the great Devereux family of Sanderby.

Each morning she walked from the lodging house without taking a breakfast, and each evening she walked back again in the darkness, being careful to use only those streets which had parish lamps. At night she was usually too exhausted for anything but instant sleep on the dirty mattress. But sometimes she could not sleep, and that was when the memories came back to haunt and hurt her. At those times she could not force Miles Devereux out of her thoughts, and the pain of losing him made her cry herself to sleep.

In the workroom she had to suffer James Ridley's taunts and Miss Chiddock's constant and unrelenting spite, spite which was due entirely to jealousy. Susannah's unprecedented arrival did not go down at all well with the forewoman, but the main cause of her jealousy was the footman. Annie told Susannah that soon after James's arrival, he had discovered that Miss Chiddock had formed a hopeless infatuation for him, and he did not hesitate to use this to his own advantage. Madame Hilary held herself aloof from the workings of her establishment and relied completely on Miss Chiddock, who for all her faults was a very good forewoman. But when that forewoman was in the clutches of an avaricious, scheming young lover, then things were apt to go very awry. James was suspected of stealing some of the expensive French trimmings which were so necessary for ladies of fashion and which were becoming increasingly rare as the war progressed, and he was known for certain to have made off with a costly bolt of cloth-of-gold one night. What else he had been responsible for could only be guessed at, for Miss Chiddock successfully concealed most of it, and no one else dared to go to Madame Hilary anyway. The outcome of such a move would surely mean Madame Hilary believing Miss Chiddock and the unhappy informer being dismissed without a testimonial—and who could take a risk like that? No, let Madame Hilary eventually discover for herself what was going on under her nose! Miss Chiddock, said Annie firmly, was a nasty old biddy and she deserved to get herself into such a pickle—and it was all because she wanted to keep a virile young lover in her bed!

So while the drawing rooms and salons of England rattled with talk of the way the war was going, or of whether Mr. Pitt would be recalled to oust the ineffectual Mr. Addington, or indeed of whether the King's return to insanity would mean an end of the Tories in power altogether when the Prince of Wales became regent and restored his beloved Whig friends to government, Susannah Garland was much more concerned with the mundane chore of keeping out of the way of both Miss Chiddock and James Ridley.

But it was no easy task, especially when she was before the forewoman's eyes for almost twelve hours each day except Sunday! Susannah's work was always criticized. Her paper patterns were said to be a little too large for the required fitting, her stay-stitching was not firm enough, her seams were on the crooked side to be sure, and she had most certainly left the lace shelves in a disgraceful state! The list was endless. And untrue. But Susannah knew that Miss Chiddock did not dare go to Madame Hilary to complain just yet; after all, Madame Hilary herself had taken Susannah on—so Susannah's dismissal would have to be planned and orchestrated with great care, so that the dressmaker would not guess the truth. So for the time being the forewoman contented herself with merely making Susannah's existence as uncomfortable as it possibly could be. The matter of Lady Ormanton's spencer proved a fine sport for a time, the disagreeable garment being stitched and unpicked with such regularity at one time that Susannah feared it would fall apart once and for all, as she informed Annie in a whisper one luncheon time over the hashed beef and cabbage. The ending of the spencer's suffering came only when a slightly miffed Lady Ormanton had the temerity to ask Madame Hilary one afternoon if she had perhaps forgotten the order. No one was expected to question either Madam Hilary's integrity or her memory, and she frostily informed the anxious German lady that the spencer would be forthcoming within a day. Miss Chiddock had to allow then that Susannah's stitches were quite adequate, and the spencer was put in a plain brown box and dispatched to Lady Ormanton's Mayfair house the very next morning.

Apart from the "ordeal by spencer," as Susannah termed it, she could for the most part close herself away from the injustices. She was given the most menial of tasks to complete, from the kindling each morning of the miserable fire, to the cleaning out of the forewoman's inkwell. But when it came to dressmaking, she soon discovered that there was nothing she did not know, for her mother's work in Chippenham had covered the same methods, stitches, skills, and trimmings—only the degree of luxury at Madame Hilary's was different. It was very hard work and she earned every farthing of her eight shillings each week.

A welcome change came when one day only she was available when Madame Hilary wished to send someone to purchase a particular shade of cream muslin from a warehouse in Conningby Street, a warehouse which was notorious for its unhelpful assistants. But unfortunately it was also renowned for the very finest selection of Indian muslins anywhere in London, and so it reigned supreme—and arrogant. With Madame Hilary's instructions ringing loud and clear in her ears, Susannah repaired to Conningby Street, where to her surprise her well-spoken voice achieved the seemingly impossible almost immediately. The young man could not have been more accommodating, bringing bolt after bolt of cream muslin until she found the exact one.

Impressed by this result, and being far from slow to seize upon anything advantageous, Madame Hilary soon began to dispatch Susannah upon all manner of errands. She was sent to scour London for the French trimmings which seemed to be used up at such an alarming rate, and she trudged through icy March rain to Nicholay's Fur and Feather Manufactory in Oxford Street to purchase ostrich plumes. Grafton House in Bond Street was a constant destination for silks, and there was not a single establishment in the city which did not receive a painstaking visit in search of a very particular Brussels lace for the Countess of Sommerton's court gown. Although the weather always managed to be inclement upon these excursions, Susannah found them a welcome relief— and a fine escape from Miss Chiddock.

Having Annie to share a laugh with made all the difference—seeing the humor in anything always tipped the balance and made anything capable of being risen above. And it was a chance remark of Annie's too which brought a new and exciting dimension to Susannah's involvement in fashionable dressmaking. The pantomime over Lady Ormanton's spencer, and Susannah's conviction that the hateful garment was entirely unsuitable for the lady concerned anyway, caused Annie to ask her why she didn't design a more suitable one herself, if she was so sure. Susannah mulled the thought over as she walked home that night, and the next day she went to a stationer's shop in Tavistock Street to buy pencils and paper. She *could* do better for Lady Ormanton, and she would prove it!

Now she always carried her drawing things in the cloth bag which she still insisted on bringing with her each day, for nothing would have induced her to leave anything at all lying around at the lodging house! At luncheon time and again at tea time she would be seen busily drawing, filling each sheet of precious paper with a succession of court gowns, wedding dresses, fancy-dress costumes, mourning and day dresses, and she was agreeably pleased with the results.

But one morning late in March, Miss Chiddock pounced at last, and Susannah's fragile new life was endangered yet again. She was sent to Nicholay's in Oxford Street to purchase some peacock feathers, and she arrived back just as the other seamstresses were going to luncheon.

Miss Chiddock's fingers tapped on the table and she nodded at the feathers. "They are fine quality," she said, which praise alone should have warned Susannah that something was amiss. "And did they have the correct buttons?"

"Buttons?"

"For Lady Cowper's pelisse."

"I know nothing of buttons."

"No? But my instructions were quite clear—here is the very paper I showed to you, Garland." The forewoman indicated a piece of paper on which was written: "Ten peacock plumes, and two dozen of the mother-of-pearl buttons kept for Lady Cowper."

Susannah stared at it. She had not seen it before, and the forewoman most certainly had not shown it to her or mentioned anything about buttons. Uneasily she looked at Miss Chiddock. "You did not show this to me," she said quietly, "and you know that you did not."

"I know nothing of the kind, Garland, and now I am afraid that I will have to see Madame Hilary about this matter. Really, it is too bad, especially when Lady Cowper is wanting the pelisse so very quickly. There will be quite a to-do about this, Garland, I can promise you."

Susannah took a long breath and said nothing more. What was there to say? The forewoman had been waiting for just such a moment as this—a rush order from an important customer, something which could be used to put Susannah apparently very much in the wrong.

"Go to your luncheon, Garland," said the forewoman, getting up with a tight smile on her thin lips. "You will be dealt with later."

Susannah turned and walked out. She was trembling from head to toe with anger and frustration. But by the time she reached the kitchen, there was no sign on her face that anything was amiss. Only Annie guessed that something had happened, but then, Annie knew the little signs to look for now.

The summons to Madame Hilary's presence came just as dusk fell. The shadows had blended as the sun sank in a blaze of crimson and gold in the west, and there was a promise of a fine clear day to follow.

Madame Hilary was waiting in her drawing room, which was on the floor above the showroom. It was a fussy room, strangely wrong somehow for the cool, detached character of the dressmaker. The walls were covered with light brown paper and there were many heavy pieces of furniture. Some very fine pieces of silver-gilt were displayed on a side table, and the sunset threw a livid glow over everything.

Some lap dogs slept on a soft rug before the roaring fire, which made the room unbearably hot, and the leaping flames threw still more reddish light over the somber figure of the dressmaker as she sat in a chair nearby. Her tray of tea was on a little table beside her, the remains of cucumber sandwiches and scones on pink-and-white plates. A large, elegant silver teapot shone in the firelight, and the dressmaker slowly set her cup and saucer down beside it as Susannah entered.

"So, Garland, I am told that Miss Chiddock has reason to find serious fault with you."

"It isn't true."

"I do not for one moment imagine that Miss Chiddock would lie to me, especially where a garment for Lady Cowper is concerned. Once before it was brought to my notice that you were possibly lacking, but the customer concerned then was only Lady Ormanton, and she does not really count for much where it matters. She is never seen at Court, or at Almack's, and apart from that, she is of a singularly unpleasant shape for one of my exquisite creations. Lady Cowper is an entirely different matter. She is a leading light of fashion, she is seen everywhere, and she comes only to me for all her clothes. I will *not* overlook your shortcomings this time!"

"I was not told to purchase the buttons, madame."

"Miss Chiddock informs me that you were, and James confirms that he heard her instruct you."

Susannah said nothing; she was resigned to her imminent dismissal in the face of such apparently overwhelming proof of her guilt.

"That pelisse is required at Devonshire House within the hour, Garland," said the dressmaker angrily, provoked by Susannah's silence, "and now I shall be forced to explain to Her Ladyship that the delay is none of my doing! I fear that I made a sad mistake the day I took you on here, Garland. I should have had you thrown out, as was my first intention! You are dismissed, and there will be no testimonial. And I shall see to it that no other reputable dressmaker in the land takes you on in any capacity!"

Susannah turned on her heel and walked out, closing the door quietly behind her. She had not really defended herself, for she knew when the odds were too great.

Madame Hilary remained in her chair. She regretted having to dismiss Susannah Garland, for the wench was very useful. And undoubtedly talented. But one simply could not have such gross negligence if one was to maintain an efficient house. She leaned her head back against the chair, gazing at the flickering flames. The man she had sent to Chippenham to make inquiries had not returned as yet, and maybe now there was no point in finding out the truth anyway. Still, it was all very curious. Very curious.

8

Still bitterly angry and fighting back the tears, Susannah hurried down the stairs to the first floor where the showroom and the private booths lay. As she reached the landing and turned to go to the back stairs, an imperious female voice halted her in her tracks.

"Ah, you there, girl, come here this instant!"

A very regal woman dressed entirely in sober dark blue stood in the doorway of the showroom. Her gray hair was fluffed and frizzed and she did not walk but glided a few steps toward Susannah. "I am the Princess Amelia's lady-in-waiting and I have to inform you, nay *complain* to you, that Her Royal Highness has been waiting here for fully five minutes now and no one has come to attend her! It is quite disgraceful that an establishment of this quality should have its doors unguarded and should further allow one of His Majesty's daughters to remain unattended!"

Susannah was stunned, her gaze going beyond the lady-in-waiting to the young woman inspecting the display of hats in the showroom. She was very handsome, although her complexion was pale and sickly. Princess Amelia was known to suffer from extremely poor health most of the time, and she was the youngest of the King and Queen's six daughters. She was also her father's favorite. She wore a red velvet pelisse and a turban which hid her hair, and she did not glance around as the enraged lady-in-waiting shooed Susannah away to bring Madame Hilary. "And then return here, girl!" she finished.

The dressmaker was still in her chair by the fire, completely unaware of her important visitor. Her face darkened with fury when Susannah reappeared. "How *dare* you—!" she began.

"Madame, the Princess Amelia is waiting for you in the showroom. It appears that she has been there for more than five minutes."

The dressmaker was on her feet in a moment. "The Princess is *here*? But she never, ever comes here!"

"She has this time."

The dismayed dressmaker swept out of the room without another word, her skirts crack-cracking with each hurried step. Susannah followed on her heels. In a cloud of black bombazine, the dressmaker sank into a deep curtsy before the Princess. "Your Royal Highness, *please* forgive this gross negligence! I do not know *how* such a terrible oversight can have occurred!"

Well, thought Susannah, at least there are *some* customers before whom even Madame Hilary must grovel.

The Princess inclined her head briefly. "You are here now, madame, so let us proceed. I have been to Carlton House to visit my dear brother, and it occurred to me that maybe the gowns I have ordered are nearing completion."

"I . . . Yes, your Royal Highness, they are indeed."

"I will see them, then."

Madame Hilary nodded at Susannah. "Bring them," she said shortly.

Susannah knew the two gowns in question and she hurried to the workroom, where a startled Miss Chiddock gave them to her immediately, and Susannah had the great satisfaction of being able to tell the forewoman that there was no time to answer her questions about the interview with Madame Hilary just yet! Oh, it had been a very sweet moment, if only a small sop after all the misery and insult she had endured at this woman's jealous hands.

The Princess had adjourned to one of the larger booths, and the lady-in-waiting snapped her fingers at Susannah. "Make yourself useful, wench, help me with the Princess's clothes."

"Yes, ma'am." Nervously Susannah followed the tall figure in blue into the booth, where Madame Hilary was fussing around the Princess like a worried hen.

The Princess and her lady-in-waiting conducted their conversation in French, as did most of the Court, and Madame

Hilary, who had only a few pertinent phrases in her vocabulary to call upon, did not therefore understand. But Susannah did, for her schoolmaster father had taught her the language from an early age, and she listened quite avidly to all that was said by the two, who thought themselves safe.

"Your Highness seems very set upon this lunacy," murmured the lady-in-waiting, dropping the Princess's gloves into Susannah's hands.

"I am, Tolly, I am. The dear King is a little better now, although the Queen is still very ill and cross—and disagreeable as ever—and my sisters and I are brought quite low by it all. I declare I shall sink completely if I do not go to my dearest angel!"

"The King may be a little better, but he will still not allow you to marry Sir Charles Fitzroy, my pet, and you know that he will not. Please do not go on with this request, for your health is so poor, and it cannot but bring heartbreak upon you."

"Tolly, the King will allow his daughters nothing! You know how dull and unimaginably stifling our lives are at Kew or Windsor. It is a nunnery. I cannot endure it, I know that I cannot. I have spoken with my darling brother now and he has promised—"

"Sweeting," pleaded the anxious lady-in-waiting, unfastening her royal mistress's tight gown, "The Prince of Wales has a noble and willing heart and he loves you so, but he is not the one to speak to the King! Indeed, he is the very *last* person! You know how his eagerness for a regency has distressed the King and Queen—they will not receive anything he says with open hearts. It is doomed from the outset, my lamb."

The Princess bowed her head then, blinking back sudden tears, and Susannah's heart went out to her suddenly. She was a princess, but she was desperately unhappy. "I do not know which way to turn, Tolly, for *everyone* is so disagreeable. Mama is rendered quite hateful because of poor Papa, and my brother the Prince of Wales is quite frenzied that Mr. Pitt will return and there will be no chance of a regency. They none of them care about me. Life is very tedious, Tolly."

"I know, my lamb. But let us turn our minds to pleasing things, let us take delight in Madame Hilary's beautiful gowns, mm?"

The Princess nodded, and when she raised her head, there

was no trace of the unhappiness she had allowed to show a moment earlier. She spoke in English to the dressmaker. "I will try on the chenille lace first, madame."

When the gown was on, the Princess surveyed herself in the cheval glass, looking critically at the tiny puff sleeves and the high waistline. "I do know now what Mama will say. She does not care for these new things. She does not care for anything at all, she is quite horrible," she added as an aside in French.

Madame Hilary tweaked the lace and fluffed the skirt out, kneeling on the floor then with a mouthful of pins to adjust the hemline. She took the pins out. "But the gown is quite exquisite, your Royal Highness, and you will look quite magnificent when you wear it."

"It is not quite . . . quite . . . Oh, I don't know, it's just not *something*." The Princess nodded at the lady-in-waiting. "I will try the white gauze."

Susannah glanced at Madame Hilary's still face. The dressmaker did not like any criticism at all, especially not of her gowns, but she did not dare raise a whisper about it to a Princess of the Blood. But she felt compelled to say something. "I think the chenille lace is quite exceptional, your Royal Highness, and upon you it cannot fail to impress. But maybe you did not think so when I sent you the two mannequins—"

"I like the gown, madame, but at the moment I am seeking something quite removed from the ordinary. I wish to look particularly fine, particularly so." The Princess glanced at the lady-in-waiting, who tutted disapprovingly.

The white gauze met with scarcely any more approval. The Princess expressed more interest in it, but still had reservations. She sighed. "Lady Cowper wore a gown at the Queen's drawing-room which Mama thought quite unsuitable, but it was *such* a gown, it caught everyone's breath. That is the sort of gown *I* wish to have!"

Both the lady-in-waiting and Madame Hilary were aghast. "But, your Royal Highness," said the dressmaker, "what I make for Lady Cowper I could not possibly make for you!"

"Why not?"

"Because," said the lady-in-waiting firmly, "you are a Princess and cannot possibly display yourself in that vulgar way. Your mama was quite correct to disapprove."

Madame Hilary looked frosty at the word "vulgar" being

applied to her gown, but managed to remain commendably silent.

The Princess was put out. "But I thought the gown looked very fine, and Lady Cowper is so very beautiful anyway . . ."

"Your Royal Highness," said the ever-patient Toddy, "I swear there was nothing Sir Jeffrey Stratton could not see when she stood with him by that fire!"

The Princess gave a sniff. "From all accounts there is nothing about Lady Cowper Sir Jeffrey has not already seen at close quarters anyway! It is the fashion to look a little naked, Tolly, and I wish to be fashionable. I cannot have much happiness in this life, and I *will* be modish if nothing else!"

"You cannot lower yourself to every vagary of fashion."

"Then I must look different in some other way!" insisted the Princess a little crossly. "Something must be done to make me feel a little happier! I am quite determined that it shall be so!" Raising her voice a little brought on a fit of coughing, and the anxious Tolly eased her distraught mistress in the only chair in the booth.

Susannah felt so sorry for the miserably unhappy Princess who was denied all the rights of other women, to wear what she wanted, to love whom she pleased. . . . Susannah wanted suddenly to help, to suggest a gown which would stop everyone's breath and yet be demure and acceptable. It was surely not beyond the bounds of possibility to give her such a little thing as that?

Impulsively she stepped before the Princess, curtsying low. "Your Royal Highness, perhaps if you truly like the white gauze we could trim it a little unusually?"

Madame Hilary's eyes flashed and she bridled instantly at this further evidence of Susannah's impudence. "Foolish chit—" she began, but the Princess held up a hand.

"Trim it unusually? In what way?"

"With black fur."

Madame Hilary snorted and then choked. The Princess stared at Susannah, and the lady-in-waiting blinked. Then the Princess glanced down at the folds of delicate white gauze, so fine and sheer over its undergown. "Black fur," she murmured. "How intriguing a notion."

"I thought," went on Susannah tentatively, ignoring Madame's baleful glare, "that it would be quite different, a blend of summer and winter. Maybe if the sleeves were long instead of short. Long and voluminous, so that they swung a great deal with the weight of the fur ... ?"

The Princess smiled then, getting up to look at herself in the mirror again. "Oh, Tolly," she said, "is that not a capital idea? And no one, *no one* could accuse me of being low and vulgar, not even my mother!"

The lady-in-waiting looked decidedly relieved that her troublesome charge had decided upon a totally safe course after all the threats of recent days.

The Princess beamed at Susannah. "Your name, girl."

"Garland, your Royal Highness."

"I think you are very clever, Garland, and very original, and I would very much like to have this gown trimmed with black fur. And I shall want the sleeves to be as you suggest. Madame Hilary, I do believe that you have found a positive treasure, and I know that you must appreciate her worth a very great deal."

The dressmaker's accommodating smile was almost savage. "I do indeed, your Royal Highness," she said in a tight voice.

Ten minutes later the royal visitor had gone in a flurry of delight over the new gown and in a lather to inform her dear Fitzroy how beautiful she would soon look for him, even if not as his bride for the time being.

Madame Hilary returned to the booth where Susannah was putting the scissors and pins away and preparing to take the two gowns back to the workroom. "Return to your work, Garland," said the dressmaker angrily, her voice shaking.

"But I am dismissed, madame."

"Consider yourself reinstated."

Relief swept through Susannah, although she showed nothing. "Thank you, madame."

"And as you have made yourself so overwhelmingly agreeable to the Princess, you may attend personally to the alterations and trimmings of her gown."

"Thank you, madame."

"Do not thank me, Garland, for I do it so that the blame will rest entirely at your feet if the Princess is displeased with the finished article. Fur on gauze indeed—the very notion is a contradiction! And to think the garment will bear *my* name!"

"And if the gown is a success, madame, yours will be the glory."

"Do not be forward with me, missy, for you are still not

secure here! Now, take yourself to your work and inform Miss Chiddock that you are still employed and that you are to work solely on the Princess's gown until it is finished."

"Yes, madame."

At that moment the dressmaker caught sight of James, and she called him angrily. "*Where* have you been, sirrah? You left the door unattended and the Princess Amelia came without my knowing anything about it!"

James gaped. "The Princess? But, madame, you . . . you sent me to deliver the Countess of Sommerton's court gown."

Madame Hilary breathed in sharply. She *had* sent him, and the fact that the door was unattended was therefore her fault if she did not see to it that a maid was on duty. With an angry flick of her skirts she swept away to the showroom, the double doors swinging wildly behind her. James breathed out slowly.

Then he grinned unpleasantly at Susannah. "Got your marching orders, then, have you?"

"No."

His smile faded. "Eh?"

"Your lying failed. I am to remain, and I am to work on the Princess's gown."

His face darkened with anger. "Got nine lives, haven't you!"

"So have you, but I believe you've used a considerable number of yours!" she retorted, holding his gaze. "And I warn you that if you do anything like this to me again I shall see to it that Madame's attention is drawn to the discrepancies between what she buys and what is actually to be found in the stock! She may not believe me, but she will wonder a great deal! So stay away from me!"

He stared at her for a long, long moment, and then turned to walk away. She knew that she had won, that he would leave her alone from now on, just in case she carried out her threat. Now for the sweet, sweet delight of informing Miss Chiddock that she had not rid herself of Susannah Garland's presence after all!

9

~~~

After Princess Amelia's singularly fortunate visit to Tavistock Street, things became a great deal better in the workroom as far as Susannah was concerned. Miss Chiddock's initial fury and disbelief on learning that Susannah had not after all been dismissed had resulted in the forewoman taking herself with all haste to Madame Hilary in search of an explanation. She had returned to the workroom much chastened and in a mood of silent resentment which signaled that she had had no success and would have to either put up with Susannah's presence or resign herself.

Annie was highly delighted with the outcome, and very impressed with Susannah's bravery in daring to speak unbidden to a Princess of the Blood. On reflection Susannah was amazed herself, for had she stopped to think of the enormity of what she was doing, she would not have been able to open her mouth at all! But it had been done, and the result had been splendid as far as she was concerned. Indeed, it could not have been better. Miss Chiddock, naturally enough, sneered at the royal gown, criticizing and ridiculing, but she did not demand the unpicking of a single stitch. Susannah had won an important battle, if not the whole war, on a field of white gauze and black fur.

When the gown was dispatched to Windsor, taken personally by Madame Hilary, Susannah waited anxiously for word of the Princess's reaction, but none was forthcoming. But as Annie pointed out, Madame was not likely to tell Susannah what the Princess had said, and anyway, the mere fact that nothing had been said was a sure sign that the Princess was delighted. Madame Hilary was not one to give anyone the satisfaction of knowing her idea had been a success. Susannah would dearly have liked to know what the gown's reception had been, but she had to content herself with accepting that what Annie said was probably true.

Spurred on, she continued to scribble designs on every available piece of paper, and it was this increasingly engrossing hobby which almost brought her back into her uncle's clutches.

It was on a cold, wet day at the beginning of April, the same day that word reached the workroom that Lady Agnes Winston had decided to definitely order her wedding gown from Madame Hilary, that Susannah hurried out through the side door at the end of luncheon to go quickly to the stationer's to purchase some more paper.

The rain was falling heavily and there was hardly a hint of spring in the bitter wind which drove the rain at her face. The people on the pavements carried umbrellas, a sea of black weaving to and fro along the sides of the busy street. There was congestion on the road itself, however, for a brewer's dray was trying to turn halfway along, and the resulting blockage had caused chaos as bad-tempered, wet and cold travelers shouted and waved their fists at the complacent brewer, who ignored them all as he coaxed his cumbersome team around. Curricles, carriages, wagons, and phaetons were all forced to wait while he accomplished his maneuverings, and all the time the rain slashed down relentlessly.

Susannah's skirts were splashed and her feet wet by the time she reached the stationer's, and she went in with great relief to the warm, dry shop, where the old assistant greeted her with a smile. He knew her well by now and had no need to be told that she had come for more paper. He passed a comment about the dreadful weather as he wrapped her purchase up and tied it with string. She left the shop, pulling her hood over her face again, but as she stepped from the shelter of the doorway, a harsh voice halted her in her tracks.

"So, it *is* you, missy!"

Her blood seemed to turn cold in her veins as she slowly turned to look at her uncle. His coat had only a little rain on it, and she guessed that he had been in one of the carriages she had passed. He stood with his hands on his hips, his eyes bright with triumph. He nodded brusquely in the direction of the barouche, the door of which still swung on its hinges. "Get in."

She shook her head, beginning to back away in terror. "No . . ." she began.

He darted forward and grabbed her arm. Her packet of paper almost fell to the pavement as she began to struggle, crying out for help, but no one took any notice. Her uncle's grip grew harder as he dug his fingers in, and then at last she found the sense to swing the rather heavy parcel of paper at his head and kick him on the shin at the same time. He released her with a foul curse and she darted away, running straight out into the street between the stationary vehicles which still waited impatiently for the dray to complete is negotiation of the narrow way, but it had now become entangled with a gentleman's cabriolet and he was shouting furiously.

Tears blinded her as she ran along the opposite pavement, pushing her way between passersby and almost cannoning into an elegant lady whose maid screamed loudly as Susannah almost thrust her mistress down into a basement. Susannah did not dare to apologize or to halt; she ran blindly on. She could hear her uncle's roar of rage echoing along the street, and fear lent her wings as she ran on, not stopping until she reached a small alley where she took refuge, leaning back against the damp wall, her heart thundering.

No one paid any attention to her. A flower woman at the entrance of the alley turned once to give her a curious look, but then returned to the more important business of selling her daffodils and violets. For a long, long moment Susannah remained in the shadows of the alley, and then at last she dared to emerge again. The brewer's dray had completed its lengthy maneuverings and the congestion was almost ended. Horses trotted and wheels crunched as Tavistock Street untangled itself at long last. Slowly she went back along the street. Her uncle's barouche had gone from outside the stationer's shop and she stared at the empty curb with relief. How close she had come to recapture! She felt faint and sick as she stood there, a hand on one of the parish lamps for support. She could not forget her uncle's hate-filled face, or his gloating triumph at having found his quarry again. Not for the first time she began to wonder what he really intended to do with her once she was safely in Ireland. Would she ever have been heard of again? After all, would it not be far better, as far as he was concerned, if Susannah Garland had conveniently ceased to exist altogether?

Closing her eyes, she raised her hot face to the soothing chill of the April downpour. The rain sluiced refreshingly over her, bringing calm and cooling her skin. Gradually her heartbeats became less frantic and the panic subsided. She had escaped him yet again. But one thing was certain: she could no longer go to the same stationer's for her paper, and she must be very careful each time she walked abroad from now on.

Several weeks later the incident seemed very far away, and spring arrived at last to lighten hearts and blow away the ghosts of winter. The chill left the air except at nights, and the sun streamed down each day from a flawless sky. It seemed that it rained only at night, and what could be more perfect than that? Leaves unfurled in the parks, and Covent Garden market was filled with flowers again. The only ominous sign on the horizon was the fact that the French fleet were gathering in Boulogne, ready to invade Britain during the summer. In political circles, it was being whispered that Mr. Pitt, so much admired and adhered to by Sir Jeffrey Stratton, would soon return to power. It was also whispered that the Prince of Wales was beside himself with fury and dismay that his old adversary should hold the reins again, for the King's illness had led to hope after hope that there would be a regency. The Prince's hopes would be dashed if Mr. Pitt was Prime Minister, for he would do all he could to thwart the future king's plans.

One morning Susannah entered the courtyard in Tavistock Street promptly at nine to find Miss Chiddock waiting impatiently for her. Susannah was sent immediately to Madame Hilary, without time even to remove her spencer.

Puzzled, Susannah did as she was told. She passed James Ridley on the stairs, but although the footman threw her a venomous look, he said nothing at all and made no attempt to bar her way. He had left her alone since the day the Princess had visited the premises.

Madame Hilary was rearranging a new poke bonnet in the window, the sun streaming in over her and the sunbeams dancing dustily across the cheval glasses. She turned slowly as Susannah entered. "I sent for you some time ago, Garland."

"I came directly I was told, madame."

"Indeed? Then I can only assume that you arrived late today, a serious fault for which you will be penalized when your wages are paid this week." The dressmaker ignored the nearby church bell, which was even at that moment striking nine. She went to sit by the fire, which looked pale and harmless in the strong sunlight, carefully arranging the heavy folds of black bombazine to her satisfaction before looking at Susannah again.

Susannah felt hot and uncomfortable in her outer garments in a room which was warmed by both fire and sunlight.

"I presume, Garland, that you would be interested to know that the Princess Amelia was very pleased with the gauze gown, indeed she caused a minor sensation when she wore it. Naturally, I took full credit for having produced such a garment."

Susannah looked at her for a moment and said nothing.

"I have found you most useful since you have been here, Garland, really most useful. And in so many ways. I suspected on that first day that you had immense talent, and now I know that to be so. I also suspected that you were very interesting—I now also know that to be so."

"Madame?"

"It must have taken a great deal of spirit to run away from Lord Devereux, to leave Sanderby and all that that entailed."

Susannah went cold, staring at the dressmaker. She knew! But how?

Madame Hilary smiled coolly. "It was not difficult to discover what I wanted to know. I sent an agent to Chippenham to inquire about a dressmaker named Garland—from there he followed the trail to Sanderby, and he learned all there was to know from a groom who rather liked too much cognac for the guarding of his tongue."

"I beg of you, madame—!"

"Not to inform your uncle that you are here?"

"Yes."

"My dear Garland, telling him such a thing just yet would hardly be of benefit to me, would it? I said that I find you useful, and so I do, but I am convinced that I shall shortly find you even more useful. Yes, indeed. So I have no intention of informing him anything—yet. But I do intend using my new knowledge about you to my own advantage. Your continued safety from Lord Devereux hangs upon your next few words, Garland." The dressmaker paused, her long, pale fingers toying with the bunch of keys. "I understand that you have been interesting yourself with . . . a little drawing, shall we say?"

Susannah had not expected the question. "I . . . Yes, madame."

"I wish to see your efforts."

"But they are mere scribbles, madame."

"Allow me to judge their worth, Garland."

Susannah opened the cloth bag and took out the drawings she had with her. "But, madame, of what possible interest can my drawings be to you?"

The dressmaker inspected the sheets with their packed designs. "*Your* drawings, Garland?" she murmured at last, a smile on her thin lips. "How very foolish you are, to be sure."

"But they *are* mine, madame!"

"They are also exactly what I have been unable to dream up myself of late—they are precisely what I need to maintain my position as the most important *couturière* in London! These drawings are mine from now on, as will be every other design you do. They are the price of my continued silence. Now, then, I think we understand each other perfectly well, don't we?"

Susannah stared miserably at her. What choice did she have? Her fear of her uncle was even greater now that she was convinced he would not be satisfied with anything less than her death. There was nothing she dared do now except meekly bow to the dressmaker's blackmail. She nodded.

Madame Hilary gave a bleak smile. "I am in a quandary about the fancy-dress costume the Marchioness of Graveley wishes to have for the annual ball at Petworth. See to it that you produce several from which I may choose before the week is out."

"I . . . I will try, madame."

"That is not good enough, Garland. You will both try *and* succeed, is that clear?"

"Yes, madame."

"The Marchioness is young and gay and likes to appear outrageous. I do not think that you need know anything else in order to produce suitable toggery."

"No, madame."

James bowed at the door. "Madame, Lady Agnes Winston has arrived."

The dressmaker nodded, and he left again. With a rustle of black bombazine she then stood and approached Susannah, smiling still. "I think you may go now, Garland, for I doubt that you wish to see your beloved cousin's betrothed, do you? And I have no wish for your quick tongue to result in a further demonstration such as I was forced to endure when the Princess came. No, from now on you shall be kept back, I shall see to that. By the way, I noticed one or two drawings a moment since which would do admirably for Lady Agnes' wedding. Would that not be exquisite, Garland? *Your* design adorning Miles Devereux's bride?"

Susannah stared miserably at her.

"You may go now, Garland. And, Garland . . . ?"

"Yes, madame?"

"I do not think this conversation need go any further, do you? One whisper, and your uncle will hear from me, is that clear?"

"Yes, madame. Perfectly."

Susannah went down the back stairs in a daze. Her thoughts milled around confusingly, and she stood in the blinding sunlight of the courtyard without being able to think clearly at all. But she must compose herself, she must carry on as before, for there was nothing else she could do. Turning, she went to the side door, wanting to escape the muffled courtyard and hide in the bustle and noise of the busy street for a moment.

But as she stepped out, she froze, for there, barely six feet away from her, stood Miles Devereux.

He was waiting by his cabriolet, having obviously conveyed Lady Agnes to her appointment with Madame Hilary, and his top hat swung idly in his hand. He wore a maroon coat and pale gray breeches, and his cravat was tied in a new way which had taken his fancy. He glanced at his fob watch, his head bowed slightly and his hair very golden in the bright daylight. The small groom who always accompanied him was having great difficulty controlling the nervous horse, and Miles glanced at him disinterestedly. His face bore no expression at all, not impatience, boredom, pleasure—nothing at all.

Susannah began to step back into the safety of the courtyard, but as if some sixth sense warned him she was there, he turned suddenly and looked straight into her eyes.

"Susannah?" His lips moved to her name although the

noise of the street drowned his voice. He came toward her, catching her cold hands. "Oh, Susannah, my dearest——"

"Don't, Miles, please."

"But why did you go? I have been out of my senses with worry over you."

"Why did I go?" She stared at him. "Surely you know that for yourself."

"Was it because I am to marry Agnes? For if it was——"

"Miles, I overheard everything which passed between you and your father on the night Sir Jeffrey Stratton came to Sanderby."

His blue eyes were full of pain then. "Forgive me," he whispered. "Forgive me for so letting you down."

"It . . . it doesn't matter now."

"But it does. Where are you living? How are you set up? I mean . . ."

"I have found work and I have taken lodgings."

"Where?"

She did not answer.

"Please, Susannah, tell me."

"No, Miles."

"Don't you trust me?"

"Should I?"

"Please don't look at me like that, Susannah, for I cannot bear it." He still held her hands, the thin, tight leather of his gloves so smooth against her skin. "I love you still," he whispered.

"That is all ended, Miles."

"No, I will not believe that."

"You are marrying Lady Agnes."

"May God forgive me my weakness."

"She is still your intended wife."

"And you are still the woman I love!"

He spoke urgently, and she glanced nervously around in fear that someone would notice them. "Someone may hear——"

"Then let them!"

"You cannot mean that. Lady Agnes is even now in there discussing her wedding gown!"

"How do you know that?" he asked quickly.

"I——"

"You came from in there, didn't you? Through that side door? Tell me, Susannah."

"Yes."

"You . . . you are *employed* there?"

"Yes."

"As what?"

"A seamstress."

"Oh, dear God . . ."

"What would you have me say, Miles? That I am sorry to bring further shame to the Devereux family?" Her eyes filled with tears then. "At least I am honestly employed, and so help me, I have not done anything to bring myself face to face with you like this. As God is my witness, I want nothing more to do with my Devereux relations, do you hear me? I just want to be free—and to stay alive."

"Stay alive? What do you mean?" he asked quickly.

"Do you honestly believe my mere banishment to Ireland would have been sufficient? Ireland is not far enough away, Miles, and you would not have left me alone there, would you?"

"No—how could I, when I love you?"

"Your father knows that too. He must rid himself completely of me if he is to safeguard his interests. While I am free there is always the danger that you and I will meet again, exactly as has now happened."

He shook his head slowly. "No," he whispered. "No, many things I can believe of him, but not that. Not that."

"Your father is the most unscrupulous man I know, Miles, and I stand in his way, no matter how unwillingly now."

He kissed her fingers suddenly, his eyes compelling her to meet their urgent gaze. "But, Susannah, I would not let him harm you. Sweet God, you must know that I would not."

"I know that you would not knowingly let it happen."

"But by my weakness and complacency I have endangered you?"

"No," she said quickly, her fingers tightening over his. "No, I do not mean that. By our foolishness we both played with fire, we both knew what would happen if your father found out. You will not be burned, Miles, but I will, if he finds me."

"I would rather burn with you than continue to exist without you!" he cried defiantly. "Susannah, can you have any notion at all how I have felt these past months? I love you so very much, you mean everything to me—"

"Not quite everything," she interposed quietly, but he ignored her or did not hear.

"Not knowing where you were or even if you were still alive was a more dreadful fate than you can possibly imagine. Now that I have found you again, I will not easily let you slip from my fingers again. I know where you work each day and it will not be difficult to find out where you live."

Resignedly she nodded. "I live in lodgings in King Lane."

"But your aunt is dead! When I went there they told me—"

"*You* went there too?"

He looked puzzled. "Too?"

"Your father was there the very night I ran away."

"I did not know that. Susannah, I guessed that you would go to your aunt if you were in distress, because you had nowhere else. I went there hoping to find you and take you somewhere safe, somewhere where I could look after you."

"As your mistress?"

"If that could ever be, then you know I would wish it to be so, but if not, then I would still take care of you—and honor you."

"But you would not honor me as your wife."

"Susannah, if you overheard the discussion between myself and my father, then you know the pressures I have upon me. And is a ring so very sacred when we love each other?"

"Oh, Miles . . ."

"Say you will meet me again."

"It's wrong."

"Damn what is right and wrong. Agnes may come out at any moment now, and I must have the solace of knowing you will keep an assignation with me."

"No."

"Don't you feel anything for me now? Have my actions so alienated you that you cannot grant me even that one small favor? It will cost you nothing and will mean so very much to me."

How could she resist him? How could she refuse when he pleaded so, and when he had stirred her great love all over again?

"You will be safe," he murmured. "My father will not know. Only we need know. Please, Susannah, indulge me in this."

She nodded reluctantly. It was so very wrong, so very wrong . . .

"When? Tonight?"

"I—"

"Tonight, then," he said quickly, giving her no time to reconsider. "I will come here tonight. When do you finish?"

"At nine."

"I will be right here, then."

"No, not right outside, for someone may see you."

"Very well, outside the church." He nodded at the nearby steeple.

"Yes, outside the church."

He smiled, his face a little flushed. "Whatever has happened, Susannah, I have loved you all along."

She gazed up into his eyes for a moment and then turned to go, opening the little side door and stepping back into the relative silence of the courtyard. It was improper and ill-advised to agree to meet him; in fact, it was very reprehensible when he was betrothed to another, but she had not been able to refuse him when all she had ever wanted was to be safe and cherished in his arms again, as she had before.

10

~~~

That day more than on any other occasion Susannah longed to finally unburden herself to Annie, but still she did not dare. It was with mixed feelings that she contemplated the coming evening—half of her so wanted the hours to pass more swiftly, the other half had grave misgivings. She was treading a delicate path between honor and dishonor, and her conscience told her she was wrong.

But she had so much else to contend with that day. After luncheon Miss Chiddock triumphantly bore the drawings of Lady Agnes' wedding gown and the gowns of the bridesmaids into the workroom and pinned them to one of the boards. Everyone crowded around the drawings, exclaiming with delight at the clever designs and saying that they were further examples of Madame Hilary's genius and inspiration.

Susannah remained at her work. They're *my* designs, she thought savagely, and *my* genius and *my* inspiration! She wanted to shout the truth aloud, to make them all turn to look at her—but she knew that she would never dare, that Madame Hilary had her exactly where she wanted her.

Annie looked curiously at her. "Are you all right, Susannah?"

"Yes."

"You're very pale—you have been since you returned from the showroom this morning."

Susannah forced a quick smile. "I think the beef stew the cook provided today was a little too heavy in such warm weather."

"Yes, it was, rather—but you went to the showroom first thing this morning."

Susannah applied herself to her work.

Annie noticed the withdrawal, but she persisted in trying to draw Susannah out of the shell she had placed around herself that day. "What do you think of the gowns Madame Hilary has designed for the wedding?"

Susannah looked at the drawings then. They had been redrawn from the originals, but they were quite definitely Susannah's; she recognized the intricate pattern of jeweled embroidery on the bridal gown's long train and the full, diaphanous sleeves gathered tightly into cuffs stitched with still more of the same embroidery. The dressmaker had even retained the same materials Susannah had chosen originally—cream satin and golden embroidery for the bride, lilac and yellow silk for the ten bridesmaids.

Annie continued to study the drawings. "I think they are very beautiful."

"Yes," said Susannah flatly, "they are."

Later that afternoon Susannah found herself being dispatched to purchase the material and trimmings for the wedding. It was the final and most crushing blow somehow—for not only had her designs been stolen, but she was forced to buy the materials for them too. She could well imagine the dressmaker's mean delight in seeing to it that Susannah and Susannah alone was sent on this particular errand.

At last nine o'clock came and the work was put away. Susannah put on her cloak very slowly. She was hesitant again now that the moment was finally upon her; she still had time to change her mind, to turn away from this illicit love which had suddenly surged back from the past to possess her once more. But she left the house in Tavistock Street and turned toward the church, leaving without saying anything to Annie.

The carriage was drawn up at the curb. It was a nondescript vehicle, dirty and unremarkable, and the coachman wore a plain gray box-coat. Only the team could have occasioned attention, for they were fine dark bays and obviously very costly.

As she reached the carriage, the door swung open and Miles stepped down, his cloak swinging heavily. He smiled. "I did not think you would come," he said softly. "Right to the end I thought you would deny me this."

"I should, I know that I should."

His hand was warm over hers. He wore no glove and his skin touched hers. Their eyes met for a moment before he helped her into the coach and told the coachman to drive on.

She sat on the beige seat and he sat opposite. The carriage jolted as the whip cracked once, and the team came up to a smart trot. She looked at Miles without speaking. Now that they were alone she could not think of anything to say. She wanted suddenly to fling herself into his arms, but conscience held her back. He removed his hat and tossed it on the seat, and by the light of a streetlamp she saw that he was smiling at her. He held out his hand then, and she took it. Slowly, oh so slowly, he pulled her toward him until she was in his arms.

He could taste the tears on her lips as he kissed her, and feel the quivering of her body pressed so close to his. He could only whisper her name over and over again as if it contained some fine and fragile magic. He unpinned her hair so that it tumbled down over his hands, warm, heavy, and scented, a moment so sensuous that he closed his eyes. They didn't speak at all then; they just held each other close as the carriage drove slowly through anonymous streets, and it was Miles who at length drew away first.

He smiled, touching her lips with his finger. "I think maybe we should walk a little, for being alone with you like this presents too great a temptation. I am only flesh and blood, and my desire for you is too much to endure." He leaned out of the window to speak to the coachman. "How far are we from the Egyptian Gardens?"

"Not much over a quarter of a mile, sir."

"Drive there, then."

"Yes, sir."

The carriage slowed and turned, the team's hooves striking sparks from the stone street.

The Egyptian Gardens were a gathering place for high society, but with the Season so young, there was hardly anyone there. They walked through the great wrought-iron gates which marked the entrance to the gardens. The grounds were brilliantly illuminated with thousands of small lamps which were suspended in all the trees and along the triumphal arches which marked the line of the narrow, straight canals which emanated from the site of a glittering central temple. Great sphinxes stood on the banks of the canals, the lights playing on their human heads and lions' bodies. There were rainbow colors everywhere and from time to time fireworks cracked and flashed in the sky, although not yet on the scale which could soon be expected when the *beau monde* flocked to the gardens.

Susannah leaned on Miles's arm as they strolled along a fairly dark, leafy walk, a high hedge to one side and a bank of pale, creamy daffodils bobbing in the night breeze. It was so good just to be with him again, to be able to put reality away to the back of her mind again and just pretend. But reality would not stay away for long; it insisted on returning to take the sparkle from the fountains and to darken the lights playing on the cascades of water by the temple. She was about to unburden herself to him, to tell him what her life was really like now, about Madame Hilary's blackmail, about the stolen drawings, and even that his bride's gown was her design, when he suddenly drew her sharply into a leafy alcove in the hedge, pulling her out of sight of the walk.

"Stratton and Emily Cowper!" he whispered, putting a finger to his lips.

She heard footsteps coming slowly toward them, and Miles drew her into his arms, kissing her so that their identities would be hidden from anyone who happened to look in.

She heard Emily Cowper's soft, teasing voice. "So, Jeffrey, your most cherished wish is about to come true and your beloved Mr. Pitt, God rot him, will probably grace Downing Street again."

"I sincerely trust so."

"You would. I confess I find you a complete enigma."

"It's part of my charm."

"No doubt. But how a thinking man can possibly cleave to a Prime Minister who wants an insane king to remain on the throne, I cannot possibly imagine."

"Better an insane King than an incompetent Prince."

Emily laughed, pausing right by the alcove and not seeing the two hidden there. "You really believe that statement, don't you, my handsome Tory?"

"I do. Besides, it is Pitt's conviction, and mine, that the King will recover his senses in due course."

"For which we all must pray."

"You could at least sound as if you mean it—otherwise do not say it at all."

"I am a Whig."

"Whigs are permitted treasonous utterances?"

"Would that they were. But you must admit, political arguments aside for the moment, that the Court is excessively dull—how much better it would be if the Prince of Wales had command of affairs, how much more gay and interesting."

"Spare me anything connected with that fat buffoon."

She smiled at him, her eyes speculative. "I think I shall spare you the Prince of Wales, but as to sparing you anything else—well, later you shall see, Jeffrey Stratton. That I promise you."

Susannah watched his face as he returned the smile. She had forgotten how very handsome he was, and how devastatingly attractive was his reputation with the opposite sex.

Emily drew coquettishly away, tapping his arm with her fan. "If you have time for me, that is—I understand your conquests multiply daily."

"You flatter me."

"I think not. The *monde*—what *monde* there is in Town as yet—positively smacks its lips over the spectacle of Miles Devereux's affianced bride making such great eyes at you behind his back. It is very quaint."

Susannah looked quickly up at Miles. His face was very pale in the darkness, but somehow he did not seem surprised or enraged by what he heard.

Jeffrey gave a short laugh. "Oh, dear, how you do lend your ear to senseless prattle, Emily."

"You know that it is far from senseless prattle."

"I also know that neither Agnes nor Miles Devereux has entered into this match because they are devoted and in love. It is a marriage of convenience of the most base kind, with neither party having any intention of remaining faithful to the other. It makes a mockery of the whole institution of marriage."

"Oh, come now, Jeffrey, how fit are you to cast stones of that kind? No, I do not refer to your own marriage, for I believe you were indeed in love with Elizabeth, but I do refer to the way in which you have taken a considerable number of other men's wives to be your mistress. Is that not also a mockery of marriage?"

He gave a thin smile. "Emily, I have never seduced a

woman who married for love. A true marriage is sacred, in my eyes. I have a code by which I stand."

"You are saying then that my marriage is one of convenience?"

"I am."

"If anyone else said that to me, I would strike his face."

"You were the one who commenced this investigation, not I."

She smiled then. "I am indeed the culprit. But to return to the matter of Agnes Winston—I would not put it past you to encourage her."

"And why would I do that?"

"To goad Lord Devereux, to put a dent in his pride. All that business in the past, when your father was ruined—some say by Lord Devereux—"

"Some say correctly, then."

She surveyed his dark face for a moment. "And it still matters a great deal, doesn't it?"

"Yes. Why should it not? I consider that most of the Devereux fortune is actually Stratton fortune. Devereux falsified evidence in order to prove my father's guilt. He proved corruption which was not of my father's doing—my father was ruined, socially and financially. And those missing funds were never discovered—they certainly did not benefit the Strattons. But, my word, did not the Devereux star ascend rapidly after that? Sanderby was a miserable villa, suddenly it was a grand estate. Yes, I believe Devereux was guilty, but I cannot prove it. But, Emily . . ."

"Yes?"

"Whatever is in Agnes Winston's mind, it is not in mine."

"I will have to believe you, won't I?"

He smiled. "You will indeed. Now, shall we progress?"

She put her hand on his arm, reaching up to kiss his lips for a moment. Then they walked slowly on.

Susannah and Miles drew apart at last. "Miles? Is it true?"

"About what?" he asked flatly. "My father's dishonesty or Agnes' lust for Stratton?"

"Both, if you like."

"As to the first, I don't know, but it would not surprise me. As to the second, yes, it's true."

"Oh, Miles—"

"For heaven's sake, don't sympathize! I could not care less

if she graces his bed three times a night! The world knows she is a whore!"

"But she is to be your wife!"

"As Stratton himself said, it is a marriage of convenience, a loveless match, a thing of paper and promises. We marry for purely financial reasons, it has nothing at all to do with affection. I thought I had made that clear to you already."

"Yes, but . . ."

"But?"

"But I cannot believe it somehow. I don't know Lady Agnes at all, but I know you—I do not understand how someone like you could enter so knowingly into such a dreadful connection."

"Don't be naive, Susannah, I know more marriages of this kind than of any other. Besides, there are pressures of a different kind upon me, remember?"

"Your debts."

"Correct. My debts—and dear Papa's."

"It is not what I would have wished for you, Miles," she whispered. "Not for you."

He caught her hands, pressing them to his lips. "I love you, Susannah."

"I know."

"Then let me look after you, let me place you somewhere safe where I may come to you—"

"No, Miles."

"But why not? It cannot possibly be to spare Agnes' feelings, not after what you've heard tonight!"

"No, it is not because of that, although I still admit to having a heavy conscience about meeting you at all like this."

"Damn your conscience. What other reason have you for refusing me, then?"

"The folly of being weak and utterly dependent upon someone else was forced most clearly upon me the night I ran away from Sanderby. I will not ever be dependent like that again."

"Are you comparing me with my father?" he asked in disbelief.

"No, of course I'm not," she said quickly.

"Then I presume you must like your new life so much that what I offer holds no lure for you," he said a little pettishly, releasing her hands.

"I like it inasmuch as I am responsible for myself."

"If you were my wife, you would be dependent on me."

"If I were your wife, then everything would be very different, wouldn't it?" she retorted, meeting his eyes squarely. "But that will never be, will it, Miles? You dare not marry me—and I have too much pride to become your mistress."

He stared at her, and she knew that he did not really comprehend what she had said. "Maybe tonight was not the time to ask you, maybe I've rushed my fences—" he began.

"If you had waited another year, then my answer would still be the same."

"You've changed, Susannah."

"I have had to."

"Then let me rescue you now, let me take care of you . . ."

She gently put her hand to his cheek. "No, Miles—but I thank you."

"You would rather be a damned seamstress for the rest of your life?" he cried.

"No, that is not what I want for myself."

"What, then?"

"I see Madame Hilary's example before me each and every day."

He stared then. "You want *that*?"

"Why should I not?"

"Because . . . because you're my cousin, dammit!"

"It is more honorable to be a dressmaker than to be your mistress," she said quietly.

He looked sharply away, biting back the anger which for a moment was so like his father's. Then he gave her a wry smile. "Damned if I can understand you."

She smiled too, glad of the small olive branch which melted the quarrel away. "Well, *I* can't understand why *you* take such pleasure in wasting your time and your fortune at the card table almost every night."

"Ah, there you have me, for there is no answer, is there? But for all that, I don't know that I like the notion of having another damned dressmaker in the family, and in Town at that! It ain't the *ton*!"

She took a long breath. "It isn't likely to happen, is it? How can I think of something like that with your father still searching for me?"

"He will only search in such earnest *before* my marriage, Susannah. After that, he won't give a damn. All that matters is getting dear Agnes to the altar—then the rats can eat you, for all he'll care. But *I'll* still care, no matter what." As if he feared to take a wrong step and launch unwittingly into another argument, he turned the matter into something more lighthearted. "So, my virtuous cousin, you will not change your mind and come to live sinfully with me?"

"No."

"But at least you will agree to meet me again?"

"Oh, Miles . . ."

"But what possible harm has this night done? We have merely walked and talked together."

"It hasn't been as innocent as that, and you know it."

"It has still been a damned sight more innocent than I want it to be!"

"That at least is honest."

"Throughout, I have been honest—with you. You gave me no chance to come to you the night you ran away, I had no chance to do anything at all."

"I know."

"Say you will meet me again, then, for I do not deserve to be thrust away like an old glove."

"Don't look at me like that."

"If I know I still affect you, and I do, then I shall persist until you agree. Oh, I know I'm not being fair, but then, I don't mean to be. I mean to have my way and make you agree to meet me—I mean to have you in the end, Susannah. You'll come to me, I know that you will, and until then, I shall move heaven and earth toward that." He caught her shoulders. "You heard what Emily Cowper said—"

"Miles, it's the *way* you all seem to be entering into it all—it's so false! Sir Jeffrey alone seems to have any sort of honesty!"

"Stratton? *Honest*? God above! If you believe that, then I fear you will believe anything. Very well, I will try another tack. You are my cousin—so, cousin, will you honor this wretched cousin with your company again soon?"

She smiled in spite of herself. He meant too much to her still for her to be able to easily shut him out of her life now that she had met him again. Against her better judgment now she nodded her agreement, and he pulled her close for a moment, his lips warm over hers. But as she returned the embrace, she knew that the magic had slipped away somehow. Maybe too much had happened, maybe she had changed more than she had realized. Maybe it was just that her faith in him had been shaken a little too much for anything to be the same again. A sliver of trust, and therefore of love itself, had drifted away from her outstretched fingers.

11

As spring gave way to a hot summer, the sun blazed down over London, giving a welcome promise of a good harvest to come, something which was prayed for at the best of times but which was doubly indispensable at time of war. Across the Channel in Boulogne the French fleet still awaited the order to invade, and Bonaparte affronted the crowned heads of Europe by declaring himself to be Emperor Napoleon. At last it seemed that other countires must soon join Britain in her lonely struggle against the French, but until that happened, then the people of Britain took what solace they could from the return of Mr. Pitt to Downing Street. Of all men, he alone seemed equal to the daunting task of leading the country against so terrible an enemy. Not that the disgruntled Whigs had the same faith in him, not in the slightest, but he had the King's approval and there was nothing they could do about that. The King had recovered from his illness, and no one could say now that he was not in full possession of his faculties once more. That year the King's birthday in June promised to be a day of great celebration throughout the land.

For Susannah there were more immediate considerations. Throughout the early months of summer she continued to meet Miles, although there could be no return to those enchanted meetings at Sanderby, stolen moments and kisses which had lifted her far beyond mere happiness. He was still her dearest Miles, but she loved him without passion now—something which he refused to accept, no matter how many times she told him. He continued to press her to leave her lodgings and allow him to provide for her; he begged her at each meeting, and his ardor was such that she found it almost impossible to withstand the pressure. He offered her dazzling luxury after the misery of her lodgings in Covent Garden, but she turned him down time after time. She had to admit to herself, when at last he returned to Sanderby barely a month before the wedding, that she felt something very akin to relief at not having to endure his constant demands and subsequent bewilderment at her refusal.

At work she had other problems, not the least of which was satisfying Madame Hilary's insatiable demands for new drawings. The Season was in full swing now, and it was the most successful for Madame Hilary yet—and that success Susannah was sure was mainly due to the freshness and novelty of the designs which were being employed now. The dressmaker's hold was as firm and unrelenting as ever, with requests for a traveling pelisse for Lady This, a ball gown for Lady That, a number of morning gowns for the Duchess of So-and-So. The Princess Amelia came to Tavistock Street again to order a new gown for her father's birthday celebration, and Madame Hilary decided to show the world—and Susannah—that she was still capable of producing a magnificent gown for such an occasion. The gown was not at all well-received by the Princess, who saw to it that word reached Madame Hilary to that effect, although Susannah did not know it, as Madame Hilary gave no hint at all of what had happened.

There was a second garment which Madame Hilary undertook to design herself—another pelisse for the unfortunate Lady Ormanton. Madame Hilary's design was elegant enough, there was no gainsaying that, but the color and embellishment she chose were disastrous for someone of Lady Ormanton's rotund proportions—a bright vermilion cloth trimmed with thick black braiding in horizontal lines across the bosom. It would be an odious garment in every way, as just about all the seamstresses in the workroom said when the drawing was first pinned up by Miss Chiddock.

As Susannah worked on the endless stream of beautiful clothes, however, she admitted more and more to herself that what she had intimated to Miles that night in the Egyptian Gardens was really becoming more and more of a dream in her thoughts—she really *did* want to be as Madame Hilary was. Oh, it was only a foolish daydream, but it was a goal which could be striven for, and when Miles had married Lady Agnes, then Susannah would be free—free of her uncle and free of Madame Hilary. She smiled ruefully then, for although she would be free in one sense, in another she was as much a prisoner as ever, for how would she ever find the money to set up as a dressmaker? Still, it was a pleasant thought to ponder upon as she stitched during those long hot summer days. And the daydreams began to be very high-flying—dreams of elegant premises in Mayfair or St. James's and of maybe being summoned to wait upon the Queen herself.

There were times, however, when being in Madame Hilary's position did not seem a desirable thing, especially when dealing with a customer as tyrannical and difficult as Lady Agnes Winston. The wedding gown was a constant problem in the workroom, the bride frequently changing her mind about irritating details which made life very difficult for the seamstress involved, whether it was Annie, Susannah, or one of the others. There must be finer trimmings, a longer train, more embroidery, and worst of all, Lady Agnes decided that she wanted an overgown of golden lace to be made to accompany the original gown. This last would not have been all that dreadfully difficult to accomplish had it not been for the proviso that the bride intended leaving London in three days' time and would not be returning until the day before the wedding at the end of July: the overgown would have to be completed in three days! And the golden lace the bride had particularly described had not been purchased and maybe did not even exist in any of the London warehouses!

An audible groan of dismay and horror spread through the workroom when Miss Chiddock and Madame Hilary announced this latest development, and the seamstresses one and all tried to avoid the eyes of the two women at the dais. No one wanted to be given the onerous task of stitching the overgown, and there was a great deal of shuffling of feet and clearing of throats as the forewoman's baleful eyes scanned the room.

Susannah knew that the forewoman's gaze would come to rest upon her, for Miss Chiddock missed few opportunities still of prodding the loathed newcomer, and sure enough, Susannah and Annie were given the awful job of making the overgown. It took a whole day to even find a lace which could be thought of as suitable, and after that it was a case of stitching hour after hour long into the night, their heads aching from concentration and their fingers sore. But on the evening of the third day they finished at last and Miss Chiddock considered the overgown ready. Madame Hilary was sent for.

The day was close and humid, and everyone in the workroom felt tired and limp, but none more so than Susannah and Annie. The clock had seemed to crawl, and nine o'clock was still an hour away—another hour before they could all escape to the slightly fresher air outside.

Lips pursed, Madame Hilary considered every last detail of the overgown, and at last she too professed herself satisfied that it would meet with Lady Agnes' approval. The overgown and the wedding gown itself must be dispatched to the bride's town house in Bruton Street directly, for Lady Agnes would surely be attending the grand ball at Burlington House tonight and there was very little time left now.

The dressmaker glanced at her fob watch. "I shall not be able to take the gowns myself, as I must go to Kew Palace to have an audience with the Princess Amelia. Garland, you must take the gown to Lady Agnes." This last was said with a certain amount of malicious pleasure which only Susannah could detect. Even now the dressmaker could not resist sending Susannah on such an errand, thinking that Susannah was still in love with Miles and would therefore be hurt even more by having to visit the woman he was to marry.

But Susannah revealed nothing as she gave a little curtsy. "Yes, madame," she murmured politely.

"I will have James procure a hackney carriage for you, for I think it may rain and there must be no risk of any harm coming to the gown at this stage."

Susannah put on her plain blue spencer, a proud purchase made with her hard-earned money, and tied on the equally new straw bonnet. Annie carefully wrapped the gown in tissue paper and laid it in one of Madame Hilary's drab brown boxes. As Susannah picked up the box, James hurried up the steps to the workroom.

"Hurry up, Garland, the coachman's in no mood to wait about!"

"I'm being as quick as I can!" she retorted, sweeping past him and down to the courtyard. There was a mist of rain in the air as she climbed into the dilapidated old carriage and sat back on the dusty seat, the box beside her.

As the carriage pulled away, a rumble of thunder spread through the western skies and the rain began to fall more heavily. Maybe a storm would freshen the air.

She gazed out at the wet streets as the carriage swayed toward Mayfair. Broadsheet sellers stood on corners shouting the headlines, and crowds of people collected to buy the publications, for London was seething with rumors on this oppressive June day. It was being said that the new government was already on the verge of defeat in Parliament. The carriage lurched over a corner curb and Susannah reached quickly to stop the box slipping to the floor and the gown spilling out. Let Mr. Pitt be defeated ten times over, anything was preferable to Madame's fury if anything happend to this wretched gown!

The trees in the squares rustled wetly as the rain fell ever more heavily, and the evening was prematurely dark as the storm swept nearer, the wind rising to sough through the branches overhanging the streets. There was hardly anyone about as the hackney carriage came to a standstill outside Lady Agnes' town house, but there were some fashionable drags driving to congregate under the plane trees outside Gunter's in nearby Berkeley Square. There were some places one had to be seen at, come rain or shine, and Gunter's was one. Susannah climbed down with the precious box, paying the impatient coachman, who said that he would not under any circumstances wait for her. Ignoring her pleas, he drove away, the wheels splashing in puddles which had already collected in the rutted roadway.

Wearily Susannah approached the basement door of the house. Not since her first mistake at Tavistock Street had she been guilty of forgetting her place again! She was shown through a house where chaos reigned supreme as everyone made ready for Lady Agnes' departure for the country the next day. Her baggage was already piled in the hallway and servants scurried here and there on various errands. Susannah followed a footman up to the first floor, and long before reaching it, could hear Her Ladyship's shrill voice.

"You *fool* of a girl! Am I expected to go to Burlington House in *that*? Not, I suppose, that anyone of consequence will be there at all tonight with all the suspense in Parliament!"

"But, my lady——"

"Where is the peach muslin? You know that I wish to wear it tonight!"

"My lady, you told me to pack it."

"Jenkins, are you suggesting that I do not know my own mind? If it has been packed, then the fault is yours and yours alone, is that quite clear? Unpack it immediately and see that it is made presentable for tonight's function. And be quick about it!"

"Yes, my lady," said the tearful maid.

"And if there is another disgraceful episode like this, I shall dismiss you!"

"Yes, my lady." The miserable maid scurried out of the blue-and-gold boudoir, stifling a sob as she ran down the stairs.

The footman who had escorted Susannah from the kitchens now looked a little warily into the boudoir, obviously wishing that he did not have to attract his mistress's attention at this particular juncture. Susannah peeped in too, curious for a glimpse at last of the woman who was to marry Miles Devereux.

Lady Agnes stood in the center of the room, a tall figure in a pink lace wrap. A rose silk gown lay on the floor at her feet where she had tossed it, and now she kicked it angrily aside. Her rich red hair was brushed loose and hung to her shoulders, and her skin was clear and pale, although two spots of high color stained her cheeks. Her green eyes were long-lashed and quite beautiful, and she was altogether a very striking woman, but the whole effect was spoiled by the petulant twist to her lips and the discontented frown on her forehead. Susannah knew instinctively that even if it had not been that this woman was to marry Miles, she still would not have liked her in the slightest—there was nothing likable about Lady Agnes Winston.

Agnes turned suddenly as if she sensed she was being observed. "What is it?" she demanded testily.

"My lady," said the nervous footman, "your wedding gown has been brought from Madame Hilary——"

"Since when have I not merited the attentions of Madame Hilary herself?"

Susannah bobbed a hasty curtsy. "She had a previous appointment at Kew Palace, Lady Agnes."

"Kew? Well, no doubt I must take second place, then. Bring the gown."

Susannah untied the string and carefully took out the gown, shaking it a little before holding it up. The green eyes moved critically over it, and there was not the slightest flicker of appreciation of the gown's beauty or of all the hard work which had gone into its making. Susannah's instant dislike deepened in those few seconds.

Agnes waved her hand. "It seems well enough—I suppose I must try it on. My wretched maid is otherwise engaged for the moment, so you will have to attend me—one presumes you are acquainted with such matters?"

"Yes, my lady."

Agnes suddenly caught one of Susannah's hands and inspected the nails closely. "You are tolerably clean. Very well, proceed."

Susannah's cheeks burned with anger as she laid down the gown and began to remove Agnes' lace wrap.

"You oafish wench, your fingers are like ice!"

"I'm sorry, my lady."

"Have you no sense at all?"

"I will try to be more careful, Lady Agnes."

"See that you are, or I shall feel compelled to complain to your employer."

"Yes, my lady."

The cream-and-gold wedding gown slithered finely over the red hair and pale shoulders, and Susannah fastened each tiny hook and eye very carefully, making certain that her fingers did not touch the other's skin at all.

When she had finished, Agnes stepped before a cheval glass and surveyed the gown more closely, turning this way and that, her full lips pursed. "I wonder now about this overgown—" she began.

"Oh, my lady," said Susannah hastily, dreading yet another change of mind at this eleventh hour, "the overgown was quite a stroke of genius!"

"You think so?"

"Oh yes, indeed I do."

"Maybe it obscures the embroidery too much—and the embroidery is, after all, one of the gown's merits."

Susannah silently agreed fully, but nothing would let her admit it now. "I can see the embroidery quite clearly

91

from here, my lady. I think it tantalizes, draws the beholder closer."

Agnes glanced curiously at her then. "You have a strange manner for a seamstress—you *are* a seamstress, I take it?"

"Yes, my lady."

The clock began to chime, and Agnes' attention was drawn away from Susannah. "Where *is* that idiot Jenkins with the peach muslin? Has she no conception of the time? You, girl, seamstress. I am satisfied with this gown—convey my acceptance to Madame Hilary. Now you may disrobe me again."

Thankfully Susannah obeyed, and five minutes later she emerged from the house. The storm was raging overhead now, the trees dragging in the wind, and the rain lashing the pavement as Susannah began to run, her head bowed against the might of the weather. But it was not of herself she thought as she ran, it was of Miles. Poor Miles, he would be no match at all for the dragon he was to marry.

She came to a sudden standstill. She had run from the end of the pavement and was in the road in Berkeley Square! She had come the wrong way, turning right instead of left when leaving Lady Agnes' house!

The thunder broke sharply, and she did not hear the carriage, and the coachman's shout came too late to warn her. The lead horse struck her forcibly to the ground and she fell heavily, striking her head on the curb. She heard the coachman's anxious voice and in a blur saw the elegant black carriage and the team of stamping black Hanoverians. The harness gleamed in the rain and there was an emblem on the coach doors, a golden eagle. . . . Pain washed over her, and she could not move. Everything was so faint now, she could not hear the thunder clearly, and even the trees in the center of the square looked vague and distant.

"What is it, John?" asked a voice she remembered from somewhere. "I wish to be at the House before division—"

"A wench, Sir Jeffrey. I did not see her." The coachman climbed down and hurried to where she lay. "It was my fault, Sir Jeffrey, I was paying more attention to the storm than to what was ahead of me!"

"God damn it all. Who is she? Have you seen her before?"

"No, Sir Jeffrey."

"Well, we can't leave her here. Put her in the carriage and we'll take her to the house!"

"*In* the carriage, Sir Jeffrey?"

"Would you have me drag her behind on a rope? Be quick about it, now, I must reach Parliament before the vote!"

"Yes, Sir Jeffrey."

As the coachman picked her up, the pain increased. Everything faded into oblivion.

12

~~~

She was lying in a bed which smelled of lavender; its fine white sheets were trimmed with lace and the coverlet was embroidered in gold. The carved canopy overhead was draped with pale brocade and the curtains at the posts were tied back with gold-tasseled ropes. The room had one tall window, the royal-blue curtains drawn tightly to close out the violence of the storm which still raged over the night sky above London. A glass-domed clock on the mantelpiece pointed to half-past two.

She turned her aching head to look the other way. The room was very elegant, furnished with a fashionable chaise longue in blue velvet, some chairs with heart-shaped backs, and a mahogany table on which stood a three-branched candlestick which threw a soft light over everything. In a far corner was a washstand, and above it a mirror in which Susannah could see her distant reflection.

Lightning illuminated the night outside for a moment and was followed almost immediately by a crash of thunder which rattled the windowpanes. The vibrations made the candles tremble slightly, and slowly Susannah sat up, putting a hand to her forehead. Gradually recollection returned. She had been knocked down—by Sir Jeffrey Stratton's carriage.

She slipped from the bed. Someone had undressed her and put on a voluminous nightrobe which was far too big, and her long hair had been unpinned and carefully brushed, but whoever it had been, there was no one in the room now. Going to the window, she looked out over the long, narrow rear gardens where the storm beat against the rambling roses and

94

flattened the delicate summer flowers in the neat beds. She could see lights in the mews where she had once hidden—so very long ago it seemed now. Turning, she went to the door, peeping out onto the landing.

The house was of almost palatial magnificence. A sweeping staircase of Portland stone rose from the inner hall several floors below, and Ionic columns reached high into the shadows overhead. She dimly saw a coffered dome of gilded plaster and glass far above. The floors were carpeted in dove gray and the walls were gold and white. At regular intervals against the walls were marble-topped console tables, and on each one a huge bowl of dark red roses which filled the still, warm air with perfume. The only light came from wall-mounted candles, and apart from the noise of the storm, the house was quite silent. There was no sign of anyone she could ask about her clothes.

Hesitantly she left the doorway, gathering the cumbersome folds of the nightrobe in her hands so that she could walk, and at the top of the staircase she looked down to the gloomy hall far below. On a half-landing there was a pool of light from an open door, and hoping that she would maybe find a maid or a footman, she began to descend. She held the nightrobe above her ankles, but it was very difficult, for the sleeves were far too long and only her fingertips protruded from the gathered cuffs.

She reached the landing and paused with her hand on the carved eagle which marked the end of the rail. Through the open door she saw with dismay that the occupant was not a servant, but Sir Jeffrey Stratton himself. The room was a study, the predominant piece of furniture being a large dark desk topped with green leather and a collection of quills and inkwells. The light came from an oil lamp nearby and she could see him quite clearly as he lounged behind the desk, a decanter of cognac before him, and a glass in his hand which he slowly swirled as he gazed at nothing in particular. His dark hair was untidy and he had undone his cravat, leaving it to hang loose. His coat was tossed over a chair and she had the impression that he had not long returned to the house.

Turning, she began to go back up the stairs, but he saw the movement of white from the corner of his eye. "Who's there?"

Reluctantly she returned, standing in the doorway, feeling both ridiculous and embarrassed.

His glance swept over her, taking in the tentlike nightrobe and the wide-eyed face surrounded by a tumble of tawny hair. A hint of amusement shone in his gray eyes. "Ah, yes," he said, standing, "now I remember. How are you?"

"I . . . I was looking for my clothes . . ." she began lamely, wishing she had remained in her room and spared herself this embarrassment.

"No doubt they are being attended to—they were somewhat wet and dirty, as I recall. Besides which I cannot imagine why you would wish to have them now, for you surely do not intend returning to your employer on a night like this?"

"I should not take advantage . . ."

He seemed amused. "Take advantage? My coachman drives carelessly and knocks you down, and you speak of taking advantage?"

"I was not looking and stepped into the road."

"That is true—but the fault lies in the main with my coachman. I feel it only right that I should do what I can for you under the circumstances."

"You are very kind, Sir Jeffrey."

"Now you have the advantage of me—you would appear to know who I am, when I have no idea at all who you are."

"I know who you are because I heard your coachman speak to you," she said quickly.

"Ah, yes. But you still have the advantage of me."

"My name is Garland, Sir Jeffrey."

"I do not particularly like this predilection for addressing ladies ungallantly by their surnames. You surely have a first name?"

"Susannah."

He swirled the cognac for a moment. "Susannah Garland? Surely I have heard that name somewhere before?"

How could he possibly know her? There was no way—it was merely a coincidence! But she felt suddenly frightened, for although Sir Jeffrey Stratton was no friend of her uncle's, he was still too well acquainted with him for comfort.

"I do not think you can know of me, Sir Jeffrey."

"Possibly not. Tell me, is there some household which should be informed of your whereabouts? Your mistress will maybe—"

"I'm not a lady's maid, Sir Jeffrey, I'm a seamstress and I live in lodgings, so there is no one who should be told."

"A remarkably well-spoken seamstress."

"Thank you."

"I presume then that you are employed by no ordinary dressmaker."

"I work for Madame Hilary."

"The Empress of Tavistock Street," he said dryly. He smiled then, a warm humor touching his eyes, and she was suddenly made aware of him in a different way. That he was handsome and almost formidably attractive she had always known, but now she was subjected to his charm too. It was almost like a shock to meet his eyes in that moment, and she understood only too well why women like Emily Cowper and Agnes Winston wanted him so. He held out his hand then. "Will you take a celebratory glass of wine with me, Susannah Garland?"

She stared. "*Me*? Take a drink with *you*?"

"Is the thought offensive?"

"No. No, it's just that a gentleman like you does not usually take wine with someone like me."

"I frequently take wine with young and lovely women. However, on this occasion I promise you that my intentions are quite honorable and I merely wish you to celebrate Mr. Pitt's victory tonight." He still held out his hand.

Slowly she took it and he led her to a chair. She sat bolt upright, feeling uncomfortable and more and more embarrassed with each passing moment. Outside, the storm rumbled around the heavens and each gust of wind billowed the heavy dark green curtains. She watched him as he poured the wine from the bottle which rested in an ice bucket on a side table. What would it be like to be wooed by a man like him? What would it be like to have his arms around her? Her face felt hot and she was glad that she sat on the edge of the arc of lamplight, for she was sure her face told too much in that moment.

He returned, giving her one of the tall-stemmed glasses. He raised his. "Mr. Pitt."

She dutifully raised hers too. "Mr. Pitt," she repeated.

He laughed. "It makes no difference to you if Pitt sinks or swims, does it?"

"I know nothing about politics, Sir Jeffrey."

"Aye, well, why should you, your lot in life will not change whoever sits in Downing Street," he said dryly.

Outside the thunder seemed to split the night suddenly,

crashing with such force that the whole house shook. Susannah's breath caught with quick fear, her eyes fleeing to the windows, where the curtains moved in the draft of the wind. She had always been a little afraid of thunder, especially thunder so violent and so close.

He put his hand to her cheek in a reassuring gesture. "Don't be frightened," he said gently.

His touch was like fire, and the hotness returned to her face. She felt quite bewildered by the strength of emotion he could rouse in her; it was like nothing she had ever experienced before. Feeling almost weak, she got up from the chair and moved away from him, her glance falling on a portrait of a man and a woman above the fireplace. She seized upon it, for she thought that she recognized the dumpy figure of the woman. "Is . . . is that not Lady Ormanton?"

"It is."

"She is related to you?"

"By marriage only. As Ulla Schwellenberg she married my cousin Lord Ormanton. He has been dead these six years or more now."

"I'm sorry."

"Don't be, he was a singularly unpleasant fellow. Poor Ulla deserved much more from life."

"I . . . I stitched a spencer for her," she said lamely.

"Indeed—I confess to having little interest in *chiffons*, Susannah."

"No. No, of course not," she said lamely, knowing how gauche she must appear to him. She wished the floor would conveniently open and swallow her, but there was no such deliverance, she was left standing with the sure knowledge that what little composure she had was swiftly deserting her. Suddenly she put down her glass. "Th-thank you for the wine and for your hospitality tonight, Sir Jeffrey."

"The pleasure was entirely mine."

"Good night."

His gray eyes moved over her flushed, embarrassed face and he smiled faintly. "Good night, Susannah Garland."

Thankfully she hurried out, almost forgetting in her haste to lift the flapping skirts of the nightrobe above her ankles. At the top of the stairs she stopped, looking back at his shadow as it moved in the pool of light on the landing. Never in her life had she felt as strongly and abruptly drawn to any man as she was to this one. Never before had she been set so completely at sixes and sevens. She had thought herself in love with Miles, but that emotion was small when compared with the desire roused by the momentary touch of Jeffrey Stratton's fingers on her cheek.

A maid brought her laundered clothes first thing the next morning, and Susannah dressed quickly, refusing the maid's offer of breakfast. One thing and one thing only was in Susannah's mind as she hastily brushed her long hair and twisted it back into a knot—she must leave this house as quickly as possible and get away from the strange, powerful emotions which had somehow been released in her.

The puzzled maid showed her down the stairs, and not knowing that Susannah was only a seamstress and therefore only worthy of the back door, she showed her out through the front door.

Susannah stepped quickly and thankfully out, but then came to an immediate standstill, for Lady Agnes Winston's traveling britska, heavily loaded with baggage, was drawn up at the curb outside, a postilion controlling the fractious team of four grays. Jeffrey stood on the pavement and Susannah thought about retreating, but already the maid had closed the door. A church bell was striking eight.

Lady Agnes leaned out of the carriage to talk with him. He had obviously just left the house with the intention of driving his cabriolet, which waited a little farther along the street. His royal-blue coat looked very bright in the morning sun, and his cane tapped lightly against his shining hessian boot as he looked up at the woman in the carriage. His head was bare and he carried his top hat under his arm.

The plumes in Agnes' mauve hat fluttered slightly in the breeze, which was all that remained of the night's storm, and her face was animated and flushed as she smiled down at him. She toyed with the pearl buttons of her green-and-cream pelisse and self-consciously adjusted the tilt of her hat, and there could be no mistaking her feelings, for they were written large upon her lovely face as she looked at him. As to how he felt, Susannah could not tell, for his back was toward her. Agnes lowered her eyes for a moment then as Jeffrey took out his fob watch and bowed low. She reached down quickly and he took her hand, putting it briefly to his lips, and then the britska drew slowly away, the harness jingling and the wheels crunching on the hard road. Susannah watched as Miles Devereux's bride left London for her stay in the country with friends.

Jeffrey remained on the pavement for a moment, his head bowed, and then he put on his hat and went toward his cabriolet. But as he did so, he saw Susannah.

"Good morning, Susannah."

Startled, she curtsied. "Good morning, Sir Jeffrey."

"I trust you slept well for what was left of the night."

"Yes." She was very conscious suddenly of having left by way of the front door, but there was nothing in his manner to suggest that he was in any way disapproving.

"And are you now *en route* for the Empress of Tavistock Street?"

"Yes."

"Allow me to drive you there."

"I could not possibly inconvenience you any more—" she began quickly.

"You will not, I assure you, for Tavistock Street lies on my way."

"Then . . . then thank you, Sir Jeffrey."

"Do you always accept with such crushing enthusiasm, Susannah Garland?" he asked lightly, offering her his arm.

"Are you always as attentive to seamstresses, Sir Jeffrey?" she countered.

He laughed. "No, but then, I confess to not having met a great many." He handed her onto the light cabriolet and the little groom climbed onto his tiny perch behind.

The magnificent white horse leaped forward at a light touch of the whip, and Susannah gripped the side of the vehicle as it spun swiftly along the square. She heard the wind whispering in the plane trees, every leaf seeming as if freshly painted after the night of rain. There was a smell of fresh earth and flowers in the warm air, and she wanted to laugh suddenly as the cabriolet gained speed, the horse's loose mane flying in the breeze as it sped along Bruton Street past Lady Agnes' house and then on into New Bond Street.

She held her bonnet on firmly, the ribbons flapping and fluttering around her chin as if they were alive, and she heard Jeffrey laugh as she squealed when the cabriolet turned a sharp corner and seemed on the point of overturning.

When at last the pace slowed and he brought the vehicle to a standstill outside Madame Hilary's in Tavistock Street, Susannah felt quite out of breath and exhilarated. He climbed down and came to her side of the cabriolet. Her hand shook a little as she took his and stepped down to the solid safety of the pavement.

"I trust you are not too windblown, Susannah."

"I have never driven that fast before in my life!" she said breathlessly.

"Does not every gentleman drive like that?" he asked.

She smiled then. "I would not know, Sir Jeffrey, for I confess to not knowing a great many gentlemen."

He returned the smile, bowing his head slightly. "There you have me, the very answer I no doubt deserved. However, much as I would like to dally in your delightful company, I fear I must go now. Good-bye, Susannah."

"Good-bye, Sir Jeffrey."

She did not remain on the pavement to watch him drive away, but escaped into the shelter of the courtyard. There was no one else around yet, no one to see as she leaned weakly back against the side door, her eyes closed for a moment. It was not just with the exhilaration of the drive that she trembled.

13

At the very end of July, the day of the wedding dawned at last. Susannah had seen nothing of Miles for over a month, and she was a little thankful for this, for in her new, rather bemused state of mind she doubted if a meeting with him would have gone at all well. He had written several times, his letters hastily scribbled in secret at Sanderby, but she could not very well reply to him there. Not that she would have known exactly what to say anyway, for his letters were full of protestations of love, full of pleadings that she should let him support her, set her up in a house somewhere. Maybe it was as well that she could not reply, for whatever she said now would surely only hurt him, and hurting him was something she would never willingly have done.

As for Sir Jeffrey Stratton, she naturally neither saw nor heard anything from him, nor did she expect to. In retrospect she felt very foolish, for a man of his experience could hardly have missed her reactions. It must have amused him a little, having a nonentity of a seamstress obviously distracted by his every glance. Yes, the more Susannah thought about it, the more foolish she felt—but no matter how foolish, she still could not forget him or discard the fact that she could very easily fall in love with him. And if "foolish" was the word to attach to her emotions so far, how much more applicable would it be to actually falling in love with a man so far above her in station?

On the day of the wedding, Madame Hilary, in an unprecedented act of thoughtfulness which startled even Miss Chiddock, announced that as the ceremony was to be held in the evening at St. George's Church in Hanover Square, then her employees could if they wished finish work an hour early in order to view the grand occasion. Naturally, however, they would forfeit one hour's wages for the privilege. Nonetheless, quite a number of the seamstresses decided that they would indeed forgo those few pennies in order to look at what was surely one of the events of the social calendar that Season.

Susannah deliberated for a long time, for she still had little desire to see Miles enter into something which could only bring him unhappiness and regret, but in the end the lure of the occasion proved too much and she decided to go.

It was a humid evening, with none of the sunshine and brightness always prayed for on a wedding day. The trees hung motionless in the squares and the horses held their heads low, shaking them from time to time to disturb the insects which filled the still air. The muted shadows were lengthening as Susannah hurried toward Hanover Square in her best pink taffeta. It seemed appropriate somehow that she should look as fine as possible, and there were not many occasions in her new life when such a dress could be worn now. Her hair was hidden beneath her crisp poke bonnet, and she had purchased new white ribbons only recently. She carried her matching reticule, and over her arms she lightly draped her white woolen shawl. It was not a brilliant cashmere shawl, as was all the rage, but it did well enough—and besides, it was all she had.

There was a closeness in the air which was breathless, and her skin felt sticky and damp as she neared the square. The streets were thronged with expensive carriages, landaus with their hoods down and ladies sitting inside with their fans wafting swiftly to and fro in an effort to keep cool. Outside the church the road was so crowded that scarcely any carriages could pass at all and many of the guests were forced to climb down to walk the last few yards to the church steps, where two young girls in white stood by the door with decorated baskets of wedding favors which they handed to each guest. Susannah watched as a lady in primrose satin accepted one of the favors, a dainty knot of white ribbons and flowers.

Every important member of Whig society had been invited to the wedding, including, of course, the Prince of Wales himself. Susannah had heard of how very corpulent he was now, but even so his appearance came as something of a shock. He was corseted so tightly that he looked very uncomfortable, and the tight, revealing fashions so prevalent at the moment did nothing to flatter him at all. His face was florid and rouged, his lips full, and his eyes a pale, rather watery blue. His gaudy crimson coat and white pantaloons emphasized his great bulk, and he looked a little pathetic as he leaned on a friend's arm to negotiate the church steps with his gouty leg. Behind him walked the equally stout and equally corseted Lady Hertford, who was whispered to be his latest mistress. Susannah watched the Prince. It was sad that there was little left now of the great beauty which had once made him the most handsome Prince in Europe, and even as she watched, his expression darkened furiously as someone in the crowd shouted out Mr. Pitt's name and called for three cheers. A ripple of delighted laughter went around the gathering and everyone obediently cheered the absent Prime Minister. The Prince halted, scowling around the sea of unrepentant faces. Lady Hertford persuaded him that it would be better to continue on his way, and he nodded, stiffly negotiating the next step and at last reaching the sanctuary of the church.

Susannah found her way through the crowd to a position by the foot of the steps, in the darkening shadows by the columns which were draped with garlands of sweet-smelling flowers. More flowers were strewn on the steps, and she could hear the choir singing inside.

A white landau, its hood down, entered the square, conveying the first group of bridesmaids. It managed to reach the church steps at last and a gasp of admiration went around the crowd as the young girls alighted, fluffing out their beautiful gowns. The yellow and lilac silks looked very lovely in the evening light, and the girls' hair was twined with matching ribbons and pretty pink rosebuds. They carried posies of more rosebuds, and were laughing excitedly together as they hurried up the steps and into the church. Susannah looked proudly at her designs, wanting suddenly to stand on the steps and shout aloud to the world that *she* had produced those gowns which everyone thought so very pretty!

The next carriage brought the bridegroom and his father to the scene, and Susannah melted back into the shadows. Her uncle looked as black-browed and discontent as ever, and he stood with his hands clasped firmly behind his back, his head hunched between his shoulders. Even though she knew he was unaware of her presence, Susannah felt suddenly afraid as she watched him. For five years she had lived in this man's terrible shadow, and five years of fear and anxiety cannot be overcome in a few months—she was afraid of him still.

Miles seemed withdrawn and pale, and although he raised his hand in acknowledgment of the crowd's cheers, the gesture was preoccupied and lackluster. He looked very handsome in a dark blue coat with yellow buttons, his cravat very fashionably full and extravagant, and he cut a fine figure as he stood there by the white carriage for a moment, his hair very fair as he removed his hat and ran his hand over his soft curls. By his appearance it could only be thought that he lacked for nothing and that by this very fortunate marriage he was about to further secure his already immense wealth and happiness—but what could be further from the truth? Susannah's heart went out to him. Poor Miles, if only he had had more strength, how different things might have been by now.

At that moment, a little earlier than expected, the bride's large-windowed carriage entered the square, and Susannah's attention was drawn away from Miles and her uncle. The crowd mobbed Agnes' coach and it was forced to a standstill, and as Susannah watched she did not know that Miles had seen her, his attention drawn by the remembered pink taffeta gown.

He hesitated on the steps, his already pale face draining of color. His father turned to look at him. "What is it, boy?"

"I . . . I . . ."

"Well?" Lord Devereux followed the direction of his son's gaze and he too saw the girl in pink taffeta. "By all the saints," he murmured in sudden fury and anxiety that at this eleventh hour his plans could be destroyed by his penniless niece.

From the crowd Sir Jeffrey Stratton watched the scene on the steps with great curiosity. What could have disturbed the bridegroom's fragile nerve so abruptly? And what could have made His Lordship's sour visage turn that strangely purple hue? Thoughtfully Jeffrey pushed his way through the crowd until he could see at last the cause of the consternation—a little figure in pink taffeta, still pathetically ignorant of the stir she had created on the steps. He was curious then, for what could the little seamstress have to do with Lord Devereux or with his spineless son?

Lord Devereux snatched his son's arm. "Go on into the church, boy!" he growled, his face suffused with a rage which he just held in check.

"I . . . I must speak to Susannah."

"Do as you are told! Remember, now, poverty is a forlorn land."

Miles stared into his father's bright eyes. The threatening reminder of the fate which could await him sent the momentary indecision fleeing like chaff before the wind then, and without another word he obeyed. He stumbled a little on the steps and entered the church just as his bride's coach at last reached the foot of the steps. Lord Devereux waited a moment and then began to descend the steps in Susannah's direction. She was still unaware of her imminent danger.

She strained to see as the four creamy-white horses stamped and snorted. They wore white ear coverings and white tassels, and the coachman's livery was also white. The whips were decorated with white ribbons and the whole equipage had an ethereal appearance in the strange, humid evening light. The air was still and at last the crowd was silent as the carriage door was opened and the bride stepped down. Then everyone cheered as the beautiful gown was revealed at last. Susannah's eye was critical, however—the overgown spoiled everything.

"You've a nerve, missy!" said a low, angry voice in her ear.

With a gasp she whirled about to stare into her uncle's hate-filled eyes. She tried to back away, but there were too many people, people who had eyes only for the bride and who saw nothing of Susannah's plight.

He caught her arm. "Not this time," he hissed. "You'll not escape again!"

"Please let me go! I mean no harm, I promise I don't!"

"I know what you mean," he said with a chill smile. "You mean the endangering of my plans. You'll be well away from here before my son emerges."

"Please," she whispered, terrified, "please let me go!"

"Never! I'll see to it that you never haunt me again, missy, do you hear me? Never!"

A hand clad in tight black leather came from the side to rest warningly on Lord Devereux's shoulder. "I think, my lord," said Jeffrey softly, "that you are offending the lady."

Susannah's frightened eyes fled with disbelieving relief to the face of her rescuer.

Lord Devereux's tone was icy. "This does not concern you, Stratton!"

"Oh, but it does, for Miss Garland is an acquaintance of mine."

Her uncle hesitated then, staring at her and then at Jeffrey. She felt his fingers loosen their grip on her arm, for he knew as well as any that Jeffrey Stratton was not a man to meddle with.

Jeffrey's smile was cool. "My lord, isn't your presence required in the church on this . . . er, auspicious occasion?"

"You go too far this time, Stratton!"

"Do I? Think carefully, my lord. I would not wish you to make a hasty action which you may live to regret at some later date."

Lord Devereux's face lost its angry color and turned white with pure hatred. His eyes glittered unpleasantly in that way which always terrified Susannah more than anything else, but even as she watched, she knew that he would step back from facing Jeffrey. The moments passed and then suddenly he capitulated, bowing low with a sneer on his face before turning on his heel and hurrying up the steps into the church just as Lady Agnes began to mount the steps on her father's arm. The crowds cheered wildly, and Susannah felt faint.

Jeffrey's arm was tight and supporting around her waist. "Are you all right, Susannah?"

She nodded, unable to speak, and he helped her through the excited crowds. She felt as if her legs had no strength, and if it had not been for his arm, she would not have been able to stand.

His carriage was waiting in a side street, and she hardly knew that he had helped her inside or that he climbed in after her and ordered the coachman to drive on. He lowered the glass in the door so that the evening air blew across her hot face, cooling and calming her so that gradually her color returned, the fear receded, and she began to feel safe again.

"I trust you are recovered now, Susannah."

"Yes. Once again I am in your debt, Sir Jeffrey."

"What are you to Devereux?" he asked abruptly.

"I . . . I doubt if you would believe me if I told you."

"Allow me to judge that for myself."

"Very well. I am his niece."

He was silent, studying her face for a long moment before speaking. "I knew you were no ordinary seamstress," he said softly. "So, you must be Georgiana Devereux's daughter, and that is why your name sounded familiar to me."

"She was my mother, but how . . . ?"

"Oh, it is a long story and goes back before you were born. My mother died in childbed and my father decided to take a second wife—his choice fell upon Georgiana Devereux, and she accepted him. But then she met you father, 'that cursed schoolmaster,' as my father called him, and ran off with him. Whispers have ways of reaching the children of a household, Susannah, and I was no exception. I knew all about Georgiana's elopement and about the birth of her daughter, Susannah Garland. But then things went very quiet and there was no more talk of Georgiana, for my father took a second wife and his choice was so disastrous that I spent a great deal of time wishing Stephen Garland had never been born so that Georgiana had married my father after all and spared me the odiousness of my stepmother. However, that is by the by." He looked out of the window at the darkening streets. "All in all, I have little to thank the Devereux family for."

"You think my uncle cheated your father?"

"I know so. I owe him no favors, Susannah, no favors at all. Do you? You came back into the Devereux fold from the Garland fields—why?"

"I was an orphan at fifteen, but on her deathbed my mother begged me to go to her brother. She thought my life would be far better at Sanderby and that I would be protected. She thought that Lord Devereux would show kindness to his sister's only child."

"And was she correct in all this?"

"No. I ran away earlier this year."

"Why?"

She avoided his penetrating gaze then, shrinking from telling him about Miles.

He flexed his fingers thoughtfully in the leather gloves. "It has something to do with today's blushing bridegroom, has it not? I see from your face that I am right. So, dear Miles would have preferred his lovely cousin to his father's choice, would he? How very interesting. But he would not dare take you for his wife, for a penniless bride is hardly suitable for a future master of Sanderby—or for a man used to squandering everything at the gaming table. Am I right, Susannah?"

"Yes."

"And Devereux has kept your existence a secret?"

"Yes."

"Why, exactly, did you run away?"

"My uncle intended banishing me to his Irish estates, but I feared that banishment might lead to something a little more permanent," she said simply. How easy it was to say it, how surprisingly simple to say that she thought her uncle would have murdered her to rid himself of any small threat she may have presented to his peace of mind.

After a moment he nodded slightly. "I think you are most probably correct; there is very little at which Devereux of Sanderby would balk. I think also that you may consider yourself safe from him now."

"Because of the wedding?"

"That—and because he knows you are involved in some way with me. On the whole, he keeps well away from me—I am my father's son, but I am far from being in my father's weak image. I owe your uncle nothing, Susannah. Are you still in love with Miles Devereux?"

She flushed. "No."

"So it was not a broken heart which brought you to the church this evening?"

"No."

He smiled then. "Will you dine with me tonight, Susannah?"

She stared at him. Nothing would please her more, nothing would be more delightful than to spend several hours more in his company, to live like one of the society belles who were so acceptable to him. But why did he ask her? Why did he show all this interest now? It could only be because of her identity, because through her he could strike at her uncle. "Would . . . would you ask me if I were not Lord Devereux's niece?" she asked quietly.

"I do believe I would, for whatever your background, you are very lovely and I enjoy being with you. Correct me if I'm wrong, but I rather think you enjoy being with me, too." He said this last very softly, his eyes knowing as he watched her reactions. He knew exactly the effect he had upon her, and it seemed to amuse him a little.

She was undecided, wanting to accept and yet knowing

that she should not. Where he was concerned, it was difficult to acknowledge even the existence of common sense.

"Your answer, Susannah," he murmured.

Slowly she nodded. "I would like to dine with you, Sir Jeffrey. Thank you."

14

~

The grand salon of the house in Berkeley Square was a magnificent room stretching the entire width of the house. The ceiling was coffered and painted in squares with scenes from the lives of gods and goddesses, the rich blues, reds, and golds glowing softly in the gentle candlelight. The door and window frames were carved and gilded, and the two fireplaces were inlaid with white and Siena marble, a winged cherub in the center of each. The walls were hung with dull golden damask and the chairs and sofas were upholstered in a similar color. The curtains were drawn back to allow the cool night air in and Susannah could hear the trees rustling slightly in the square outside. A carriage drove slowly past, somewhere the Watch called the hour, and she could hear the sounds of laughter from the small gathering outside Gunter's.

She stood in the center of the room and looked around at the dazzling beauty which in its way excelled anything at Sanderby, because in spite of its undoubted grandeur, this room was also intimate, a room where one could be at ease.

The butler placed an ice bucket containing a bottle of champagne on a small table, and Jeffrey nodded at him. "That will be all."

"Very well, Sir Jeffrey."

"And tell Monsieur Laurent that his cooking was, as ever, quite exceptional."

"Yes, Sir Jeffrey." The butler retired.

Susannah ran her fingertips over the inlaid surface of a beautiful mahogany table and picked up the gold-framed miniature which stood there. It was of a young woman dressed in virginal white, her almond-shaped eyes looking almost challenging as she gave a half-smile. Her dark chestnut hair was draped with tiny strings of jewels and she held a fan in one hand, the other resting on the head of a large hunting dog. The minature was so exquisitely executed that Susannah felt she could have rearranged the folds of the muslin gown. "Who is she?" she asked.

"My wife."

She looked at the portrait again then. What was the truth behind all the whispers? How exactly had Elizabeth Stratton met her death? Susannah glanced at him as he poured the iced champagne. What did she really know of him? She was more than halfway in love with him already, and yet all she knew was based on rumor—his reputation had preceded him. There was a hardness in Jeffrey Stratton, a depth which she could not even begin to sound as yet—if ever. And he did not do anything without good reason, as witness her presence here with him tonight.

He turned and saw the pensive look on her face. His glance went to the minature. "You should not lend your ear to gossip, Susannah," he said with some irritation, "for it ill becomes you. My wife died of consumption, as have countless thousands of other unfortunate souls—your own father included, if I'm not mistaken. The hand of mortal man does not lie behind that dreadful death. Now, then, what else can you have heard of me? Ah, yes—I was left exceedingly rich by my wife's death. That is very true, but the fact that I was hardly a pauper before marrying her has conveniently slipped most memories in the cause of good gossip. It is also true that she died very quickly after marrying me, but I assure you that the two facts are quite unconnected. Six weeks after our marriage, she fell gravely ill and the doctors gave her perhaps half a year to live. She died within three weeks, not because I aided her departure but because the medical prognosis was quite incorrect and she was far more ill than anyone knew." He pushed one of the glasses into Susannah's hand, his face still angry. "There must be more you have heard—but of course, the duels! They most certainly took place, and two men lie dead at my hands—if they had not died, then they would have killed me, of that there is no doubt. I have also wounded several others, death not being required to defend the honor of ladies who could not lay claim to any. I have taken many mistresses and have lived a

112

most sinful existence—which makes your decision to spend this evening with me decidedly questionable!"

"There was no need to say any of that, or to say it the way you did. It is not my fault that you have a reputation which reached my ears long before I first spoke to you. And besides, I know full well that I should not be here with you tonight, that propriety most definitely demands more correct behavior from a respectable young lady, and it ill becomes you, sir, to pass comment upon my lapse."

The anger melted from his eyes then, and he bowed. "Why, I do believe that I've been put firmly in my place, and quite rightly so. Forgive me. But if propriety has already been offended, then it can make little further difference to pursue the point and discover why you chose to behave as you did tonight. Why did you come, Susannah?"

"A very foolish reason, really, and one which you will no doubt find extremely amusing."

"Allow me to be the judge of that."

"I came simply because I wished to behave like a fashionable society lady for this one evening. I wished to sit at a magnificent table in an elegant room, to be served dishes fit for a queen, and to enjoy the company and attention of one of London's most eligible gentlemen. For that I thumbed my nose at convention."

He came to her, removing her glass and placing it on a table beside them before taking her hands. "I do not find it amusing, Susannah," he said softly. "I find it charming and more appealing than is good for me. I am also flattered, but would tell you that I wish I were less of a gentleman right now and more of a rogue, for then I would have no compunction whatsoever about seducing you. Rakehell I may be, but I have yet to destroy innocence." He touched her hair gently. "But I swear that you tempt me greatly, that making love to you would surely be the sweetest of pleasures." He kissed her on the lips, pulling her into his arms and holding her close.

She closed her eyes, knowing in her heart that had he chosen in that moment to continue, then she would have been powerless to refuse him. The torrent of emotion that single kiss released in her was almost bewitching in its power, and there was no innocence in it at all.

Slowly he released her, his eyes dark as he looked into her flushed face, and his voice was barely above a whisper.

113

"Temptation personified, and with Devereux blood in her sweet veins." With a short laugh he turned away, crossing to the open window, where he stood staring out into the dark night.

She watched him, battling to gather her scattered senses and to hide the pain his last words had brought to her. It had been a timely reminder, a warning that his only reason for bothering with her was that she was a Devereux—beyond that he would still not have glanced at her. Blinking back the tears, she glanced down at his wife's portrait again.

"What do you want from life, Susannah?" he asked suddenly. "I cannot see you as a seamstress until the end of your days."

"W-want from life?"

"You surely have some prized goal, some fantasy about how your future should be?"

"Yes. I do."

"Tell me."

She raised her eyes to him. "I would like to be as Madame Hilary is. I would like to be a leading dressmaker. No, *the* leading dressmaker! I would like to clothe all the greatest ladies, including the Queen herself. I would like to have my own establishment in somewhere like St. James's . . ." She broke off. "Maybe I *do* wish to be a seamstress after all, albeit an exalted one."

He turned toward her. "It would appear that you have indeed given thought to the matter."

"Thoughts cost nothing."

He smiled. "To clothe the Queen you would have to be a German, and besides, Her Majesty is already quite content with the stodgy, old-fashioned garments her present Teutonic *Kleidermacherin* produces with tedious irregularity. To clothe *anyone* of consequence, come to that, you would first have to have a flair for original designs as well as an ability with needle and thread."

"I have that ability."

"Oh, such modesty!"

"But it's true." She told him then of her life at Madame Hilary's, and of how many fashionable ladies were already wearing garments which had come originally from the busy pencil of Susannah Garland, not Madame Hilary.

He listened in silence, speaking only when she had finished. "Such infamy among the fripperies," he said dryly. "Who would have thought it. And this is the woman you wish to emulate? You surprise me."

"Not her personality, just the position she now holds. She has achieved a great deal and I am forced to admire her for it, although recent events must make me wonder exactly how much she has achieved by her own merit. She has used me quite ruthlessly, playing on my fear and blackmailing me into doing exactly as she wishes—I cannot admire that in her. I believe that I could reach her position—but by my own endeavors, not by anyone else's."

"I rather believe you could too—I saw Princess Amelia's gown."

"You liked it?"

"It was surely the first gown the Princess has worn that I have found even remotely attractive. She is a very pretty young woman, but she dresses appallingly, for the most part. If your hand lay behind that cleverness with the black fur, then I salute you, and I am quite prepared to believe you have all the qualities needed to achieve your ambition."

She smiled.

"But how would you go about achieving it all?" he asked then, his eyes half-closed as he watched her.

"It's all purely hypothetical and I have not thought about that side of it."

"Nonetheless, you must have some thoughts in mind."

"Well, I suppose I would have to find suitable premises, a house similar to that owned by Madame Hilary—but there the similarity would end. I would have a showroom which would be welcoming and elegant, somewhere for ladies to sit and be at their ease as they discuss their wishes with me." She glanced at him, feeling suddenly a little foolish for revealing her innermost thoughts.

"You see?" he said. "You've thought about it more than you will admit."

"There was little else to do when I was stitching endless garments which should have been acknowledged as mine but which were stolen by someone else."

"Ah, a spark of resentment, I do perceive."

"Would you not resent it?"

He smiled. "Oh, I would indeed—fate has dealt a very unreasonable hand to you, Susannah. But maybe fate can relent occasionally."

"What do you mean?"

"I could grant you your wish."

"Why?"

"There has to be a reason?"

"You do nothing without good reason."

"Am I becoming transparent to you already? I must rectify that. However, as you so swiftly point out, there is indeed a reason. Setting you up as the second dressmaker in the illustrious Devereux family would gall your damned uncle quite superbly. There would somehow seem to be something very appropriate in giving you all you desire while at the same time giving him cause for a seizure."

In that moment she wished that he knew nothing of her background, that he was offering her this dazzling prize because of herself and not because of the blood flowing in her veins. But it was not to be, and he had been honest about it—so why did she not snatch the chance so suddenly presented to her? She had nothing to lose and oh so much to gain by accepting. "There . . . there would be a condition," she said slowly.

"You lay down conditions?" he asked incredulously.

"It is not one which should displease you."

"Name it, then."

"I wish to eventually pay every penny back to you."

"That could take a lifetime, and I must insist that there is no need. The amount of money involved may be a fortune to you, but it is nothing to me, and I do not really wish to set this thing on a business footing."

"I would still prefer it that way. You have a reason for your actions, Sir Jeffrey, and so do I—I do not wish to accept such a gift from you, but I will accept a correct financial arrangement."

He crossed the room toward her. "Is this the belated appearance of propriety?"

"Why not?" She gave a short smile. "I rather think my fanciful evening is at an end, isn't it?"

He put his hand gently to her cheek. "I think it best."

She said nothing, drawing away from him. *I don't. I don't think it best at all, for I love you.*

"So, it is agreed," he said, picking up her glass again and giving it to her. "No doubt you will wish to begin making arrangements concerning this house of fashion as quickly as possible," he said in matter-of-fact tone which could only signify more definitely the new relationship which was to exist between them from now on, "and you will certainly not wish to remain in your odious lodgings a moment longer than necessary."

She gazed down at her glass until she was in command of herself. "I . . . I don't know where—"

"I leave for Walmer Castle in the morning, I am to be the Prime Minister's guest for a while, so there is no reason why you should not remain in this house until you have found suitable premises for this venture."

"I believe that must bring us back to propriety again, sir."

He smiled at that. "How can there be *im*propriety if you are in London and I am the other side of Kent? Besides, it will soon be quite pointless to worry about rumor and conjecture concerning the relationship between us, for once my involvement is known, you will have overtones of scandal to contend with constantly. Such whispers could be the making of you, for to have such a connection with me will make you very interesting and therefore worthy of a visit or two. It is the precise nature of scandal which marks the line between what is acceptable and what isn't. The *beau monde* is fickle—it can adore a courtesan and despise a virgin. Lady Jersey is known to have been the Prince of Wales's mistress, but she is still welcome at Court and is acceptable to the Queen. A young lady named Lavinia Sherwood was suspected, quite wrongly, of having taken a groom for her lover, and it ruined her. So, you see, it is what form the scandal takes which is the criterion, not merely the fact that there is a soupçon of eyebrow-raising. If, however, you should eventually be called to the Queen's presence, Susannah, then it will be a little different for you than it is for Lady Jersey. You will be a dressmaker, without title and in the end without influence—any hint of scandal then, and you will be finished. For the moment, however, you need not concern yourself with such matters. All you need to do is prove that you are no nine days' wonder and that you are worthy of reaching for Madame Hilary's crown. It will need considerable strength of will on your part, for society can be tyrannical and cruel, and Madame Hilary is not about to sit idly by and watch you succeed to her throne. Whatever happens will not worry me particularly, but the effect upon you is another thing entirely. I believe this vocation of yours to be the paramount thing in your life, but even so, I advise you to think most carefully before finally accepting if you have any anxiety about your reputation."

She looked at him, longing to blurt out that *he* mattered far more to her than any ambition to be a great court dressmaker. Oh, if only he knew how much more he mattered. Had he offered to set her up as his mistress, as Miles had done. . . . But that was not what he was offering, and so she told him nothing.

"Is it still agreed, Susannah?" he asked.

"Yes," she whispered. "Yes, it is."

The glasses chinked together.

15

Before leaving for Walmer Castle for his stay with Mr. Pitt, Jeffrey sent for his agent to explain that Susannah was to be accommodated in whatever plan she made in connection with the setting up of a new house of fashion. The agent received the news without flinching, writing laborious notes and bowing a great deal, and he departed without his facial expression seeming to have changed in the slightest.

Later in the morning Jeffrey took his leave of Susannah, and his manner gave her no reason to hope that his attitude toward her had changed at all. Indeed, she detected a slight reserve in him now, as if he had decided to put their relationship firmly on the business footing she had insisted upon the night before. Since leaving Sanderby she had become past master at hiding her feelings, and if that mastery had slipped a little when confronted with her love for him, then she had regained control now. She gave him no cause to wonder if perhaps he had made a mistake in becoming involved with her, and he climbed into his waiting carriage without knowing that there were tears in her eyes. She watched the carriage drive away. It was better to have his friendship in this way than to risk losing him entirely.

She crossed the magnificent hall and mounted the staircase, conscious of the curious gaze of the two footmen who closed the door. She turned, a hand on the banister. "I shall need a chaise in about one hour's time," she said.

"A chaise, madam?"

"Yes, I must see what properties are available. I shall require someone to escort me."

The nearest footman bowed low. "Very well, madam."

She went on up to the drawing room, where the morning sunlight streamed in through the windows. She picked up Elizabeth Stratton's miniature and stared at it for a long time. The enigmatic face gazed back, revealing nothing. Slowly Susannah put the little picture down again. Maybe Elizabeth was the only woman who would ever possess Jeffrey Stratton entirely. Emily Cowper was his mistress, but she had no hold over his heart. She was one of the most dazzling women in London, beautiful, vivacious, and delightful company, and yet she could not make sure of Jeffrey Stratton. And then there was Agnes Winston—no, Agnes Devereux now— maybe he would amuse himself with her for a while. Susannah looked around the sumptuous room. There had been many women in his life and there would be many more. Susannah Garland was but a fleeting interest and she must accept that hurtful, incontrovertible fact. With a last glance at his wife's portrait, she turned on her heel and left the drawing room.

At the end of that first day, when she had been shown over no fewer than ten different premises by one agent alone, all of them unsuitable in one way or another, she ordered the chaise to go to Tavistock Street. The church bell was sounding nine as the carriage drew up at the curb near Madame Hilary's house. Susannah did not intend visiting her former employer; she would eventually, but not just yet. She sat back in the shadowy vehicle, watching the little side door, and a few moments later the seamstresses and milliners emerged, hurrying away along the street to their various homes. At last she saw the one face she sought, and she opened the door quickly as Annie walked past.

"Annie?"

"Susannah?" Annie halted, glancing curiously at the carriage. "But where have you been today? Madame was furious when you did not come, and Miss Chiddock swears she will punish you—"

"She will not, for I will not be there for her to punish."

"Not be there? What do you mean?"

"Annie, will you drive with me for a while, I have rather a lot to tell you."

Annie smiled. "The truth maybe? Oh, I know there is

something, for you are obviously no ordinary seamstress, are you?"

Susannah smiled too. "No, and if I tell you that to begin with I am Lord Devereux's niece, what would you say?"

Annie stared at her, and then without a word climbed into the chaise.

They drove for a long time as Susannah told her everything she had so wanted to tell her all along. Annie listened in stunned silence as the tale progressed, and her eyes were huge when at last Susannah finished.

"You . . . you are to set up as a dressmaker? With Sir Jeffrey Stratton's help?" she asked in amazement.

"Yes. And I shall need a forewoman, Annie Jones."

"Me?"

"Yes."

"I'm only a seamstress!"

"You know the work inside out and back to front, Annie, and you're good. I know that I am not set up yet, and I know that I may fail—but I would like you to come with me, Annie. You're my good friend and I love you dearly, you made my life at Madame Hilary's bearable, and now I want to do something for you in return. I am looking for a suitable house, indeed I have seen so many today that I am in a daze with them all, and when I find it there will be room there for you. At least say that you will consider my offer."

Annie sat back weakly, trying to absorb everything. She gave a little laugh. "Of course I will consider, but—"

"I don't expect you to say anything just yet, at least not until you've seen my new premises for yourself. But if you come then, and look over everything, and discuss with me what we must do, then you will decide?"

"Susannah, I have a safe place with Madame Hilary—"

"I know. I know, Annie, and I shall quite understand if you decide you dare not risk coming to me. You have a great deal to consider, and maybe I will not provide the security you need for that."

Annie reached over and put her hand over Susannah's. "I *will* consider it very carefully, Susannah, and I know you do me a great honor by asking me to be your forewoman. I've seen all those drawings you do, and now that I know Madame Hilary forced you to give them to her, then I know for certain that your designs are the best there are."

"Oh, I don't know about *that*—"

"They are. Why else would Madame want them for herself? I hate that workroom, Susannah, and I shall hate it all the more if you are not there. I would *like* to come with you, truly I would."

"When I have found the right building, then I shall come to see you again."

Annie nodded, smiling. "Yes." She pulled a little face. "I am afraid that I am not at all adventurous, Susannah. Indeed, I am rather meek. I think you're very brave."

"Brave?"

"Well, taking such a gamble upon something like this. And then, you are risking your uncle finding you—indeed, he *must* find you once the story gets about. Aren't you afraid of that?"

"A little. But now that Miles is married safely . . ."

"And now that Sir Jeffrey Stratton is your protector?" said Annie, smiling.

"Yes."

"You love him, don't you?"

Susannah looked away, nodding. "Yes."

"The most notorious man in the kingdom, and you have to fall in love with him?"

"Yes."

"And is he as wicked as they say?"

"I don't know."

"He's certainly very handsome—he accompanied Lady Cowper to Madame's once, and I saw him."

"Well, he's made it quite plain that his real interest in me is because he wishes to use me against my uncle."

"But you'd still come running if he were to crook his little finger, wouldn't you?"

"Yes. If I thought he wanted me, I'd show no pride whatsoever—but he doesn't, so my pride can remain outwardly intact."

"I can only say that I'm glad I'm so plain that someone like that would not pause to give me a second glance!" said Annie with feeling.

The chaise came to a standstill at last outside the tiny lodging house where Annie had a room on the ground floor. Annie climbed down, standing on the pavement looking up at Susannah. "Thank you for telling me everything, Susannah, and thank you for thinking of me."

"And I think of myself—you would be an excellent fore-woman."

"Me—another Miss *Chiddock*?"

"Well, no, not exactly—I was thinking rather of you being the first Miss Jones. A workroom under your control would be a cheerful place, wouldn't it? Somewhere where everyone would be eager to work instead of resentful? Oh, Annie, I've such plans, such ideas—and I do so want you to be there with me."

Annie smiled then. "You know, I somehow think that I will be."

Over the next few weeks Susannah drove out each day, accompanied by a footman, to inspect the seemingly endless supply of premises which would possibly be suitable for her purposes. Agents led her over countless thresholds, up numberless steps, and into a maze of gracious rooms, some far too grand, some equally as insignificant. Each night she returned wearily to the empty house at Berkeley Square without having found just that certain building which would embody everything she was seeking. She could see it in her mind's eye, but it simply did not seem to exist, even in the largest city in the world.

Occasionally she saw Annie, and it was through her that she first realized that already rumors were beginning to circulate. Word had reached Madame Hilary about Susannah's activities, and Susannah could only imagine that it was because of the ever-efficient, ever-alert London grapevine, past which little, if anything, ever slipped. The servants at Jeffrey's town house met with other servants from other town houses, and soon those other houses' masters and mistresses were *au fait* with the interesting tale. Jeffrey's agent became a little unguarded when attending an annual dinner where the wine flowed a little too freely, and before that riotous night was out the tidbit had spread still further. Susannah had not even found the right premises yet, but already society was rattling with the curious story of Lord Devereux's secret niece who was a dressmaker and who was somehow involved with none other than Sir Jeffrey Stratton. All the old rumors about Georgiana Devereux's elopement and misalliance began to circulate again, closely and inevitably followed by memories of the terrible animosity which lay between the families of Devereux and Stratton. Susannah realized how rife the whisperings were beginning to be when she noticed how each house agent she visited reacted immediately to her name—it was quite alarming to be so notorious without having done a thing.

She knew exactly how far her fame had spread when one morning she sat alone at the breakfast table reading the newspaper to which Jeffrey subscribed and found a small item in the fashionable but exceedingly gossipy *on-dits* column. It concerned a certain noteworthy Sir Jeffrey S. and a lady of *Dev*-ilish connections. The item did not say a great deal beyond that; it was what it did *not* say which spoke volumes! But as yet the suggestion was merely a little spicy; she had not progressed beyond the point of acceptability. Jeffrey had warned her about the stir which would be created, but even so she had not expected quite this. She put the paper down. Now that her name had reached the newspapers, how long would it be before she received a visit from her uncle? Or possibly Miles? Lord Devereux would not allow the matter to proceed uncontested in some way, for it was not in his nature—and all the whisperings presented him in a very poor light indeed.

She sipped the strong black coffee, glancing at the paper again. The name Devereux caught her eye yet again, a little farther down the same column. It appeared that Miles had not lost any time at all in beginning the squandering of his new wife's fortune. In one evening he had lost many thousands at a gaming hell, and more, had had to be carried back to Sanderby quite insensible. He may not have wanted to marry Agnes, but he did not shrink from using her money. Susannah suddenly lost her appetite, and pushed the half-finished egg away. It was a fine August day, the breakfast room was bright and sunny, but she felt very low all of a sudden.

On a morning at the beginning of September she at last found the premises she was looking for. Number fifteen Catherine Lane was an elegant building, its stone-fronted facade rising impressively between a private dwelling belonging to the Duke of Glenbeigh and a house belonging to the East India Company. Catherine Lane was reasonably select, the Duke's presence being more due to a desire to keep away from fashionable society than to the address being sought after, but for Susannah the popularity of the area had little to do with it just as yet. She alighted from the chaise, the weary footman coming to stand obediently at her shoulder. As at Madame Hilary's, the door of the house was approached by a flight of shallow steps, and there were wrought-iron railings bordering the pavement. Susannah could almost see a shining brass nameplate beside that door. Instinctively she knew that she was looking at her future address.

The house agent, well aware of her identity and a little uncomfortable because of it, kept clearing his throat rather noisily as he showed her inside. On the ground floor was a very large salon which stretched from the front of the house to the back where it overlooked a long, narrow garden which was overgrown but which could easily be returned to its former neatness. The salon was an airy room, catching the morning sun and then the afternoon, and for cold winter days it had two pink marble fireplaces—the same marble which decorated some of the rooms at Sanderby. Susannah gazed around it excitedly, picturing clearly how elegant this room would be and how well she could display her fashionable gowns in it. Across the hallway there was another room, a darker place which would make an excellent stockroom, the poor light giving protection to the fine and delicate materials she would keep there.

On the first floor was a collection of rooms which would serve well as places for fittings, for they were small and private—but could be so much more pleasant than the little booths Madame Hilary used. On the top floor were the rooms she would use for herself—and for Annie, if Annie came to her. There were attics too, and a large basement which contained a kitchen and laundry room, as well as pantries and various other necessary offices for a house of this size. At the back, stretching a little way into the garden, was a large addition which had been used by the previous occupiers as a ballroom. It was high and spacious, and had windows stretching from floor to ceiling, as well as extremely elegant chandeliers and silvery brocade walls. It was very grand—quite the most grand *workroom* in the whole of the realm! Susannah smiled as she stood in the center of the polished floor. The agent cleared his throat very noisily yet again, shuffling his feet and jingling his keys.

Susannah smiled at him. "I believe, sir, that this is the very thing." She saw the expression of relief pass over the face of the footman who had patiently accompanied her over the past few weeks.

The agent blinked. "It is?"

"Why, most certainly."

"For . . . for a dressmaking concern?"

"Yes."

"I thought it a little too large—too *ornate!*"

"Nonsense, it will do very well. Very well indeed."

Oh, yes, she thought, taking a last look around the house. Yes, it would do *very* well indeed.

Two days later, on a very fine evening when the sun was just beginning to sink in a blaze of gold and crimson, Susannah sat in the small garden of Jeffrey's house. She was working on the new morning dress she had purchased that very morning from Grafton House in Bond Street, and everything was very peaceful. The roses which filled the garden released their heavy perfume into the warm, still air, and a blackbird sang its heart out in the mulberry tree. Her needle flashed from time to time as she stitched the dainty lawn cotton, and she felt a vague sense of excitement. Jeffrey had still not returned from Walmer, but he had sent word that very day and was expected before nightfall.

She had dressed very carefully, putting on her new gown of red-and-white-striped muslin. She was proud of the gown, and secretly very pleased with the material, for it was unusual—and, she hoped, eye-catching. Her months at Madame Hilary had not been spent idly, and she possessed several gowns now—her small wardrobe was becoming quite presentable. She had taken particular care with her appearance today, wanting to look her very best when Jeffrey returned. In a journal she had seen an illustration of a new coiffure, and she had labored for a very long time before her mirror to achieve the correct effect. *À l'égyptienne* it was called, and her hair was brushed back and caught with a tall comb, falling in heavy coils at the back of her head. She was pleased with it, feeling that it suited her very well—and all in all she felt very good. She hummed a little to herself as she worked, her head bowed over the needlework.

The butler gave a polite, slightly uncomfortable cough. "Madam, Lord Devereux has called."

She turned sharply, her cheerful mood evaporating as if it had never been. In spite of the warm evening, she felt suddenly cold.

"Will you receive him here, madam?"

Hesitantly she put down her work, nodding. "Yes. Yes, I will receive him here." She watched the butler walk away. She had always known that at some point she must face her uncle, but in spite of Jeffrey's assurances that she would not come to harm now, she still felt suddenly very afraid—and very unprepared. Jeffrey's absence made her vulnerable.

Looking around the garden, she tried to compose herself for the ordeal, but she only half-saw the roses and the mews buildings, for her uncle's face seemed to hover in the air before her. Her heart was beating quickly and she felt faint.

"Lord Devereux, madam."

She turned with as much tranquillity as she could muster. But it was not her uncle who stood there; it was Miles. He was dressed in deepest mourning, with black weepers tied to his hat and black gloves which he removed to drop into the upturned hat to hand to the waiting butler.

"Miles!" she cried with relief and pleasure, but then the import of the mourning clothes was borne in on her. "What has happened?"

He glanced at the butler and said nothing. She nodded. "That will be all."

"Very well, madam."

Miles's eyes flickered coldly. "How very at home you are, sweet coz. I see that all the rumors are correct for once, you and friend Stratton are exceeding cosy."

She deliberately avoided the taunt, but she felt very wary suddenly. He was so very cold. "Why are you wearing black, Miles?"

"You see before you the new Lord Devereux of Sanderby."

She stared at him. "Your father is dead?"

"That is the general drift of things, yes. Dear Papa is no longer with us."

Her hand went slowly to her throat. "But what happened? I have heard nothing . . ."

"No doubt," he said dryly, "there is so much else on your innocent little mind of late, is there not? However, on this occasion you can be forgiven for being unaware, as the bereavement occurred only yesterday." He gave a faint smile. "My adoption of the title is a little premature, I grant you."

"You still haven't told me how he died."

"A riding accident. He went out once too often on that brute of a stallion. I believe he was a little vexed at reading your name in a certain scurrilous publication."

She bit back a retort that the blame was probably equally Miles's for achieving notoriety in the same publication. "I'm sorry about your father, Miles."

"I'll warrant you are!"' he said smoothly. "But do not let us pretend to be grief-stricken, mm?"

"I wasn't—I expressed my sympathy for you, not for myself. I found your father quite the most unpleasant and disagreeable man I ever came across, and I shall not miss him in the slightest. Is that honest enough for you?"

"It will do." He leaned against the trunk of the mulberry tree. "I have come to remove you from here, Susannah."

"Don't Miles—"

"If I cannot persuade you to come to me, then you must come openly to Sanderby."

She stared at him, completely taken aback. "You would have *me* at Sanderby? I cannot believe it! You actually imagine Agnes would be pleased to have me under her roof?"

"*I* am master of Sanderby and you are my cousin!"

"And Agnes would welcome me with open arms?" she asked dryly.

"Agnes—and her father—are a little disturbed to discover your existence," he admitted slowly, avoiding her eyes.

She smiled. "If it were not in bad taste, I would lay odds they're more than merely disturbed! They're downright furious, aren't they? And for differing reasons. The Earl no doubt is justifiably miffed to find a scandal so swift upon the heels of the wedding. But Agnes has other reasons for wanting me out of this house, hasn't she?"

"I don't give a damn what Agnes' reasons are," he said shortly. "*My* reasons are the ones which matter."

"And my wishes are of little consequence?"

"I see no reason why you will not let me do for you what you are apparently willing to let Stratton do."

She maintained her calm, but was finding it very difficult. "Sir Jeffrey does not keep me in the way you seem to imagine, Miles."

"No? I wasn't born yesterday, Susannah."

She pressed her lips angrily together and did not reply.

"Of course," he went on, "I realize that Stratton is so much the philanthropist that he makes a habit of offering hospitality to single ladies—without question and, of course, without payment of any kind!"

"I don't want to quarrel with you, Miles, but I will if you continue—"

"Nor do I wish to quarrel, but it is unavoidable if you remain here in this house."

"I shall be leaving soon, which would appear to remove the obstacle, would it not? And no, I am not being set up by Sir Jeffrey as his mistress, I am to be a dressmaker!"

"What does he mean to you?" he asked suddenly, coming a little closer.

"Nothing."

"That was said a little too swiftly, coz-of-mine. You've given to him that which you never gave to me, haven't you?"

"If I have, Miles Devereux, then it is not your business, is it? You made your choice and you married Agnes. What *I* do with my life from now on is *my* concern!"

"It's my concern when it touches upon *my* life!" he cried, his temper snapping. "I intend putting an end to this damned idiocy of yours, do you hear me? You are bringing dishonor on my family's name and I will not have it! Not only are you living openly with someone, the man you choose has a reputation which is extremely unsavory and he is the avowed enemy of Sanderby! Do you really imagine the reason has escaped me why he should choose to involve himself with someone like you? A *child* could divine the truth without difficulty! He simply wishes to humiliate the Devereux family for imagined past grievances, and that is *all*! It pains me that you should lend yourself to his low plans, Susannah."

"They are my plans, too. I *want* to be a dressmaker, to have my own premises. I *want* to be another Madame Hilary!"

"I little thought you could be so selfish, Susannah."

"Selfish! *Me?* I think that that coming from you is—"

"I am here to defend my family's honor, Susannah," he interrupted, "and you are set upon the debasement of that same honor."

"Tell me what debt I owe your family, Miles. Tell me, and maybe I will be able to find it in me to do as you ask."

"That you hated my father, I can understand, but not that you hate me too. *I* am the one who must bear the brunt of all this now, not him, he's beyond it!"

"My activities don't harm the family name any more than do yours!" she said more quietly, attempting to take the heat from the bitter argument. "Mine was not the only name in that newspaper, was it? I think you are a slight case of the pot calling the kettle black, aren't you?"

He flushed at that. "My behavior has nothing to do with this."

"No? If losing thousands and then getting blind drunk so that you had to be carried home isn't putting a stain on Sanderby's reputation, I fail to see what is. I *will* eventually be a court dressmaker, Miles, it is my dearest wish and nothing will make me willingly give it up! I see no reason why I should turn my back on that wish simply because of what you have said to me today."

"You forget your duty," he said pompously, his face white with anger still.

"Don't *you* prate to *me* about duty, Miles Devereux!" she cried, her anger erupting again, "You, who willingly stood aside to let your father consign me to whatever fate he wished! Oh, no, don't *you* dare to point a finger at me!"

His eyes were very cold. "And what right did you have to expect anything more of me?" he asked quietly, his voice shaking with emotion. "Why should *I* have risked everything for you?"

She stared at him then, unable to believe she had heard him correctly.

He closed his eyes weakly, putting out a hand to her. "Dear God, forgive me, Susannah, I didn't mean that. . . . Susannah, please."

She was trembling, on the verge of tears, but she didn't move away when he caught her hand and pulled her close. "Forgive me," he whispered, his cheek against her hair. "You made me so angry that I did not know what I was saying. I would cut off my tongue rather than mean anything like that." He cupped her face in his hands, looking anxiously down into her tear-bright eyes. "Susannah, I love you still, and want you still. I have failed you in the past, but I will not fail you again. Don't shut me out of your life, for I am part of you and I will always be."

"Miles, I don't love you in the way you wish."

"I won't believe that." He kissed her, his lips hard over hers. Tears burned her eyes now as she tried to push him away, and at last he released her, his face very pale and tense as he stared in disbelief. "It's Stratton, isn't it?" he cried then.

"It has nothing to do with him," she said truthfully. "I have tried to tell you before that it had all changed, but you would not listen to me. I *do* love you and I always will—but I do not want you for my lover, Miles."

He was very still. "Very well, I am forced to accept that, aren't I? Must I also accept that you refuse to leave this *business* venture?"

"Yes," she whispered.

His eyes were very blue in the evening sun as he looked at her for a last time before turning on his heel and walking away toward the house, his figure very black among the summer flowers.

She blinked back the tears, wanting so much to call him back, but she knew there would be no point, for she would not agree to do as he wished, and he would remain angry.

A moment or so later a voice spoke behind her. "My poor Susannah, how very fraught life can be at times."

She turned sharply and saw Jeffrey. He looked a little travel-weary, having obviously just at that moment arrived from Walmer and having for some reason decided to alight from his carriage in the mews lane instead of at the front of the house.

Brushing some overhanging roses aside, he came toward her, his gray eyes taking in every detail of her appearance. He took her hand and raised it to his lips. "You look enchanting this evening, Susannah."

"Th-thank you," she said lamely, wondering how much of the conversation he had overheard.

"I saw the Devereux equipage drawn up at my front door and thought it more discreet to come by way of the rear entrance. I also noted that the coachman was wearing black from head to toe—as was friend Devereux."

"My uncle is dead." She watched his face for a moment. "Does that make a difference?"

"Should it?"

"I thought that my uncle was the one you—"

"Miles merely steps into his father's shoes. There is no difference, Susannah, until he renders unto Caesar that which is Caesar's."

"Miles isn't like his father."

He smiled a little. "No, it would appear not. His interest in you is very, very different."

She went a little red and went to the bench to fold away her needlework. "How . . . how was your stay at Walmer?"

"Most agreeable—but then, Pitt is a most agreeable host."

"Is the Prime Minister in good health?"

"No, he is overworked and most unwell. Poor Billy's spirit is indomitable, but his flesh grows perilously weak."

"Billy? Is that what you call him?" she asked, knowing that she was making conversation for the sake of it. "I thought that nickname was the preserve of the balladeers and caricaturists."

He smiled, retrieving a small pair of scissors which had fallen on the path. "Aye, well, maybe I restrict myself to a more polite 'Pitt' to his face. However, the health of our Prime Minister is no doubt of little consequence to you, for you have other, more important things on your mind—such as the finding of a home for your display of elegancies. Have you found somewhere?"

"Yes. In Catherine Lane."

"Ah, not quite St. James's. You surprise me. I had thought ambition as burning as yours would not have been content with anything less than somewhere next to the palace itself!"

"That will come."

"Such confidence!" He laughed. "No doubt the Queen is already in a lather of impatience for your dazzling career to progress sufficiently that she can bestow the royal warrant upon your deserving name and thereby benefit from the undoubted glamour of your designs."

She folded the last of the needlework and pushed it into the ever-present cloth bag. "There is no fairy magic about my gowns, Sir Jeffrey. They are indeed as beautiful as they appear to be."

He smiled at that, loosening his cravat a little as he went to sit on the bench, lounging back to look around the peaceful garden for a moment. "I had almost forgotten how very beautiful this place is at this time of year," he said after a moment, running his fingertips over a heavy yellow rose, disturbing loose petals so that they fell to the grass.

"I enjoy sitting out here," she agreed.

"Yes. Elizabeth did too."

She watched his face. He was looking at the garden but did not seem to be seeing it somehow. It was as if he was remembering times lost forever. She realized in that moment how very much in love he had been with his wife.

"I . . . I think I will go in now," she said quickly.

He watched her slender figure hurrying away along the path between the crowding roses. His expression was thoughtful. He had overheard far more of her confrontation with Miles than she would have wished, and he could hear her angry words even now. *I will eventually be a court dressmaker, Miles, it is my dearest wish and nothing will make me willingly give it up!*

He lowered his pensive gaze to the grass by the bench. There was a gleam of silver there, a pin which had fallen unnoticed from her needlework. Slowly he picked it up, turning it between his fingers for a moment so that the rays of the dying sun flashed on the polished metal. Then he tossed it away.

16

The house in Catherine Lane was still at sixes and sevens, with most of the rooms completely bare or scattered with half-opened packages and crates. Men whistled as they worked in the showroom, and maids were busy scrubbing the walls and floors of the kitchens in the basement.

Annie walked from room to room, her plain little reticule held tightly in both hands and her eyes large as she stared around. She said nothing, not even when faced with the magnificence of the ballroom which was to serve soon as a mere workroom.

Susannah led her at last up the last of the stairs to the haven which was already taking shape as her own little drawing room. The high windows looked out over the city rooftops where a haze of smoke hung in the gray autumn morning. A fire crackled in the hearth, the light leaping over the rust-colored carpets and gray upholstered chairs and sofa. The cat which had apparently decided to adopt Susannah lay peacefully at sleep before the fire, and a pan of bonailie bubbled on the hot coals. A selection of lace was scattered on the table, and colorful silk threads were tangled in a box on the floor. Susannah's inevitable piece of needlework spilled over one of the chairs, and the room was a pleasant jumble.

Annie stood by the window looking at the gray city, and in the distance the green expanse of Hyde Park. It was a vantage point, high above the noise, and with a clear view which would be quite spectacular in the summer.

Susannah poured the bonailie into two dishes and handed one to her friend. "Well? What do you think of it?"

"It's very grand."

"Will you come to me?"

Annie took the dish. "I would be the world's greatest fool to refuse. Of course I'll come, Susannah." She smiled.

Susannah laughed with delight then, twirling around once so that her muslin skirts fluttered. Then she raised her dish of bonailie. "To us, then, Annie, and to the devil with Madame Hilary!"

"I'll drink to that."

"And talking of Madame Hilary, I suppose that I shall have to go and see her."

"I don't see why you should."

"Well, I *am* supposed to be employed there still. And so are you."

"Then I shall have to face her too. I cannot let you go alone."

Susannah shook her head. "I'll go for both of us, Annie, there's no need for you to. Besides, I am quite capable of holding my own, and I shall take great delight in thumbing my nose to her."

Annie grinned. "I'd like to be a fly on the wall—she's absolutely furious, you know. When that newspaper mentioned your name, she was practically unbearable. Even Miss Chiddock was on the point of putting on her bonnet and pelisse. The workroom was more like a tomb than ever before for a day or so."

"*My* workroom will never be like a tomb, Annie."

"No, it won't. But, oh, Susannah, there is such a lot to do here yet, so much to buy and to arrange. There are seamstresses to hire, and the stockroom to take care of . . ."

"Faint heart, Annie Jones?"

"Yes."

Susannah nodded, sighing. "Yes, I know what you mean. Right now it feels almost too much to take on, doesn't it? But we'll manage, we'll open the doors of Miss Garland's New House of Fashion at the beginning of next Season, you see if we don't!"

She alighted from the chaise outside the house in Tavistock Street. The throng of endless traffic still seemed to choke the thoroughfare, and the noise was all around as she stood on the pavement looking at the front door. The *front* door! With a smile she went up the steps and knocked peremptorily on the shiny paint.

James opened the door, his mouth dropping when he saw who stood there.

"I trust I am not to be kept waiting on the doorstep this time, James," she said sweetly, stepping past him into the cool green hallway. "I wish to see Madame Hilary."

He stared at her, slowly closing the door and shutting out the noise of the street. The remembered smell of the house folded over her, bringing mixed memories, and bringing back more especially a remembrance of that other time she had dared to come to the front door. But now it was all so different. "I said that I wished to see Madame Hilary," she repeated.

Without a murmur he went up the staircase, returning a moment later. "Madame will see you in the showroom," he said, running an uncomfortable finger around the starched neckline of his shirt.

Madame Hilary was standing by the fireplace when the bemused footman showed Susannah in. The cold eyes moved critically over her former seamstress's clothes. "Well, now, Garland—" she began.

"*Miss* Garland," corrected Susannah smoothly.

James hurriedly closed the double doors, and she heard his steps moving swiftly away. If there was to be a confrontation, he intended being well out of it!

The dressmaker's eyes were hooded. "One presumes that you and Jones are no longer employed here."

"One presumes correctly."

"Why have you bothered to come at all?"

"It is only good manners, surely."

"And a desire to lord it."

"No."

"What, then?"

"To inform you that your power over me has gone—my uncle, as you must know, is dead and buried. The new Lord Devereux is fully aware of everything about me, even to my present whereabouts. You, madame, can whistle for new designs from now on."

"And you don't think you owe me anything?"

"No."

"The fact that I gave you employment when you were destitute counts for nothing at all?"

136

"I have more than repaid that *kindness*, Madame Hilary, as you well know. Your reputation has enjoyed a considerable fillip this Season because you used my drawings and claimed them to be your own. Well, maybe I should thank you for that—for because of you I know that my designs are successful, that fashionable ladies find them agreeable. I don't feel in your debt at all, and will be able to open my new premises with a completely clear conscience."

"You will be sorry for this, missy. I shall see to it that you never open in opposition to me. Never!"

"I do not see that you can stop me."

"You think that Sir Jeffrey Stratton's name is the passport to everything, don't you? Well, you will find that you are wrong. *I* am a force to be reckoned with, *Miss* Garland, as you will very shortly discover. You will not succeed in this city, be warned of that. You have me to contend with from this moment on."

Susannah turned to the door, pausing with her hand on the cold knob. "And you, madame, have me to contend with from now on, and I rather think you already know my ability. Good day to you."

The dressmaker's eyes flickered coldly and she said nothing. Susannah went out.

Interest in the proposed new palace of fashion continued unabated, and autumn settled in with anticipation still at fever pitch. Snippets appeared in the newspapers from time to time, each one calculated to keep everything simmering. The feud between Sir Jeffrey Stratton and the new Lord Devereux was guaranteed to create interest, and several encounters between the two gentlemen concerned did little to cool matters. Miles rather peevishly refused to sit at the same table as Jeffrey in a club, and once, when considerably in his cups, he had had to be physically restrained by friends from striking Jeffrey, who remained aloof throughout and who had not even deigned to utter a word. Sober, Miles would not have run such a risk with a man of Jeffrey's dangerous reputation, but unfortunately he was drunk a great deal of late. Indeed, the fact that he had been aggressive because he had consumed too much port wine had been the saving factor; but for that, Jeffrey would have called him out.

Susannah felt helpless. And guilty. Had she known that it would be Miles, not his father, who would be affected by her agreement with Jeffrey, then she did not know that she would have accepted. Miles was weak and selfish, he was a great many things which were not admirable in a gentleman, but she still did not wish to hurt him, even when he behaved as he did now. But it was too late and her capitulation now would not have made much difference, for the enmity between Miles and Jeffrey moved on other planes besides the one involving her; it moved in the past and in the present, and even the new Lady Devereux had to bear part of the blame now, for her obvious and exceedingly tactless preference for Jeffrey cannot have helped Miles in the slightest. All that would still have been there even if Susannah Garland had ceased to exist, and so she went patiently on with her preparations of the premises in Catherine Lane. Beyond the shores of England, the war with France continued, but the *beau monde* was more interested in the titillating spectacle of the Great Feud than with Mr. Pitt's painstaking efforts to raise a coalition in Europe against the might of France. Society waited eagerly for the doors of the New House of Fashion to open; the humdrum echoes of a war which hardly touched the English homeland were not half so interesting as what was going on between Sanderby, Berkeley Square, and number fifteen Catherine Lane.

Susannah sat wearily in the middle of the confusion which would one day soon be her first showroom. New mirrors cluttered one corner, a rolled carpet lay across the middle of the floor, and the two maids were attempting to hang some pink velvet curtains. Outside it was raining heavily, a poor beginning to the new year of 1805, which was a mere two days old. She shifted her position, moving a little closer to the fire which crackled in the nearest hearth.

Annie sat on the floor beside her, a sheaf of papers in her hands. "Shall I order the embroidery silk in vermilion too, Susannah?"

"Yes, I think so."

"Vermilion is not at all the rage at the moment."

"There will always be someone who wants it if we don't have it."

"That's true."

"What next?"

"Netting and mending needles, gilt and steel beads, tassels and slides."

"Ah, yes. See that they are stocked in ivory, pearl, and tortoiseshell too."

"*All* of them?"

"Yes, all of them. Have you got that list of muslins?"

"Yes. No, I can't find it!" Annie searched busily through the papers. "Here it is. No, that's the laces. Oh, where is it?"

Susannah saw a sheet of paper on the dusty floor and picked it up. "Here. I think we're a little tired, don't you? Perhaps we should call a halt for a while."

"Yes, I think that is a sensible idea."

Susannah pulled a face. "Oh, Annie, I don't know what I shall do if this proves to be a disaster—how shall I ever pay him back?"

Annie smiled. "I don't think he would ask you for anything, Susannah."

"I know, but that does not make any difference. I *will* pay him back—somehow."

"He doesn't come here at all, does he?"

Susannah looked down at the papers in her lap. "No. But then, I did not really expect him to. All my dealings go through his agent. I do not see him at all."

"You hoped, though."

"Yes. It's the old, old story, is it not? Unrequited love? Still," she went on more brightly, "I have a great deal to keep me occupied." She waved the papers, smiling.

"Too much, I think, sometimes. I worked at Madame Hilary's for quite a few years, but even I did not realize what exactly was involved in setting up a concern like this." She got up, brushing the dust from her brown skirts. "I think I will go up, then. Shall you come? I believe there is a fine stew for luncheon . . ."

"In a while, Annie. I'll just check some of the stockroom before that."

"And then I'll brave Grafton House this afternoon in an attempt to slip past Madame Hilary's all-enveloping net."

Susannah smiled wearily and nodded. "She has been very thorough, hasn't she?"

Annie laughed as she left. "She always was—remember?"

Susannah crossed the hallway, which was now painted pink, white, and gold and which smelled strongly of the new decorations, and she entered the stockroom opposite. She surveyed the full shelves, feeling very daunted suddenly. Those shelves had been filled at great expense and trouble, for

Madame Hilary's hand had been detected many a time raised against the New House of Fashion. Many of the most fashionable warehouses and manufactories refused to do business with Miss Garland, because they feared losing Madame Hilary's influential patronage. Nicholay's Fur and Feather Manufactory, once so obliging to Susannah, now closed its doors on her. Madame Hilary had not uttered her threats lightly, and she was indeed proving a formidable obstacle in the path of the new enterprise.

Finding the appropriate sheet of inventory, Susannah began to check the first shelf. French ribbons and blonds, Grecian lace, British blonds, English tulle. She paused by this last item, her pencil rattling on the wood. She wanted French tulle too, but in the whole of London it would appear that only Pearce of Henrietta Street possessed it—and Pearce was more concerned with pleasing Madame Hilary than with being obliging to a newcomer. Well, the English tulle would have to do, she thought regretfully, passing on. Worked collars, caps and flouncings, foundation net and linen, colored and figured gauze.

"Madam?" The younger of the two maids spoke from the doorway.

"Yes?"

"Lady Devereux is here."

Susannah turned then, looking beyond the little maid to the tall red-headed woman in the hallway. Taking a deep breath, she put down the inventory and went out.

"Good morning, Lady Agnes."

Agnes stared at her. "You! *You* are Miss Garland?"

"I am."

"I wonder at your impudence, miss. You said nothing to me, and yet you knew I was to marry your cousin!"

"I had good reason at the time, my lady."

Agnes gave a withering snort, and went into the showroom, a startling figure in her pink velvet pelisse and the beaver hat with its scarlet plumes. Susannah followed her and dismissed the maids and the men who had begun to unroll the carpet. Agnes glanced critically around before dusting a chair with her gloved hand and then sitting down. "And how long am I expected to endure this charade?" she asked coldly.

"Charade?"

"This house of fashion, or whatever it is you say you will call it."

"It is no charade, Lady Agnes, I fully intend conducting a dressmaking business here."

"I do not think you can be serious."

"I am perfectly serious."

"But you are my husband's cousin!" cried Agnes furiously. "You are supposed to be a *gentlewoman*! You cannot possibly enter into business."

"I can and I will."

Agnes' handsome green eyes flashed. "I will *not* be associated with such a *low* connection! I *won't*! Already it is said that I have made a misalliance!"

"But Miles Devereux is hardly a misalliance," protested Susannah in surprise.

"No? As far as I am concerned, the whole match is an unmitigated disaster—when I married him I acquired a *seamstress* for a relative!"

"I am not a seamstress, but a *couturière*."

"There is a difference?"

"I believe so."

"I do not. How much are you after, Miss Garland?"

"I beg your pardon?"

"How much will you take to go away?"

"Lady Agnes, I don't think you quite understand—"

"Oh, I understand perfectly. Everything you have done has been with a calculation to punish Miles for having spurned you in favor of me."

Susannah stared at her. "It hasn't."

"Come, now, don't pretend with me. I have made inquiries at Sanderby—"

"Of the servants, no doubt."

Agnes flushed. "I have made inquiries and I know full well that you and he were . . . were . . ."

"Lovers, Lady Agnes?"

"Precisely."

"That depends upon the interpretation you put on the word, my lady."

"You know perfectly well what I mean."

"No. I do not. You will have to explain so that I am under no illusion."

"I shall not lower myself—"

"I was under the impression that you already had."

"And I repeat that I wish to know what sum would be involved to get rid of you. I do not want any more public humiliation, I wish both Miles and myself to be left alone."

"How noble you make that sound," said Susannah softly. "But thoughts of Miles never enter your head, do they? Oh, I grant you that you are disconcerted by my existence and my plans, but not so much that life becomes unbearable for you. No, your reason for wanting to be rid of me is that you fear I may be just that little too close to Sir Jeffrey Stratton, isn't it?"

"How *dare* you!" cried Agnes, leaping to her feet.

"I dare when you come here as you have today, my *lady!*"

Two spots of high color stained Agnes' pale cheeks and she raised her hand to strike Susannah, but then thought better of it. "You will regret the day you were born. I swear that one way or another I will destroy you. No one, *no one*, will come to this establishment to purchase from you, and believe me, I have the power to see that that is so. And if you nurse dreams of ensnaring Jeffrey Stratton, then you may forget them. By the time I have finished, he will not come near you even with a ten-foot barge pole!"

Without seeming to flinch, Susannah held her ground. "Do your worst." She made no attempt to hide the dislike she had always felt for this unpleasant shrew of a woman.

But when Agnes had gone, Susannah bit her lip miserably. She would not have changed the way she had conducted that conversation even had she felt able to, for being polite to Agnes Devereux in any way simply was not in her nature anymore. But Agnes had not uttered her threat lightly; she did indeed have great influence in society, especially in Whig society. On top of everything else, it was almost too much. Susannah closed her eyes wearily for a moment, but then opened them again. She would not bend under the pressure, she would *not!* Taking a deep breath, she returned to the stockroom to continue checking the inventory.

Susannah and Annie alighted outside Grafton House, the premises of Messrs. Wilding and Kent, the fashionable drapers. Annie's visit during the early afternoon had been fruitless, as had been expected, for Madame Hilary was considered to be far too important for them to risk incurring her wrath by serving Miss Garland. After enduring Agnes' visit and subsequent insults and threats, this proved the final straw for Susannah, and she determined that she would face Grafton House herself and create a positive mayhem if she was not sold the crepe flowers she wanted! She would *not* sit back anymore and let Madame Hilary's wishes prevail! After all, she reasoned as she stood on the drafty pavement, the mere fact that her former employer felt compelled to behave as she now did was proof positive that she feared the New House of Fashion—and that was reason enough for Susannah to fight.

But the short drive from Catherine Lane to Bond Street had not been without incident. Susannah had seen Jeffrey Stratton for the first time since leaving his house in Berkeley Square. He was driving his cabriolet, with Lady Cowper seated beside him. Emily had been laughing, leaning her head against his shoulder for a moment in an intimate way which told Susannah that she was still his mistress. And he seemed happy in Emily's company, laughing too as he brought the white horse up to a fine pace and passed from Susannah's sight.

Inside the shop was still thronged with customers, in spite of the late hour and the onset of darkness. The harassed young gentlemen behind the counters strove to cope with the various demands, and Susannah waited with seeming patience for her turn. She glanced around at the well-stocked shelves, which were burdened with bolts of cloth, some draped down to the counter for ladies to inspect more closely. There was a babble of noise and the sound of brown paper crackling as purchases were carefully wrapped.

At last it was Susannah's turn and a red-faced young man who was dressed bang up to the mark in a beige coat with brass buttons and a frilled shirt with a voluminous neckcloth bowed his head imperiously to her, looking down his nose in a way which provokingly reminiscent of James the footman. "Yes, madam?"

"I wish to purchase some crepe flowers."

"Yes, madam, any particular . . . ? *Crepe* flowers?" His eyes widened a little as he caught sight of Annie behind her. He flushed immediately and he glanced nervously around. "I . . . er, I'm afraid we have none." Again he glanced at Annie, lowering his eyes quickly to the counter.

"Really?" asked Susannah smoothly. "But a lady purchased some not a moment ago. I saw her select her purchase from a *vast* drawerful!" Her eyes were bright with a readiness to make a stand.

"They . . . they have all been ordered, madam," he said

lamely, unable to stop glancing at Annie, who was also thoroughly flustered by now—a fact which Susannah could not miss even when she was as angry as she was.

"Sir," said Susannah in a voice which quivered, "I believe you are being less than honest with me. I demand to see whoever is in charge!" Her voice rose a little, and the shop was suddenly quiet, all eyes turning toward her and the unfortunate young man across the counter.

He cleared his throat, mortified at the way things had gone. "We have no crepe flowers available, madam."

"And I say that you have, they are in that drawer there."

His face was quite crimson now and he was obviously in a quandary from which he did not know really how to extricate himself. His soft hazel eyes bore a mournful expression as he looked at Annie again, as if imploring *her* to come to his aid!

Disturbed by the sudden silence, a man with a quill behind his ear emerged from a room at the back of the shop. "Is something wrong, Mr. Normans? Do you have some difficulty?"

"I—"

But before the young man could tip him a wink, Susannah spoke again. "I wish to purchase some crepe flowers, sir, but this assistant tells me that you have none."

"Have none, Mr. Normans? *Have none?* But of course we do, madam, in every size and color imaginable, in every quality and material, indeed there is no finer selection in the entire realm!" He snapped his fingers at the thoroughly miserable Mr. Normans, who went heavily to bring the drawer, setting it on the dark counter in front of Susannah. As she inspected the contents, Susannah was once again conscious of the glances passing between a suddenly coy Annie and the tall young man who was obviously wishing himself anywhere and everywhere but in Grafton House at that particular moment.

She nodded at the gentleman with the quill. "I will take them all."

"*All?*" He gaped a little.

"That is what I said."

"Very well, madam." He nodded curtly at the assistant. "Attend to it, Mr. Normans."

"But—"

"Attend to it, I said!"

"Yes, sir."

Mr. Normans put all the flowers into a large box, his face

still scarlet. Gradually the hum of conversation returned to the shop and the small disturbance Susannah had managed to create was forgotten as the ladies went on with their purchases. Susannah paid the exorbitant sum asked, and with Annie helping her, she spirited her purchase triumphantly to the door. In the doorway Annie hesitated, almost upsetting the box as she glanced back yet again at Mr. Normans. She smiled a little, and after a moment he smiled back.

In the hired chaise, Susannah looked across at Annie. "I do believe you are smitten, Miss Jones."

"Nonsense."

"I didn't think it was possible to go pinker than you already are, but you are, you know—you're positively glowing from head to toe!"

"So are you," countered Annie. "You look as if you should be waving a battle banner over your head or something."

"I *do* feel a lot better for having ruffled a few feathers," admitted Susannah. "After enduring Madame Hilary's interference and Lady Agnes' visit, I simply had to poke someone's snout for them. Unfortunately, it was your Mr. Normans'."

"He's not *my* Mr. Normans." But Annie smiled as she looked out at the street.

17

Susannah counted the last of the tiny silver buttons into the last of the little boxes on the table, and she closed the lid firmly, sitting back wearily then. It was two in the morning, the night was bitterly cold, and the fire had almost gone out. A very displeased cat sat on the rug, fixing her with a reproachful gaze, silently demanding that she leave foolish things like buttons and attend to more important matters like stoking up the fire. It had been sitting there for over an hour, its amber eyes hardly moving from her, but she had withstood the animal's indignation, for the wretched buttons were more important than the comfort of a thoroughly spoiled cat which had grown exceedingly plump of late.

She sighed, glancing at the little boxes again. They had claimed her undivided attention since seven o'clock. Annie had gone to her bed at midnight, but Susannah had remained, determined to finish counting and grading every single button ready for the stockroom. Now they were all neatly put away according to their size, quality, and color, and she felt justifiably pleased with herself. It was a long, tedious job well done. With a delicious stretch she got up, contemplating the agreeability of a warmed bed, but as she did so, she heard someone knocking at the front door. Who on earth could be calling at this late hour?

Puzzled, she hurried along the landing to the empty room overlooking Catherine Lane at the front of the house, as a disgruntled, sleepy maid went grumbling down the stairs. A black carriage was drawn up outside in the dark, freezing night, a carriage drawn by black horses. Jeffrey.

She ran back to the drawing room to hastily attend to the smoking fire, and a highly delighted cat rubbed around her, purring loudly to convey its approval of her eventual obedience. Brushing her muslin skirts quickly, she stood, just as the maid showed him in. "Sir Jeffrey Stratton, ma'am."

He wore evening dress, a dark blue velvet coat with gilt buttons, the top of his pale gray waistcoat undone to reveal the frills of his shirt, and he paused to tease off his gloves. "Good evening, Susannah—or is it more correct to say good morning? I see that I have not roused you from your bed."

"No, I was finishing something."

"Something connected with dressmaking, no doubt."

"Yes."

"I should have guessed as much."

She glanced quickly at him, catching the edge in his voice; then she dismissed the maid, wondering as she did so what could have happened to bring him to her at such an odd hour.

He glanced around the room, toying with his cuff. "My first view of my . . . er, investment, is not at all disagreeable, Susannah. What I have seen of the house has been furnished most tastefully. And it goes without saying that it is also original. A preponderance of pink in an entrance hall could so easily have been disastrous, but is instead a triumph."

"Thank you. I am surprised you noticed such a detail."

"I notice a very great deal, Susannah."

"May . . . may I offer you some refreshment? Cognac maybe?"

"That would do very nicely. Thank you."

She went to the cupboard and took out the decanter which she had placed there on first arriving at the house. But he had never been here to sample it until now.

"Working until such an hour shows a remarkable degree of dedication," he said, accepting the glass.

"I had something in particular to do. I assure you that I do not always keep such hours, Sir Jeffrey."

"I'm glad to hear it."

"I have the impression that you do not think dedication to be very admirable."

"I did not say that."

"No, you didn't *say* it."

He smiled. "You keep excellent cognac, Susannah."

"I keep the same cognac that you keep."

"I'm flattered."

"Don't be, it is the only cognac I know."

"How observant you are."

"I had thought you might want to visit your investment and I wished to be prepared."

"Ah, well, maybe I have been a little remiss in that direction."

"There really is no reason at all why you should come here," she said lightly, picking up the still-purring cat and cradling it in her arms, "for you have already accomplished that which you set out to do."

"Which is?"

"Causing a considerable disturbance in the Devereux camp."

"That is putting it mildly. Your cousin is a very foolish, erratic being, and I think you may consider yourself well out of any involvement with him."

"Miles is not very happy, Sir Jeffrey."

"He is a great deal unhappier tonight," he said, putting down his glass. "And that is the reason why I have come."

"Something has happened to Miles?" she asked quickly, suddenly anxious.

"How touching that you should feel such concern over him," he said dryly. "No, Susannah, nothing has happened to him, at least nothing physical, and I think it better that *I* tell you rather than you should hear it from someone else."

Her fingers moved very slowly over the cat's silky fur. "What is it?"

"I was at Carlton House tonight, a place I usually avoid at all costs, for the Prince of Wales has little liking for me, due to my political leanings in general and my adherence to Pitt in particular. However, London out of Season is a dull concern, Susannah, and I do believe His Royal Highness wished to enliven it and possibly see a little fur fly at the same time—he saw to it that your odious cousin was also a guest."

"And did the fur fly?" she asked quietly, almost afraid of what his reply would be. Miles's behavior of late had been so unpredictable, and so foolish . . .

"It flew, in a manner of speaking, but you need not look so alarmed, for I promise that I did not touch a hair of his little golden head, although God alone knows I have had provocation enough recently."

"I know—but he believes he has been provoked too."

"That much is patently obvious, but even if he is correct, he is certainly overplaying the part of the martyr and I no longer feel obliged to behave with saintly tolerance. Tonight I decided that I had had enough, he arrived the worse for wear and was damned offensive from the outset—I taught him a most salutary lesson."

Slowly she put the cat down, pressing her shaking hands against her skirts as she waited for him to continue.

"The Prince's latest passion is poker, a game he plays exceeding badly, as he has not the necessary temperament. Neither has your cousin, but then, I doubt that *he* has the necessary temperament for anything! However, much as I did not wish to, I obeyed the royal command and took my place at the same table as your odious relative, the Prince showing an indecently delighted anticipation about what my close proximity might provoke from him. I found myself with a very tolerable hand, and I kept raising the odds until only your cousin remained in." He paused, looking steadily at her. "Finding himself without sufficient funds to see my hand, he foolishly decided to wager Sanderby on the outcome."

She stared at him, her eyes widening. "Oh, no . . ."

"You see before you the new master of Sanderby." He sketched a mocking bow.

She couldn't speak. A numb shock gripped her, and she turned away, clutching the back of a chair. How could Miles have done it? How *could* he? He loved Sanderby so very much, and now he had lost it—lost it to the man he hated most. "So," she said at last, "he has rendered unto Caesar that which is Caesar's."

"He has—albeit most unwillingly. He thoroughly deserved his punishment, Susannah, it was long overdue."

"It is punishment indeed, Sir Jeffrey, for he loves that house."

"Then he should have controlled himself a little more, shouldn't he?"

She turned to him, tears in her eyes. "Yes." she whispered at last, "yes, I supposed he should."

"I make no apologies. If the same situation presented itself again, then I would repeat my actions. Devereux needs to grow up somewhat, Susannah, and maybe now at last he will."

"I would not expect you to refrain from your actions, Sir

Jeffrey, and I thank you for coming to tell me. It was thoughtful and I do appreciate it."

"Sanderby was your home for five years. I felt it only right that you should hear from me."

"Will you live there?"

He hesitated, looking away for a moment before meeting her gaze again. "There was a time when I would have answered yes to that question. Not because I find the house to my liking personally, but because my late wife always admired Sanderby above all other houses in England. For her I would have lived there, but for myself . . . no."

"You'll just close the house up?"

"Probably. I haven't exactly had time to consider the matter in detail yet."

"No. Of course not. Sir Jeffrey . . . could I see the house just once more? When I ran away I did not ever think I would go there again, but now . . ."

"Of course you may visit Sanderby, Susannah. I will inform you the moment I have taken possession. I will take you there myself if you wish."

"That would inconvenience you—"

"Not at all, it will be my pleasure."

"Thank you."

"I bid you good night then, Susannah."

"Good night, Sir Jeffrey."

She heard the maid close the outer door behind him, and then she bent to scoop up the purring cat again, stroking it a little as she sat down by the fire. She gazed into the gyrating flames. It was a year to the day since she had left Sanderby. A year to the day.

The April sunshine was bright and warm as the landau bowled along the road to Sanderby. Catkins and pussywillow decorated the hedgerows, and the fresh leaves of spring were beginning to unfurl here and there as the unusually clement weather laid a warm hand over the countryside.

Susannah looked out at the passing scene, the breeze in her face, rippling the fringe of her blue-and-white parasol. The hoods of the landau were lowered and she could smell the freshness of the spring all around. Her blue spencer was bright in the sunshine, and the hem of her white muslin gown fluttered a little.

Jeffrey sat beside her, his long legs stretched out on the seat opposite. He wore a brown coat and white breeches, and the tassels of his hessians swung from side to side with the motion of the carriage. He had removed his hat and his dark hair was ruffled by the breeze. He said very little, and his mood was pensive.

She had left the New House of Fashion in a state of last-minute confusion, for the doors were to open in a week's time and there was still so much to do. The delivery boxes she had ordered had not yet arrived, and there were still seamstresses to take on, but the very capable Annie had insisted that Susannah accept Jeffrey's invitation when his running footman had brought it the night before. Since the night he had won Sanderby, she had not heard anything from him, indeed she had thought he had forgotten his offer, or had chosen to forget it. But he had not, and here she was driving along the stretch of the London road which led to the wrought-iron gates of Sanderby. She watched the remembered countryside with mixed feelings. Maybe coming here again was not a very good idea, for everything would be different now. She lowered her eyes to her lap. She had written to Miles, just a small note to tell him how sad she was for him, but he had returned the note unopened, with a curt message asking that she not communicate with him again.

The landau halted at the gates, and the lodge keeper came out, staring up in surprise at her. "Miss Susannah!"

"Good day, Rogers."

"But how . . . where . . . ?" The man glanced at Jeffrey and said nothing more, turning the great key in the lock and swinging the gates open, snatching his hat belatedly from his head as the landau passed into the grounds.

The wheels crunched on the drive, where in a few weeks the weeds would pierce the gravel. The waterfall by the rustic bridge chattered softly to itself, and the sunlight sparkled on the lake. The smell of spring was everywhere in the great park, and the grass was covered with drifts of pale yellow daffodils. The house looked so very beautiful presiding over the grounds which swept so gracefully down to the Thames.

The landau halted at the foot of the portico steps, and the footman jumped down to lower the iron rungs and open the door. Jeffrey climbed down, turning to hold his hand out to her.

As they went slowly up to the front door, some white-winged seagulls soared high in the dazzling spring air above the house, their screams echoing over the park and the rippling waters of the lake.

The housekeeper hurried to open the door, curtsying in some confusion as she recognized both Susannah and Jeffrey. "Miss Garland! Sir Jeffrey! Oh, forgive me, sir, I did not know you were coming—I've nothing prepared . . ."

"That is quite all right, for we require nothing. You may return to whatever it was you were doing."

She curtsied again. "Yes, Sir Jeffrey." Her keys jingled busily as she left them.

He tossed his hat on the same pink marble table he had used on the night Susannah had run away, and he glanced around at the palatial hall. "Much as you and my late wife may like this place, Susannah, I fear it is not to my taste at all."

"But you would have come here for her?"

He nodded. "Yes."

"You must have loved her very much indeed."

His gray eyes were unfathomable. "I did."

There was a silence for a moment.

He spoke again. "Sanderby is too grand—Southwood is perfection."

"Southwood?"

"My estate in Leicestershire—the estate which was purchased with what was left of my family's fortune after your late uncle had been at work. At first I did not imagine I could be satisfied with such a small house, but I grew to love it. To modern taste it is probably too dark and confined, for it is a fourteenth-century castellated house, built by a man who was exceeding nervous of large windows and the distinct possibility of an enemy arrow finding a target."

"He was probably very wise, then."

"Indeed so—offering a target is the very essence of foolishness, is it not?"

She stared at him, sensing something else beyond his words. But what?

He turned away, surveying the magnificent hallway again. "I may not wish to live here myself, but I *am* considering letting it to someone."

"Oh." She felt vaguely sorry somehow, although she had no right to any opinion concerning Sanderby.

"I assure you that the tenant I have in mind is most illustrious and fully deserving of such an . . . er, honor."

"Who?"

"Pitt. His health requires him to enjoy as much of the country air as possible, and yet he must remain within easy reach of London. I thought Sanderby might fit the bill for him, although I do know he is seriously considering a house on the edge of Putney Heath."

"Sanderby *is* near London," she said without enthusiasm.

"I detect that you do not approve."

"This house should have someone who cares living in it."

"And Pitt would not?"

"Why should he?"

"I'll warrant he would care a damned sight more than your precious cousin appeared to, for all that you say dear Miles loves this place!" he said shortly.

"I do not think we should talk about Miles."

"Nor do I—he is a most contentious subject." He smiled then. "And I do not wish to spoil today."

Oh, if only she could read more into that last sentence. If only . . .

He offered her his arm. "You must show me around this great pile of stones, Susannah, for now that it is mine, I suppose I must at least *look* at it."

There were dust covers over all the furniture, and the curtains were drawn to keep out the sunlight. The rooms echoed, and everything was so quiet, but she could still hear voices from the past. She paused in the doorway of the green silk drawing room, and suddenly it was a dark January evening again:

. . . And I tell you, boy, that you'll do as you are told! . . . I was not consulted! . . . If you think I am about to jeopardize this match because you have an itch for Susannah Garland, then you are sadly mistaken. . . . I love her. . . . I fully intend making certain that any further notion of heroics on your part is squashed from the outset. . . . I intend sending Susannah Garland away . . . away . . . away. . . .

"I was saying that this room appears very cold and drafty," repeated Jeffrey, a hint of amusement in his eyes as he watched her.

"Mm? Oh, yes . . . yes it is a little."

"Ghosts?"

"Yes."

"Tiresome ones, I'll warrant," he said, crossing the room to draw the curtains aside. The sunlight swept in strongly, almost hurting her eyes. She looked up at the great portrait of her uncle above the fireplace. It seemed that his cold, unpleasant eyes were staring straight at her. She turned on her heel and walked away.

She waited outside beneath the portico, her heart still beating a little swiftly. It *had* been a mistake to come here, for the only memories were bad ones.

She heard his step behind her and turned to look at him, smiling apologetically. "That was foolish, forgive me."

"There is nothing to forgive," he murmured, drawing her hand through his arm, "and nothing which cannot be set right by a glass or two of chilled hock."

"Hock?"

"I came well prepared today, Susannah. I thought we could take luncheon *al fresco*, the weather seeming to call for such an activity."

The footman put the large hamper down on the embankment, and Susannah sat down among the daffodils, removing her bonnet as she looked across the river. The tide was in and the water lapped noisily around the little jetty where swans floated majestically, necks arched and feathers proudly fluffed. Willows trailed their branches in the current, and a sailing barge swept downstream, her crimson sails full as the breeze and the current carried her toward London.

"The last time I looked at this river like this, I thought that it was impossible to imagine we were at war. Now it is a year later and still I must feel the same."

"Spend any time in poor Pitt's company and you would not think the war a figment of the imagination."

"It does not touch us, though, does it? Not really. Oh, I know there are taxes because of it, but the war itself seems so very far away."

He opened the bottle of hock he took from the box of ice in the hamper. "The Channel is a perilously small ditch, believe me. Would you have the war come closer, then?"

"No."

He smiled. "No, be content with your *chiffons*, Susannah, and leave the damned war where it is—the other side of the Channel."

They dined very well on cold chicken, an excellent piece of smoked ham, crisp fresh bread, and soft cheese, and the hock was the perfect accompaniment. It was very pleasant indeed to sit there in the sunshine by the river, the daffodils all around, and with Jeffrey Stratton to keep her company. She could not have planned anything finer—except that she would have him love her.

She lay back, gazing up at the sky, the pins holding her hair loosened a little. He watched her for a moment. "If you could turn back time a year, would you still have run away?"

"Yes."

"There is always the possibility that your cousin would have found a little backbone from somewhere."

"I doubt it—I know Miles."

"From what I gather from Agnes, he is as in love with you as ever."

She looked at him. "You've seen Lady Agnes?"

"I have. She is in a mighty pet about a number of things—about you in particular."

"I know. I had a visit from her."

"Yes, she told me. You have an exceedingly acid tongue, Susannah. Poor Agnes was still smarting when I saw her."

"Poor Agnes indeed! She was positively odious."

"She was somewhat more pungent in her description of you."

She smiled. "She should not have been so false, coming bleating to me about humiliation and derision when what she was really anxious about was . . ." She broke off hurriedly, for she could hardly tell him how her meeting with Agnes had really gone.

"Yes? Do go on now that you have embarked upon it."

"I do not think that I should."

His gray eyes moved lazily over her face. "What she was really anxious about was that I might be your lover."

She looked swiftly at him then, a dull blush touching her cheeks. "Yes."

"And you, of course, said nothing to allay her fears."

"Of course not. Why should I?"

"Why indeed?" he murmured, smiling. "Why should you wish to give crumbs of comfort to the woman who married your cousin?"

"That had nothing to do with it."

"No?"

"No. But tell me, Sir Jeffrey Stratton, *are* you her lover?"

"God forbid."

"Why do you say it like that?"

"Susannah, Agnes Devereux is too strident and too damned obvious for me. I like a little more subtlety in my women."

"Gossip has it—"

"Wrongly, as it frequently does," he finished for her. "I would have to be completely tipsy to involve myself there."

"You became interested in me because through me you could really upset my uncle. How much more could you have upset him if you had taken Agnes from under his nose and thus ruined his careful plans for a grand Whig match."

"You are wrong to think I became interested in you only because of your family—it was not *only* that. And as to stealing Agnes, can you but imagine the price my sanity would have to pay? Susannah, twisting old Devereux's thieving, conniving tail was to be a pleasure, not a penance."

"She isn't *that* bad. In fact, she's very lovely."

"And quite unpalatable." He leaned over her. "You, on the other hand, are most palatable and at times virtually irresistible. You break all my rules, Susannah—all of them." His fingers coiled in her warm hair as he kissed her, and she could smell the bruised petals of the daffodils all around.

Then, quite abruptly and without warning, he drew sharply away. "You will always break those rules," he whispered, getting up.

She felt as if he had struck her, but none of the hurt showed as she picked up her bonnet to put in on, her face averted toward the sparkling river.

She smiled, a little too brightly perhaps. "I . . . I think I should return to Catherine Lane. There is so much to do still, and they need me."

He inclined his head. "Very well."

Her fingers felt cold and stiff as she buttoned her little spencer. What were his rules? In his eyes she might be an innocent still, but there was no innocence in the way she felt about him. Maybe she simply fell into the wrong category because she was a Devereux and therefore cursed. Or maybe it was simply that she was a pale shadow when placed beside the ghost of his beloved wife. Yes, that had a great deal to do with it. Susannah Garland could not compete with Elizabeth Stratton's memory and would therefore always be beyond the pale, always outside his heart.

18

~~~~~~~

The showroom was finished at last. Susannah held a spill to the candles and looked around with great satisfaction as the warm glow flickered into life and fell across the beautiful room. Shadows moved softly on the pale pink walls and turned the dusky curtains to a deep rose. The dove-gray velvet chairs looked elegant, and perfect in such a setting. Her glance came to a halt on the carved golden initials which twined together above the two fireplaces. S.G. Was it an affectation? A little too presumptuous? She turned to look at the delivery boxes, which had arrived at last. They were striped in pink and gray and they too displayed her initials very prominently in one corner. All dressmakers used plain brown boxes, but Susannah wanted the origin of her gowns to be proclaimed aloud when they were delivered. She smiled a little uncertainly, for she was assuming that her garments would be in demand. What if no one came? What if Madame Hilary's campaign should prove successful in the end? Susannah knew that apart from trying to close all the fashionable shops and manufactories against the New House of Fashion, her former employer had also lost no time in telling of Susannah's multitudinous "inadequacies." Each customer at Tavistock Street had been left in no doubt that Miss Garland had been dismissed for inefficient work and manners which left much to be desired. Lady Agnes had not been idle either. True to her word, she had made Whig drawing rooms ring with her shrill criticisms of her husband's low niece. There was nothing good to be said about Susannah as far as the new Lady Devereux was concerned, and Agnes was determined that that opinion should be shared by the rest of the *beau monde*. Whispers reached Catherine Lane of Agnes' activities, but of what Miles said or thought, there was no hint, for his name was never mentioned at all. Susannah's face was anxious as she stood there in the candlelight looking at the room which would be the focal point of all her dreams. This was what she had yearned for, planned for, somewhere welcoming and gracious in which to display elegancies; but what if not a single customer crossed the newly scrubbed threshold?

No, she mustn't think like that, she must be at all times confident that they *would* flock to her—and she must do all in her power to see that they did. She picked up her gloves and pulled them slowly on. What she had in mind now was very impudent, and it was not something she really wished to do after her last meeting with Jeffrey Stratton at Sanderby, but once the notion had struck her, it refused to be denied and she knew that she would have to put it to the test. She tied the silvery ribbons of her dainty hat and inspected her reflection in one of the cheval glasses.

Sapphire blue was one of her best colors, she thought, for it emphasized her eyes, and this Indian muslin was so delicate and fine that the slightest movement made it cling. She buttoned the cream spencer and brushed some fluff from the black velvet cuffs. She must look her very best if she was to persuade Jeffrey to do what she wanted. Taking a deep breath, she went out into the hall, where Annie stood waiting with her reticule.

"Good luck, Susannah, I fancy you'll need it."

"I need encouragement from you, Annie Jones, not pessimism."

"I'm just glad I'm not going to ask him."

"Do . . . do you think it a little *too* bold?" asked Susannah, hesitating uncertainly.

"No, not really."

"But?"

"But it's not usual to ask a man to speak to his mistress."

"If I want the *beau monde* to come, then I must have some bellwether to lead them—and what finer bellwether could there be than Emily Cowper? She is a great lady of fashion and influence, she is a patroness of Almack's, and if she came here for her gowns, then I would have no difficulty in attracting a great deal of custom."

"*If* she comes. She's a Whig, don't forget, from the same set as Lady Devereux."

"Yes . . . if she comes." Susannah took the reticule and opened the door to step out into the chilly spring night. "I'll just have to ask him. It's too important not to."

Annie watched her go down the steps to the waiting post-chaise. She took a long breath as the hired vehicle pulled away along the street. It *was* an impudent notion on Susannah's part, but as she said, it *had* to be at least tried.

The chaise turned into Berkeley Square and came to a standstill outside Jeffrey's house, where the lights blazed reassuringly. At least he was in. Now that she was here, however, the idea seemed a little too outrageous, and he would surely be exceedingly annoyed with her. She climbed down, nodding at the yellow-jacketed postboy. "Wait, if you please, I shall not be long."

He touched his beaver hat. "Yes, ma'am."

She glanced nervously around the quiet square where the trees rustled their spring leaves and a seagull perched unceremoniously on the statue of the King.

Jeffrey received her in the gold drawing room. He stood before the fire, a glass of port in his hand, his black-clad figure illuminated by the flames. She realized with immediate dismay that he was not alone, for a tall man she did not know rose from a nearby chair as she was announced. He wore a sober dark blue coat and she guessed that although his hair was prematurely white he was only a little over forty years old. There was an air of tiredness about him, and that fragility which goes with poor health. His face was not startling, being thin and pale, but his eyes were very large and handsome, their gaze shrewd and penetrating. His expression was cold and aloof as he put down his glass of port and bowed stiffly to her.

She curtsied uncertainly, for now she could not possibly speak to Jeffrey as she had intended.

Jeffrey approached her. "Good evening, Susannah."

"Good evening, Sir Jeffrey. Forgive me, I did not realize you had a guest."

"Not at all," he murmured, leading her to the other man. "Besides, now you are here, I may be able to enlist your help in persuading this stubborn fellow that he must rest more."

"My help?"

He nodded. "This is Miss Garland, Pitt, about whom you

159

may or may not know. Susannah, Mr. William Pitt, who needs no further identification."

She stared, shocked into silence at finding herself face-to-face with the man who had become Prime Minister at the age of only twenty-four. He had held office for most of her life and he was still a young man, but as Jeffrey's words suggested, he looked very tired now. And ill.

The Prime Minister seemed a little amused at her obvious alarm on being faced with so unexpected an introduction. He took her hand and raised it to his lips. "Miss Garland."

"Sir."

"Do not look so full of horror at the prospect of maybe having to debate with me, Miss Garland, for no matter what friend Jeffrey avers to the contrary, I do not need persuading of anything at all."

Jeffrey led her to a chair and then turned back to his friend. "But you do, Pitt, you do. You are working too hard and your constitution has never been that of the proverbial ox. If you continue at this pace, then you will wear yourself out—"

"Jeffrey," said the Prime Minister patiently, "I believe I am fully aware of what is and is not good for me, just as I am aware of what must be done for Britain's struggle against the French. Before I can begin to think about resting, I must see to it that I raise a coalition between Austria, Russia, and the Prussians—until then we stand alone. Bath and the cure must wait, and that is a fact which I face quite knowingly."

"You are fighting not only the French. You have an enemy closer at hand than that."

Pitt smiled. "Do you refer to the port or to the Prince of Wales?"

"Both."

"The first I refuse to do without, the second I refuse to do with. He will not become regent while I have anything to do with it. At the moment, he contents himself with holding grand political dinners to which he invites only my opponents. I survive most happily without the royal loquacity to add an aching head to my other problems. Besides, the King's health improves with each day, and the prospect of a regency fades accordingly—thanks be to the Almighty." He picked up his glass of port and raised it with some feeling toward the heavens. Then he looked suddenly at Susannah. "Miss Gar-

160

land, have you, like your troublesome cousin, imbibed too much Whig chatter?"

Her eyes widened that he should have heard of her at all. "No, sir, I have not imbibed any at all."

"I am most relieved to hear it. One Devereux is more than enough. Your cousin has come into his title with a considerable amount of noise, taking his place in the Upper House with new-broom fervor and attending with monotonous regularity those political dinners of which I spoke."

"Miles?" she asked in surprise, for it did not sound at all like her cousin, who was more interested in an idle life of luxury than in the heat and hard work of politics.

"Yes, a more fervent little Whig disciple I have yet to meet. His father was a thorn in my side, but the new Lord Devereux is a positive stake!" Pitt glanced shrewdly at Jeffrey. "I had wondered at this sudden enthusiasm, but now that I have seen the beautiful reason for myself, I think it all a great deal more clear."

Jeffrey flushed a little. "You see nothing of the kind."

"No?" The Prime Minister smiled, finishing his glass of port and preparing to leave. "Duty calls me, I fear, and I thank you most sincerely for an excellent dinner. As to that other matter we were discussing earlier, be assured that I have no objection to your acceptance of another invitation to Carlton House. I realize full well that it is impossible to refuse such requests, and our friendship will not be impaired if you go. Be warned, however, that the Prince is most anxious to harm me in any way he can, and he will stop at nothing to achieve that end. I stand in his way on too many issues—I am a Tory, I oppose the regency, and I support his most loathed wife, from whom he would dearly wish to be divorced. He will quiz you continuously and make strenuous efforts to persuade you to his view, in the fond hope that you will then use your considerable influence with me."

Jeffrey laughed. "As if my considerable influence would take effect!"

Pitt spread his hands with an air of hurt innocence. "But the world knows that I am the most reasonable of men," he protested.

"When you wish to be."

"Aye, and there's the royal rub." The Prime Minister glanced at his watch. "And now I really must go. Good night, Jeffrey, and thank you again for a most enjoyable evening.

To dine *tête-à-tête* with a good friend is surely one of life's great pleasures." He turned to Susannah, taking her hand. "Good night, Miss Garland, I trust that we shall meet again soon."

"Good night, sir, and I trust we shall meet again too."

"And please rest easy concerning Sanderby, for I shall not be granting it the dubious honor of my presence, that honor is reserved for Putney instead." He smiled at her.

Her face flamed immediately, and she shot Jeffrey a reproachful glance.

Pitt went to the door. "It would seem, Jeffrey, my friend, that you have a penchant for ladies who in turn have a penchant for Sanderby. First Elizabeth, and now the delectable Miss Garland." With a last bow, he left them.

She looked accusingly at Jeffrey. "You should not have told him what I said."

"I knew it would amuse him. I did *not* know he would ... er, split on me."

"He isn't at all how I imagined he would be, quite the opposite in fact."

"There's no greater man in the realm than Billy Pitt. But he's not up to the strain of it anymore, his health is failing badly."

"He looks very tired."

"He's damned well worn out. He's forty-six years old, and for fully nineteen of those years he has been first minister—for most of your life, in fact. However, enough of him." He lounged back in a chair, looking at her. "You look extremely lovely tonight, Susannah. Am I to be dazzled into submitting to some request or other?"

"Something of the kind," she said, a little uncomfortably, for his words were a little too close to the truth.

"Surely there is nothing to hold up your grand opening?"

"No. Actually my purpose is very impertinent, and I do not really know how to put it to you."

His smile faded. "I trust it has nothing to do with your damned cousin!" he snapped suddenly.

"Miles? No. Why would you think that?"

"Because he's in Town again and because he wants Sanderby back."

She stared. "Sir Jeffrey, I don't think Miles would come to me at the moment, and least of all to intercede with you on his behalf."

162

He nodded and then smiled a little. "I rather think my title gets in the way a little, Susannah—just plain 'Jeffrey' will do very nicely, I am sure. And no doubt this impertinence, whatever it is, will not alter that."

"I trust so." She took a deep breath. "A dressmaker is only as good as the customers she attracts to her showroom. All the interest already shown could still go against me as easily as it could work for me. I have seen to it that the premises in Catherine Lane are all that anyone could wish, and I have placed announcements in the newspapers, but I still need to be sure that on the very first morning I receive a visit from a lady of great eminence. Someone like Lady Cowper."

He stared at her, completely taken aback. "It *is* impertinent, isn't it?"

"Where fashion is concerned, she has few equals," she said, "and I know that you are . . . are acquainted with her."

"You really are quite remarkable, Susannah Garland. No sooner do you enter my life than I find myself making you dizzy offers to further your enterprise in the world of fripperies, and now I find myself being importuned to speak to my ex-mistress on your behalf!"

"*Ex*-mistress?"

"All good things come to an end."

"Forgive me, but once the idea occurred to me—"

"Spare me any more of your ideas, then. Do you really expect me to approach Emily on such an errand? She would think I had taken leave of my senses, and she would be correct!"

She smiled ruefully, wishing she had taken heed of Annie's doubts and refrained from this visit entirely. "No, I didn't really think you would be persuaded to such a thing, but I simply had to try."

He got up, leaning a hand on the mantelpiece and looking into the fire. "I go to Windsor later in the week. I'm acquainted with the Princesses and with the Queen—shall I put a timely word in there too?"

"I did say that I was sorry, and you have already made your point sufficiently well without resorting to sarcasm."

He smiled in spite of his anger. "I do believe that somehow or other *I* am being put in my place, and I do not see the justice of that on this occasion. But you are right, I *was* being sarcastic, and it is alleged to be the lowest form of wit." He looked at her. "You really could not resist the thought of one

163

of your gowns gracing Almack's, openly acknowledged to be yours this time, could you?"

"No. I couldn't."

"Don't look at me like that, for I am not being a bear."

"No, I think you a very subtle man, Jeffrey," she said, getting up, "and very persuasive, even with an ex-mistress. I know that she would be most intrigued and would come to see me out of curiosity. After that, it would be up to me, wouldn't it?"

He caught her hand suddenly. "You are scheming and calculating, and your damned audacity amazes me. Very well, I will do what I can with Emily, but I can promise nothing, as she is most certainly a law unto herself."

Her eyes shone then. "You will?"

"I will—God help me. But if anyone had told me I would be such a damned fool, I believe I would call him out! Jeffrey Stratton, a dressmaker's messenger boy—what *would* the Whigs make of that, mm?"

"But Lady Cowper is a Whig."

"She is also a woman, very much so, and that makes all the difference," he said softly, "and I do believe that your supposition concerning her reaction is the correct one."

"I hope so."

He gave a short laugh. "So do I, Susannah, so do I! Believe me, for if not, then the Whigs will have a gala day with my name!"

"Will that bother you?"

"Not immensely, I suppose."

She picked up her reticule. "I think I had better go, then. I will not take up any more of your time."

"Yes, well, you have accomplished that which you came to do, haven't you?" he said dryly.

"Thank you for agreeing—"

"Not at all, I merely see to the welfare of my investment."

She lowered her eyes momentarily at the sharp reminder. "Good night, Jeffrey."

"Good night."

When she had gone, he went to pour himself another glass of the cognac, standing before the fire with it without drinking. He looked down at the amber liquid and then suddenly threw the glass into the fire with all his might. The cut crystal shattered and the cognac spilled in a burst of roaring flames before dying away again.

164

She drove home in the chaise, and she was at once elated and miserably unhappy. She was elated because she knew that Emily Cowper *would* come to Catherine Lane; she was unhappy because what really mattered was Jeffrey Stratton, and he had placed a barrier between them which was so real she could almost feel it.

She gazed out as the chaise passed St. George's Church, where Miles and Agnes had been married the previous summer, and as she looked at the beautiful portico where all the flowers had been strewn on that day, a familiar figure caught her attention. Quickly she lowered the window glass and called to the postboy to halt.

As the chaise came to a standstill, she climbed down and ran toward the church and the man leaning so drunkenly against the foot of one of the pillars. "Miles?"

He turned, swaying a little. "Well met, coz," he said, his voice thick.

"What on earth are you doing out here in this state?"

"Drowned me sorrows tonight, drowned 'em one an' all."

"You can't stay here alone."

"Holding up St. George, coz, might fall down if I moved." He patted the pillar, smiling crookedly.

She glanced helplessly around. She couldn't possibly leave him in this condition. Indeed, it was a wonder he had survived this long without receiving the attention of footpads or worse. "Come with me, Miles," she said, taking his arm.

His blue eyes met hers. "I love you, Susannah," he said softly.

"Where are you staying?"

"You'd take me back to Agnes? Oh, cruel heart . . ."

She helped him down to the chaise with great difficulty and he slumped against the wheel, shaking his head. "Not Agnes."

"But she'll worry!"

"She don't give a damn," he said, his knees suddenly giving beneath him so that he fell heavily to the ground.

She called the disgruntled postboy, and with a struggle they managed to drag Miles into the carriage, the little coachman grumbling under his breath about not being paid to shift coves with a skinful. She had no alternative but to take him home to Catherine Lane, for since he had lost Sanderby she did not know where he stayed, and he obviously did not want to see Agnes at all tonight. Maybe it would be better to let him sleep it off and take himself back to his wife when he was sober.

She had to pay the postboy well over the odds for his extra duties, for if she had refused, he threatened to simply dump His Bloomin' Lordship on the pavement like a sack of coal! She took him at his word and agreed to pay him for his trouble if he would help her carry Miles into the house.

Then, with Annie to help too, they carried him up to the drawing room and laid him carefully on the sofa. Susannah loosened his cravat and unbuttoned the top of his shirt before putting a soft cushion carefully beneath his head. She looked down at his pale, drawn face and at the shadows under his eyes. He was sadly changed from the laughing, carefree cousin she had fallen in love with at Sanderby.

Annie stood with her. "He's going to feel absolutely dreadful when he comes around, Susannah."

"I know. Heaven knows how much he has drunk tonight. A skinful, the postboy said."

"And that is about right. You should have had the postboy take him home, Susannah. It was not wise to bring him here."

"He didn't want to go home, and anyway, I don't know where home is."

"He's not in any condition to know what he wants."

"He knew that, all right," said Susannah quietly, sitting beside him and taking his hand in hers. "I had to bring him back here, Annie, I couldn't ignore his wishes."

"He still means something to you, doesn't he?" asked Annie curiously.

"I don't love him, if that's what you mean."

"No, but it's something very close, isn't it?"

"I suppose so. Oh, if you knew him, Annie, you wouldn't condemn him out of hand."

"Yes, well, I'm not likely to get to know him that well, am I?" Annie smiled. "Will you be all right alone with him? I'm so tired I think I shall fall asleep where I stand unless I take myself to bed."

"Of course I'll be all right."

"How did you get on with Sir Jeffrey?"

"He agreed."

Annie stared. "He didn't!"

"Yes, he did."

"Well, you must be creeping into his heart for him to do something like that for you, truly you must."

"No," said Susannah softly, "he's just taking care of his investment."

Annie said nothing to that, leaving her still sitting on the sofa with Miles's hand held gently in hers.

Several hours passed before she managed to rouse him sufficiently to ply him with strong black coffee. He sat back wearily on the sofa, grumbling as she held out yet another cup. "Must I? Dear God above, it tastes like sewer water!"

"Drink it, Miles. I am determined to send you back as sober as a judge."

"As a matter of interest, do you know any judges?"

"No."

"Drunkards one and all."

She smiled. "How are you feeling now?"

"As the proverbial newt—I shall have a head and a half in due course."

"I've never seen you quite so intoxicated before."

"I've never had anything to be so intoxicated for before. No doubt you are fully cognizant of my losing Sanderby . . ."

"Yes."

"From the horse's mouth, no doubt."

She said nothing.

"Still as close as a bug on a hide, are you?"

"It's not like that, Miles."

"I know, sweet coz, it's a *business* arrangement."

"Yes, it is. Drink the coffee, it will help to clear your head."

"It's clear enough already, too damned clear in fact, for I prefer my edges a little blurred these days. It helps, don't you know."

"And how long have you been getting in this state?"

"Does it matter to you?"

"You are my cousin—"

"Ah, I see. Good old family concern!"

"Yes."

"How very exciting. I have been getting in this state, as you so delicately put it, since I realized what a god-awful mistake I made when I married my dear wife. I lost you, married her, and lost Sanderby—three body blows which became a little too much to stand. I've squandered Croesus' fortune, Susannah, and paid a few prices for my pains. Oh, I still have an income of sorts from the Irish estates, but Croesus ain't left much of a shadow where yours truly is concerned at the moment. My in-laws are displeased with me, to say the least. Old Winston thought he was getting a good match for his dear daughter, a rich husband *et cetera et cetera*, and Agnes thought she was acquiring a decorative armpiece to escort her to all the masques and drawing-rooms so that she could view prospective lovers. Dear Agnes is very like my old man, you know, determined to make me do her bidding in all things. Well, my behavior has put paid to such thoughts, and now she wants more than anything to be rid of me. I believe her papa is making inquiries about having the marriage set aside—*nonconsummation*, would you believe! Well, Agnes knows the lie of *that* charge, for I swear that between the sheets was the one place where I pleased her!"

"Don't, Miles . . ."

"Too improper a topic for you, coz?"

"Miles Devereux, I believe you are wallowing in self-pity, and I feel I should point out that all that has happened to you is your own fault."

"How unfeeling you are," he murmured, smiling a little. "But you see, you and Sanderby went to the same man, God blast him, and to know that my wife would like to follow suit ain't exactly conducive to giving a man pride, is it? Stratton is the demon sent by old Nick to plague me—all roads seem to lead to his door." He raised his cup in mock toast. "Your ill health, Stratton, may you rot in hell!"

"You are blaming someone else for your own sins, Miles."

He ignored her. "We make quite a circus to amuse the *monde*, don't we? I love you, you love Stratton, Agnes wants Stratton—and Stratton wants . . . ? God knows who, and that's a fact. Maybe he's still in love with his wife."

She looked quickly at him. "I thought you believed him to be responsible for her death."

He smiled ruefully. "Ah, that was just a nasty Whig rumor, put about to cause him discomfort. He's a damned Tory, one of the worst outside office, and something had to be said about him. That was as good as any."

"It was despicable, then."

"All's fair in love and politics, sweetheart. Lord, how you swoop to defend him, don't you?" He studied her face for a moment, his large eyes a little sad. "You love him, but does he love you, Susannah?"

168

She drew her hand away. "No."

"Because if I thought he did . . ."

"You'd what?"

"I'd do all I could to destroy it between you. Look at me and know that I mean it, Susannah. I want you for myself, and if I can't have you, then I swear I'll see to it that Stratton doesn't either."

"Miles," she breathed, horrified at the venom in his low voice, "don't speak like that, for it isn't you."

"On the contrary, coz, I assure you that it's very much me of late."

At that moment she heard someone at the front door, and after a moment the maid dutifully emerged from her room and hurried down the stairs.

Miles pursed his lips a little suspiciously. "Now, who could that possibly be at a time like this?" he asked slowly.

"I don't know."

"No?"

In the ensuing silence, however, they both heard Jeffrey's voice in the hall.

Miles stood immediately, his face suddenly angry. "How very late for a social call," he said acidly.

"I don't know why he has called," she said, her face flushing at the insinuation in his tone. "I'll go down—"

He restrained her quickly. "Not at all, don't you know by now that it ain't the thing to receive so honored a guest anywhere but in the drawing room?"

"Don't, Miles, I think it would be better if you didn't see him, don't you?"

"Afraid I'll make a *thing* of it, coz?"

"Yes, yes, that's just what I'm afraid of," she cried, trying to pull her wrist away from him.

"I shall be the soul of discretion," he said softly, releasing her. "I promise I will not say a word out of place."

Uncertainly she remained in the room; besides, it was too late now, for she could hear the maid leading Jeffrey up the stairs. But as they approached the door, Miles suddenly caught her hand again, dragging her swiftly into his arms and holding her so tightly that she could not move. He kissed her passionately on the lips, timing his action to a nicety so that Jeffrey stepped into the room to witness what was apparently a tender embrace. Miles took his time over the kiss, and then slowly released her again, smiling a little as he did so.

Her face was flaming with mortification as she turned at last to look at Jeffrey's cold face. "Jeffrey, I—"

He inclined his head coolly. "Pray, do not let me interrupt your evening *à deux*," he said, glancing once more at Mile's smiling face before turning on his heel and walking out again, followed by the startled maid.

Susannah followed him to the top of the stairs, anxiously holding the banister. "But why did you come? Was there something . . . ?"

He didn't glance back. "I rather think, Miss Garland, that my reason is now a little immaterial, don't you?"

Miserably she stood there watching him, and when the front door closed, she turned back into the drawing room, where Miles stood by the table. "Get out of here," she whispered. "Just get out of here, Miles."

"I warned you that I would stop at nothing to keep you away from him, Susannah."

"Get out," she repeated. "I wish I had left you there tonight."

He looked at her. "I love you, Susannah."

She said nothing, her eyes tired and accusing as she waited by the open door. He picked up his hat and gloves and left. She closed her eyes then and the tears welled hotly down her cheeks. She didn't make a sound; she wept her misery in silence.

19

On the eve of the grand opening, Susannah and Annie took a last look around the showroom before retiring. Susannah felt almost sick with apprehension now that the moment was almost upon her after all the months of preparation, and her hand trembled a little as she held the candlestick high to survey the result of all the industry.

The showroom was just perfect, she thought, taking in the display of jewel-bright velvets in one corner and the dainty mannequin dolls in their rich ball gowns. Lace tumbled over a shelf in apparent confusion, but it had been carefully arranged to show off each lace to the best advantage. Several gowns had been completed and were hanging from the special rail Susannah had placed on the far wall. She looked at the gowns for a moment and then at the mannequins.

"You know," she said at last, "just think how much better it would be for garments to be displayed on living mannequins."

Annie stared at her. "*Real* women?"

"Why not?"

"But you can't do that, what *would* everyone say? It wouldn't be proper, Susannah."

"No, I suppose not—but it *would* show off the gowns." She smiled then. "Perhaps I had better confine myself to the innovation I have already put into effect here."

"Yes, I think you better had," agreed Annie. "There is quite enough already with displays of material, special delivery boxes, and all these comfortable chairs. Madame

Hilary didn't have anything like it and I think you've gone quite far enough with all your new ideas for the time being."

"Too far?" asked Susannah quickly, dreading from her friend's remarks that maybe there was too much that was new and different.

"No, not too far. Just far enough. It all looks very well indeed, and when the ladies come tomorrow—"

"If they come."

Annie went to a table and picked up the newspaper which lay there. She turned the pages quickly and then pointed to the announcement prominently placed in the very center column.

Miss Garland begs to solicit special attention to the opening of the New House of Fashion in Catherine Lane, which exists with the view and intention of rivaling and surpassing every dress establishment in the Kingdom.

"That cannot fail to be noticed, Susannah," she said, "and when Lady Cowper comes . . ."

"Ah, well, I think that after the other night there may be little hope of that now."

"You think Sir Jeffrey will go back on his promise?"

Susannah put the candlestick down and nodded. "Yes, I think there is a great likelihood. Oh, Annie, it was dreadful, I will never forgive Miles, truly I won't. Why did it have to happen like that? Why did Jeffrey have to come here?"

"Why indeed," said Annie thoughtfully. "It could be that he had seen the light after all."

Susannah gave a short laugh. "Well, if he had, then it has of a certainty gone out again now! Extinguished once and for all, I would imagine. He called me 'Miss Garland' and was so very cold, and I suppose I cannot blame him, for what he saw when he came in—"

"Was not your fault."

"No, but he is not to know that. Anyway, I mustn't think about it, for there is no point. Come on, let's go to bed and see what tomorrow brings, mm?" She smiled brightly, picking up the candlestick again and taking a final look at the splendid showroom before going up the stairs.

The crash woke Susannah with a start, and the cat jumped down from the bed beside her with a low warning growl.

172

Staring around at the dark bedroom, Susannah listened for a moment, half-thinking that she had been dreaming. But the cat growled again, its hackles rising and its tail swishing warningly as it stared out at the deserted landing. Everything was quiet, and outside, the cold spring night was perfectly still.

Then there was another splintering crash from somewhere downstairs. In an instant she was out of the warm bed and running out to the landing. Far below she could see a light shining from the showroom. She ran down the stairs in her bare feet, her white nightrobe flapping wildly behind her, and at the door of the showroom she halted in horror. By the light of a lantern, a cloaked figure was in the act of wrecking the whole room, slashing at the furniture and decorations with a knife.

Susannah gasped, first in fear and then in sudden anger at the wanton and deliberate destruction of all their hard work. The figure heard her and turned sharply, dropping the knife and lunging toward her before she could move. She was pushed violently across the hall, where she struck her back on the handle of the stockroom door, and she sank to her knees a little winded as the mysterious figure ran to the front door and out into the dark safety of the night. She heard the footsteps hurrying away along the street, and then there was silence again.

Then Annie and the maid came running down the stairs, crouching anxiously beside her. Annie caught her by the shoulders. "Susannah?"

She could only stare in silence at the showroom.

Stunned, they all looked through the open doorway at the wreckage. Ink had been thrown at the delicate pink walls and the golden initials above the fireplaces had been gouged and destroyed. The mannequins lay trampled on the floor and all the chairs except one had been cut badly so that their stuffing spilled out. Similar slashes had cut the display of velvets into ribbons, and the costly lace had had more of the dark blue ink poured over it. The mirrors were all shattered, and the fragments of glass were shining brightly in the lantern light.

Slowly Susannah got to her feet, and Annie went with her into the room which only a short time before had been so perfect in every way. "Who would do such a thing, Susannah? Who?"

"There is more than one who would prefer these premises never to open."

"Madame Hilary?"

"I do not think her above such a thing, do you?"

"No. Nor is Lady Devereux."

Susannah looked quickly at her. "No, I suppose not."

"What do we do now? We can hardly open the doors tomorrow."

Susannah glanced at the maid. "Go and see if the workroom has been touched." She crossed the hallway then and opened the stockroom door. The lantern light fell across neatly stacked shelves and drawers. The intruder had not got that far before he was disturbed. The maid returned with the news that the workroom was intact too.

Susannah smiled grimly. "And all my drawing folders are upstairs in my drawing room. Only the showroom has been destroyed, Annie. We can still open tomorrow."

"But we'll never tidy this mess in time!"

"We can try. I know I shall not sleep any more tonight, and I would prefer to begin clearing up than sitting back on my heels doing nothing at all. I won't give in, Annie, I won't!"

Lady Cowper's barouche halted outside early the next morning, and Susannah turned away from the window, not really knowing whether to be pleased or dismayed. Jeffrey had kept his word after all, but what would Lady Cowper's reaction be when she saw this dreadful chaos? Susannah looked sadly around the once-beautiful room. The ink stains had proved impossible to remove and the walls would have to be painted again. The golden initials would have to be completely replaced, and the jagged glass in the mirrors shone sharply in the slanting light of the morning sun. The shattered cheval glasses stood in a corner and the two mannequins lay like sleeping children on the floor beside them. There were no pretty displays of lace and velvet, no discreet, welcoming elegance—just devastation. But she took her place before one of the fireplaces, plucking the folds of her new pink muslin gown and clasping her hands neatly before her. The New House of Fashion was most definitely open!

Followed by her rather superior lady's maid, Emily Cowper entered the showroom, halting then in instant amazement as she saw the state it was in. Holding up the hem of her lilac pelisse, she came farther in, carefully avoiding an ominous ink stain in the center of the carpet.

"Well," she said at last, "I was promised a startling new *maison de modes*, but I do not think that this was what was in mind."

"I fear the premises have been viciously attacked, Lady Cowper."

"So it would seem. You must be the famous—or infamous—Miss Garland."

Susannah curtsied. "I am."

The sharp, lovely eyes moved slowly over her. "You bear little family resemblance to your cousin Devereux."

"I bear none at all."

"There are wicked Tories who would say that that cannot be a bad thing for you," murmured Emily, sitting on the surviving chair and handing her reticule to her maid, who took up a dutiful position at her shoulder. "So, at last I come face to face with the interesting Miss Garland," she went on, "and find her more interesting than ever this morning, but then, no doubt there are many jealous rivals who would wish to be rid of your competition."

"There are."

"And not all are rivals in dressmaking, are they?"

Susannah met the shrewd gaze. "No, my lady, they are not."

"Society has rattled about little else but you of late, Miss Garland. The poor little war has been hard put to raise its head above the more lip-smacking tales concerning the late Lord Devereux's secret niece. And of course the resurgence of acrimony between Devereux and Stratton has seen to it that interest in you has been kept at a fine pitch. I confess that when I first heard of you I was a little skeptical that such a skeleton could rattle its way from Sanderby's cupboard—but it has, and now it stands before me garbed most becomingly in pale pink muslin. You are a very fetching skeleton, Miss Garland."

"Thank you, Lady Cowper."

"Very fetching—and very surprising."

"Surprising?"

"Surely the object of your enemy in destroying this room was to force you to close before you could open—but with you it has had the opposite effect. Here you stand, in the midst

175

of all this mayhem, calmly greeting me to your New House of Fashion. You are surprising, therefore, Miss Garland, and you most certainly have style. It must have taken a considerable style to persuade a Corinthian like Jeffrey Stratton to come upon an errand concerning *fashions*. I salute you for being so very enterprising." Emily sat back in the chair, surveying Susannah's still figure for a moment. "Which brings me next to the *other* style you evince—to wit, the amazing blend of Whig and Tory which pervades this palace of modes. On the one hand you are Whig—what else could someone who is half-Devereux be? And on the other hand there is your tantalizing connection with Sir Jeffrey Stratton, a terrible Tory if ever there was one. If you are a success, you will draw Whig and Tory alike to your door, and neither will feel they are offending political allies in any way. It is very neat."

"But not as intentional as your words would seem to suggest."

"Probably not—but it is elegantly done, for all that. I have personally found it all quite interesting. I have heard Agnes Devereux denigrating you as if you were Beelzebub's right hand, and Madame Hilary telling me with a mouthful of pins that you were the most discourteous employee it had ever been her misfortune to come across. Then I am visited by Jeffrey, who assures me that on the contrary, you are a most talented and brilliant lady and that if I visit you I shall be assured of a most exquisite selection of fripperies. All in all, Miss Garland, I am inclined to take Jeffrey's version for the truth, for to have made your enemies make such a tantrum about you must mean that you are indeed a force to be reckoned with." There was a momentary pause. "Mind, if I were still in love with Jeffrey, I wonder if I would still have come? A moot point, *n'est-ce pas?*"

Susannah flushed a little. "I . . . I don't know, my lady."

"Nor do I. However, I shall treat myself charitably and say that I would not have been swayed in the slightest and would still have come to honor this new *maison de modes* with my presence." Emily smiled. "But I am still intrigued, Miss Garland, to know exactly what *is* your relationship with the desirable Jeffrey."

Susannah was taken completely aback by the directness of such a question from a woman she hardly knew and with whom she had no connection whatsoever. Moreover, Emily

Cowper was a patroness at Almack's, that temple of manners and exclusiveness, and it came as a considerable shock to Susannah to be faced with such out-and-out unambiguousness. "There . . . there is no relationship, Lady Cowper. Indeed, at the moment, Sir Jeffrey finds himself unable to be particularly civil to me."

"*Jeffrey*? I confess that that does not sound in the least like him. However, no doubt there is much more to it than meets my curious and penetrating eye." Emily smiled again. "Well, maybe my eye is not all that penetrating after all. I am surprised at what you say, however, for on the last occasion I saw him he was extolling your many virtues in a way which quite vexed me, for I am sure my qualities were never praised like that. Indeed, I was under the impression that he was coming on around here afterward to . . . to . . . Well, it does not matter now."

Susannah wanted her to say more, but Emily had obviously made up her mind that she had said enough. Susannah hid her frustration admirably, and was suddenly distracted by the maid moving slightly. The maid! She had forgotten all about her presence, and the conversation had been very indiscreet!

Emily laughed. "Oh, do not be afraid, Miss Garland, she is completely deaf—a positive advantage on occasions, don't you know. She is also the soul of discretion. I love her dearly and would not be without her for all the world. Now, then, I have shilly-shallied enough and must come to the point of my visit—your designs. It will no doubt please you to learn that I wish to order a new gown for the coming Season, one which I fully intend displaying at Almack's. And if I am pleased with it, which I have no doubt I will be, I shall not hesitate to spread the good word about you, that I promise."

Susannah could not hide her great joy. "You are very kind, Lady Cowper!"

"Not at all, it is a pleasure to find you to be a dressmaker who is not determined to out-Queen the Queen!" Emily leaned forward more confidentially then. "Besides, I do have an ulterior motive. I suspect that some of your designs have been used by Madame Hilary of late, for she was a tired dressmaker who suddenly began to produce again some quite exquisite gowns—like the one Princess Amelia wore. I have a very special reason to wish to look my very best this coming Season, Miss Garland. There is a certain Lord Palmerston who is quite the most beautiful young man you ever did see in your life, and if I do not win his heart, then I think I shall die of misery."

Susannah smiled. "I am sure that I can make you more eye-catching and stunning than ever, Lady Cowper."

"Yes, I do believe you can, Miss Garland. Oh, and it must be in sea green."

"Sea green?"

"Palmerston is very fond of that color, and if I can be a little naughty at the same time . . . ?"

"I think that can be arranged to your satisfaction, my lady."

Emily beamed. "Jeffrey Stratton is wickedly handsome, but I rather fancy Palmerston has the edge on him."

"I think he must, my lady."

Emily nodded. "There is another reason for coming to you, of course."

"Yes?"

"Yes. I never could stand Agnes Winston."

Night was beginning to fall when at last Susannah locked the door of the New House of Fashion at the end of its first day. She leaned back wearily on the door, smiling as Annie carried a large pile of paper patterns in from the workroom and laid them on the hall table before sitting on the bottom of the stairs with a great satisfied sigh.

"Our first day was far more successful than I dared to dream, Annie!"

"And more exhausting."

"You are surely not grumbling already!"

"Of course not."

"Oh, when only Lady Cowper came this morning, I feared Agnes' campaign and Madame Hilary's contribution had counted for too much, but then, this afternoon . . . ! Word traveled very quickly that Lady Cowper had come here, didn't it?"

"Word *always* travels quickly, and we have orders for three day dresses, a pelisse, a riding habit, and full mourning for Mrs. Baxter to prove it. To say nothing of Lady Cowper's Palmerston-bait. Is she really going to have a *décolletage* as low as that?"

"Yes."

"She'll frighten him away!"

"Oh, I don't think so." Susannah began to laugh then. "Do you know who my last customer was?"

"No."

"Lady Ormanton. And do you know what she has ordered?"

"Not another spencer!"

"Oh, yes. And she was wearing that dreadful thing I worked so hard on for Miss Chiddock! The very same horrible garment, and it *did* look as odious as I thought it would!"

Susannah went to inspect the patterns on the table, but stopped almost immediately, for a noisy outbreak of barking from the back of the house made her turn sharply. "What's that?"

"Dogs."

"I know, but they sound as if they're on the premises!"

"They are."

"Why?"

"I think we need guarding," said Annie, getting up. "We cannot be sure we won't be broken into again, and I thought we should do something to protect ourselves."

"Whose dogs are they?"

Annie cleared her throat then. "They . . . they belong to Mr. Frederick Normans."

Susannah stared. "Mr. *Normans?* Of Grafton House?"

"Yes."

"Well, I did notice how often you seemed to look at each other, but I hadn't realized things had progressed to such a degree."

"It's not all that much of a degree," protested Annie, "and it only began when you sent me for some yellow silk. I couldn't find the right shade anywhere and decided in the end to go back to Grafton House. There wasn't anywhere else, and when I got there, the shop was virtually empty. Mr. Normans served me again and he was most kind. It . . . it was his afternoon off and he asked me if he could walk me back to Catherine Lane."

"He did not waste his time, did he?"

Annie's flush deepened. "He asked me most politely, indeed he was quite the gentleman. I enjoyed his company."

Susannah smiled then. "And when he asked you if he could call on you again, you agreed."

"Yes. He comes to the back entrance, which is why you

179

have never seen him. I . . . I've walked out with him five times now."

"My, my, things *have* been progressing!"

"I saw him earlier this morning and told him what had happened last night. That was when he suggested—no, *insisted*—that we have his dogs here. He assures me that they are very fine guard dogs, Susannah."

"They sound it," said Susannah, listening as the dogs began to bark again at something. She went through to the back of the house and held a lace curtain aside to look out.

Two large brown hounds padded around, noses to the ground and ears twitching for the slightest sound as they inspected their new territory. As she watched, her cat appeared on the wall which bordered the mews lane. It began to slink warily along the top of the wall, making toward the workroom roof nearby. The hounds detected the dark shape immediately and leaped furiously at the wall, snapping and growling as they tried to reach the horrified cat, which erupted along to the safety of the roof. There, perceiving that it was safe, it sat tantalizingly out of reach, a disdainful look on its face. It began to clean itself from head to toe as the hounds kept up their frenzied noise at the foot of the wall.

Susannah lowered the curtain. "If our intruder should return, he will have something of a surprise, won't he? That is—if he comes by the back way."

"That's the way he came before."

"How do you know?"

"Mr. Normans had a look around this morning. He found marks on the wall where the ivy had been torn when the intruder climbed in. He had to escape the front way, though, for there wouldn't have been time to climb the wall once you had discovered him. He'll come the back way again, I'm sure of it."

It was four o'clock in the morning when the hounds began to raise the alarm again, and Susannah awoke immediately. She slipped from the bed and hurried to the window which overlooked the back garden. A shadowy figure was struggling against the foot of the wall, trying to fend off the excited hounds. As she called for Annie to come quickly, the cloaked figure managed to extricate itself and make a desperate lunge for the wall, where it hung for a moment before heaving itself up to the safety of the top. It paused there, the hood torn back from its face, and the moon came from behind a cloud to reveal James Ridley's face quite clearly.

Annie was at Susannah's shoulder. "We should have known! This is just the sort of miserable thing James would do!"

"At least we know our enemy," murmured Susannah, watching the cloaked figure drop out of sight into the mews lane. "I wonder how long she will keep trying?"

"She *does* have a lot to lose if you become established, doesn't she? And she's bound to know already how well your first day has gone, isn't she? News like that travels like wildfire. She won't give up easily, Susannah, that much I can tell you."

"I know," said Susannah softly, "I know."

20

Susannah was working on Emily Cowper's sea-green gown the next morning when she was hastily summoned to the showroom.

Lady Ormanton was pacing up and down in a state of great agitation, the tall feather in her scarlet hat trembling a little on her hennaed head. She wore girlish cream muslin and the unbecoming spencer upon which Susannah had once worked so hard and long. She always used a great deal of rouge, and today her upset condition made her face flame. Her short, wide figure moved restlessly and she toyed constantly with the strings of her lozenge-shaped reticule. Her impassive German maid stood solidly by the window, her face as expressionless as her mistress's was mobile.

When Susannah entered the room, Lady Ormanton uttered a cry of relief and swooped upon her.

"Oh, Fräulein Garland, Fräulein Garland, you have come at last! I am qvite alarmed, and I do not know vot I shall do!"

"Please sit down, Lady Ormanton," soothed Susannah, ushering her to a chair, "and tell me how I may help you."

"I must go to Vindsor! To *Vindsor*! I am to join the Qveen's household and I have no court gown! It is too bad, I am given no vorning, no time to prepare myself for such a position! All these years and I am not summoned, and now I am given only two veeks!"

Susannah smiled. "Oh, I think we can make you a court gown in two weeks, my lady."

"*Ja?*" Lady Ormanton collapsed back in the chair, the scarlet feather wobbling. "Oh, I am so relieved! You do not know how better I feel already! The messenger came to my house this morning and I am straight avay at sevens and sixes. The Qveen likes to have her fellow Germans around her still, and I am a Schwellenberg."

"Schwellenberg? Was not a Madame Schwellenberg Her Majesty's Mistress of the Robes?"

"*Ach, ja*—she voz my aunt. A terrible voman, a dragon! To think that I had to marry an Englishman to escape from her!" said Lady Ormanton with great feeling. "But then, I must not speak ill of the dead—either of them."

Susannah suppressed a smile, for both the late Lord Ormanton and the formidable Madame Schwellenberg must indeed have been ogres to bring forth such a statement from the inoffensive Lady Ormanton.

"Fräulein Garland, you can indeed make me a court gown?"

"Of course. I will bring my folder and we will see what appeals to you."

Lady Ormanton was delighted. "It is so refreshing to find a dressmaker who is both helpful and polite. Such a change."

It did not take long for the design to be chosen, and it only remained for the correct material to be decided upon. Lady Ormanton was quite set to have a virtually transparent tiffany gauze which would not have suited her, and it took all Susannah's ingenuity to persuade her that a dainty satin-striped silk could be so much more flattering. Changing a customer's mind without really appearing to do so was quite an art, for it was so difficult not to give offense.

Lady Ormanton felt the silk. "I vill not look like a . . . a zebra?"

"No, not at all, my lady. But if you are in doubt and really would prefer the tiffany, then of course I will make it up for you. The silk *is* quite exquisite, though . . ."

"Fräulein Garland, I am persvaded that you are correct and the silk is the very thing! Yes, I must have it!"

Relieved, Susannah began to roll up the bolt of silk again, and as she did so she noticed a carriage drawing up outside. She paused, staring out at the crest on the carriage's black door. Jeffrey Stratton! As she watched, the footman opened the door and Jeffrey alighted.

Lady Ormanton was taking her leave, once again eliciting a firm promise from Susannah that the gown would be ready in good time. Susannah reassured her and then waited in the showroom for Jeffrey to be shown in. But he did not come immediately, as he encountered his cousin's widow on the doorstep.

"*Guten morgen*, Cousin Ulla," he said, bowing.

She halted in surprise, being so preoccupied with her thoughts that she had not noticed him barring her path. "Jeffrey! How agreeable it is to see you again."

"You are looking very well."

"Vot you mean is that I am looking very fat!" she said with a fond smile, patting his arm. "But today I am in so fine a mood that I shall not be cross with you."

"Your visit to Miss Garland would appear to have put you in an excellent humor."

"Indeed it has, she is qvite a treasure, your Miss Garland. Such a change from that *Hündin* Hilary."

"She is hardly *my* Miss Garland."

"But of course she is, your money finances her! You have come to see the terrible damage that dreadful person did here?"

He glanced at the showroom window, his face expressionless. "I have."

"She is such an angel—to think that anyone could do such a thing!"

"Oh, she is indeed an angel."

She looked sharply at him. "If *I* am in good humor, sir, it vould seem that you are most certainly not."

"My humor is always excellent, Ulla. Now, then, what is all this I hear about you being summoned to the Queen?"

"Ah, yes, at last the Qveen vishes another Schwellenberg to attend her!" said Ulla proudly.

"And the prospect obviously pleases you."

"It is my duty, Jeffrey, my bounden duty."

"That isn't what I asked."

"Of course I am pleased, she is my Qveen—and besides, I must say that my terrible aunt is no longer there to plague me, so of course I vill be pleased. Aunt Schwellenberg alvays treated me as if I voz still a little girl in Hanover. Oh, it was marvelous to escape into marriage, even such a marriage! An Englishman!"

"You are not particularly complimentary to my race, Ulla," he reproved, smiling.

184

"Ah, but you are different, Jeffrey, you could be taken for a German."

"And that is a compliment?"

"You know perfectly vell that it is." She looked more closely at him then. *"Sie sehen etwas bleich aus."*

"Pale? Ulla, I am not pale, I am in perfect health."

"You spend too much time with your Mr. Pitt, you begin to look as ill as he does, poor man."

"I sallied forth this morning feeling in fine fettle, and now you have set me quite back. That is most unkind, Ulla."

"You still look pale."

He glanced at her rouged cheeks, thinking that virtually everyone would look pale to someone who liked such a high color.

"You should take herb tea," she went on. "It is very good for you."

"I am not in need of herb tea, beef tea, or any other kind of tea. I swear to this day that my late cousin Ormanton was speeded on his way by too much of your currant tea."

She smiled. "I assure you that if I had thought I could speed him by such a method, then I vould indeed have done so, for he voz qvite the most odious of men."

"There I will agree with you. He was not a feather in the family cap."

"Vell, I must go now, there is so much I must do before I go to Vindsor. *Auf wiedersehen*, Jeffrey."

"Auf wiedersehen, Ulla."

She hurried away along the street to her waiting carriage, the stony-faced maid following obediently four paces behind her.

Susannah stepped away from the window as she saw Lady Ormanton take her leave of him. Her heart was beating swiftly as he knocked at the door.

He inspected the damage in silence. He had walked past her with the briefest nod and she knew that nothing had changed since the night he had seen Miles kiss her.

"We . . . we have tidied up as much as possible," she said at last, feeling she had to say something as the minutes dragged leadenly by, "but everything will have to be decorated again."

"Naturally. I am surprised you opened your doors at all, Miss Garland, but then, nothing must interfere with your plans, must it?"

She stared at the bitterness in his voice. "You think I should have delayed?" she asked.

"I don't think anything, Miss Garland," he said coldly, glancing around again. "Have you any notion who may be responsible for this?"

"I believe it is Madame Hilary."

"You only believe?"

"We saw her footman. He came again last night."

"How very determined. Well, I regard these premises as my concern, and I do not appreciate such damage being done. I shall see to it that Madame Hilary receives fright enough to deter her from further activities. A war of words is one thing, an out-and-out attack quite another."

How very cold he was; it was as if their previous friendship had never existed. And it was all because of Miles.

He looked at her. "You would appear to have achieved miraculous success on your first day."

"I have you to thank for that, for you spoke to Lady Cowper."

"I am a man of my word."

"Yes."

"But I cannot take the credit for your success—you have your own talent to thank for that. No doubt when I return to London you will be very well established and in full command of society's every fashion foible."

"You speak as if you will be away some time."

"I trust that I will be. I am shortly to be the Prince of Wales's guest, as you know, and after that I am returning to my country seat in Leicestershire—I have been conspicuous by my absence of late." He gave a slight smile which lacked any warmth at all. "But I feel you do yourself an injustice to presume that your rise to glory will take a long time, Miss Garland, for it seems to me that you have already commenced what is bound to be a meteoric ascent. I believe barely two Seasons should see to it nicely."

"Two Seasons? I think that very unlikely, Sir Jeffrey."

"If it did not matter so little to me, I would lay odds on it."

"And if it did not matter so little to me," she said stiffly, "I would be interested in your activities, whether gaming or anything else."

"That was known to me already, Miss Garland." He

walked past her. "I shall see to it that Madame Hilary is frightened off."

"Why do you bother?"

He turned. "Because we have an agreement, Miss Garland. Good day to you."

"Good day."

She turned her face to the door as he left, pressing her forehead against the cool wood and closing her eyes. She fought back the tears, and when she was a little steadier and more composed, she picked up the drawing Lady Ormanton had decided upon, and the bolt of white silk, and she took it through to the workroom.

She gave Annie brief instructions, her voice still taut, and Annie glanced up at her pale face. Annie knew Sir Jeffrey Stratton had paid a visit, and she knew now that the confrontation had been a disaster as far as Susannah was concerned. Quickly she put her hand over Susannah's, smiling a little, and Susannah managed to smile back before going to the table she used herself. She picked up Emily's gown again, bowing her head as she worked. Her needle flashed in and out, pins rattled and scissors snipped busily, and the low drone of talk hung in the industrious chamber where once had echoed the strains of music.

There was a happy atmosphere among the seamstresses; they were not regimented, not restricted, and they gave of their best. The only unhappy one among them was Susannah herself, and everyone thought she had more reason to be just the opposite. No one but Annie knew that in the midst of her apparent good fortune, and with great success imminent, Susannah Garland was more desperately unhappy than ever, and more miserably in love with Jeffrey Stratton.

The first Season of the New House of Fashion was the unmitigated success Jeffrey had so cuttingly predicted. It seemed that as far as society ladies were concerned, Susannah could do no wrong, especially after the triumphant appearance of Emily Cowper's sea-green gown at Almack's. The gown had the desired effect as far as Emily was concerned, for it soon helped her to ensnare Lord Palmerston—and as far as Susannah was concerned, it set the seal on her arrival. A steady stream of ladies passed through the door of the house in Catherine Lane throughout that long summer, and the pink-and-gray boxes she had so daringly introduced became a common sight being delivered at Mayfair doors. Ladies considered it to be a positive advantage to have such a box be seen to arrive, and before many months had passed Susannah found herself being mentioned in that most important of fashion publications, *The Ladies' Magazine of Modes*. In one fell swoop she had joined the ranks of court dressmakers like Madame Hilary. Where others had had to labor over many years to achieve her position, she had stepped in unfairly high on the ladder, and there were many to point out that it was hardly just that she should have the financial patronage of a man as wealthy as Sir Jeffrey Stratton. But there were equally as many to say that had she not had great talent, no amount of financial support could make her the dazzling success she was.

Of Jeffrey himself she saw nothing. She heard from tittle-tattle in the showroom that his visit to the Prince of Wales had not been the royal master stroke it was intended to be. Using Jeffrey as a lever to alter Pitt's course concerning the regency and the troublesome matter of the Prince's loathed wife, Caroline of Brunswick, proved impossible, as the lever had no intention of being in the least obliging. Jeffrey was dismissed from the royal presence, and the Tories curled up with mirth over the whole episode. Everyone knew that Jeffrey's loyalty to Pitt was impenetrable, and consequently the Prince of Wales had shown lamentable judgment—a further indication to the Tories that Pitt's verdict on the would-be regent was entirely the correct one. The Whigs were naturally less pleased, confining themselves to dark utterances about Jeffrey obviously having more interest in needles and thread of late than in the welfare of the future King of England. The present King of England, however, thoroughly approved of Pitt, and therefore of Jeffrey's actions, as Susannah learned from Lady Ormanton, who was now installed most happily at Court.

But Susannah gleaned little satisfaction from having her named linked, however tenuously, with Jeffrey, for she knew that she could not have been further from his thoughts. After his encounter with the Prince, he left London for Southwood in Leicestershire, closing his Berkeley Square house at the very height of the Season. She already felt his alienation most keenly, but now his departure for the country had to be endured as well. She knew she had no hope of ever winning his love, but at least knowing he was close by had been a comfort. Now she did not even have that. She was the darling of the *monde*, welcomed and fêted by that fickle society, but the only man who mattered didn't care in the slightest.

To keep her unhappiness at bay, she worked very hard, giving each garment her personal attention and working many times late into the night to finish a special order. Of all the important dressmakers, she alone still wielded a needle. Nothing slipped past her eagle eye, and she could recall instantly all the details of an order. Her increasing success meant that Madame Hilary's power over shops and warehouses fell away, and doors were opened swiftly to the New House of Fashion. Grafton House could not have been more obliging—or anxious to forget the past—and Nicholay's scoured their shelves for obscure items simply to please her. There was no more trudging the streets to find the nearest comparable button or lace; now she could always find exactly what she wanted each time.

No one was given cause to complain about the service given by the New House of Fashion, or the pains taken by Miss Garland herself over each and every order. The atmosphere there was such a change from the showrooms of other dressmakers that ladies, Whig and Tory alike, said it was a positive pleasure to linger there and discuss *modes*. Susannah received orders for the King's birthday celebrations, and fashionable ladies felt quite at ease conducting conversations with her as they received fittings. After all, they told themselves, it was quite in order to do so, for was she not a cousin of Lord Devereux's and therefore perfectly above the salt and acceptable? All the rumor and conjecture which had been rife at the outset had gone to Susannah's advantage, and now the premises in Catherine Lane were fast becoming *the* place to be seen for ladies of quality.

The grumpy Duke of Glenbeigh in the house next door became steadily grumpier at the constant intrusions upon his much-prized peace and quiet. He had chosen Catherine Lane because it was *un*fashionable, and now this odious temple of fripperies had put an end to it. The Duchess continued to patronize Madame Hilary and was quite vociferous in her condemnation of the premises adjoining, and so the Duke's mood was an unrelieved one of gloom. All in all, he did not enjoy that summer in the slightest and was heard to say so quite loudly from time to time at his club—a refuge he sought increasingly as the weeks passed and the clatter of carriages in Catherine Lane became unendurable. Before the end of July he had determined to move from the area entirely, *anything* to escape the Castle of Calicoes, as he called number fifteen Catherine Lane.

If being Miles's cousin had helped Susannah, which she fully acknowledged it had, she still could not bring herself to make up her bitter quarrel with him. She rebuffed his few approaches, feeling too angry and resentful still for his part in the breach of her friendship with Jeffrey. He had forfeited her affection that night and she did not think she would ever be able to forgive him for it. Her rebuffs were made in no uncertain terms, and she wondered if she would force him over into the camp of her enemies, but not once did she hear his name mentioned in that way. Whatever else he may have been guilty of, Miles Devereux did not turn upon her or raise his voice against her in any way.

Beyond the walls of the New House of Fashion, the war still dragged on, but as in the previous year, the dreaded invasion did not take place. Now that she had met the Prime Minister, Susannah was more aware of the war, and she knew the ailing Mr. Pitt was working tirelessly to raise a coalition against France. But by the time war broke out at last on the Continent too, he had been only partly successful, and how long Britain's new allies could remain at her side was a matter of conjecture.

The streets of London were filled with red uniforms by September, and the ships of the Royal Navy lay at anchor in the Thames. For once the chitter-chatter in the showroom turned upon the war, and Susannah knew within an hour that Admiral Lord Nelson had been to Downing Street for instructions. Afterward he had been afforded the unprecedented honor of being escorted to his waiting carriage by the Prime Minister himself. Emily Cowper had laughed as she related the tale. It was, she remarked, much more than the Tory Mr. Pitt would have done for a Prince of the Blood—but then, everyone knew Mr. Pitt's opinion of Princes of the Blood.

When the door closed that night, Susannah stood in the window of the showroom to look out over the rain-swept street where the September evening was gray and dark. A terrible storm had raged over London all day, trees were bent by the force of the gale, and gentlemen passing by had to hold on tightly to their tall hats. Umbrellas blew inside out and ladies' skirts flapped unbecomingly around their legs as they struggled against the storm. The rain lashed across the street and puddles rippled like small seas. It seemed as if summer had ended, she thought, holding the lace curtains aside. An officer on a fine bay horse rode smartly by, his saber swinging and his scarlet coat a bright splash of warm color. Emily's news had brought the war that much closer again, but Admiral Lord Nelson would defeat the enemy upon the high seas; his name was synonymous with victory.

21

~

Trafalgar. The name was on every lip, for it had been a victory of dazzling brilliance, leaving Britain firmly in command of the seas and safe from invasion, and it had come as an almost delirious relief after the disastrous news of a French triumph which had split the fragile new coalition asunder. Britain was once again almost alone against the French empire, and her new allies were in disarray. But Trafalgar was tinged with sadness too, for it had been won at the cost of Nelson's life.

In the foggy parks the guns had boomed out in salute on the day the news reached London, and that night there were illuminations, fireworks reaching high into the dark night above Hyde Park. The celebrating went ahead, but Nelson's death dulled the enthusiasm felt for his great victory. Houses were decorated in his memory, wreaths of bay leaves hung on doors, and the initials L.N. were lighted by candles in windows.

Susannah put the finishing touches to a large bow of black satin ribbons and then took it to the door of the New House of Fashion. The fog swept over her and she could hear the fireworks popping and spluttering in the distance. A rocket burst overhead in a scatter of crimson sparks and she glanced up into the night before tying the bow to the door knocker and arranging the loops carefully. She heard the carriage approaching and turned as it came to a standstill near where she stood.

Miles climbed down, his heavy black cloak swinging, and

he paused as he saw her. "May I come in, coz, or is my presence still an anathema to you?"

She stood aside without a word, and he entered the house, bringing with him a smell of coal smoke from the damp night. She led him to the showroom.

"So I'm relegated to this public place, am I?" he said, removing his cloak and flinging it over a gray velvet chair. "No cozy drawing room for your wicked kinsman this time?"

"You do not deserve anything else."

"Possibly not." He looked around at the showroom, which had been decorated some time now and was restored to its former glory. "So, my Lady Innovation, you are become a resounding success at the end of your first Season, and I stand at last in the temple of chiffons from which no lady worth her salt will dare stay away." He bowed to her. "You neglected to show me this elegant chamber when last I was here."

"I neglected many things last time you were here, Miles, not least to keep my wary eye on you."

He smiled. "Aye, well, it cannot be undone now. But I congratulate you upon your success and I do not begrudge you the leeway you have made because of your connection with me."

"Thank you."

"Not at all, I think I have behaved most graciously—my father would not have stood aside so obligingly. Mind you, I believe I have heard Agnes' teeth grinding from time to time—usually when she hears of yet another lady of quality deserting the ranks and fleeing to you. I do not believe my dear wife will be honoring you with her presence."

"You do not surprise me. She would not be welcome here anyway."

"That I can well believe. She had used her clacking to great effect in some quarters, I believe, but not in as many as she would have wished. It was a master stroke to have Emily Cowper dragooned across your threshold—she is a lady of much influence."

"Why have you come here tonight, Miles?"

"This day of Pyrrhic victory cries out for the healing of our differences, coz."

She was still suspicious. "And?"

He looked hurt. "Surely you do not believe I have an ulterior motive?"

"I have little reason *not* to think you have."

"Well, I have not. Tonight just seemed the right time to try to set things right between us, that is all. Besides, the itch to gamble away what is left of my fortune is rather strong still, and I need someone to keep me in line. I have, as you well know, a very great fondness for you, Susannah, and I believe that in spite of your crossness with me you still like me a little."

"I feel slightly more than mere crossness toward you, Miles Devereux."

"So it would seem. That don't alter my course or my wishes tonight, though."

"It makes a great deal of difference to my course and my wishes."

"Oh, come now, Susannah, can we not be a little more friendly than this? We meant a great deal to each other once." He ran his fingertips over the fringe of a delicate silver gauze gown she had displayed on a ground of black brocade. "You are right, of course, I do have another reason for coming to see you."

"Ah."

"But it is quite innocent. I merely wish to celebrate." He touched the spangles on the gown's little sleeves, and they moved, catching the candlelight. "On two counts, actually."

"Well?"

"First, I have snapped my Whig teeth successfully at the government and caused them some discomfort—but as you are imbued with Stratton's politics now, no doubt that does not impress."

"Should it?"

"Your sarcasm is almost worthy of Pitt himself! He would hug himself with delight if he knew that the lady who holds such sway over London's fashion is a dedicated Tory." He gave a faint smile. "To be sure, our pure Prime Minister hugs no one else but himself."

"You said there were two counts."

"So I did. Now, what was the other? Ah, yes. I am to be a father."

She stared at him. "Agnes is with child?"

"I *am* capable," he said with mock hurt. "Many things I may fail at, but in this I have yet to . . . admit defeat, shall we say?"

She was forced to smile. "I wish you would go away, Miles

Devereux, for I don't wish to be friendly with you, and you are making it difficult for me."

"That is the general idea," he said with a disarming smile.

"As you say, you *are* my cousin. I will not withhold my friendship, but there is nothing else in my heart for you. Nothing at all."

She could not tell if he accepted her words or not, for he turned away in a pretense of looking around the showroom again. "So, you will celebrate with me on the second count, cousin? You will come out to dine with me?"

"Have you any idea how late it is?"

"I realize that staid Tories retire to their warm beds at sunset, but we Whigs have a greater sense of fun. We consider the night to be just beginning at eleven. Susannah, I want to enjoy myself tonight, I want to drink iced champagne and toast both Trafalgar and my forthcoming state of parenthood."

"Then should you not do so with Agnes?"

"Ah, well, maybe I have not been entirely truthful tonight." He gave a wry smile. "There are three counts to celebrate, and maybe the third is the most joyous of all. She has left me and gone back to dear Papa."

"She's *left* you?"

"That is what I said, and I do believe the phrase describes precisely my present situation, coz."

"I'm so sorry."

"Don't be, for it is a blessed relief, I promise you. She has made it depressingly clear to me of late that she considers me to be a misalliance in every way, indeed she misses no opportunity for telling me as much. Her preference for Stratton had become an embarrassment to me anyway, especially in view of all the other circumstances pertaining to my relations with him. Dear Papa Winston was moving heaven and earth to try to have the marriage annulled, but I am afraid that his daughter's condition rather put paid to all that, and they are stuck with me, as they say. He signed far too many documents, agreed to far too many things at the time of the betrothal for him to wriggle out of it, and I have no intention of divorcing her now. I have my child to think of, his or her future, and there shall be no divorce to mar that, not while I live and breathe." He came closer, studying the expressions crossing her face in the candlelight. "I *am* the father, Susannah, I know it for a fact, and I promise you that Stratton

195

showed a remarkable degree of intelligence in spurning my wife's every advance."

"It would not concern me—"

"Fibber," he said softly, putting his hand to her chin and raising her face toward his. "It would concern you very much, for you are in love with him. However, I must reassure you that as far as Agnes is concerned, he is now very much in the past tense. Her insatiable searchings have taken her elsewhere for affection—to a dainty little French *émigré*—the Comte de St. François. He trails obediently around in her wake like a small dog and she in content to let him join her in her kennel at Winston Hall. It is all very neat and very cozy—and a world away from her fruitless pursuit of Jeffrey Stratton. *I* am here tonight, Susannah, not he, and I very much want you to favor me with your company at dinner. Mind you, I will be disgustingly honest and say I would very much like to do more than just dine with you, but I must be content with what kindness I can wring from your hard little heart." His lips brushed softly over hers, and then he moved away, suddenly picking up the spangled gown. "If my eye serves me as well as it once did, this delightful confection should fit you to a T. Wear it, Susannah, for one of us at least should sparkle tonight."

She could see the love in his eyes as she slowly took the gown from him. "You do not play fairly, do you?" she said softly.

"No Devereux ever does—surely you have digested that particular pill by now," he said with a faint smile.

The Thames was almost invisible in the fog, although as Susannah walked slowly with Miles she could hear the wavelets of the swelling tide lapping against the embankment. The sound reminded her of Sanderby, and she wondered if Miles felt the same. But if he did, he said nothing.

It was almost dawn now, and after dining they had joined the other countless citizens in the streets on this momentous night. There was an atmosphere of bewilderment, for Britain did not know if she should laugh with joy or weep with vexation. Bells echoed all around in the foggy darkness, and for every one that pealed with triumph, there was another to toll for Nelson.

A carriage rumbled slowly past them, halting a little farther along the embankment. The footman jumped down and opened the door for the single passenger to alight. The tall, white-haired man climbed down awkwardly, leaning on a walking stick as he went to the wall overlooking the river. He stood there staring out over the dark water, a dejected air about the set of his shoulders and the loneliness of his solitary figure.

Miles halted abruptly, suddenly recognizing him. "Great God above, it's Pitt! Of all the damnable coincidences! Come, we'll walk back the way we came—"

"No, Miles," she said quickly, "I would prefer to walk on, perhaps speak to him."

He stared at her. "Approach the Immaculate P.? You cannot be serious!"

"But I am."

"Then I can only presume that your friendship with Stratton has meant an introduction to him."

"Yes."

"What lofty circles you move in now, Susannah," he said a little stiffly, glancing at the figure by the wall. "Or maybe they are far from lofty, according to one's persuasion."

"Miles, please . . ."

"If you intend speaking to him, then I cannot forbid you, but nothing will induce me to attempt civility to the leader of the most iniquitous government ever to hold office. You proceed as you wish, but I shall remain here."

She was taken aback by the vehemence in his voice and by the obvious loathing with which he regarded the Prime Minister, and she could not help wondering if a great deal of his reaction was due simply and solely to his hatred of Jeffrey Stratton. "You . . . you will wait for me?"

"I shall not leave without you."

She turned then and walked on toward the Prime Minister, hesitating a little nervously as she came closer. "Mr. Pitt?"

He glanced around sharply, not recognizing her immediately, and there was a chill in his expressive eyes which was meant to intimidate.

"It's Miss Garland, sir."

"Miss Garland?" The chill went away and he smiled, bowing. "Forgive me, I did not know you."

She stared at him, silenced by the dreadful change she saw in his face. His eyes were still bright and commanding, but something seemed to have gone out of them. It was as if the constant hard work and the systematic destruction of all that he had striven to build had struck deep into his frail health.

Apologetically he indicated his walking stick. "Forgive me if I do not bend a leg to you, but my gout will most definitely not permit such a salute," he said wryly. "The cure, as ever, awaits me in Bath, and soon I shall be forced to give in and take myself there."

"I trust the condition is not too distressing, sir."

"I endure, Miss Garland, I endure." He glanced beyond her toward Miles. "I see that you are accompanied by the omnipresent Whig stake—should anyone see London's queen of fashion tonight, they will not be able to accuse her of political bias, will they? You walk out with a Whig and exchange pleasantries with the worst Tory of them all."

She smiled. "That was not my intention, sir."

"No, I do not imagine that it was. Tell me, why are you out at this unfashionable hour? Does sleep evade you as it does me?"

"Everyone seems to be out tonight because of the victory."

He glanced away across the river again. "Trafalgar comes with a sting in its tail, does it not? Nelson was a great man, and a friend of mine—which is why you find me seeking solitude tonight instead of the company of my fellowman."

"Oh, I hope I am not intruding . . ." she began hastily.

"Not at all, Miss Garland. I believe the circumstances of our introduction more than allow for such an approach on your part, and indeed I would be grieved to think you would *not* speak to me as you have done tonight." He smiled again, and she saw the great charm which bound men like Jeffrey Stratton to him. The private side of William Pitt was a world away from the cold, aloof, proud side he showed in public. "And speaking of our introduction leads me to ask if you have any idea at all when Jeffrey Stratton will return to London?"

"I know nothing at all of Sir Jeffrey's plans, sir."

"No?" He seemed surprised.

"No."

"Then it would appear that my judgment has proved faulty yet again."

"Judgment, sir?"

"It is of no consequence, Miss Garland, merely an idle observation which has proved quite incorrect." His glance wandered thoughtfully toward Miles again.

She felt herself begin to flush a little at what she saw as the implication behind his words. "It would be equally as wrong to conclude that my friendship with my cousin is anything other than platonic, sir."

He smiled at that. "Oh, *I* have not concluded anything incorrect on that count, Miss Garland, but I rather think someone else may have, and that is maybe after all more to the point as far as you are concerned. I believe that after all, my first idle observation was the correct one. Not only do you have the ghosts of past quarrels and of a past wife to contend with, you also have male obstinacy, do you not?"

She stared at him, her face flaming with embarrassment now.

He smiled again. "Do not look so taken aback, Miss Garland, for my reputation for being disinterested in the fair sex is unfounded, and I am quite well aware of what goes on around me. I miss very little." He took out his watch then and flicked the lid back. "I fear that I must take myself back to Downing Street now, I have little desire to be found abroad at the moment."

She recovered a little at the change of subject. "You will be fêted, sir."

"That is what I fear, for I little deserve praise at the moment."

"Trafalgar is as much your victory as Lord Nelson's. One could not have achieved anything without the other."

"You are wrong, Miss Garland, but I thank you for saying it." He took her hand, raising it gently to his lips. "Never admit defeat in anything—until now that has always been my maxim, and now I hand it on to you, Miss Garland. Always be optimistic, and in the end you will gain what you want. And now I must bid you good night."

"Good night, sir."

She watched him climb painfully back into the carriage, assisted by the footman. He raised his hand to her once more as the carriage drew away, moving slowly along the embankment, where the air was luminous now as the freezing cold gradually became dawn over London.

She turned as Miles came to her, and she saw that his face was dark with anger and impatience. "Forgive me, Miles, I did not mean to leave you for so long."

"And what on God's earth had the Virgin Minister to say which kept you enthralled?" he said stiffly.

"Nothing I think you would wish to hear, Miles." She linked her arm determinedly through his. "I really must go home now, for there is a great deal of work to be going on with, and unless I have a little sleep . . ." She smiled up at him, quite set that she would not allow a quarrel to begin.

He hesitated, obviously still angry, but then he returned the smile and they walked back along the embankment.

22

Susannah's chaise could move only slowly through the congested streets. There was snow in the air, and an icy wind whipped through the heavy winter clothes of the passersby like freezing needles. Christmas turkeys were suspended in rows above the doors and windows of a poulterer's shop, their feathers ruffled by the wind as they swayed to and fro over the pavement. It was the sort of bitter December day which gave no pleasure and made the thought of Christmas shopping something to be shied away from, but it was the sort of day too which suited the mood of the city. A month had passed since Trafalgar, but the news which came out of Europe was only bad, culminating in a great French victory at Austerlitz which had shattered Mr. Pitt's hard-won coalition once and for all. Once again Britain was completely alone; her fainthearted allies had scattered before the might of France, and that solitariness was reflected in the stern faces of the people in the streets.

A large pink-and-gray-striped box lay beside Susannah on the drab upholstered seat, and it made a cheering splash of color on such a dismal day. Inside it lay Lady Ormanton's new Christmas ball gown, a garment which would grace the Court itself over the coming weeks. Susannah glanced at the box again, knowing that she had a secret hope that the Queen would notice the gown and inquire of Lady Ormanton where she had obtained it. Many of Susannah's gowns had been seen at Court, but the ladies who wore them were not as close to Her Majesty as Lady Ormanton now was—Ulla Ormanton was a German, a Schwellenberg no less, and the

201

Queen liked her. Susannah smiled then, for how was it possible not to like Lady Ormanton? She was so unaffected, so natural and genuine, her delight in each new garment was not forced, and Susannah always took great pleasure in delivering her orders in person. It was not always possible to deliver every garment to every customer, but for Lady Ormanton Susannah always made a special effort. And this particular ball gown was a very singular creation, one of which Susannah was justifiably proud. It was made of dark green silk, a stuff so fine that it took on a watery sheen, and it was rimmed with black lace which was threaded with bright silver. The lace covered the bodice and was looped richly at the back of the high waistline to trail down over the gown's small train. Silver sequins flashed here and there among the silken folds, making it very eye-catching without being overpowering, as it could so easily have been with someone as large as Lady Ormanton.

Susannah felt a deep satisfaction about this gown, both for the delight it would give its wearer and because the unusual lace had been stolen from right under Madame Hilary's nose. Hind's, the lace men, had been keeping it for the Empress of Tavistock Street, but once Susannah had spied it, she had been determined to have it for Lady Ormanton's gown. It had been a very sweet moment when Hind's had given in to her demands and had packed the lace and had it sent around to Catherine Lane. The arrival of the lace had signified to Susannah that the New House of Fashion had indeed arrived too, and was of sufficient importance to defy Madame Hilary over a length of reserved lace. Susannah had employed tactics which were less than honest, but then, as far as Madame Hilary was concerned, she did not think the niceties were required.

The chaise drove through the quieter streets of Mayfair now, entering a small square where Lady Ormanton's house stood. Lady Ormanton was at home for a few days, taking a little time off from her duties at Court, and the windows of her house were the only ones blazing with light in the otherwise deserted square. The chaise halted and Susannah climbed down, shivering in the bitter cold. It was only eleven o'clock in the morning, but it was gray and dismal; the lights glittering in the windows made a welcome, cheering sight.

As she turned to approach the entrance of the house, however, Susannah caught sight of a black carriage drawn up a little farther along the square. Jeffrey Stratton must be visiting his cousin's widow. Her immediate joy on realizing that he was back in Town was swiftly replaced by dismay, for she could not possibly contemplate delivering the gown to Lady Ormanton in person now. Coming face to face with Jeffrey Stratton was out of the question as things stood at present, and so no matter how much she hungered just to see him again, she would merely content herself with handing the box in at the door.

She smoothed her blue-and-white-checkered skirts and fastened all the many buttons of her white velvet spencer very carefully. With a final fluffing of the royal-blue ribbons of her bonnet, she picked up the box and went up the steps to the front door. But as the footman opened it, Lady Ormanton came hurrying down the staircase at the far end of the hall in a flurry of beige dimity. The large white day-cap on her hennaed hair wobbled to and fro as she crossed toward Susannah, and several little brown lap dogs pattered busily behind her to snuffle eagerly around Susannah's ankles.

Lady Ormanton clasped her hands in delight on seeing the box. "Ah, it is finished, *ja*? Come up vith me now, Miss Garland, I vont you shall take a glass of *Schnapps* with me to celebrate Christmas."

"Oh, but you must have guests . . ."

"Not at all, only Sir Jeffrey, and you know him already, *ja*? Come, now, it is vorm in the drawing room."

Without waiting for Susannah's reply, she turned on her heel and hurried back to the staircase. Slowly Susannah did as she was told, following her up the stairs with the little dogs still sniffing around her. The solemn footman brought up the rear, the pink-and-gray box held before him like an award placed on a velvet cushion.

Jeffrey was lounging on a sofa in the luxurious drawing room, and he got up immediately as they entered. His face was expressionless as he saw Susannah, but he bowed. "Miss Garland."

"Sir Jeffrey." She gave a curtsy which matched his bow for chill and reserve. Her heart was thundering but she kept her eyes averted as if he were of little consequence to her.

Lady Ormanton waved her toward a chair, but beyond that was far more interested in gaining entry to the box than with anything else. Susannah perched on the edge of the chair, her

203

reticule in her lap and her hands clasped neatly to stop them fidgeting nervously.

Lady Ormanton at last took the dark green gown from the box, and she gave a gasp of delight. "*O, sieh einmal*! Look, Jeffrey, look! Vill I not be very fine at Vindsor this Christmas?"

"You will look very elegant indeed, Ulla."

"Such a gown, so very beautiful, so very delicate!"

"Miss Garland has indeed excelled herself," he said politely.

"I must try it on," said Lady Ormanton with sudden decision. "Nothing vill do but that I try it on immediately!"

Susannah looked at her in dismay, for if Lady Ormanton went, then she would find herself alone with Jeffrey.

Lady Ormanton bore the gown to the doorway and then hesitated. "Jeffrey, you must entertain Miss Garland until I return."

"Naturally." He bowed.

The door closed, and silence swamped the room immediately. He cleared his throat. "May I offer you a drink, Miss Garland? Ulla would no doubt insist upon *Schnapps*, but that is not a very ladylike beverage."

"Thank you, but I do not want a drink, Sir Jeffrey."

"Would you have me in Ulla's black books? A sherry perhaps?"

She nodded. "Thank you."

He poured her a glass. "How providential that my one day in London should bring me to the very house where I will encounter you again."

"Providential?"

"Now I may ask you how does the New House of Fashion."

She met his gray eyes without flinching. "It does very well, sir."

"That is good—I may continue to Bath without further delay."

"Bath?"

"I am to visit Pitt."

"Oh, yes, of course."

"Formal conversation can be very embarrassing at times, can it not?" he said, flicking some fluff from his sleeve in a bored manner.

"It passes the time," she replied with commendable

204

coolness, for inside she felt as if her heart was breaking yet again.

His smile was disinterested as he turned to go to the window, looking out for a moment at the snow which had begun to fall. The heavy flakes curved past the glass on the ice-cold wind, sometimes clinging to the glass for a moment before being whisked on. The skies were a uniform lowering gray, and the lights in the drawing room made the day seem prematurely dark. She studied him for a while, wondering if her feelings had undergone any change at all, but she knew that they had not. As she looked at his weather-tanned face and the figure which was the epitome of masculine elegance, she knew that she was as attracted to him as ever and that had he shown any kindness at all she could not have hidden her feelings for a moment. But he was cold, his whole demeanor told her that his opinion of her had not altered, the indiscretions of which she was thought to be guilty were not to be forgotten or forgiven. Maybe even if they had, then she would still have lost the battle, for Elizabeth Stratton's memory was too strong and fresh still, and what chance would a mere dressmaker have against such a rival? Or against the other insurmountable obstacles which would forever separate Jeffrey Stratton from a woman with Devereux blood in her veins. She pondered a moment on Mr. Pitt's maxim of always being optimistic. No, she could not be optimistic in the face of all the overwhelming odds stacked against her.

To her relief, Lady Ormanton returned at last and the silence was broken by her delighted cries as she hurried into the room in the rustling silk gown. She turned, her eyes shining happily as she showed off the black lace bow and the dainty train. "There!" she cried. "Does it not look vell?"

Jeffrey went to her, taking her hand fondly. *"Du Eva,"* he murmured.

She flushed with pleasure. "A temptress? *I* am a temptress?"

"Undoubtedly—and if what I hear of his proclivities of late, you will have to flee from the Prince of Wales when he claps eyes on you in this wondrous creation."

Lady Ormanton beamed at Susannah. "Miss Garland, I cannot tell you how delighted I am vith this, you have made me a very happy voman."

"I'm very glad to have pleased you, my lady."

"I promise I shall *flaunt* it at Vindsor for you, the Qveen herself must admire it and know how excellent you are."

Susannah smiled, putting down her glass and getting to her feet determinedly. "I trust you have a most excellent Christmas, my lady."

"You are leaving now?"

"I must return to Catherine Lane, there is so much to do."

Jeffrey smiled faintly. "The work of the rising *couturière* is never done," he murmured.

Lady Ormanton took his remark at its face value, clasping Susannah's gloved hand firmly. "Of course, of course, how foolish of me."

Jeffrey went to the door, turning to offer Susannah his arm. "Allow me to escort you out, Miss Garland."

She paused, unwilling to offer him any advantage of her in the slightest, but he took her hand and drew it through his arm.

Lady Ormanton swirled the rustling silk gown again. "*Frohe Weinacht*, Miss Garland, *Frohe Weinacht*."

"A happy Christmas," translated Jeffrey for her.

"Oh, yes—and a happy Christmas to you too, Lady Ormanton."

They descended the curving staircase. "You have made Ulla very happy, Miss Garland, and for that I thank you."

"There is no need to thank me, sir, for I am only too glad to do all I can for Lady Ormanton, as I find her a very agreeable person."

He paused then beneath the swaying ball of Christmas greenery suspended high from the ceiling above, its scarlet ribbons fluttering in the rising heat from the chandeliers in the hallway. "Tell me, Miss Garland, how is your *disagreeable* cousin?"

Stiffly she withdrew her hand. "As far as I am aware, he is well enough, but I have not seen him for a month now."

"Perhaps you have had a surfeit of each other's company."

She stared at him, a flame of anger spurting into sudden life as she raised her hand and struck his face hard. She would have struck him again had he not caught her wrist. "That is quite enough," he said softly, his face dark.

"How dare you say what you have just said!" she cried, tears springing to her eyes. "How *dare* you!"

"I said nothing untoward. I fancy rather that it is your guilty conscience which leads you down the wrong path."

"I have no guilty conscience, and I came to the very conclusion you fully intended I should!" she cried angrily.

He gazed at her flushed face, her violet eyes bright with unshed tears and her honey-colored hair lying in gentle curls against her cheeks. "It's a pity you're so much the Devereux," he murmured, "for a man could make quite a fool of himself over you had he the inclination. But to make a fool of himself over a woman who is not only a Devereux but is also a whore is going beyond mere foolishness into the realms of insanity itself."

She felt cold then, her anger evaporating, to be replaced by a despair which she hid only by looking away from him. Without another word she went on down the staircase, hurrying blindly across the hallway to open the door without the aid of a footman. She didn't glance back once as she ran down the steps to the waiting chaise.

The postboy looked curiously at her as she entered the carriage, and as he closed the door behind her he saw her turn away, her face hidden in her hands as she wept. He glanced back at the door of the house, and then with a philosophical shrug he began to whistle as he climbed back onto the horse and urged the animal away along the square, where the swirling snowflakes soon swallowed it from sight of the house.

23

The snow lingered over that dreary Christmas, but melted swiftly in the new year of 1806. January was a wet month, the deluge of rain which followed the snow leaving great pools of water in the streets and forcing harassed pedestrians to Herculean effort in order to avoid being saturated by passing carriages and in order to cross from one side of a thoroughfare to the other. Stepping out-of-doors at all was not to be recommended, unless positively essential, and that, together with Mr. Frederick Normans going down with a feverish cold, had put paid to any progress in the warm friendship between him and Miss Annie Jones. Christmas had been anything but dreary for Annie, for she was convinced that Mr. Normans was on the point of proposing to her, and the excited anticipation was quite unbearable for her—and for Susannah, who had put up with her constant chatter about Mr. Normans' undoubted qualities. Annie was quite determined that the moment the weather relented, and Mr. Normans' cold had gone, the friendship would be resumed so that the much-awaited proposal would materialize at last.

To this end she cornered Susannah in the showroom one morning late in January.

"I . . . I was wondering . . ."

Susannah smiled. "Mr. Normans again?"

Annie flushed, smoothing down her simple blue skirts nervously. "I don't talk about him *that* much."

Susannah merely raised a quizzical eyebrow and said nothing.

"I was wondering if I could possibly . . . *we* could possibly invite him to dinner one evening soon."

"I hardly think you require my presence."

"It isn't proper if I dine alone with him."

"Annie Jones, you have been walking out with him alone, sitting in his house alone with him, and so on, these few months now. I believe it is a little late to begin considering propriety, don't you?"

"Please, Susannah."

Susannah smiled fondly. "By all means invite him here, and I will play gooseberry for a while. But I swear that I shall then find something absolutely essential to do and I shall leave you to hold hands. Oh, go on with you, don't look at me like that, for I know full well that at the very *least* you hold hands!"

"Susannah Garland, I don't know what you mean!"

"No? Well, not even my cat looks quite as smug as you do of late, Miss Jones, not even when she's been at the cream, too!"

Annie grinned then. "I think I will return to my duties in the workroom before I have to endure any more of your insults." But before leaving, she hugged Susannah quickly, and then turned to hurry out, her skirts swishing behind her.

A short while later, the rain tamping on its roof, a carriage bearing Emily Cowper arrived in Catherine Lane. Susannah looked out in surprise, for Emily was hardly one to step out in such weather merely to come to her dressmaker! Gathering her pink skirts carefully, Emily emerged from the carriage and under cover of the large black umbrella her coachman held over her, she hurried up the steps into the New House of Fashion, followed by her maid.

The maid immediately began to remove the costly pale pink pelisse which Susannah had produced the previous summer, while Emily fidgeted crossly, shaking the woman's arm to attract her attention. "Have a care," she said, moving her lips exaggeratedly for the maid to follow, "I must go to Holland House afterward and there must not be a single crease, not a single mark upon that pelisse."

Affronted, the deaf maid draped the garment over her arm, giving a loud, disparaging sniff as she did so. She stalked to a position by the showroom window and stood with her back to her mistress, her whole body quivering with rage. Her stiff attitude said as loudly as any voice that *she* knew perfectly well

209

how to treat costly velvet garments and that there had been no need at all for the warning!

Amused, Emily came toward Susannah. "Ah, how very pleasant it always is to come to this place."

"Please sit down by the fire, Lady Cowper."

Emily took one of the chairs, stretching out her dainty toes to the warmth and sighing deliciously as she settled back in the comfortable chair. "I have, on this very auspicious morning, decided that a ball I have long intended holding shall now go ahead with as much speed as possible. It shall be as grand an affair as can be managed out of Season."

"That is a very sudden decision."

"The decision has been made a long time, it was merely a case of waiting for the moment," said Emily mysteriously. "But now I must come to the highly embarrassing part of this interview."

"Embarrassing?"

"Well, what else can it be called, and how can I face myself, let alone the rest of the *monde*, when I have to admit to you that I want a gown like that dark green silk you made for Lady Ormanton? Really, Miss Garland, it's too bad of you to clothe that Tory German dumpling in a gown so glorious that it was the envy of Windsor at Christmas. I *must* appear at my ball in just such a gown—not the selfsame green silk, of course, for I must not be too obvious."

"Of course not."

"You have the silk in another color?"

"I'm afraid not, there was only that bolt in the stockroom. Maybe one of the shops can supply something . . ."

"I do not wish to wait at all. But surely you have something else which would be just the thing? I wish to look especially well at this ball."

"For Lord P.?"

"Who else? Oh, he really is the most gloriously beautiful of men," she said with a sigh, her large eyes soft as she thought of her lover. "I know, I will inspect the contents of your stockroom myself!"

"My *stockroom*? But it is a very dismal and uninteresting place, Lady Cowper."

"You could be secreting something exceedingly desirable in that Aladdin's cave, and if you are, then I fully intend discovering it. This gown has to be perfect in every single way."

Susannah laughed, leading her important and persistent

customer across the hallway to the stockroom. *All* Emily's orders were very special, very different—and there hadn't been one yet which had not been urgently needed for some reason or other. She seemed to live life at a great pace, hurrying excitedly from one grand moment to the next.

She drew back the curtains which protected the stockroom from the daylight, and the pale winter morning fell faintly over the cluttered shelves and drawers. Emily stood in amazement, shivering a little in her flimsy gown after the warmth of the fire in the showroom.

"But there's so much here!" she said at last.

"An establishment like this requires many things, my lady."

"So it seems. Ah, what is that!" Emily pounced on a bolt of lawn cambric in the most delicate of pale greens. She pulled it from the shelf and put it on the table, unrolling it a little and running the dainty cloth over her fingers. "I do believe that in one moment I have found the very thing for my gown. It's so fine I declare it to be positively wicked!"

"It will be if you neglect to wear an undergown and then stand with the light behind you," warned Susannah, smiling.

Emily's eyes were impish. "Really? How very naughty that would be of me." Her smiled faded a little then. "Has anyone else had this cloth yet?"

"No, I only purchased it just before Christmas. It was at Grafton House, somehow or other they had discovered it at the back of their store. They told me that it was originally intended for the poor French Queen."

"This was for Marie Antoinette?"

"That is what I have been told."

Emily was even more delighted then, holding the filmy cloth against her body to study the way it fell into soft folds. "Oh, this wonderful day goes from good to even better."

Susannah glanced at the rain driving dismally past the window. "This is a *wonderful* day?"

"Why yes—oh, surely you've heard the news?"

"What news?"

"The reason why every Whig heart bursts with joy today! Pitt is dead! That is the reason for the ball, a ball I have been intending to hold ever since the odious fellow showed signs of ill health!"

Susannah felt quite numb. Mr. Pitt was dead? "It cannot be so," she said softly. "It just cannot be so . . ."

"I assure you that it is. We are free of the Tory yoke at

last, for with Pitt gone there are no Tories of stature. The way is clear for the Whigs—and for the Prince of Wales, of course. If the King should ever become . . . er, ill again, then there will be no obstacle to a regency anymore. Oh, this coming Season is bound to be the very best ever!"

"Yes."

"I swear your face is as long as Jeffrey Stratton's undoubtedly is at the moment! You should not show such woeful Tory leanings to your Whig customers, Miss Garland, for that does not do at all."

"I . . . I just find it hard to believe that he's dead."

"Yes, I do agree that the fellow seemed to be first minister for positively *ever*! However, it's all done with now and there are surely much more pleasing times ahead for us all. Oh, no, look at the time—I'm expected at Holland House and I've chitchatted with you so long that I haven't time to look at your drawings now!"

"I will have my folders sent to your house, my lady."

"Oh, that would be capital. Now, where is that maid?" Emily hurried back to the showroom.

Susannah remained in the quiet of the stockroom for a moment. She wasn't hearing Emily's twittering voice, she was hearing Mr. Pitt as he spoke to her on the night of Trafalgar: *I deserve little praise at the moment. . . .* Little praise? How could that be so, when he had worked himself to death itself in the service of his country?

But she managed a bright enough smile as Emily took her leave, and she promised faithfully that the bolt of pale green lawn would be set aside exclusively for the wonderful ball gown Emily intended dazzling the *monde* with at the celebratory ball. A *celebratory* ball. . . .

Susannah stood on the doorstep, the cold sweeping over her and the smell of the rain all around. There were no bells tolling for poor Mr. Pitt as they had tolled for Nelson, no windows and doors decorated in his memory. She lowered her eyes to the rain-washed streets.

For one day toward the end of February the bells of London tolled for William Pitt. On that cold winter's day he was laid to rest in Westminster Abbey and the nation mourned the passing of a second hero.

That night, as the bitter wind blustered through the streets and howled over rooftops, Susannah dressed in her warm bedroom. A fire crackled in the little hearth and the mellow light of candles moved gently over the bed and on the silk-clad walls. The only sound apart from the fire was of hairpins dropping into a little silver dish on the dressing table as Annie put the final touches to Susannah's hair.

Susannah had dressed with special care, paying close attention to every detail of her appearance. She wore a dress of damson satin, trimmed at the hem and on the little puffed sleeves with guipure lace dyed to match, and a silver comb was the final touch in her tawny hair. She had used her precious box of Chinese papers to put a blush on her pale cheeks, and in spite of the warmth in the little room, she felt cold. She smiled as her glance fell on the lacquered box of colored papers. It was strange that she still felt it to be so precious and to be used so sparingly, for now the price of replacing it would not have concerned her as it had when she had purchased it those years ago at Sanderby. She caught a glimpse of Annie's disapproving face in the mirror, and to stop her from chiding her yet again for what she intended doing that night, Susannah caught her hand to admire the ring which adorned the fourth finger. "It truly is a very fine ring, Annie, he's done you proud."

"It was his mother's ring. And don't change the subject."

Susannah sighed. "Please, Annie . . ."

"You're a fool to go, he'll not thank you for it, and after the last time you were unfortunate enough to come face to face with him—"

"I just feel that I should go tonight."

"Why? Why give him the opportunity of being unpleasant to you again? He made his feelings quite plain before Christmas at Lady Ormanton's. I've never seen you as upset as you were when you came back here that day, Susannah, and I'll never forgive him for doing it to you."

"Annie, I would not be being true to myself—or to poor Mr. Pitt—if I did not go to Sir Jeffrey and just express my sorrow. That's all."

"He'll have the door closed in your face," said Annie shortly, anxious at this eleventh hour to spare Susannah further pain at Jeffrey Stratton's hands. "Or better still, I pray that he won't be in and you'll be forced to just leave your fool card!"

"He is in Town, he attended the state funeral today." Susannah stood, shaking out the damson satin and studying

213

her reflection in the mirror. "I'm definitely going to Berkeley Square tonight, Annie, and that is the end of it. Oh, I *do* appreciate why you've been nagging me all day, and I confess that your misgivings are probably very well founded, but I must do this. You do understand, don't you?"

"No."

"Now you are being deliberately unhelpful." She picked up her gloves and reticule, and Annie draped the jewel-colored cashmere shawl over her shoulders.

A short while later she emerged from the house to enter the waiting chaise. But she trembled as the carriage conveyed her toward Jeffrey's house.

The lights blazed in the windows of the house as she alighted, but as she approached the door she felt suddenly quite composed. Let him do his worst, she knew that she was doing the right thing, and that was what really mattered tonight.

Contrary to Annie's expectation, the door was not closed in Susannah's face, and she was shown immediately up to the magnificent drawing room on the first floor. The room was in semidarkness, the chandeliers unlit, their crystal drops moving gently in the rising warmth from the bright fires. The only other light came from a many-branched candlestick on one of the small tables.

Jeffrey stood as she was shown in, and she saw immediately that he was alone. His black coat had been tossed carelessly over a chair and his cravat was undone. The front of his frilled shirt looked vividly white and the dull black satin on his waistcoat shone just a little in the candlelight. Slowly he bent to replace something in the pool of light by the candlestick—the miniature of his dead wife. Susannah's heart sank, for she realized that she had interrupted a very private moment.

The butler cleared his throat and at a slight nod from his master closed the door and left. Silence descended over the room. "Well," said Jeffrey at last, "I did not for one moment imagine I would ever again find myself receiving an unsolicited visit from you, Miss Garland."

"Nor would you, had this terrible thing not happened to poor Mr. Pitt."

He gave a short laugh. "That is honesty for you."

"I'm very sorry he died, Sir Jeffrey, and because I know how very close you were to him, I came here tonight to tell you how I felt. I saw him again, you see, on the night the news of Trafalgar reached London, and—"

"I know. He told me."

"I liked him very much."

"All those who saw the real Pitt liked him. But he's gone now, and there's no bringing him back. Would that there were, for Britain is now governed by incompetents."

"Surely they are far from that."

"They have laughingly been termed the Ministry of All the Talents," he said scathingly. "*Talents*! Between them they have less talent than Pitt had in his left hand! A coalition of gray Tories and even grayer Whigs!"

She did not know what to say, and she felt uncomfortable in his presence because of the bitter echoes of their last meeting. She swallowed. "W-well, that was all I came to say, and I will not impose upon you further tonight, Sir Jeffrey." She turned to go.

His cold voice halted her. "You dressed so very finely and made yourself so exquisitely lovely merely to say a few sentences of condolence to me? How very flattered I should be!"

"No, sir, you should not be. The care I took with my appearance was on Mr. Pitt's account—you did not enter into my thoughts."

He gave a grim smile at that. "Oh, you'll do very well at Court with that imperious manner when the time comes. Let me see, now, how did I prophesy it would go for you? Ah, yes—two Seasons should do it. Well, you have one tucked under your dainty belt and another soon to begin. And it is rumored that the Queen's dreadful German dressmaker is on the point of retiring—which should smooth your path to glory once and for all. I wonder you can contain your excitement."

She said nothing.

"Silence, Miss Garland?"

"There is more dignity in silence than in pettish outbursts, sir."

"You would appear to bring out the very worst in me."

"I'm very sorry to reduce you to such a desperate low, Sir Jeffrey," she said, continuing to the door. She was blinking back the tears. Outwardly she was cold and aloof, but each hard word he uttered cut straight through to her heart.

"Susannah?"

She hesitated, and then turned.

"It was unforgivable of me to turn this into yet another verbal brawl. I am sorry."

She stared at him. His mercurial changes confused her. One moment he was harsh and derisive, and the next warm and gentle. He came closer, and saw the unshed tears in her eyes.

He caught her hand then, raising her palm to his lips. "Forgive me for that, and for those other occasions when I have hurt you. I know that I do not deserve forgiveness, that my conduct cannot be justified in any way, but nonetheless I ask it of you."

His touch was like fire, and her breath caught. Oh, how easy it was for him, how simple to cause such pain and then cast his spell over her again, to bring her to the edge of tears and then rescue her with a single gesture. But he must not know how he affected her still; she must hide it if she was to salvage her pride.

She drew her hand away. "Of course you are forgiven, sir," she said lightly. "What possible good would it do me to be continually at loggerheads with my . . . er, business associate?"

There was a light in his eyes as he nodded. "What good indeed?" he murmured. "For the smooth running of the New House of Fashion is of paramount importance, is it not?"

Paramount importance? No, not *paramount*—it would always come second. But she smiled. "Naturally it is, sir."

"Then do not let me delay your speedy return to your Castle of Calico."

"Good night, Jeffrey."

"Good night, Susannah."

24

~~

Spring arrived late that year, the watery sunshine of April doing little to warm the air, but with the approach of May the *beau monde* began to return to London for the new Season. But the arrival of fashionable society saw the departure of Jeffrey Stratton for his country seat. He said nothing to Susannah, choosing instead to inform her through his agent. Why even that gesture could hurt so was a mystery, for she knew that she could never win him, that he had never given her any reason to hope to the contrary—and yet receiving the brief message from the agent had cut deep. For all her resolve, she could not shut Jeffrey Stratton out of her heart, no matter how much she tried. He had told her that she broke his rules—yet when she made rules of her own designed to exclude him from her life, she broke the rules herself by thinking of him constantly and allowing each thing he did to reach her. But outwardly she hid her heartbreak well, immersing herself in the world of high fashion and working so hard that only Annie Jones guessed the truth.

But fate had a surprise in wait for the New House of Fashion, a surprise which Jeffrey would have done all in his power to avert had he known of it. It happened on a night late in April, when the air was bitterly cold outside but the dying fires in the showroom took the chill from the night.

Susannah and Annie were working late to rearrange the room. Some fine new silks had been purchased and Annie was draping a particularly handsome primrose taffeta to make a display in a corner. Susannah put daffodils in the crystal vases which would greet her customers the following morning. The flowers smelled so fresh and clean and they reminded her of that last visit to Sanderby with Jeffrey. Thinking of Sanderby brought thoughts of Miles too, for in March the birth of his son had been announced, although the baby's arrival had not meant a reconciliation between Miles and Agnes. The opposite rather, for the estrangement seemed more rancorous than ever. There was no hope of Miles changing his mind about a divorce, and so Agnes consoled herself with her French lover, a lover who, as the *on-dits* would have it, was ever hopeful of the possibility of divorce so that eventually the Winston fortune would come his way.

Annie gave the primrose taffeta a final tweak and then stood back to survey it critically. "Will that do?"

Susannah nodded without looking.

"Brooding again?"

"Mm?"

"I asked you if you were brooding again."

Susannah looked up then. "I'm sorry . . . yes, I suppose I am brooding a little."

"What about this time? About Madame Hilary maybe receiving the royal warrant?"

Susannah picked up the journal which had been published that very day. The tiny paragraph seemed to leap out at her.

We await with baited breath the onset of the new Season, more especially to see what delights emerge from the New House of Fashion and what the *beau monde* is to make of the whispers that a certain Madame H— is to receive at last the ultimate royal accolade. Windsor calls and Tavistock Street answers.

Annie smiled. "It *is* only a rumor, you know."

"Sir Jeffrey said that the Queen's German dressmaker is thinking of retiring—and the Princesses already go to Madame Hilary."

"The Queen will not do something simply because her daughters do," said Annie firmly. "Everyone knows that there is precious little royal love lost between them. You heard what Princess Amelia says about her mother, she absolutely *hates* her!"

"I know, but this paragraph does seem to have a ring of truth about it, that's all. And anyway, what right have I to hope for anything from Windsor? I have had one successful

Season—much more successful than anyone has a right to expect, and I must be content with that." Susannah put the journal down again and took up some more of the daffodils which had been purchased in Covent Garden market that morning.

"It's not just this business of the royal warrant, is it? It's that odious *man*, isn't it?"

"I don't think about him at all."

"No—which is why you cry yourself to sleep at nights."

Susannah looked swiftly at her and then returned her attention firmly to the daffodils.

Annie turned suddenly as a new sound reached her ears. "Listen, isn't that a carriage?" She hurried to the window and held it slightly aside to look at the shadowy vehicle drawn up at the curb. "It's a lady and her maid, but they're so well cloaked that I can't recognize them."

There was a knock at the door, and Annie smoothed her rustling brown skirts and straightened her day-cap before hurrying to open it. Susannah listened, but could not tell anything from the low voices. Then Annie returned quickly, her face pale and startled as she stood aside in the entrance of the showroom.

"It . . . it's the Princess Amelia," she said faintly, curtsying very low as the two women entered the room.

Stunned, Susannah sank into a curtsy too, rising then to look in surprise at the two heavily cloaked figures. Her surprise sharpened when the Princess threw back her hood to reveal that her face was further concealed by a small mask, which she now removed.

"Miss Garland."

"Your Royal Highness."

"I come at this hour because no one must know that I am here. Tolly, my cloak." She said this last in French.

The lady-in-waiting removed the cloak.

The Princess wore a gown of deep crimson brocade, and rubies sparkled in her ears and at her throat. Her fragile beauty was quite breathtaking, although Susannah could see that her health had deteriorated a little and she was more frail now, the telltale flush of color on her cheeks that little bit more pronounced.

The lady-in-waiting was anxious, conducting her conversation with the Princess in what she thought was the safety of French. "Your Highness, I beg of you to reconsider."

"Nothing shall stop me this time, Tolly, nothing at all. I shall marry my beloved angel, and not you or anyone else shall stand in my way."

"And if the Queen should discover—or, God forbid, if the King himself . . . Would you have a recurrence of his illness on your conscience, my dearest one?"

"They will *not* find out, though, will they?" The Princess turned away a little angrily. "I am forced to live like a nun and I will no longer submit. Look at me, Tolly, how many years do I have left?"

"Please don't say that," whispered the lady-in-waiting, tears springing to her eyes.

"But it must be faced, Tolly, and I will not face it alone. I will marry Sir Charles Fitzroy, because anyway I am his wife in everything but name already."

"Highness!"

The Princess's eyes flashed. "Make of that what you will, Tolly, but it remains that I wish our union to be blessed in the sight of God, and if I must resort to this lying and subterfuge in order to do what is the right and Christian thing, then I will do it!"

A little belatedly the lady-in-waiting glanced at Susannah's expressionless face, wondering if maybe a woman with Devereux blood would have more than a mere sprinkling of fashionable French phrases at her fingertips. But Susannah's face reassured her somehow, and she returned her attention to the agitated Princess.

"Please do not upset yourelf, your Royal Highness, you know that if you do you will maybe bring on the coughing."

"Then simply reassure me with your loyalty, Tolly."

Tolly sank into a low curtsy. "Always you will have that, your Highness. I will never desert you or play you false."

The Princess smiled then, putting a gentle hand on the bowed powdered head. "I know, Tolly. And now . . . the wedding gown."

"Highness, I must beg of you to be discreet."

"Then we shall tell fibs about it. Who is to know anyway?" The Princess smiled at Susannah then. "Miss Garland, I wish to order an especially fine ball gown—for my father's birthday in June. The gown must be a complete secret, no one must hear the tiniest whisper about it, and so I have come to you. Madame Hilary cannot be relied upon now that she seeks the warrant from my mother the Queen. Besides, I recall that I was once very well pleased with your suggestion about putting black fur upon one of my gowns, and I would like you to dream up something just as wonderful for me this time."

"Yes, your Highness."

"I will come to you for my fittings, I will come late at night like this, and the gown when finished must be delivered to Tolly here in a plain box—none of your well-known pink-and-gray stripes."

"I understand, your Highness," said Susannah, her heart beating swiftly, with both excitement and fear. This was something bordering on the dangerous; she would be aiding and abetting a Princess of the Blood to make a clandestine marriage. What could be the possible outcome for the New House of Fashion of such involvement?

"I will see your drawings, if you please, Miss Garland."

Susannah ushered the Princess into one of the chairs by the still-glowing fire and then hurried to bring her folders. Briefly her glance met Annie's. When she returned, the Princess was recovering from a brief bout of painful coughing, and her already flushed cheeks were flaming. Beads of perspiration stood out on her forehead, and Tolly was fussing around anxiously. Annie brought some water and in a while the Princess recovered sufficiently to begin perusing the drawings.

After a moment she glanced across at the display of silks in the corner, nodding at the primrose taffeta which Annie had so painstakingly arranged only a little earlier. "I know which material I shall have, Miss Garland. May I see that primrose taffeta more closely?"

Susannah took down the heavy bolt of cloth, and the Princess inspected it for a moment before nodding, a smile on her lips. "This is the very thing, Miss Garland. Please set it aside for me."

"Yes, your Royal Highness."

"And this is the gown I have chosen." The Princess took out one particular drawing.

Tolly was horrified. "It is very exquisite, Highness, but for a *bride*?" The conversation lapsed swiftly back into French now that it touched upon such private matters again.

"What is wrong with it, Tolly?"

"It is very *décolleté*."

"But far from vulgar."

"Oh, it isn't *vulgar*, it's—"

"I find it quite perfect, and it will go so well with my necklace."

"Necklace?"

"The one I saw in Christofier's, the one I shall of a certainty purchase tomorrow."

"But, Highness, that necklace was impossibly expensive," cried the lady-in-waiting. "You have already borrowed four thousand pounds from the Prince of Wales—"

"Nonsense, Tolly, that four thousand pounds was a gift. I shall have the yellow diamond, I am determined on it."

Poor Tolly fell silent. Her mistress was hopelessly extravagant, and her cloistered, impossible life at Court had made her willful as well. She had been restrained and confined too much, and her present behavior was the inevitable result. But as Tolly looked at her mistress's flushed cheeks and delicate appearance, she knew in her heart that the extravagance would soon stop. It would have to when ill health took its final toll.

When all the arrangements had been made, measurements taken, and final details agreed upon, the Princess prepared to leave again. She put on the mask and drew the hood over her face. "And remember, Miss Garland, no one must know of my visit, no one at all."

"You may rely upon my discretion, your Royal Highness."

"Not even your seamstresses must know my identity," said the Princess, glancing at Annie.

"Miss Jones is my forewoman, your Highness, and I trust her completely."

"Very well. Send word to Tolly whenever it is time for a fitting. But the gown must be completed as swiftly as possibly—I require it one month from today."

"Yes, your Highness."

Susannah and Annie sank into deep curtsies again as their royal visitor took her leave.

Afterward Annie looked at Susannah. "Why all the secrecy about a ball gown? Why must no one know of her visits, and why does she want the gown so quickly? The King's birthday isn't until June and it's only April now."

"It isn't a ball gow, Annie, it's a wedding gown."

Annie stared then, her hand creeping to her throat. "But . . . but there hasn't been any announcement."

"There isn't going to be one. She's marrying Sir Charles Fitzroy, and the whole affair is most definitely a close secret."

"But, Susannah—"

"We've been told that it is a gown to wear at the King's birthday celebrations, and that is what we must work by. Only you and I must know, Annie, and I must have your word on that."

"You have it, of course. But I think you may say farewell to any hope of having the warrant to the Queen if your part in all this becomes common knowledge. I know that you speak French, that your father taught you—how long before someone else realizes that little fact too?"

"I know, Annie, but what else can I do? Would you have me refuse her?"

"Perhaps you should have done."

"That is far easier said than done, Annie Jones."

"It will still be a very hot kettle of fish for you if you're found out."

"You saw her, Annie—how long does she have to take any happiness from life? For that reason alone I will make her the very finest gown any bride ever had, and she will marry the man she loves knowing that she looks as beautiful as it is possible to look. I will help her, for I feel so sorry for her— just as Tolly helps her when she knows that it is wrong."

Annie put a hand over Susannah's then, picking up the chosen drawing and looking at it for a moment. It was of a high-waisted tunic gown, its long train falling so that the front of the gown parted a little to reveal a delicate under-gown of the finest white silk, which with the primrose taffeta would look so fresh and springlike. The trimmings were to be of strings of tiny seed pearls, stitched one by one on the sleeves and hem in the shape of leaves and flowers.

"Well," said Annie with a smile, "in this gown she will indeed be the most beautiful of brides, Susannah Garland. I wish only for your sake that it was to be a joyous public occasion instead of the clandestine and illegal affair it will undoubtedly be."

The fashionable carriages thronging Bond Street were decked with garlands of flowers and the coachmen all wore new livery to celebrate the King's birthday. There was a lightheartedness about the capital on that fine June day, for the Royal Navy was still master of the high seas and the French were kept at bay. The summer months had arrived, the Season was in full swing, and the element of unease and danger brought by the war seemed somehow very far away.

Susannah and Annie alighted from their chaise outside Grafton House, and Susannah smiled to see how quickly Annie retied her bonnet ribbons and straightened her skirts. "I'm sure he will be so dazzled simply by seeing you that he will not notice if your ribbons are a little awry."

"But *I* must know I look my very best."

The shop was very busy, but this time Susannah's arrival was a far different matter than from that other time when she had been prepared to make a great scene about some artificial flowers. Now the assistants flocked to greet her, eager to be as accommodating as they possibly could for the mistress of the New House of Fashion. But Susannah had gone there on a very particular mission and it was Annie's Mr. Frederick Normans who led the two women through to the storerooms at the back of the shop.

He drew out a large drawer in a dark cupboard and stood aside, indicating the rare and costly French lace which lay there, its soft creamy threads caught in the dusty light from a rear window. The sunbeams danced over the delicately worked whirls of flowers and stars as Susannah lifted the lace out and held it up, her breath held in wonder at the magnificence of the work. Her eyes shone as she glanced at Mr. Normans. "I hardly dare to ask you how much this is or how you managed to come by it, sir."

"Mr. Pitt's taxes did not deter all the Kentish smugglers, ma'am."

"So it would seem. The quality of this lace is quite superlative. I do not think I have ever seen finer, even from the French."

"The price is, I fear, accordingly high."

"I'll warrant it is. However, French lace is an absolute necessity in high fashion, sir, so I will bow to your exorbitant demands and agree whatever is asked,"

He glanced around and then leaned confidentially closer. "They're asking seventeen," he whispered, "but they'll take fifteen, of that I'm assured. I . . . er, told Madame H. that they would take fourteen, and that is what she has offered." He winked at Annie, who blushed immediately.

Susannah smiled. "You are truly very kind, sir."

"No, ma'am, I have given my heart, and that is what matters," he said gallantly, bowing over Annie's hand. Annie dissolved into complete flusterment, and Susannah took the opportunity of leaving them alone for a moment.

She returned to the main shop. A tray of new ribbons lay on the dark wooden counter, and she drew it closer to sort through the contents, always alert for something a little different and eye-catching with which to trim her garments. The drone of conversation drifted around her, but she paid little heed. The bell above the door tinkled and she didn't glance around, holding up a particularly dainty strand of silvery ribbon and pondering whether it would look good upon Lady Ormanton's latest order. Suddenly a voice she knew only too well leaped out at her from among the low murmurings in the shop.

"Well, there's such a to-do at Court, I can tell you. After a very odd and unexplained illness, the Princess Amelia has now sent word that she is still too unwell to attend the King's birthday drawing-room tonight."

Susannah turned slowly to look at Agnes Devereux. Miles's wife had regained her slender figure after having her son and she looked quite lovely in her rose-pink muslin gown, her red hair almost hidden by a leghorn bonnet tied with crimson ribbons and decorated with roses. Her shawl almost dragged on the floor as she turned to her companion, Lady Cynthia Greville, a Whig hostess of some standing and Agnes' close friend and confidante. Susannah knew instinctively that both women were fully aware of her presence, although there was nothing to tell that that was so from Agnes' stance as she snapped her fingers at a waiting assistant. "Bring those shawls, if you please."

He bowed and dutifully brought an armful of the colorful cashmere shawls, which he displayed over the counter before her.

Lady Cynthia held up a particularly gawdy shawl. "The Princess is unwell?" she asked in a falsely loud voice which was guaranteed to continue holding the attention of everyone in the shop.

"That is what we are supposed to believe, but I must say that she looked in the very pink of it when I saw her yesterday," said Agnes, glancing for the first time at Susannah, her lovely eyes malevolent.

Susannah's unease deepened as she returned her attention to the drawer of ribbons.

"Her health isn't perfect, my dear," murmured Lady Cynthia.

"There's nothing wrong with her *à ce moment*, of that I can assure you—at least, nothing which would normally have kept her from the King's birthday. Actually, there is a very interesting rumor . . ." Agnes glanced around the shop in a way which was so ridiculously conspiratorial that had Susannah not been so very anxious suddenly then she would have laughed aloud. "The rumor is, my dear, that the Princess has upped and married Fitzroy."

The silence was so stunned that the traffic in the street outside seemed suddenly much nearer. Susannah's hands shook as she continued determinedly sorting through the ribbons, as if she had heard nothing. The ribbons slithered over her gloved fingers as if alive.

"Is that so?" murmured Lady Cynthia, shaking out the shawl. "Well, perhaps that would be no surprise—making illegal marriages would appear to be the forte of our royal family, as witness the strange affair of the dear Prince of Wales and Mrs. Fitzherbert. However, Agnes my dear, how can you be so sure about this particular rumor?"

"Because I've seen the dress she wore."

A stir rippled through the listening shop, and Susannah's heart seemed to stop for a moment as she gazed blindly at the blur of ribbons. Where was Annie? Oh, *why* didn't she come quickly?

Agnes shook her head at the shawl, and Lady Cynthia put it down and lifted another. Agents sighed heavily. "Oh, I wasn't meant to see the wretched rag, that Tolly person made all haste to slam the door in my face, but I saw it clearly enough—*and* the veil. That was what gave it away, you see, the veil. I mean, she wasn't dressing like that to attend confirmation, was she?" Agnes gave a trill of brittle laughter.

"What was the gown like?" asked Lady Cynthia.

"A tunic of primrose taffeta with an undergown of white silk. Quite extravagant and unsuitable for someone of the Princess's coloring. Most definitely not Madame Hilary." Agnes looked deliberately along the counter at Susannah then. "It had the mark of a lesser dressmaker, don't you know. Quite distinctive in its vulgar way. Do you not agree, Miss Garland?"

226

All eyes moved to Susannah, who turned slowly to face the opposition. "I beg your pardon, Lady Agnes?"

"The garment in question is surely vulgar and quite unsuitable for the Princess."

"Vulgarity has different meanings for different people . . . my lady."

"Come, now, you need not be coy with us, Miss Garland," purred Agnes, ignoring the barbed reply. "Admit that the gown is your handiwork."

Susannah felt very cold inside, but she had steeled herself so often now to hide her feelings that neither of her antagonists could tell from her face the effect they were having upon her. "I do not discuss my work with anyone, Lady Agnes, least of all with the woman who is so sullying my cousin's good name by her *vulgar* behavior with a certain Frenchman."

The room gasped delightedly at this unexpected counterattack, and Agnes' eyes flashed with bitter fury. "I *know* that that gown came from you, madam, I know it for a fact! Oh, those secret visits at night were not the secret they were intended to be—and you threw out fragments of cloth which could be collected quite easily and kept for use at a later date." She opened her reticule and took out some tiny offcuts of primrose taffeta and sheer white silk. "You aided and abetted the Princess, Miss Garland, and you will suffer for it. You have been too clever this time, too eager to reach above yourself."

To Susannah's immense relief, Annie emerged at last from the rear of the shop, glancing swiftly at the silent room and the two women facing Susannah along the counter.

Susannah smiled at Agnes. "What a quaint picture your words summon up, my lady—Lady Devereux scratching around among the rubbish to find little fragments of cloth with which to stir up trouble if she can. How the mighty have fallen, my lady. Good day to you."

Agnes' face was stony. Coming so unexpectedly upon Susannah like that had seemed a golden opportunity, but somehow it had not gone as had been intended. There were smothered laughs in the shop, and they were not directed at Susannah Garland. Agnes replaced the precious pieces of silk back in her reticule, for they never left her sight now. She would prove the complicity of the New House of Fashion, she would ruin her hated husband's even-more-hated cousin once and for all!

The chaise drove slowly through the crush of traffic in the busy street. "What happened, Susannah?"

"Oh, dear Agnes has been rifling through our rubbish and she has found incriminating pieces of primrose taffeta and white silk."

"Oh, no!"

"But, oh, yes. Well, it's done now, and all I can do is hope for the best." Susannah stared out at the passing street. "And pray that the Princess will stand by her tale to me about wanting the gown for her father's birthday."

"Of course she will."

"You think so? Maybe turning some of the wrath on to me will save her a great deal of misery, Annie."

Annie said nothing then, gazing instead at the little package of French lace which rested on her lap.

25

~~~~~~

"You are vindicated, coz," said Miles, leaning his head back wearily against the landau's mauve upholstery, his eyes half-closed as he watched her. "You are vindicated because the Princess admitted to Papa that she told a morsel of a fibling to you. But then, she and the dreaded Tolly speak in French, do they not, and guess who speaks French to perfection? Why, you, sweet coz-of-mine."

Susannah folded her hands in her lap. "That isn't fair, Miles."

"I know—but it's second nature to me, I fear. Still, having become *au fait* with the veritable tizzy of interest this whole affair has created, and with your apparent part in it, I thought it only right to come directly I knew the outcome. After all, it was because of me that my dear wife interested herself in it all anyway."

"What do you mean?"

"She wants a divorce, I've told you that already, and she was hoping and praying that she would be able to detect your involvement with me. In short, she was having number fifteen Catherine Lane watched all the time, and instead of discovering my visits to your abode, she discovered instead that a certain Princess of the Blood was going to great lengths to come secretly to you. Agnes is like a dog with a bone at times, she will not let go—she kept her disgusting nose to the proverbial ground and discovered a very interesting royal trail. Unfortunately for her—and most fortunately for you—the Princess had told you little white lies about the purpose of the gown. Hence your present state of vindication. It was badly done, though, very badly done."

"What would you have had me do, Miles—refuse to make the gown for her?"

"I wasn't refering to your part in it, for I doubt that there was much you could have done. No, I was referring to the Princess's behavior. If she wanted a secret marriage, then she should have kept it secret. There should not have been any doubtful conversation in front of you, and there certainly should not have been all this fussing with nonexistent illnesses, and the number of people who had seen her who could testify that she was as healthy as it was possible for her to be was tantamount to a small nation in itself! Still, it's done now, and she's tied the proverbial knot with Fitzroy, God help her."

"It's to be acknowledged?"

"Good God, no! The marriage stands, but it will be denied in public. She's got herself her husband, but as far as the world is concerned, she is still spinning thread. The upshot of it all is that the King has decided to hold a private celebration next week—now that his favorite daughter has recovered her 'health'—and That Gown will be displayed there. The fib she told you in private, coz, will be perpetuated in public at a royal function. You've slipped out from under quite well, your reputation more enhanced than tarnished, and I fancy that there will be many a fine lady wanting a similar tunic gown before the Season is out."

"I pray you are right. Oh, Miles, I've been so worried about it all."

"I know—but you may console yourself that you are undoubtedly still in the running as far as Her Majesty is concerned."

Susannah pulled a face. "I think Madame Hilary will come up with trumps on that score."

"Because foolish journals twitter about it?"

"Yes. And because Madame Hilary is an established dressmaker, she already holds royal warrants and she is good."

"She's dreary. As is the Queen, I suppose, now I come to mention it. Oh, enough of the Court and its damned machinations. Tell me how you are, Susannah, for I have not seen you for some time now."

"I'm very well, as you see."

His eyes moved over her neat figure in its lilac-and-cream

cotton lawn, the flounced ribbons of her poke bonnet trembling a little under her chin as the landau swayed through Hyde Park. "I see that you are as lovely as ever, sweetheart," he said softly, "and if ever a man had cause to rue a decision, then that man is myself. I remember . . . I remember those meetings in that damned boathouse . . ." He didn't finish the sentence, leaning across instead to take her gloved hand and raise it to his lips.

Her fingers tightened around his. "You have asked me how I am, Miles, and now I must ask the same of you, for when I look at you I see that you are not well."

He released her with a short laugh. "And here I was thinking I am quite the swell."

"Is it because of Agnes?"

He shot her a cross look. "As if my wife's activities could have any bearing on *my* constitution!"

"Your son, then."

"Ah, well, that is maybe another matter. I shall have him away from her yet, you mark my words. I'll not leave him in the tender clutches of the Winston clan a moment longer than need be. They seem to imagine that they alone have the prerogative to commence litigation, and they will shortly discover that that is not so. I will not allow a son of mine to be brought up with Winston notions—or morals—in his Devereux head. Or French notions and morals, for that matter."

"Miles, I do not think it becomes you to point a finger at others on those counts," she reminded gently, remembering how often he had importuned her to let him "set her up."

He smiled. "That was before I fathered a son, sweet coz. I've taken the first steps in law already, and I intend making quite a thing of it to get custody of him."

"But where will you live? You've lost Sanderby, Miles . . ."

"I still have the Irish estates."

"You'd go there?"

He nodded slowly. "Oh, yes. I'd go there. Look at me, Susannah, don't you see a change? And don't you think that I am now a more fitting person than my wife to bring up a child to know what is right and wrong? Maybe in the past I've not shown a particularly sensible or admirable face to the world, but I've learned my lesson. There isn't a gaming hell in London where my face has been seen these few months now, and I've remained praiseworthily sober, too. I have also watered down my extreme Whiggishness so that it is contained within tolerable levels now. In short, I have become an upright citizen who is well worthy of having the upbringing of his son and heir entrusted to his care."

She stared at him. "Do . . . do you have a halo too?"

"Vixen. Was I thumping the lectern a little?"

"Just a little."

"I feel most strongly about it all. I am kept at arm's length from Winston Hall, Susannah, as if I had no part whatsoever in my son's existence! I will not forgive that. Not that." He leaned back in his seat, tipping his top hat back on his golden hair. "I shall make amends to you for my harangue by taking you to Gunter's for an ice."

"There is no need," she began quickly, for Gunter's was in Berkeley Square . . .

"I will not hear any argument. Besides, I happen to know that a new shipment of ice arrived from Iceland only yesterday, so that today's ices will be most fine. Come on, now, coz, admit that a fine June evening under the trees with a Gunter's ice is just the very thing!"

She smiled. "Very well. A Gunter's ice it is."

As the landau turned out of the park and into Park Lane, Susannah glanced at Miles a little more closely. He was undoubtedly a lot thinner, and there were shadows beneath his handsome eyes, shadows which spoke of long nights without sleep. He was pale, too, an anxious sort of pallor born of the sudden and final realization of the way his life had gone. He had made many mistakes and paid the price of each one. Now he had a child to consider, and all that must be put aside. But Miles Devereux was by nature easygoing and funloving; this new, self-imposed abstemiousness could not be easy.

He sensed the close perusal to which he was being subjected. "Do I pass muster, coz?"

"You'll do, Miles, you'll do."

"I take heart from the softness in your eyes, then. And therefore I must wonder about the opposition."

"Opposition?"

"Stratton."

She looked away. "I don't want to talk about him."

"Why not? Has he spurned you again?"

Her face felt hot. "It's none of your business."

"I'm making it my business—as head of the family."

"Go to hell."

He pretended to be shocked. "Miss Garland, that is hardly dainty talk for a fashionable young lady! You should be thoroughly ashamed of yourself. Dammit, you're still very touchy about the fellow, and I cannot for the life of me see why. It's obvious he don't care for you, he ain't even been in London for a couple of months now. Let me see, when was it—ah, yes, a week or so after Sweet Billy Pitt's funeral!"

"Miles, I enjoy your company except when you persist in talking about Sir Jeffrey Stratton, and unless you stop it at this very moment, then I shall get out of this carriage and make my own way home to Catherine Lane!"

He smiled at that. "You would, too, wouldn't you?"

"Yes."

"Then I shall say no more on the subject—except this. I am still dangerously jealous of your love for him, Susannah. That at least has not changed in me."

She met his bright eyes for a long moment, and she could see that he spoke the truth. Miles had made strenuous efforts to become a different man, but in this one thing he could not change. Her thoughts went winging back to a night when he had forced her to kiss him so that Jeffrey could witness it.

The old sign of the Pot and Pineapple still hung outside Gunter's. In the windows of the teashop were displayed giant wedding cakes under glass domes, and a small boy was actually inside an empty dome cleaning it meticulously with a cloth. A number of fashionable carriages were drawn up in the square outside, and waiters ran continuously to and fro across the road to deliver trays of ices and sherbets to the ladies sitting in them. Glasses tinkled and people talked together in low voices beneath the rustling plane trees. The gentlemen who accompanied the ladies lounged against the railings nearby, and the scene was one of unadulterated lazy luxury, thought Susannah, as the landau came to a standstill almost opposite the door of the teashop. Across the square she could see Jeffrey's house. She sat forward suddenly, staring across the grassy square at the black carriage which had at that moment halted there. Was Jeffrey back in London, then?

Miles hadn't noticed the carriage, or her reaction. "Now, then, what shall it be, Susannah? Peach sherbet? Or maybe lime? And I believe the strawberry ice is superlative."

"S-some lime sherbet, please."

He kissed her hand. "Your wish is my command." He

beckoned to the waiter who hovered nearby, but as he gave the order the smile on his face became distinctly cooler as a dark green barouche turned into the square and drew up a little way away. Susannah followed his gaze, and her spirits sank as she recognized the occupants. The Earl of Winston sat with his daughter, Agnes, and opposite them lounged a small dark-haired man who, judging by his Gallic appearance, must be the Comte de St. François.

"Miles," she began quickly, "maybe we should leave—"

"No."

"Please, Miles, don't let it all be spoiled by a scene!"

"I have promised you one of Gunter's ices, and that is what you shall have, coz."

Susannah looked at the barouche again, and as she did so, Agnes looked straight at her. The wide green eyes sharpened and she leaned to touch her father's arm, whispering close to him. The Frenchman looked across too, his dark eyes narrowing speculatively. Susannah became aware then that the occupants of the other nearby carriages had noticed what promised to be an interesting development in the continuing saga of the Devereux marriage.

"Please, Miles," she whispered urgently, "please let us go now."

"No, Susannah," he said shortly. "I will not run like a cur with my tail between my legs simply because I am faced with my wife and her damned frog lover!"

Susannah closed her eyes faintly, for his words must have been heard by the occupants of the other carriage. Her fear proved correct, for the Frenchman stiffened and a moment later climbed down from the barouche, pausing elegantly to toy with his lace cuff for a moment before approaching the landau. His eyes were a dark, melting brown and his lashes were long and curved. He wore a coat of pale green with brass buttons which were surely almost the size of crowns; his breeches were white and skintight and his waistcoat was a rich ruby red. His smile was insolent as he halted by the landau, sketching a brief bow.

"*Milord* Devereux?"

"*Milady* Devereux's lap dog?" inquired Miles coolly, his glance withering.

"I do not like your tone, sir."

"I have no intention of adopting any other with you."

234

"Then such rudeness shall not go unchallenged, Lord Devereux," said the Frenchman stiffly.

But before Miles could say anything and before the inevitable challenge could be issued, another voice interrupted them. "I believe, *monsieur*, that the Earl requires you."

Susannah turned with quick relief as Jeffrey stepped between the Frenchman and the door of the landau.

The Comte hesitated, torn between his desire to punish Miles's taunts and his uncertainty of the mettle of the newcomer. But after a moment looking into Jeffrey's cold gray eyes, the Frenchman stepped back and bowed. *"Monsieur."*

Jeffrey inclined his head briefly, and then, as the Frenchman walked away, he turned and opened the landau door, holding his hand up to Susannah. "Get down, Susannah."

Miles sat forward angrily. "You go too far, Stratton!"

"And you are the one to stop me? I watched everything from the beginning, Devereux. I saw how Susannah asked you not once, but three times, if you would leave. Each time you refused. That was not the behavior of a gentleman, sir, and so I have taken it upon myself to relieve Susannah of your presence. Susannah?"

She stared down at him and then slowly slipped her hand into his and climbed down from the landau.

Miles's face was a dull red and he avoided Susannah's eyes then. What Jeffrey had said was completely true, and he could not deny it. He had forced her to remain with him while he deliberately sought a confrontation. He nodded at his coachman and the landau pulled swiftly away, just as the startled waiter returned with her lime sherbet.

Consious of being watched from all sides, Susannah kept her eyes lowered as Jeffrey led her away from the crowded part of the square outside Gunter's. He drew her hand gently through his arm.

"I believe it is fully five minutes since I returned, five little minutes, and already I find myself involved in your affairs, Susannah Garland."

"You did not have to involve yourself, then, sir."

"No, that is very true—but neither could I honorably stand by and watch things develop. The Frenchman is a fine swordsman, and he would have called your foolish cousin out."

She said nothing for a moment. "Are . . . are you back in Town for long this time?"

235

"I have no idea. I came back because I heard rumors about Princess Amelia and a certain damned millstone of a wedding dress. If I had not seen you now, then I would have come to Catherine Lane tonight anyway."

She halted. "You came back because of that?"

"Yes. You are, after all, my responsibility—to a certain extent, anyway."

"Indeed!"

"Yes—*indeed.*"

"If you feel so involved, I wonder you dare leave London at all for fear of my next *faux pas.*"

"I stay away for my own peace of mind—which peace has been disturbed a little of late."

"Well, you need not concern yourself on this particular count, for I understand I am exonerated from blame."

"By the skin of your little white teeth." He smiled. "The language of the Court would not pass over your head, Susannah, even though the Princess and her fool of a lady-in-waiting would undoubtedly think it would."

"They still think that."

"You sailed close to the wind this time, Susannah."

"I had little real choice."

"I know. He walked on. "From all accounts, the gown is a triumph."

"I am pleased with it."

"So you should be. My dearest Susannah, where would I be without you to brighten my dull, safe little life? If nothing else, I have been jerked out of my complacency by your energetic and unpredictable presence. So, here we are, well on the way through your second Season and still on course for your final royal goal. The Queen still has not sent for Madame Hilary, you know."

"She hasn't?"

"No. And I believe that Her Majesty has been most impressed by the Princess's dazzling gown now that it has been brought out and displayed openly for them to admire."

"The Queen has seen it?"

"Yes," he said, pausing outside his house, his gray eyes moving slowly over her face, "so I think you may still hold out hope for your cursed ambition."

His choice of words stung her. "You say that as if it is somehow despicable."

"Despicable? How could it be that, when, as you will no doubt remind me, I have a vested interest in your success?"

"I was not about to say anything of the kind, but since you mention it . . . yes, you do have a vested interest, and for someone who is involved as you are, sir, you would appear to have an unfortunate lack of appreciation of my endeavors!"

"Oh, I assure you, Susannah, that I fully appreciate your endeavors—I doubt if you will ever know how much." His face was unsmiling as he turned to call to his coachman. "John, see to it that Miss Garland is conveyed back to Catherine Lane."

She looked quickly at him. "There is no need."

"Indeed there is. I may have an unfortunate lack of appreciation, but I do not forget my manners this time. I removed you from Devereux, and it is my duty to see that you are delivered safely to your door."

For a moment she felt that she could not hide her feelings, but as he bowed stiffly to her, she managed to give a light smile before turning and walking toward the waiting carriage. But the tears shone in her eyes as she sat back on the pale blue upholstery.

He watched the carriage pull slowly away. "Damn you, Susannah Garland," he whispered. "Damn you to hell and back."

26

~

Susannah's slippers made only a small sound in the echoing drawing room of the empty house in Duke's Row, St. James's. The hem of her chestnut velvet pelisse was heavy with leopard-skin trimming and so it swung a little with each step as she slowly looked around at the rolled-back carpets and the furniture which was covered with protective white sheets. There was elegant golden scrollwork on the pale blue walls and two chandeliers were suspended from the ceiling with its molded plasterwork of cherubs and laurel wreaths. Everything was shadowy, for the shutters were closed, but as she opened them, the cold sunlight streamed in to dazzle her for a moment. She gazed out at the tall red-brick walls of St. James's Palace, a mere few yards away from this exclusive address. Oh, how exclusive an address for the New House of Fashion, she thought, watching a curl of smoke from one of the palace chimneys. Autumn leaves scuttered along the cobbled road, and she could feel the chill on the glass. It was only the end of September, but already winter was in the air.

She turned as she heard Jeffrey come into the room behind her. He removed his top hat and tossed it onto one of the covered chairs; then he slowly teased off his gloves in that oddly thoughtful way which always reminded her of the very first time she had ever seen him. At Sanderby. He dropped the gloves into the upturned hat, and the brass buttons of his wine-red coat flashed suddenly in the sunlight as he turned toward her. "You would be reaching very high indeed this time, Susannah."

"The house is perfect for my needs."

"I'll warrant it is!" he said with a small laugh. "Right opposite the palace itself! Was ever a mere *dressmaker* that impudent before? And after a mere two Seasons at that!" He smiled at her. "But I suppose your outstanding success gives you a certain standing, the *beau monde* would probably accept the audacious from you where it would throw up its hands in horror were anyone else to be even half as bold."

"Is that your honest opinion? You think I could do this and get away with it?"

"My opinion is of any consequence?"

"Yes."

"Then, yes, I think you will probably survive. You rose triumphantly above the matter of the royal wedding dress, and so I would imagine you are capable of this decidedly cheeky removal to St. James's. But a word of warning: you *may* be being too clever for your own good, and this latest escapade could be frowned on at Court—in which case you will be ruined."

"But all in all, you think the risk is worth taking?"

"That isn't what I said—I said I thought you could succeed."

"I do so want to do this, Jeffrey, I just feel that it's right."

"Catherine Lane to St. James's is a rather meteoric rise, Susannah, even for the darling of London's fashions. Maybe the climb would be better made in easy steps."

"No, Jeffrey," she said quietly, "I will not be satisfied with anything less than St. James's. I promised myself that I would reach this sort of exclusiveness, and so I shall."

"And one must not deny such an ambition, must one?" he said dryly.

"Why should one, if there is no need?" she countered.

"Why indeed."

She was determined to ignore his sarcasm. "The premises in Catherine Lane have become cramped now, I had so many orders this past Season that I shall definitely need a larger workroom for next year. It simply isn't possible to enlarge the workroom I have now, and so where shall I put all the extra seamstresses I shall have to employ? And then, there is the millinery . . ."

"Millinery?"

"I think that I should widen my business a little. Madame Hilary is dressmaker and milliner."

He sighed. "Is there no end to it?"

"Not yet," she said, smiling a little.

"Well, for the multitudinous purposes you seem to have in mind, then this mansion would appear to fit the bill."

"It's hardly a mansion!"

"Susannah, that room you wish to turn into a workroom is large enough to house a damned *army* of needle-and-threaders! And while we are on the subject of the changes and advances you wish to make, there is one which has come to my attention of which I most definitely do *not* approve!"

"Which one?"

"The displaying of your gowns upon the persons of young women who will parade up and down in them like courtesans."

"But—"

"No buts, Susannah, it is a very ill-advised notion and one which I wish you to set aside immediately. You run a house of fashion, not a house of ill repute, and if you hold my opinion to be of any value whatsoever, you will desist from this particular plan."

She stared at him. "If . . . if that is what you want . . ."

"It is."

"Then of course I will do as you wish."

He inclined his head. "Thank you."

"But the gowns would have been shown to their best advantage," she added, smiling at him.

"No doubt," he said dryly, "and so would the charms of the young women—which would attract the male of the species to your doors, Susannah, not the female. However, we digress from the purpose of this visit. By all means take the house—it is a very fine property and furnished very elegantly, it could hardly be in a more fashionable neighborhood, and the accommodation it provides would appear to be everything any aspiring dressmaker could desire."

"I had to have your approval, though."

"Why? Because you have not paid back all that which you borrowed from me? I think the sum outstanding is hardly worth mentioning, don't you?"

"I am still in your debt, and if I take this house . . ."

He drew the cover off a sofa and sat down, lounging gracefully back and holding his hand out to her. "I am quite content to have you in my debt, Susannah, for it at least gives me the right to curb your more startling notions, and it brings me into your company from time to time, which experience is far from unpleasant, I do assure you."

No, but no matter how pleasant, you will not take it further. She avoided his gaze. Why could it not be different? Why could she not slip within those cursed rules?

"Who would have thought," he said softly, "that the little seamstress I so providentially knocked down would in so short a time have become the queen of London's fashion? You lead a charmed life, Susannah, everything you touch seems to turn to gold."

"Not everything," she said quickly. For a moment she was on the verge of telling him the truth, of setting aside the mask she so sought to hide behind.

"No? Come, now, but for the stubborn presence of a German dressmaker at Windsor, I truly believe you would now possess the royal warrant you so desperately want. Even in this new nineteenth century when women are becoming ever more free of their shackles, your success is quite astounding. You are almost dauntingly admirable."

Admirable? I don't want your admiration, I want your love—your love, Jeffrey Stratton. Again she wanted to tell him; the words were burning to be said.

He glanced around the room. "I met Elizabeth here."

The confession died unsaid, and she could only stare at him in dismay. "In this room?"

"The house belonged to a mutual friend, Lady Hesterhouse." He got up and went to the window, leaning a hand on the shutter as he gazed out at the cold day.

Susannah closed her eyes momentarily. In this house, in this very room! "Forgive me, I did not know."

"There is nothing to forgive, the memory is not a sad one. I may have lost her, but what time we had together was more happy than any man could ever dream possible."

"Did . . . did you not say you had an appointment at midday?"

"Ah, yes, so I did." He picked up his hat and gloves. "By the way, I think you should know that I am on the verge of selling Sanderby."

"Who to?"

"I fancy you will not care for my answer. I am considering selling to the Earl of Winston."

"You can't possibly!"

"I most certainly can if I wish. He is offering an excellent price and I have no quarrel with him beyond the fact that his politics are odious."

"Could you not sell to someone else?"

"Why? To spare dear Miles?"

"I did not say that."

"No, but that is what you meant. Well, I have little desire to spare Miles Devereux anything, any more than he would spare me."

She stared up at him. The morning, which had begun so well, was suddenly sour and alien. She felt close to tears, both for how Miles would feel when he heard about Sanderby and for herself. Of all the houses in London, she had to select this one, the very place where Jeffrey Stratton had first met the only woman he had ever loved.

Annie sat back wearily on the red velvet sofa, heaving a sigh of relief as she glanced out of the window at St. James's Palace. The early-winter evening was closing mistily in and there was a gray indistinctness about the scene beyond the frozen glass. A fire crackled in the hearth and the cat from Catherine Lane was sitting before the warmth, busily trying to lick the butter from its paws.

Susannah looked doubtfully at it. "Are you certain that that will stop it from wandering away?"

"My mother swore it worked. Anyway, if it doesn't, let the horrible feline wander off if it wishes."

"Just because it won't sleep on your lap." Susannah laughed.

"It is a creature of little taste. Oh, I don't think I've ever been more tired in my life than I have been these past few weeks. Setting up in Catherine Lane was bad enough, but this has been ten times worse! Is there *any* warehouse or manufactory in London you haven't been through with a fine-tooth comb? I think that those storerooms in the basement here are filled to overflowing—and all that silk thread!"

"Ah, well, there is a good reason for purchasing that."

"What, for heaven's sake?"

"Well, Bonaparte has decreed that there shall be no trading with Britain, and that means no silk. That's why I bought all I could find as soon as I heard."

"It will take us fifty years to use it all up."

"Not if we receive the orders we received last year."

Annie groaned. "My fingers and back ache at the very thought."

"You will have a month or so of peace and quiet before the rush starts."

"I shall need it. Still, we're here now." Annie gazed around at the drawing room, which had been redecorated in Susannah's pink-and-gray colors. "Number three Duke's Row, St. James's," she murmured. "It's very grand, isn't it? I wonder what the *beau monde* will think when they open tomorrow's journals and read your announcement?"

Susannah shuddered involuntarily, picking up the little piece of paper on which she and Annie had written and rewritten the advertisement.

Miss Garland, Dressmaker, late of Catherine Lane, begs leave to inform ladies of fashion that the above business will in future be carried on in Duke's Row, St. James's, and takes this opportunity of returning the most grateful thanks for the numerous and distinguished favors hitherto so liberally conferred upon the New House of Fashion, and most respectfully solicits a continuance of the same.

She smiled wryly. "Well, the announcement at least is dignified and restrained, even if this momentous move has not been. It's too late now, anyway, there's no going back."

"We'll swim, not sink," said Annie firmly, pushing the cat with her toe so that it rolled over, stretching luxuriously on the carpet.

The maid tapped at the door and came in. "Madam, Lady Cowper is here."

Annie hastily pulled on her discarded slippers and straightened her cap, and Susannah went to the door as Emily was shown in. "Good evening, Lady Cowper, what a very pleasant surprise this is."

Emily smiled, handing her large black fur muff to the maid. "Well, when Jeffrey told me you had taken yourself to St. James's, I could not believe it, but here you are." She looked around at the familiar colors of the room and at the pile of cloths in a corner waiting for Annie to put on display. "Here you are indeed! This is more like a palace than a dressmaking establishment! I doubt if dear old Lady Hesterhouse would recognize her old home."

"Please sit down, Lady Cowper."

"No, I cannot stop, I merely came to pass on two messages from Jeffrey." Emily smiled. "He knew that I was going to the palace tonight and told me that it would do me no harm to take a step or two farther and come to see you."

"It is most kind of you."

"Nonsense, I am merely being nosy. I wished to see how you had done out this place. I must be first with such snippets, you know. Anyway, to the messages. First of all, he says I must tell you he is no longer thinking of selling Sanderby to the Earl of Winston."

"But why?"

"I cannot say that I know, Miss Garland—but I *can* say that this news coming on top of all his other problems has infuriated the Earl completely. He is in a pet to end all pets."

"Coming on top of what other news?"

"My dear, you have obviously been far too engrossed in the business of removal—it's all the chatter at the moment. Agnes Devereux has run off with her Frenchman."

Susannah stared at her. "What of the baby?"

"He remains at Winston Hall." Emily sighed. "Well, she's played into Miles's hands, of course, he's almost bound to be granted custody of his son now. This coming Christmas promises to be a black time at Winston Hall. No one seems to know where Agnes and her lover have gone, and I doubt if anyone but the Earl cares anyway."

"You . . . you said there were two messages."

"Oh, yes. The Queen's German dressmaker is definitely going at the end of February next year, the gout has proved too much for her after all. The Queen will be considering a new dressmaker then—Ulla Ormanton told Jeffrey this very morning that the decision had been made."

"It's quite certain, then?" Susannah almost held her breath.

"There's absolutely no doubt. Just as there is no doubt that there are only two houses of fashion in the running at all. Madame Hilary is one, and you, Miss Garland, are the other. The fact that you have been audacious enough to move in here caused hardly a ripple at Windsor—you never can tell, can you?"

"No."

Emily took the muff from the waiting maid. "I must go now, I have literally squeezed you in between appointments."

"I am most grateful to you."

"Jeffrey was quite determined that I should run this errand for him; he didn't have time to come himself."

When she had gone, Susannah remained staring at the closed door in a daze. Jeffrey would not have sent word to her at all unless it was all quite genuine. But who would it be in the end? Madame Hilary? Or the New House of Fashion?

27

The new year of 1807 began well for Susannah. If society had wondered whether to be affronted or not by the removal of the New House of Fashion to St. James's, then the silent approval from the Court removed all threat. Even though the Season was far away still, through January the house in Duke's Row received visits from those ladies of fashion who were in Town for one reason or another. But there was no further news from Windsor. All Susannah knew was what she had been told in Jeffrey's message.

Then, halfway through February, on a windy day which rippled the straight canal in St. James's Park and almost bent the trees to the ground occasionally, Ulla, Lady Ormanton, arrived in a very grand carriage bearing the royal crest.

Almost weak with anticipation, Susannah received her in the beautiful drawing room. It was obvious from the outset that Lady Ormanton had come on a matter of importance and not merely to order a new pelisse. She refused Susannah's invitation to take tea.

"*Nein*, Miss Garland, that I must not do on this occasion."

"But you will at least take a seat, Lady Ormanton."

"That I vill do." Ulla lowered her bulky form into the chair. "I am here on the dear Qvéen's business, Miss Garland."

Susannah clasped her hands nervously in front of her. "The Queen's business?" she asked as lightly as possible.

"*Ja*, but then, I think you must know vot that means." Ulla smiled fondly. "Her Majesty has been very impressed vith your vork, Fräulein Garland, as indeed have all ladies of qvality been since first you set up here. So, Her Majesty has charged me to come to you and tell you that she vishes you to come to Vindsor in two days' time, bringing vith you your folders of drawings. You can do this?"

"Yes." Susannah's pulse was racing, almost unbearably now.

"Do not read too much into this, Fräulein, for it could be that Her Majesty will not find anything to appeal to her. However . . ." Lady Ormanton leaned forward. "I think she vill, *ja*? Of this I am determined, however, and that is that she vill *not* send for that *Hündin* Hilary! No indeed, not ven Ulla Ormanton lives and breathes! That odious *person* will not gain anything!"

Susannah couldn't speak for excitement now. It was happening—at last it was happening!

Lady Ormanton took a long breath. "Maybe I vill not have time to speak vith you on the day, Miss Garland, and so I vill explain things to you now. I vill conduct you to the Qveen as she is dressing for the day. Please do not speak vith her in monosyllables, for this is something she dreads. Frequently she complains that she has difficulty in getting any conversation, for not only must she alvays start the subjects, but then she must entirely support them, too. She is a dear lady, with many trials to endure, and a little thing like that can make such a difference, *ja*?"

"Yes, I suppose it must." Susannah had not thought of the Queen in that light and it somehow made her seem a great deal more human than her reputation would suggest.

"You vill know you are dismissed from her presence because she vill say to you, 'Now I vill let you go.' That is alvays her vay, Miss Garland."

"I understand."

"And now to the time. Each morning she, the dear King, and the Princesses go to prayers in King's Chapel in the castle. She begins formal dressing for the day at a qvarter before vun. I think it best that you come the day after tomorrow at a qvarter after vun. You can manage this time?"

"Yes, Lady Ormanton."

Lady Ormanton beamed. "I think you vill do very vell, Miss Garland, for already Her Majesty has noted my toggery—and, of course, particularly the beautiful tunic dress you made for the Princess Amelia."

Susannah felt suddenly cold at the mention of that particular garment.

Lady Ormanton studied her face for a moment. "Care must be taken at all times, Fräulein, great care and much discretion, *ja*? It vould not do at all for a slip to be made."

Susannah could only stare at her.

"Do not say anything, my dearest Miss Garland, for there is no need. Ve know that it vas not your fault, that there was a lamentable deception by persons who should have known a great deal better. But if you had done that vich you should not have done, then you vould not be being summoned to Vindsor now, you realize that, don't you?"

"Yes."

Lady Ormanton smiled again and the smile put an end to the unease which had crept into the interview. "Now, I have to go, for my verk at Court is never-ending. It is said by unkind souls that life at this Court is nothing but stupefying boredom, so dull that the *monde* dreads a royal invitation. But *I* cannot find it so, for there is alvays so much to do, so many things to remember! I cannot think how I would live now if I did not have all those things to do—vot *ever* did I do before? I ask myself."

Lady Ormanton took her leave a moment later, and Susannah returned to the showroom. Her heart was still thundering so much that she could hear her pulse in her ears. It had happened; she was being summoned to Windsor, and she didn't have anyone she could tell, for Annie was spending the day with Mr. Normans. She felt she would burst with excitement; then, lifting her skirts up around her ankles, she danced wildly and exultantly around the room. The Queen had chosen the New House of Fashion after all!

Susannah felt almost sick with nervousness as the royal carriage conveyed her the final few yards into Windsor Castle. She had hardly slept at all the night before and had had to resort to the Chinese colors again to put a little color on her pale cheeks. It seemed that she had spent the entire night worrying over what outfit to wear for such an important interview. She had finally chosen a cream cloth pelisse with capes and a black silk lining. Her pale pink hat was embellished with aigrette plumes and she carried a black satin reticule. Beneath the pelisse she wore a demure morning dress of oyster wool, but as the carriage began to slow she wished she had worn the blue wool instead. She clutched her folder of drawings tightly, her kid gloves drawn tightly over her knuckles as she glanced out at the sweep of gray medieval wall which enclosed the roadway now. Her breath was misty in the chill of the February morning, and she shivered a little as the carriage came to a standstill at last.

A footman in royal livery opened the door and lowered the iron rungs for her to alight, and it was almost with a rush of relief that she saw Lady Ormanton's comfortingly familiar figure emerge from a nearby doorway.

"Ah, Fräulein Garland, how punctual you are! *Komm, komm*, the Qveen vill receive you in her powdering room."

Taking a deep breath, Susannah followed her into the castle. The Queen's rooms were on the ground floor, overlooking the Round Tower, and everything was so quiet that Susannah's steps sounded unnaturally noisy on the stone-flagged floor.

Outside a door which was guarded by another footman, Susannah waited in increased nervousness as Lady Ormanton preceded her into the Queen's presence. After a moment Lady Ormanton returned. "You may go in now, Miss Garland."

Swallowing once, Susannah stepped at last into the royal presence.

Queen Charlotte sat at her dressing table, a voluminous robe concealing her rather plump person. A dusting cloth rested over her shoulders and a woman was busily powdering her fine darkish hair. By no stretch of the imagination could it be said that the Queen was a handsome woman; indeed she was rather plain and her low forehead was marred by a permanent frown. She was sorting through a large jewelry box, lifting out first this necklace and then that, and she did not immediately see Susannah, who had sunk into a very deep curtsy.

At length the Queen looked up shortsightedly and saw Susannah's reflection in the mirror. "Ah, Miss Garland," she said in a guttural German voice.

"Your Majesty."

"Please rise, and let me look at you. Ah, how very pretty you are, every bit as pretty as Sir Jeffrey said you vere. But I do not see any Devereux in you at all . . . no, not one little bit." The Queen nodded almost to herself. "But then, who vould vish to look like your uncle, *ja*?"

"I certainly would prefer not to resemble him in any way, your Majesty."

The Queen chuckled at that. "But then, maybe your handsome cousin is another matter, even if he supports the Vhigs and the Prince of Vales." Her voice became decidedly cold on mentioning the heir to the throne.

In spite of Lady Ormanton's warnings about keeping up a conversation, Susannah was suddenly tongue-tied. Besides, what could she say in the wake of a remark about the Prince?

The Queen sniffed. "I trust that you have brought all your designs for me to see."

"I brought everything I thought your Majesty would like to inspect, but if what you have in mind is not there, then . . ."

"Then you vill produce it immediately for me?" The Queen smiled and turned to wave the powdering woman away. "Now, let me see vot you have brought. You see, Miss Garland, I think now is an excellent time for me to change my appearance. The other day I saw a portrait of myself which was executed only six years ago, and there I voz, still dressed as I voz at seventeen! I am over sixty now and if I cannot look young, then at least I must look as if I can move a little vith the times. I vish a new appearance of neatness and simplicity, but I do not vish to come into public as if I am *en chemise*. It is only too easy for a lady to look as if she has just emerged from her bed, don't you think, Miss Garland?"

"I do indeed, your Majesty, and with everyone liking light muslins so greatly, then it can be so much worse."

"There you are very right! The dear King said to me that he thought ladies today could lack all pretense at modesty when they step out in such naked materials. Now, then, let me see vot you have brought me. . . ." The Queen snapped her fingers and Lady Ormanton quickly brought her her spectacles and a small enameled snuffbox. The Queen put on the spectacles and then took a pinch of snuff, inhaling deeply up both nostrils and then wrinkling her nose for a moment, her eyes screwing up as she resisted the urge to sneeze. Then with a sigh she settled back to go through the sheaf of drawings.

After a while she looked up. "Are there no trains on your gowns, Miss Garland?"

"Trains went out of fashion last Season, your Majesty," said Susannah reluctantly, for having to say such a thing to the Queen of England was not at all easy; it smacked of criticism somehow.

But the Queen was not offended at all. "Indeed? I had not even noticed! Oh, Lady O., I really have been remiss, have I not? Ah, now this gown I really like!"

Lady Ormanton took the sheet of paper the Queen held out to her. "It is very elegant, your Majesty. And very fashionable."

"Well, that is vot I vish to be!" scolded the Queen, tutting a little as she snatched the drawing back again. "Vhy else vould I send for a fashionable dressmaker if it voz not to look fashionable? Miss Garland, of vot material would you make this garment?"

"Plowman's gauze, your Majesty."

"*Plowman's* gauze? Oh, surely not!"

"It is a very beautiful gauze, your Majesty, very delicate and fine, quite perfect for an evening dress. The spots are of satin and they shine quite exquisitely. In fact, I have some in my storerooms now which is particularly fine. It is of a very pale green and the spots are silver."

"It sounds very nice, Miss Garland." The Queen put the drawing aside and then went on through the folder.

After about half an hour there were four sheets set aside. The Queen closed the folder and gave it back to Susannah before holding up the separate sheets. "I think I like these greatly, Miss Garland, but first I vould like to see them on the fashion dolls, *ja*?"

"Yes, your Majesty."

"Lady O. vill give you the measurements. When I have inspected the dolls. I vill give you my final vord."

"Does your Majesty wish to see the fashion dolls in any particular order?"

"I vould like to see the white satin and blue ribbon first, the others you can do as you vish."

"Very well, your Majesty."

"It has been a pleasure meeting you, Miss Garland, for you know how to converse, and it is not alvays my pleasure to hold a conversation. Now I vill let you go."

"Thank you, your Majesty."

"And, Miss Garland. . . ?" Susannah halted. "I tell you now, in advance, that I do not think I vill be sending for another dressmaker." The Queen smiled graciously.

Susannah's heart lurched with joy and she was unable to

resist glancing delightedly at Lady Ormanton, who beamed and nodded. With a final curtsy, Susannah backed out of the royal presence, pausing then in the outer room to regain her breath and composure.

Lady Ormanton followed her out and together they began to walk to where the carriage awaited. "There, Fräulein Garland, it is—how do you say?—in the bag?"

"Sh-she will appoint me?" Susannah hardly dared to utter the words.

"I do not think there is any doubt, Fräulein, any doubt at all." At the carriage Lady Ormanton halted, her hand on Susannah's arm. "The only thing vich vill prevent you gaining the royal varrant is if your name is involved in some dreadful scandal. But then, that vill not happen, vill it, Miss Garland?"

Susannah shook her head. But as the carriage drove her back toward London again, she felt a vague sense of unease. She was about to realize her final dream—but instead of feeling over the moon with joy, she suddenly felt a sense of foreboding.

28

The shadows were lengthening as Susannah and Jeffrey walked back across the grounds of Sanderby toward the waiting carriage. Her parasol twirled a little and the pink silk kerchief at the back of her gypsy bonnet fluttered in the light spring breeze which swept up the Thames on that fine April evening. Her white muslin skirts dragged against the daffodils which once again spread in drifts across the grass. The house was caught in the dying sun and the stone walls looked golden, with the windows flashing like diamonds as the rays caught them. How beautiful it was here, how perfect in every way.

"I'm so glad you didn't sell it to the Earl," she said suddenly, "but I still don't know why you changed your mind."

"Nor do I, to be perfectly honest. Winston even upped his offer to sway me, but I declined." He gave a faint smile. "Maybe it was simply that I could not bear the reproach in your eyes—it certainly was not that I had any thought of your irrelevant cousin in my mind."

"I did not for one moment imagine that you had."

"He's won in the law courts, you know—he will have custody of his son. Had you heard?"

"No. I'm glad he's won, though."

"No doubt."

"I'm still very fond of him, you know."

"Oh, I *know*. Was ever a cousin more fortunate than he? I vow that he does not deserve even a passing thought, least of all from you."

"He can't help the way he is."

"Would you still say that if you were incarcerated in that odious lodging house and trudging to and from Madame Hilary's each day? And *anyone* can help being as feckless as he would appear to be. He is the most selfish, undeserving, spineless individual I have come across, and I think it little short of a miracle that you can still think kindly of him at all."

She said nothing, and they walked on in silence. The subject of Miles Devereux was always fraught, the more so perhaps here at Sanderby. She looked at the house again. "Why don't you live here sometimes? Southwood is so very far away from London, and you could come here for a day or so if you wished."

"I still care little for the place." He smiled then. "And I did not for one moment think you would wish to spend this day here."

"I hope you don't mind too much."

"No."

"It's such a lovely day and Sanderby is always so beautiful in the springtime."

"That I will grant you."

The carriage was a black silhouette against the house, and by chance it occupied the very same place it had on that night over three years earlier when she had run away. As she sat back on the blue upholstered seat she gazed up at the house again, remembering the fear and uncertainty of that dreadful time. So very much had happened to her since then.

The whip cracked and the carriage moved away. She turned in her seat until she couldn't see the house anymore as the team came up to a smart pace and the carriage skirted the edge of the lake. The wheels crunched and rattled on the gravel drive and the harness jingled richly.

She smiled at Jeffrey opposite. "Thank you for today, I did enjoy it so."

"You are very easy to please."

"You should not grumble at that."

"Oh, I'm not grumbling. Far from it. I enjoy your company, Susannah, I find you most refreshing and never, ever dull."

"Considering I am a dressmaker?"

He laughed. "Among other things. And talking of dressmaking, how is the royal affair coming along?"

"I've sent off three of the fashion dolls. The last one is almost finished. I will sew on the spangles tonight when I return." She pulled a face. "My fingers and back ache at the thought of all that kneeling!"

"A *couturière* of your eminence should surely set someone else to do such a mundane task."

"I somehow feel I should do this particular one myself."

His eyes flickered. "Naturally—it is, after all, the pinnacle of your *métier*."

"Or it could just be that we have had an enormous rush of other orders very early in the year and I am the one with most time to spend on such work."

He inclined his head. "I cannot argue with that, can I?"

"No." Why was there always this slight friction? Why did he seem resentful and adopt this sarcastic tone when this topic arose?

He toyed with the frill at his cuff for a moment. "I gather the Queen was quite charmed with you, particularly with the fact that you made an effort to converse with her."

"I was very well briefed by Lady Ormanton beforehand."

"Being well briefed on something does not necessarily mean that the desired conversation is forthcoming. You, apparently, were successful."

"Only because of Lady Ormanton's help."

"The delightful Ulla. Well, *she*, of course, likes you immensely and loathes Madame Hilary with equal fervor. She would do all she could to smooth your path to the royal warrant."

"I haven't got the warrant yet."

"I shouldn't imagine there's much doubt that you will."

"No." The sense of foreboding returned momentarily. *Would* she ever realize that final goal?

"So, Susannah, here we are in April 1807, with the New House of Fashion poised on the brink of its third successful Season and you poised on the brink of absolute glory. I congratulate you."

"I could not have done anything had it not been for your help."

"How very gratifying to be told that." His eyes moved over her. "You know, I have never much cared for this rage for wearing white muslin, but on you it looks quite exquisite. You are a very beautiful woman, Susannah, so how is it that you remain unattached? You have connections which make you quite acceptable in most circles, in spite of the nature of your occupation, your loveliness would grace any society occasion and certainly dazzle most warm-blooded males—and yet there is no attachment, no one whose name is linked with yours."

"Except yours," she said lightly.

He paused. "That is hardly what I meant."

She gazed out of the window. Why couldn't he see the truth? Or was it that he *wouldn't* see it? He must surely be able to tell still, merely by the warmth in her eyes, that he was the only man who had ever mattered. Oh, she had tried to conceal more and more, but it was impossible to draw a complete veil over the love she felt. If he didn't want to acknowledge the truth, why did he bother with her at all? When he was in Town he came to see her, he escorted her and enjoyed her company, and she knew that he was not indifferent to her, for it was there in his glance, in his touch. But that was all. The barriers were there constantly, so cold and strong that she could almost reach out to touch them. She so wanted to brush them aside, but she was too afraid, afraid of losing what little of him she had. *I'm beyond your rules, Jeffrey Stratton, but you made those rules, not me. Not me.*

It was dark when at last the carriage drew up outside her house in Duke's Row. Tendrils of mist curled in the cold air as Jeffrey handed Susannah down and walked with her to the stone porch. There in the shadows she turned to smile at him. "Thank you again for taking me to Sanderby. I know you do not like the house, but I do very much, and the day was quite perfect for me."

He said nothing, slowly loosening the ribbons of her bonnet so that it slipped back from her head and her hair tumbled down from its pins. He pulled her close suddenly, kissing her roughly on the lips, and then he held her tightly for a moment before releasing her and walking quickly back to the carriage. She watched him leave, and her lips still tingled from the kiss. But he had said nothing at all, not one single word.

Slowly she entered the house. Everything was in darkness, as it was the maid's evening off, and Annie was spending a little time at Mr. Normans' parents home prior to her wedding in June and would not be back until the following morning. Susannah lit a candlestick in the showroom on the first floor, glancing around to see that all was in order before going up the stairs to her own rooms on the floor above. The cat was sleeping before the fire which the maid had kindled earlier before leaving, and Susannah removed the guard and poked it vigorously into life. The flames roared and the cat sat up quickly as a shower of bright sparks scattered over the hearth.

Susannah drew the curtains and then slowly removed her bonnet. In the mirror she could see the tawny curls which had so willfully refused to remain pinned. The cat rubbed around her ankles as she stood there for a moment gazing at her reflection. If she closed her eyes, she would feel his lips on hers again. . . .

Behind her in the center of the floor stood the last of the royal fashion dolls. The little mannequin stood stiffly in its ridiculously rich and fashionable gown of plowman's gauze. The satin spots gleamed in the candlelight and the pale green was touched here and there with a dancing pink from the fire. Beside it lay the dish of spangles waiting to be stitched on one by one, a skein of silk thread, some needles and new papers of pins. With a sigh, she took off her spencer and put it on the table with the parasol and bonnet; then she knelt by the doll and picked up the first spangle.

As she did so, she heard the stairs creak stealthily. The cat's fur stood on end and it spat. Susannah froze with instant fear. The landing was in darkness and the pale light from the candles did not extend to the top of the staircase. Again she heard the stairs creak. Someone was there!

Frightened now, she called out, "Who's there? Who is it?"

A black shadow emerged into the light. "Why, coz, you've gone quite pale!"

"Miles!" She didn't know whether to be relieved or furious. "Why on earth did you steal in like that? Why didn't you. . . ?" Her voice died away as he came into the room, for he was once again wearing black and the weepers from his top hat streamed as he removed it and sketched a bow.

He smiled at the surprise on her face. "I am widowed, coz, dear Agnes is no longer with us."

She stared at him. "Agnes? But how. . . ?"

"She and the Frenchman were killed when their carriage overturned—somewhere in darkest Westmorland I believe. The scene of the miracle is immaterial, I care only that I am relieved of a damned encumbrance." He removed his cloak and draped it over a chair, and then he gave her a slight smile before going to the cupboard where he knew she would

257

keep the decanter of cognac. "In the absence of a civil welcome from you, or an offer to take some refreshment, I will avail myself of the necessary beverage. Ah, I see that it is Stratton's favorite poison—well, well. However, I'll say this for him, he has an excellent palate."

She watched him, unable to think of anything to say. She was stunned by learning of Agnes' death, and more than a little uneasy at his mood.

He sipped the cognac. "Well, aren't you going to congratulate me on winning my court battle? Don't disappoint me, coz, tell me how damned delighted you are that I have custody of my son."

"Of course I'm pleased for you."

He bowed. "Thank you."

"Are . . . are you leaving for Ireland now that you've won?"

"All in good time, all in good time."

"Why have you come here, Miles?"

"That's not very gracious."

"I don't feel very gracious! You frightened me by creeping up the stairs like that. Why did you do it?"

"Shall we say that it seemed like a good idea at the time?"

"I don't think it was at all clever."

"So it would seem. My apologies." He glanced around the room. "You've certainly come up in the world, Susannah— this address is very much the *ton*, is it not? And now I am given to understand that you have been summoned to Windsor, no less. My, my, how far away now a certain lodging house in Covent Garden." He dragged the toe of his boot gently across the hem of the fashion doll's gown so that the satin spots seemed to move with light. He swirled the cognac a moment more and then looked at Susannah. "Actually, I have a very special purpose in coming here tonight, coz. I have come to put right a wrong which was perpetrated over three years ago now."

"Wrong?"

"The wrong I did you when I deserted you for Agnes. I've come to propose to you, coz, to ask for your hand in marriage."

She stared at him, her lips parting with surprise. "But, Miles—"

He put a finger against her lips, smiling a little as he did so. "I may not have what old Croesus left to me, but I have

258

my title and there are always the damned Irish estates. I love you, Susannah, I always have done and probably always will, and now I am in a position to make you my wife."

"No, Miles."

"I ask you to reconsider your answer. Very carefully." He was not smiling now, and the strange mood was more apparent than ever.

"Miles, I still feel very deeply for you, but how many times must I tell you that it is the wrong kind of love? I could never be your wife, and you deserve far more than I could ever give you."

He gave a single cool nod. "Well, I warned you once before that if ever I had reason to believe Stratton returned your love then I would do all I could to destroy that love."

"What do you mean?" she asked quickly, a coldness spreading through her now.

"I mean that I shall now carry out that threat."

"But he doesn't love me!"

"Oh, come now, I've spent this day in your wake, sweet Susannah. I watched you at Sanderby—"

"You've been following me?" she asked angrily.

"And I saw that touching scene beneath the porch here not half an hour since," he continued as if she had not spoken. "I came up now to ask you just once more to come with me, but you have refused. Now you must face the aftermath." He put on his cloak and hat, and she watched him, unable to move, she was so shocked.

He smiled then, cupping her chin in his hand and kissing her very gently on the lips. "You should have accepted me, Susannah, it would have been so much tidier all around. I have endured it all long enough and will endure it no more. I have never denied that there were only two things of any consequence in my life—Sanderby and you. The one I have lost forever and can never recover, but you are another matter entirely."

"What . . . what are you going to do?"

"You will discover that soon enough."

"Please, Miles . . ."

"All you need do is accept me." He waited.

"But I don't love you!"

"It doesn't matter, for you will be forced to come to me in the end anyway. You will have nothing and no one but me,

259

Susannah—that is, if I survive. Good-bye, coz." He inclined his head and then left her.

She heard his light steps on the stairs and then the heavy front doors closed. The echoing died away, and all was silent again.

29

The dawn was bloodred, the sunrise piercing the partially drawn curtains and falling obliquely across Susannah as she knelt by the fashion doll. The fire had gone out and the room was cold now, but she felt nothing. The dish of spangles was untouched and not a single pin had been removed from its place in the paper. She stared out at the flame-colored sky. Why hadn't Jeffrey come? She had sent a message immediately Miles had gone, but still he was not here. Miserably she lowered her eyes. What was she to do now? Miles had been so strange; his veiled threat could mean practically anything.

A carriage drew up outside, and she was on her feet in a moment, hurrying almost eagerly down the curving staircase. But as she flung open the doors she saw a hired hackney carriage at the curb, and Annie and Mr. Normans alighting at the end of their journey from his parents' home.

The disappointment was almost bitter. Susannah's shoulders were bowed and she lowered her eyes to the pavement for a moment, trying to muster the willpower to smile and greet them cheerfully. But she couldn't.

Annie hurried anxiously to her. "Susannah? What's wrong?"

"Annie," she whispered, "I just don't know what to do . . ."

The fire had been rekindled and a pan of bonailie bubbled on the crackling flames. The smell of cloves hung in the air, and Annie and Mr. Normans listened in silence as Susannah told them about Miles Devereux's visit.

"I sent a messenger to Berkeley Square," she finished, "for Jeffrey has to be told what has happened, but he wasn't there.

My note was left, but it's hours now and I still haven't heard from him. I don't know where Miles lodges, either, so I can't go to him and try to reason. I feel so helpless, as if I must just sit here and wait for the inevitable!"

Annie glanced at her fiancé. "Can you think of anything, Freddie?"

"Well, maybe Lord Devereux is staying at his club. He must have a club."

Susannah shrugged. "I only know that his father used Brooks's."

Freddie got up. "That's only around the corner more or less, isn't it? I'll go there directly and see if he's there."

Susannah's eyes brightened with hope. "Thank you."

"Not at all. And don't worry, we'll find him somehow."

When he had gone, Annie poured a dish of the bonailie and pushed it into Susannah's hands. "Drink this, now, it will make you feel better. I'm sure everything will be all right and that you're worrying unnecessarily."

"You weren't here, Annie, you didn't see how he was." Susannah looked at the unfinished fashion doll. "I somehow knew something would happen, I had this dreadful feeling . . ."

"Nonsense."

"*If I survive*, he said. *If I survive.*"

"It was just talk to frighten you into accepting him."

"No, I think he meant it."

Someone knocked loudly at the front door, and again Susannah jumped hopefully to her feet, but Annie put a restraining hand on her arm. "Let the maid go and see. Sit down, now, and finish that bonailie."

But it wasn't Jeffrey's voice they heard, it was unmistakably that of Lady Ormanton. Susannah looked at the fashion doll again. It would never be finished. The thought came starkly into her head without warning. On this terrible day, everything was coming to a dreadful conclusion.

Lady Ormanton did not look at all her usual self. She had neglected to put on any rouge and as a result her face was oddly pale beneath its frame of hennaed curls. She did not smile at all and neither did she bother to waste time on idle pleasantries.

"Fräulein Garland, I have vorried all night about vot I must do, and all I could think of voz coming to you. Something very terrible is going to happen unless you are able to stop it."

262

Susannah's hand crept slowly to her throat.

"Fräulein, such a thing as this is out of the qvestion, it is against the law of the land and achieves nothing. Nothing!"

"I don't understand, Lady Ormanton . . ."

"No? There is to be a duel, Fräulein Garland, a duel between your cousin, Lord Devereux, and Sir Jeffrey Stratton. And you, Miss Susannah, are the cause of it all."

"But I've done nothing!" cried Susannah. She felt faint suddenly, as if the room was moving. Gradually the feeling passed. "I've done nothing," she repeated, "I swear that I have not."

"Vell, Lord Devereux evidently thinks differently." Lady Ormanton sat heavily in a chair. "I know about it only because Jeffrey kindly agreed to escort me to the opera house last night, and I returned vith him to his house and voz there ven Lord Devereux's seconds came. The challenge voz couched in such a vay, and the claim so strong, that Jeffrey could not refuse it."

"What was the challenge?"

"Oh, come now, Fräulein, let us be done vith this playacting! You know perfectly vell vot the challenge is."

"But I don't, Lady Ormanton! I'm not playacting, I truly don't know!"

Lady Ormanton stared at her then, her face changing. "Oh, my dear, I have wronged you. I have thought badly of you ven you are innocent! I really thought . . . Vell, it does not matter now. I vill tell you about the challenge. Your cousin claims that you and he are to be married—"

"That's not true!"

"Nonetheless, that is his claim. He says that Jeffrey has dishonored you and therefore has dishonored the Devereux family. That is vhy Jeffrey has been called out."

Susannah closed her eyes and Annie quickly put a hand over hers. Susannah looked at Lady Ormanton again. "What did Jeffrey say?" she asked in a voice that was barely above a whisper.

"Nothing. He said nothing at all, Fräulein, he merely nodded that he accepted the challenge. It is all very unpleasant, very unpleasant indeed, and if it gets out over Town . . . Vell, you vill have no reputation, no reputation at all. God forgive me that I should have thought you guilty in any vay, but I thought that there could not be smoke vithout fire."

Susannah looked away. "All I am guilty of is loving the wrong man," she said dully.

"I came here intent only upon stopping the duel, because I know that Jeffrey vill kill your foolish cousin. I still vish to stop it for that reason, but also now because I vish to help you extricate yourself from this disaster. You do realize how serious this is for you, don't you? A scandal like this vill ruin you completely. Dueling is against the law—oh, I know it still goes on, even the late Mr. Pitt vas guilty of this particular crime—but your name vill be involved in such a vay that the *beau monde* vill spurn you. The King and Qveen disapprove very much of dueling and so the Qveen will have nothing more to do vith you. You vill have nothing, Fräulein Garland, there vill not be a New House of Fashion anymore."

You will have nothing and no one but me, Susannah—that is, if I survive . . . survive . . . survive . . . Miles's parting words seemed to echo in Susannah's head.

Lady Ormanton sighed heavily. "The duel has to be stopped, Fräulein Garland, Lord Devereux must be persvaded to retract the challenge. He issued it and only he can withdraw. Jeffrey vill pursue the matter to its conclusion."

"The only vay I can achieve that is by accepting my cousin as my husband."

"And that is so bad?"

"I don't love him, Lady Ormanton, I love Jeffrey Stratton."

Lady Ormanton stared then. "I feel very sorry for you, Fräulein, and I vould not ever vish to be in your sad position," she said quietly, getting up. "But my advice is this. Accept your cousin, become Lady Devereux, and thereby save both yourself and him. I made a marriage I did not vish, and I vill not pretend that it vas happy, but at the same time it voz not so bad that it could not be endured. You have so very much to lose that I cannot see you have any sensible alternative but to marry Lord Devereux."

Susannah could only look at her. She felt numb, as if she would wake at any moment and find that it was all a terrible dream, some dread nightmare which would vanish with the sun. But there was no waking, it was all happening.

"Fräulein Garland?"

"Yes?"

"I voz saying that you vill have to marry your cousin—it is

qvite the most intelligent thing you can do in such a situation."

"I . . . I will consider what you say."

"Consider? My dear young lady, you must act, not merely consider, if you vish to survive in society and most certainly if you vish to clothe the dear Qveen. Vot has happened may not be your fault, but on your shoulders falls the strain. However, it is your affair and I have done vot I can—now I have to go back to Vindsor and there are things I must attend to first. Remember, now, Fräulein Garland, you are the very best *Kleidermacherin* in England, the vorld of fashion lies at your feet—provided you do the sensible thing now. Good day to you, Fräulein."

"Good day, my lady." Susannah's voice was a mere whisper.

Lady Ormanton nodded and swept out. Susannah stared at the door when she had gone. It all seemed so clear to Lady Ormanton, a disastrous marriage was by far preferable to such a scandal as was about to break. How could so sweet and charming a lady be so calculating about so important a thing as one's future life? How could she shrug her plump shoulders with an air of *c'est la vie* and then become virtually hysterical for fear that a court gown would not be completed in time? The two things bore no comparison, and yet for Lady Ormanton the decision was quite simple and clear—marry Miles, prevent the scandal, and live unhappily ever afterward.

Annie looked sadly at her. "Oh, Susannah, what can I say?"

"Nothing."

"But you must not blame yourself—it *isn't* your fault."

"It is, Annie," said Susannah heavily, turning to look out of the window at the green, misty expanse of St. James's Park. The walls of the palace looked rosy in the sunrise and the straight canal stretched in a pale line between the avenues of trees. There was a thin vapor clinging close to the ground after the cold night, and she watched as a white dog moved swiftly over the ground, a ghostly shape which was suddenly lost in the haze. She lowered her eyes. "It is my fault, for I did not obey the rules, did I? I was warned about the form the scandal would take, and now I must face the consequences."

Annie felt helpless. "Then . . . then marry your cousin."

"Would you?"

"I don't know . . . maybe I would if I stood to lose as much as you do."

Susannah shook her head. "I don't love him and I won't marry him unless that is the only way to stop him dying. That is what it comes down to, isn't it? It has nothing to do with what I have built, what could still be mine—it is simple blackmail yet again. He knows full well that Jeffrey will kill him, and he is relying upon my conscience. He knows me well—as I know him."

"You don't hate him even now, do you?"

Susannah smiled a little ruefully. "No, I can't hate him. Listen . . . isn't that Freddie?" She hurried eagerly to the door, hoping against hope that he had somehow found some miraculous remedy. But one glance at his pale face sent such hopes fleeing in a second.

"You did not find him?"

"I found him, he was just leaving Brooks. Do . . . do you know what it is all about? What is to happen tomorrow?"

She nodded. "There is to be a duel."

"I told him that you wished to speak to him, but all he would say was that if you wished to prevent the duel from taking place, then you must agree to what he asks and you must be at Sheppard's Dell, Putney Heath, at dawn tomorrow. He wouldn't tell me where he could be found in the meantime, even though I begged him to tell me. That was his final word—you must be there tomorrow."

Yes, she thought, she would have to be there, so that Jeffrey would be forced to see that she had chosen Miles Devereux after all. Except that Jeffrey would not care in the slightest. Jeffrey. Why had she heard nothing from him? He must surely have received her note by now.

As if he had heard her thoughts, Freddie Normans spoke again. "After trying with Lord Devereux, I thought I would take a chaise to Berkeley Square and see if I could speak to Sir Jeffrey."

"Did you?"

"No. Oh, he has been given your note, I ascertained that much, but immediately afterward he left the house and gave instructions that they were not to expect him home for several days. Again, no one knew where he had gone."

Susannah turned slowly away. She could not speak to either Miles or Jeffrey; her hands were tied until the very moment the duel was set to commence. "I have little choice, have I?" she murmured. "I must go to Sheppard's Dell to-morrow morning as Miles wishes."

"Will you accept your cousin?" asked Annie softly.

Susannah stared at the misty park again without answering.

It seemed that the day and night before the duel took a lifetime to pass. Time hung so heavily that when dawn was at last approaching, Susannah felt as if she carried the weight of the world upon her shoulders. She gazed blindly out of the window of the chaise as it bowled swiftly along toward Putney.

She could see her reflection in the dark glass. How carefully she had dressed—but for what? She did not really know why it had seemed so important to look her very best, but somehow that was how she had felt as she prepared for the short journey. She wore a brown velvet pelisse lined with crimson silk, and carried a reticule made of the same stuffs. There were little crimson plumes in her dainty hat, and her whole appearance was one of fashionable perfection. The *queen* of fashion, she thought wryly, the arbiter of London's modes. But for how much longer now? And did it really matter anyway? Somehow the world of fashion was of little consequence when she was faced with trying to prevent this senseless confrontation between the only two men she had ever loved.

She stared at her reflection. Why could she not hate Miles and let him consign himself to the devil? The answer was simple: the bond between them was too strong, and the memories too fond.

The Thames was invisible in the darkness and the trees and houses slipped silently past like wraiths. There was a chill in the air, but Susannah felt even colder now that they were nearing the end of the journey. She felt as if there was ice inside her; her hands were without feeling and she was conscious only of a frozen emptiness.

A solitary barouche stood at the edge of the dell as the chaise came to a standstill and Susannah prepared to climb down. She shook her head at Annie and Freddie as they prepared to climb down with her.

"No, I must see them alone."

Annie was anxious. "Please, Susannah . . ."

But Susannah walked slowly across the wet grass toward the small group of men by the barouche. Their heavy cloaks dragged in the dew as they turned to look at her, and she recognized Miles's golden hair as he removed his hat. There was no sign of Jeffrey yet.

The seconds moved away to a discreet distance as she approached, and Miles bowed, smiling a little although she could see how nervous and tense he was. "Good morning, coz. Have you changed your mind, then?"

She halted a few feet from him. His face was very pale in the gray light. "Don't go on with this, Miles. Please."

"I must, if I am to keep you from Stratton."

"What good will that do you if you are dead?"

He smiled. "It just could be that Lady Luck will choose to smile upon yours truly for once, or had that not occurred to you?"

"Luck does not enter into this, Miles, it is skill which matters—and you are not skilled enough to defeat Jeffrey. Please withdraw the challenge, for my sake if not for your own."

"Withdraw and prevent ruining you?"

"That is not what I meant and I believe you know it full well, Miles," she answered reproachfully.

He glanced away. "Marry me, Susannah, and then I will gladly withdraw."

"What sort of marriage do you honestly imagine it would be?"

"You loved me once and you will love me again."

"No."

"Then why have you bothered to come here now?"

"You have responsibilities, Miles, you have a son to think of, a baby with no one else in the world but you!"

He gave a harsh laugh. "No one else? He has his Winston grandfather!"

"You fought through the courts to gain custody of your son—was it all in vain then if you now willingly wish to hand him back? You prated to me about how changed you were, about how fit you were to be a father—now you prove that you haven't changed at all! The Devereux leopard is still the same, he is selfish and weak, and quite prepared to throw his life away wantonly on a pointless duel which is entirely of his own seeking." Tears shone in her eyes and she brushed them angrily away. Why could he not see reason? *Why*?

"Maybe I am all of those things, Susannah," he said softly, "but this duel is far from pointless to me. Stratton is my *bête noire*, he has taken everything I love most dearly. He'll not

268

have you if I can prevent it, Susannah. If I must die to achieve this, then so be it—this duel will create a scandal from which you will never rise, and he will not come within a mile of you afterward."

"Can't you see that you will be hurting me and hurting yourself? He will not be affected at all, Miles, he doesn't love me!"

"I have the evidence of my own eyes, sweetheart," he said softly. "He'll not have you." He reached out to touch her face gently for a moment, and then his hand fell away again.

She felt a bitter desire to laugh suddenly. "Tell me something—if you had not wagered and lost your inheritance on the turn of a card, Miles Devereux, would you still have challenged him like this?"

He avoided her eyes. "Probably not. One I can endure losing, but not both." He smiled at her. "Being supremely selfish is yet another Devereux trait I would have thought you knew well enough by now, coz."

She turned away then, the tears wet on her cheeks. But as she began to walk back toward the chaise, Jeffrey's black carriage approached through the rising mist, the first rays of the sunrise glinting on the harness.

She halted in the center of the dell, her heart thundering. Would he even speak to her? Could she attempt to convince him where she had failed with Miles?

The carriage halted, the horses stamping a little, sweat gleaming on their coats and billowing in thin clouds around them as the coachman jumped down to fling blankets over them. Slowly the door opened and Jeffrey climbed down, accompanied by his seconds. He did not see her at first, until one of his companions touched his arm and pointed. He turned then, gazing at her without expression for a moment, and then he nodded at the seconds before leaving them and walking toward her.

"Good morning, Jeffrey." How lame the greeting sounded.

"And why would you be here, I ask myself," he said coldly.

"Did . . . didn't you receive my note?"

"I did."

"Then why. . . ?"

"There seemed little point."

"You believe what Miles said, don't you? You believe that I have accepted him in marriage.

269

"Let me put it this way: what reason have I *not* to believe it? You've never made any pretense at loathing him, in fact I would say you have behaved in quite the opposite way. Being Lady Devereux would most certainly have sent your stock up to new heights, wouldn't it? No doubt the only thing to mar the coziness was that you wouldn't have been Lady Devereux of Sanderby, but then, we must not be too greedy all at once, must we? I'll warrant you little thought dear Miles would be fool enough to endanger it all by forcing this duel. But he has, and so here you are, no doubt quite determined to stop the duel in any way possible so that you can save your precious lover, your chiffon empire, and your pure, unsullied reputation—to say nothing of your titled future, dancing attendance on the Queen."

She listened without saying a word, trying hard to hide how deeply each successive barb penetrated.

His expression was contemptuous. "Are you not at least going to deny it?"

"Believe what you will of me, Jeffrey, it really doesn't matter anymore. But you are right to think I am here to stop the duel."

"Then take yourself off to dearest Miles—he issued the challenge and is therefore the one to stand down. I care little one way or the other, but I do assure you that I am quite prepared to extinguish him once and for all."

"I know that."

"What a pity for you that he does not appear to be as enlightened."

"Oh, he knows it full well, but he is banking upon me bowing to his will."

"And what might that entail?"

"He wants me to marry him. You see, Jeffrey, you were wrong and he was lying when he said that I had already accepted him."

"Then I suggest you rectify the omission immediately and save us all the trouble of this charade."

She looked away miserably. Never had the barrier between them seemed more real, or so impenetrable. "I have tried to reason with him already, and I have failed. I have also failed with you. And it is all so very foolish, he is only doing it because he thinks you have both me and Sanderby."

"I know."

"You know?"

"He was very voluble when he came to issue his damned challenge. I chose to let the fool think as he pleased. His caperings have become tiresome in the extreme, and I no longer have either the patience or the temper to endure him. He has deliberately set out to force this issue with me, he knows my reputation and my ability, he knows that I have weathered the fact that I have already put an end to two men in duels, and still he has pursued this idiocy. So be it."

She stared at him. "You are right, of course," she said softly, "I cannot defend him. But he was kind to me once— he was the only one who was kind to me."

"That he loves you in his own odd way, I have no doubt."

"He loves Sanderby more. He told me that had he not lost both the house and me to you, then there would have been no challenge."

"How very flattering for you."

She bridled a little at that. "Between you I have been forced into a position from which I cannot escape—I must accept him or see him die. He does it for his own reasons, but you are guilty too, Jeffrey Stratton! Well, maybe you do not see my actions clearly. I do not believe you ever have, but I have a conscience over this and I cannot live afterwards knowing that I could have done something to save him."

"He can save himself. And no doubt you will manage to come to terms with yourself after becoming a martyr to his cause. The delights of his bed will surely compensate for the loss of your freedom!"

His words goaded her. "You wrong me greatly, Jeffrey!" she cried, her eyes flashing. "The *only* reason I would have for accepting him would be to prevent his death. It has nothing to do with loving him, with protecting myself or my so-called chiffon empire! I just don't know what else I can do!" Her voice almost broke and she looked quickly away from him again, biting her lip as she fought back the tears. She must not cry, not here in front of him.

He paused. "So, correct me if I'm wrong, but if his miserable life is to be spared and you are to be released from a fate worse than death, you wish me to sacrifice my honor and step obligingly down like a coward from a duel which was not of my making in the first place! If you think I am about to look that foolish and weak in the eyes of the world, then you are sadly mistaken!"

She closed her eyes. How could he behave as he now did?

271

How could he be both so cruel and so cold? He was still blind to the truth about her after all this time—he still *wanted* to believe the worst. "Maybe," she whispered, "I have been as wrong about you, sir, as you have been about me, and as this is probably the last time I shall speak to you, then I will tell you how it really is. It is not at all how you have chosen to picture it, you know. I am very fond of Miles, it's true, but I haven't *loved* him for a long time. On the other hand, I have loved you since almost the first time I saw you. All that I have achieved at the New House of Fashion has come a very poor second to the way I feel about you, but you think I only dream of my ambitions, that I love nothing but my *chiffons*, as you so scathingly call them. You have misunderstood me throughout, and sometimes I truly believe you have done so quite deliberately. Well, it doesn't matter now, does it? You don't love me and you never have, and so the outcome of this day's work is quite immaterial to you. But it matters a great deal to me because now I am losing what little I had of you—and God knows that was little enough. I break your rules, don't I? Why? Because I am a Devereux? Because I cannot be compared with your wife's bright memory? Because I am a schoolmaster's daughter and therefore beneath consideration? Or maybe because I have proved that I can succeed in my chosen world? Who knows what other reasons you could have for despising me as you so obviously do now, but I will tell you this, Jeffrey Stratton, you do not break my rules even though I tried so very hard to see that you did. You are still everything that I love, everything that I will ever love. Go ahead with this duel—put an end to Miles, for he deserves it, does he not? Make certain of my ruin, for that is no more than I obviously deserve as well in your eyes. Live with your precious honor afterward and know that above all you behaved correctly. But you will also know that you wronged me, Jeffrey, and that whatever you may think, I have never wronged you."

She began to walk past him, but he caught her hand suddenly. "Oh, Susannah," he said softly, his hand warm over hers, "I would to God you had said all that a long time ago."

"What difference would it have made?"

"All the difference in the world, for then my damned pride would not have got in the way. At first the only rule you sinned against was that your mother was a Devereux. It was that simple. Except that it refused to be simple because I wanted you so very much. But I am not a man to take second place in any way, either to your love for Miles Devereux or to your muslins and lace, and it seemed to me that I would always have been second to both."

"No—"

But he put his finger to her lips to silence the words. "I don't despise you, Susannah, I despise myself for loving you and still hurting you. I have tried to close you out, but I could not. Time and time again I've wanted to come back to you, but each time I managed to convince myself somehow that you didn't really mean anything to me after all. But you did, damn you, you mattered more and more. I've hurt you because I wanted you completely, body and soul, and believed that I could not have either."

Her eyes were bright. She could not believe that he was saying it, that he was telling her he loved her. "You could always have had me, Jeffrey," she whispered. "You would never have come in second, because there was always only you."

He drew her closer then, one hand firmly on her small waist. "Will you come to me now, Susannah? Can you forget the past and begin again now?"

"Yes."

His lips brushed hers, and she felt that the air was singing around her. A great warmth flooded through her after the long cold of the past day, of the past years, and the tears were hot on her cheeks.

He released her slowly then, glancing across to where Miles stood motionless, watching them as they stood so close together in the center of the narrow dell. "But first, Susannah, there is something else I must attend to."

Her eyes widened. "Please, Jeffrey . . ."

"Spare him?"

"Yes."

He wiped the tears on her cheeks with his fingertips. "Do you think I will jeopardize our future now by spilling his damned blood? He may be a fool, my love, but I am not."

She watched him as he walked across the damp, dewy grass to where Miles was waiting by the barouche.

Miles straightened, his mouth a tight line and his eyes cold. He bowed stiffly. "Stratton."

"Devereux."

"If you think I will retract—"

Jeffrey raised an eyebrow. "You would if you had any sense, but then, sense is a commodity in which you are sadly lacking, it seems. You've lost, man. Your heroic death at dawn will not achieve that which you so dearly wish to achieve. She's mine, whether you live or die, and believe me, your existence is entirely inconsequential as far as *I* am concerned."

Miles's eyes were steely. "As far as you are concerned, maybe, but not as far as Susannah is concerned—*she* would suffer if you snuff me out today."

Jeffrey controlled his anger and loathing admirably, giving little sign of how dearly he would prefer to go ahead with a duel the outcome of which was so pleasantly certain. But for Susannah's sake, Miles Devereux must be spared if possible. Jeffrey glanced back at her lonely figure, so dainty and fragile, and so very anxious still. For her he would try to avoid this confrontation with her cousin, but for no one else on God's earth would he have sacrificed so much. He looked at Miles. "What will it take to call you off, Devereux?"

"I want Susannah."

"Really? You have a very odd way of showing your love. But I was not thinking in terms of Susannah on this occasion—more of Sanderby."

"Sanderby?"

"I see that the name communicates something to you."

Miles flushed a little at the sarcasm. "You are offering me my own birthright if I take back the challenge."

"Ah, well now, I quarrel with your choice of words, dear fellow. As far as I am concerned, Sanderby is, if anyone's, *my* birthright, seeing that it was made what it now is on the proceeds of my family's losses at your father's hands. However, be that as it may, I am still prepared to give you the house and the land if you will retract now and then stay well away from me and from Susannah ever afterward. And when I say stay away, I rather think you had better believe I mean exactly that—to the very letter. I am not prepared to put up with your misdemeanors ever again, Devereux, and if you should cross my path or harm Susannah, then you will regret it." He gave a cool smile, and the expression in his eyes was enough to quell the bravest man. "Susannah would know nothing of your extinction at my hand the next time," he said very softly. "Do we understand each other?"

274

Miles said nothing, swallowing a little as he looked away at last from those steady gray eyes.

The moments passed. "Now, then," went on Jeffrey, "I think you have had time to digest the main points of the offer. What is it to be then—the duel, or Sanderby?"

The trees stirred a little with a breath of wind which stole into the sheltered dell as Miles spoke at last. "I will take Sanderby."

"I somehow thought that you would."

Miles managed to bite back the hot retort which leaped to his lips.

Jeffrey watched and smiled. "Yes, it would be a little unfortunate if you provoked another skirmish at this eleventh hour, wouldn't it? Be warned now, toe the proverbial line, dear fellow, or you will rue it. And if one whisper of this gets out, if Susannah's reputation suffers in any way because of your clacking little Whig tongue, you will still rue it."

"No word will get out," said Miles quickly.

"Very well. You may expect to receive the deeds and so on within a day. And now . . . your presence is no longer required."

Miles turned sharply to get into the barouche, and his puzzled seconds followed him. The whip cracked and the team strained forward.

Susannah watched as it approached her. Miles was leaving—it was all over. But as the barouche passed, Miles did not glance down at her, he averted his pale face until she could not see him anymore. The barouche passed the chaise where Annie and Freddie still waited, and then it was on the rough track which led to the London road, and the team was brought up to a smart pace.

Jeffrey walked back slowly to where Susannah stood waiting. The morning sun shone on the crimson plumes in her hat as she took one step toward him, and then she was running into his arms. He held her tightly, his eyes closed as he rested his cheek against the foolish, fluttering plumes. He could feel her heart beating. He would never lose her again, never. "I love you, Susannah," he whispered, "and I had no idea how much until now." He could taste the salt on her lips as he kissed her again.

ABOUT THE AUTHOR

SANDRA HEATH was born in 1944. As the daughter of an officer in the Royal Air Force, most of her life was spent traveling around to various European posts. She has lived and worked in both Holland and Germany.

The author now resides in Gloucester, England, together with her husband and young daughter, where all her spare time is spent writing. She is especially fond of exotic felines and, at one time or another, has owned every breed of cat.